Robin Blake was born in Lancashire. After teaching at home and abroad in the 1970s, he became a producer in independent radio and then a full-time writer. He has written non-fiction books, many radio programmes and a previous thriller, *Fat Man's Shadow*, which is also published by Penguin.

ROBIN BLAKE

THE GWAILO

PENGUIN BOOKS

PENGUIN BOOKS

Published by the Penguin Group
Penguin Books Ltd, 27 Wrights Lane, London W8 5TZ, England
Penguin Books USA Inc., 375 Hudson Street, New York, New York 10014, USA
Penguin Books Australia Ltd, Ringwood, Victoria, Australia
Penguin Books Canada Ltd, 10 Alcorn Avenue, Toronto, Ontario, Canada M4V 3B2
Penguin Books (NZ) Ltd, 182–190 Wairau Road, Auckland 10, New Zealand

Penguin Books Ltd, Registered Offices: Harmondsworth, Middlesex, England

First published by Viking 1992
Published in Penguin Books 1993
1 3 5 7 9 10 8 6 4 2

Copyright © Robin Blake, 1992
All rights reserved

The moral right of the author has been asserted

Printed in England by Clays Ltd, St Ives plc

Except in the United States of America, this book is sold subject
to the condition that it shall not, by way of trade or otherwise, be lent,
re-sold, hired out, or otherwise circulated without the publisher's
prior consent in any form of binding or cover other than that in
which it is published and without a similar condition including this
condition being imposed on the subsequent purchaser

*For Catriona Sword*

# Note

The word *gwailo*, which is now in everyday use among Hong Kong expatriates when referring to themselves, demonstrates the mild mixture of contempt and fear with which native Chinese view Western foreigners.

In Cantonese *gwai* is a devil, demon or ghost; *lo* is a colloquial term for a man – a 'guy', we might say. A *gwailo* is therefore literally a 'devil-guy'. It is, however, used exclusively of foreigners of white Western extraction.

In Lancashire there is no such place as Moxon. Nor anywhere, as far as I know, is there a bank such as Trans-Africa Finance. There are, of course, many Hong Kongs, factual and imaginary. Much of mine is imaginary.

I would like to record my thanks to Beth McKillop for her technical assistance in the writing of this story.

# I

The vast field had been freshly ploughed, ready for winter wheat, and in the moonlight its corduroy ridges shone, polished by the sharp ploughshares. Moving by ungainly jerks over the field was a man, his town shoes slithering from furrow to furrow. The man's whispered curses and panting breath fell softly on the night as he laboured towards the far hedgerow. His feet carried twice or three times their usual weight as, with every step, more of the sticky earth coagulated under the soles.

Mid-way across he reached a solitary oak tree. It was the last remaining standard of a hedgerow grubbed up to increase the farm's acreage of cultivation. He stopped, leaning on the trunk to catch his breath. His fingertips found and tapped at his breastbone, where the usual indigestion was releasing fish-bubbles of pain into his chest. He regretted now that take-away supper. The fish had been dry as cardboard, while the chips had drooped with grease.

Swivelling around, he looked back at the gateway where his car was parked, then, turning again, he saw ahead of him two shadow blots pushing into the sky beyond the far hedge. These were the isolated cottage with its rounded, cap-like thatched roof and, 20 yards from it, the birch spinney where, earlier in the week, he had hidden the kit necessary for tonight. He checked his watch: it was 3 a.m. He knocked the toe of each of his shoes against the trunk of the oak to dislodge at least some of the compacted mud and began once more to trudge over the wet field.

He pushed his hand behind the iron drainpipe, feeling a fur of rust that turned to powder as his fingers groped up and down. There was no key. His foxy face twitched with satisfaction, for it meant the family were at home. Taking a duplicate key from his pocket, he moved to the front door. Weekenders always left a key somewhere about the place for repairmen and cleaning women – he remembered as much from his old burgling days. You never had to search long to find it, nestling on some convenient ledge or under a flowerpot. The original, from which he'd had this copy made, was hung on a rusty nail behind a rickety down-spout. He'd found it during his reconnaissance, when he'd left his gear among the trees. He slid the key, a Chubb mortise type, into the keyhole and turned. The lock's mechanism plopped gently, but the door did not open. *Shit!* It was bolted on the inside. He relocked the door and moved away to inspect the windows.

There were no bars on the one looking out towards the back from the sitting room. The glass broke with a dry rattle, and he froze, listening for any sound of disturbance. There was none. His hand went inside to release the catch, then he swung the casement open, stepped up on the ledge and dropped inside, pulling both rucksacks behind him.

He stood in the low-beamed cottage room and listened again, mouth dry, heart rate beginning to pick up as the adrenalin pumped. From somewhere in the house he ought to be able to distinguish the sound of two sleepers. One would be a child's shallow, mucous breathing, while the other would be the respiration of its mother, fetching on a more measured and profound cycle. Yet he could not hear it. The whole place seemed to be muffled in silence, with not even a fox or an owl breaking through. It was a waiting silence, a hush of suspense, maybe. He shook his head. Stupid. *He* knew what was going to happen in about ten minutes' time. To anyone else it would be merely the silence of the night before dawn.

He put the two rucksacks together on the floor – he wouldn't need them till later – and moved towards the box staircase. When he tested the lower steps they creaked a lot more than when he'd tried them on his previous visit. But that had been daytime, and he'd had the house to himself. At night noises doubled and redoubled. So yes, he would make a noise going up, but only by contrast with the depth of the surrounding silence. By the time he reached her, she would not have woken to anything more than half-consciousness.

He knew exactly where he would find her. His mud-caked feet took the stairs two at a time. The stairhead faced a bathroom, and the bedroom door, he knew, was round to the left. He would have to pass through the kid's room to get to the mother. So should he deal with the kid first? No, reach the mother and make her safe, *then* get the youngster. Children sleep through anything, don't they?

There was an old-fashioned iron latch which clacked as he pressed down the thumb-plate to free the door. Its hinges creaked and he made himself go quickly through the room. He had time to register a dim night-light, a child's bunk bed with humped quilt, and the perfume of washed clothes and talcum powder. Then he was on the threshold of the mother's room. The door was ajar and the room beyond was quite dark. But he could hear the chafe of bedclothes as a body turned in bed.

'Josh?'

It was the woman's voice calling her son's name, just a mumble really, a half-hearted inquiry, hoping for no answer, hoping it would not be necessary to get out of the warm bed. He froze, waiting beside the doorframe, listening for the rustle of a sheet being pushed aside or a toenail on a floorboard. He waited until he heard her breathing, slow and regular again. Then he forced himself to wait another ten minutes. She had to be asleep when he went in. She must never know what hit her.

The pain in his stomach throbbed again, but he dared not rub the spot. A droplet of sweat had formed on his forehead and he waited in agony for it to fatten and roll unmolested into his eye. The effort at supreme and unaccustomed control passed the time. The sweat had still not rolled when the luminous green figures on his watch told him ten minutes were up. He placed a hand in his side pocket and inched out a wad of cotton. Then cautiously he drew on the zip of the breast pocket. Trying to do it slowly, he extracted a bottle of colourless liquid. His fingers trembled as he unscrewed the cap. It seemed to take a long time to reach the top of the thread – then, when it did, he was taken by surprise and dropped the cap.

It fell to the floor, where there was a sheepskin rug underfoot. The bottle-top bounced and rolled away.

Gingerly he got down on hands and knees and placed the wadding and open bottle, whose pungent smell was already reaching his nose, beside him. Groping, and in an escalating state of panic, he searched for the fugitive cap. He looked for its dull, golden glint in the faint night-light. He must have it – he would need the stuff later as well as now and couldn't risk spillages.

At last he had it, tucked into a corner of the room. Quickly he slopped some of the liquid on the wadding, screwed back the bottle-top and, after he'd replaced it in his zipped pocket, listened. Behind his back the child still pushed its snuffly breath out and pulled it in with no noticeable disturbance. And the mother's breathing was still regular as a metronome. He pressed on the door and, with the wadding held at the small of his back, walked into the room.

In the darkness, it seemed larger than he remembered. The bed was a high, old-fashioned double with a brass head, and seemed heaped with more bedclothes than should strictly be necessary. He inched forward until he stood beside her heap of pillows, then reached down and, grasping a pillow which had partially slipped out of place, slid it from beneath the dark smudge which he took to be her hair. He wanted her head to be resting on a flat surface so that it couldn't slip out of his grasp. He put the pillow aside.

He saw her face, saw that it was beautiful in the flawless way that oriental beauty always presents itself. He would have to go down on the face smoothly and without hesitation. If she clocked what was happening, she would twist and thrash and scratch like a hellcat. He would, of course, prove stronger, but he didn't want this. He wanted her to slide under never knowing a thing.

He moved over her, brought the wadding round and lowered it by millimetres towards her face. She caught the pungency, moved slightly in her sleep. He dropped it over her nose and mouth and held it firmly with the clamp of his hand.

But she was not going under quietly. Instantly her voice came, muffled and mewing from beneath his palm. She was bucking and twisting, trying to dislodge him. Relentlessly he rose up and planted his knees on her shoulder, riding her torso as it fought him. The muscles in his neck had tightened with a surge of effort as he pressed down, and gradually all the strength ebbed and left her and she lay still.

For some seconds it went exactly as he'd planned it. But suddenly his senses were flashing warnings, at first just a danger signal, a blip at the edge of his vision. Then it was a full-scale, screaming alert. Some unaccountable dark shape had reared up in the bed beside the woman. This was something which should not, *could not*, be! A shape with a voice attached, a *male* voice. The bitch had been making the beast with two backs. All the people he'd talked to – in London, in Hong Kong, everyone – said she'd never do that with the child in the house!

'Hey!' said the shape. 'Hey, what the fuck's going on, Lizzie?'

The intruder found he was paralysed, like a rabbit in headlights. He was still pressing the pad down as the voice came again.

'Josh? Is that you? What you doing to your Ma, Josh? Hey! Can't you sleep, old feller?'

The woman's partner got no answer. It didn't take him long to work it out for himself. The first hypothesis of his half-awake brain was quickly discarded, for this was something rougher than horseplay between a small child and his mother, and there was a smell of something chemical. With horrifying intensity the truth took its place. An intruder was in the room, sitting astride his girlfriend, the woman he had made love to only three or four hours earlier. What was happening to her? The young man gave a wild, hollow, terrible scream, a scream with an awful question in it. Then he lunged madly at the intruder. His hand reached out and flailed at the other's wrist, while another hand, a fist in fact, was trying to find the stranger's face. It got hold of his ear and started to twist. The intruder felt pain burning him as the tissue connecting his earlobe to his face began to tear. He tried to concentrate on the job under his hands. He heaved down on the woman's face more intensely than ever while, in the corner of his eye, he tried to keep track of the boyfriend's movements. The boyfriend slid to the edge of the bed, braced a foot against the floor and then launched towards the intruder again, still wrenching at the ear in his right fist and pummelling the heavily muscled body with his left.

In fact the boyfriend was not particularly big or notably strong, but he was young and certainly he was brave. Something decisive would have to be done about him.

The intruder raised his palm from the woman's face and slashed upwards and sideways at the boyfriend, who overbalanced and slid away. He was immediately kicked off the bed. Then the men were grappling on the floor, their breath coming in grunts and sobs, their spit flying. The intruder had been in fights like this before. He got one hand to the boyfriend's throat, withdrew the other to his chest and, straightening his index finger and pinkie, straight-fingered the other man's eyeballs with three sharp jabs. A squeal of pain told him he had hit target. As the boyfriend rolled over, burying his face in his palms, the intruder stood and lashed out with his foot, catching some part of the boyfriend's head. Then he scanned the room. On the mantelpiece was an array of objects, old metal household implements. One was an antique flat-iron, which he picked up, gauging its weight for a second. He bent his knees, leaned his left elbow on one knee and brought the iron down with his right arm, a sharp, single blow. There was the dry crack of an eggshell fracturing, and then the boyfriend lay permanently still.

The intruder turned his attention back to the woman. She had sat up in bed and, in a thin, remote, doolalli voice, was repeating a name over and over.

'Sean? Sean? Sean?'

The intruder picked up the wad of cotton from the floor beside her. She was only half-conscious. He knew he had plenty of time.

But when the intruder turned away from the bed the child, Josh, was there in the doorway, looking at him. His bandy-legged, dwarf-like figure was silhouetted by the golden light from the bedside lamp, designed to chase away his night fears. The man flashed his torch into the chubby face. It was topped with spiky black hair, the face of a child maybe two years old. That was much younger than he'd been led to believe, younger than he would have wanted to mess with if he *had* been told. But it was too late for misgivings.

'Mama! Mama!'

Josh (God, how the intruder hated to know its name) was dressed in a red zip-up sleeping suit. A black and white soft toy dangled from his fingers. The glare that beamed out of his flawless deep-brown eyes was accusatory. The man took a step towards the child, but Josh dodged back into his room. Lurching after him, the man gave chase, slamming the mother's bedroom door behind him. By the time he had crossed the room Josh was at the top of the stairs. He hesitated for a moment, looking down into the unfriendly darkness of the stairwell. But the intruder was advancing cautiously down the short landing, his hand edging along the wooden balustrade that protected the stairwell, ready to grab the child.

Suddenly little Josh jerked and teetered, waving his arms with the movement of a circus acrobat at the summit of a human pyramid. Then his feet slid from under him on the shiny wooden floor, and he was gone. He bounced down the stairs feet first, crying once before his skull cracked against a tread. The rest of the way he descended more slowly, and in silence. At last he rolled off the bottom step and lay still. The man took the stairs three at a time and lifted the limp body, cradling it awkwardly. He searched in desperation for a sign of life – the wrist, the mouth, then, gratefully, he found a pulse in the neck. He laid the child carefully on a sofa and fetched the rucksacks he'd brought in from the spinney. He had work to do before they left.

The service area, with space for 1,000 cars, had only a few dozen early breakfasters. He'd made 60 miles, going as fast as he dared along country roads. At last they had joined the motorway, with its endless, anonymous, smoke-belching ant trail of distance truck-drivers and early commuters. Some 20 miles on, the services came as a relief. He needed a coffee, and he needed to look at the child.

He jerked up the handbrake and turned in his seat. As he'd carried the unconscious boy with stumbling haste across the field, he was spurred on by the need to go quickly, for flames in the cottage, though not yet visible, would be building inexorably behind them. Reaching the road at last, he'd dropped his burden gratefully on the back seat, pulled a rug over it and scrambled the car into the crown of the road. He hadn't thought whether the child might be badly hurt. Kids were tough, he thought, and people got KO'd all the time. But then, the more he drove, the more he dwelt on the way the boy had first bounced and then slithered down the stairs. Pulses of dyspeptic pain, brought on by tension and physical effort, came and went between his throat and his stomach. From somewhere came the voice of a National Service instructor. *Nasty things, head injuries, very nasty. Death may ensue with unwonted suddenness, always remember that. Unwonted suddenness!*

He was aware of his heart beating as he reached back and

lifted the rug. Now it looked like a child lost in a daydream. The face was tilted upwards towards him, yet the opened, half-oriental eyes were gazing not at his face but into some impalpable, inner distance. They did not flicker even as he stretched closer in the grey dawn light. There was no sign of hurt. The skin was not broken, no blood flowed from its mouth or nose. It was perfect and complete in every respect except in just the one: it was dead.

He let the rug fall and got out of the car, feeling sick in his stomach. So this was what it felt like. He leaned with both hands on the side of the bonnet and dropped his swimming head. To kill a child. He had never faced up to the possibility. He'd planned and carried this whole thing out, and never admitted that possible outcome. But it was always on the cards, something going wrong.

'Hey! You all right, mate?'

For a moment he may have lost consciousness. It wasn't long enough for the knees to buckle, but sufficiently long to make him realize – as he heard the voice addressing him – that he must pull himself back together.

'I say, you all right?'

The man was in dark blue with peaked cap and leather gloves. He stiffened, retrieving control over his legs.

'No, I'm OK, thanks. Just –'

*Just what? Just killed a kid? Just torched his home, orphaned him, then let him die?*

But he was a pro, a charmer. He forced his breeziest smile.

'No, no, I'm fine. Just needed a breath of air. Bloody heater was on too high.'

The man was not a policeman but a chauffeur. Still the pest hesitated, so there was nothing for it but to lock the car door and walk away towards the cafeteria. He waved his arm in nonchalant farewell.

'*Kill* for a cup of coffee. Bye.'

## 2

The cage doors of the huge industrial lift clashed shut. Madeleine felt her stomach lurch as the upward journey began. The lift was crowded with Chinese standing silent, their faces turned towards her. All the faces were male. They ranged from those criss-crossed with a fine mesh of wrinkled age to the caramel-fudge smoothness of extreme youth. They were dressed in pyjamas, overalls, jeans or city suits and carried bags of tools, briefcases, bundles of laundry, schoolbooks.

She was glad she had started the tape-recorder in her bag before entering the building. There would be no chance of doing it undetected now.

The elevator clattered up floor by floor, stopping at each to offload some of its cargo. As they neared the top stage, Madeleine, with slight furtiveness, unfolded the scrap of paper on which Ed Craike, in his careful, italic hand, had written the details of her meet: 'Swann – Apartment 33C, Golden Fortune Boarding House, 6th floor, 36 Fuk Tsun Street.'

The gates clattered open at the sixth landing. The remaining passengers hung back for a moment to let Madeleine step out. She felt their eyes on her back as she did so. Then the men bustled past her, some towards washrooms whose plumbing could be heard beyond a swing-door at the far end of the landing, others straight through the high entrance opposite the lift, with its massive steel doors doubled back against the walls. Madeleine followed them through.

The low-ceilinged sixth-floor warehouse had been designed to store bushel-sacks of grain, huge bolsters of plastic foam, bales of cloth and man-made fibre, crates of boxed plastic toys for shipment to America, Europe and Australia. But the room's construction was flawed. In rain, at points where it ought to have been watertight, it leaked: its concrete walls glistened then with damp. In heat the room was stifling and infested with rats and cockroaches. At all times the air was crapulous and sour. So the warehouse proved unsuitable to the storage of any merchandise, except for just the one. It now stored people.

Madeleine had heard of these places but never seen one. At first sight it seemed to be a battery for giant chickens. The cages, 6 feet long, 30 inches wide and the same high, were stacked in fours and arranged in five rows, at least thirty stacks to the row. The stacks were no more than 2 feet apart, the rows separated by walkways a yard wide. Each cage contained a mattress, a pillow and an assortment of plastic shopping bags hanging from the wire mesh.

As Madeleine walked the length of the room, looking for stack 33, she did a rough calculation. If all the cages were occupied, the Golden Fortune Boarding House was home to more than 700 people.

Many of them were here now, lying behind the wire, sleeping, smoking, listening to personal stereos, writing, studying. Some watched small battery-powered television sets. Others gossiped or argued. She saw two old men engaged in Chinese chess, moving the wooden discs across a paper chessboard unfolded on the floor between their cages. She saw one surreptitiously taking a fishball from a paper bag and popping it into his mouth. He caught her eye guiltily, like a boy eating gobstoppers in class. All round the walls were signs forbidding the consumption of food on pain of summary eviction.

Apartment 33C was second from the floor in its stack. It had the usual assortment of bulging carrier bags lashed to the rectangular mesh, beyond which she could see the bedding, heaped up over the shape of a man. Only his grey hair was showing.

'Excuse me?'

She spoke in English and there was no response. Madeleine reached her fingers through the wire and lightly plucked at the topmost blanket.

'Excuse me, are you Mr Swann?'

This time the bundle shivered slightly. She heard a voice, muffled but distinctively American.

'Waddya want?'

In Hong Kong the Golden Fortune Boarding House was as low as you could go without abandoning all claims to independence. At 1,500 Hong Kong dollars a month the cages were a strictly Chinese solution to poverty and homelessness, an indoor shantytown. So what was an American doing here?

'Mr Swann, my name's Madeleine Scott. I'm Ed Craike's associate. He assigned me to come and meet you.'

The bedding underwent a further quake as Swann turned over. Now he lay facing her, the head still cowled by blanket, but with his eyes visible from within the shadow of the covering. They gazed at Madeleine steadily and brightly. Then a veined and elderly hand emerged to stick its fingers through the wire.

'Hi, I'm Jim Swann. I'm a bit crocked up here. Got a fever. Got to be careful. You got any money?'

Gingerly, Madeleine touched one of the fingers. Ed Craike had said nothing about paying him money.

'He claims he's got some information,' Craike had told her. 'It could be useful to us, I don't know. Just go down and see him, would you, Maddy? Gauge the strength of it.'

She decided to act as if she'd not heard the mention of money. Instead she tapped with her knuckle on the square section of mesh which acted as the bunk's sliding door.

'Can I open this a little?'

'No. Leave it be.'

The voice was low, but rough and throaty. It struck a note of deep suspicion. On Madeleine's part the feeling was mutual.

'Well, look. You contacted Ed, my boss. What can we do for you?'

'First off, keep your voice down. Most of these people are bums with no schooling, right? But some of them do speakee English. Savvy?'

Madeleine dropped her voice to a whisper and repeated her question.

'You wanted to see someone. What's it about? What can we do for you?'

The staring eyes burned inside the huddle of bedclothes. She looked away from them momentarily. The resident of a bunk across the walkway was gazing meditatively at her, his fingers buried up his nose as he mined for some elusive nugget of bogey. Then Swann spoke again, his gravelly voice a little stronger.

'How do I know who you are?'

Madeleine produced a business card. It gave her name above the words CRAIKE COMMERCIAL SECURITY LIAISON, along with the Hong Kongside address and telephone number. He took it, pushing his head a little way out of the blankets to read it in the gloom. He gave out a grunt, which sounded like acceptance.

'Can you tell us something about yourself, Mr Swann?'

She looked around, and up at the ceiling. It was crowded with hanging signs screwed into the mould-stained concrete. In stark red characters they barked out the rules of the Golden Fortune Boarding House.

RESIDENTS, DO NOT SNORE! WASH DAILY!

LOCK THE BUNKS FOR SECURE LIVING.

MAKE NO NOISE SPITTING.

ALCOHOL DRINKERS WILL BE THROWN OUT.

DRUGS INCUR IMMEDIATE EVICTION.

GAMBLING EXPRESSLY FORBIDDEN.

There were many other ordinances which defeated her powers of translation. She said: 'For instance, what brings you to this awful place?'

'It's not so awful if you ever lived in an army billet or a POW camp. Anyways, I'm broke. I'm sick. I got no relations. I came here from the PRC with nothing.'

Madeleine was puzzled. 'You mean you come from China – from the mainland?'

'You got me. I shouldn't *be* here. I'm illegal.'

It took her aback. There were scores of illegals coming over every week, she knew. But none of them was ever American.

'What on earth were you doing there?'

'Look, my health is fucked. I got no time for this. Figure it out. I got some information which I guess is valuable. I'm offering.'

'What price tag is on it?'

'One you can afford. You bus me out of here: money, passport, ticket to the States. I'm being hunted. Got to keep out of sight. You could cover my ass for me.'

'I can't *promise* any of that. But if the information's good, we might be able to swing something. We're a private organization, you know.'

'Not what I heard. You have friends in very influential places. You can trade on at a nice profit.'

Madeleine felt in danger of going out of her depth. That bastard Craike. Why hadn't he taken the assignment himself? It was pure malice. He said he thought the tip-off was suspect and he'd sent her down here only to rub in her junior status.

'Where did you get our name?'

'From a guy in a bar. Policeman.'

'Well, I can't make any promises. Not without some idea of what you've got for us.'

'*Will* you trade it on?'

'It's possible, yes. We sometimes – we have had dealings with official sources.'

'Well, OK then. Makes no odds to me either way. I can give you the detail when I know you're gonna do something for me. The bones of it is this. It concerns one of the big shots in Hong Kong business.'

'What's his name?'

Swann's head shook under the blanket. 'For the moment I forget the name. One of the *biggest* shots, OK? And it's like this. He's being targeted by the Chinks' secret service. They don't like his plans, they don't like his methods. They don't like him period. Come 1997 they don't want to take over this dump and find him still in a position of influence.'

'What are they going to do with him?'

'They'd like to bust his ass open. But he's too rich to be screwed financially.'

Swann's whisper was one of laryngeal suffocation, a tortured affair of sputtering and puffing. Now he took a deep breath and continued. 'And his personal security is hot as dragon spit. So instead of trying to nail the feet of the man himself, they're gonna do some very shitty things to certain members of his family.'

Madeleine was thinking, this could be something rather bigger than Craike had imagined. Hong Kong's industrialists were among the richest people in the world. Their businesses were often worth more than the national products of most countries in equatorial Africa.

'Can you give chapter and verse?'

'Sure I can. Whistle the tune, too, if you want.'

'I want the name. Who are they going to hit, how and when?'

There came a sigh from the bed, half regretful, half bored.

'Not today, sweetheart.'

She stiffened. That 'sweetheart' had a fake Bogart twang about it and false notes always made Madeleine want to kick something. She managed to subdue most of the reflex. Her foot swung out, but gave no more than a light tap to the steel upright of Swann's stack.

'All right, when?'

'I want you to go away now and speak with your boss. Tell him what I just told you. Tell him the price and then come back to me. And don't wait too long. Right here I stick out like a banana in a bowl of beans. I need out.'

Madeleine was going to speak again, as if to delay her dismissal, but she thought better of it. The man was on the skids – he wasn't going anywhere but down. Just as long as he didn't die on her, she'd know where she could find him.

'I'm on my way. I'll try and get you an answer by tomorrow.'

She moved into the walkway and picked up her bag.

'Hey! Come back here.'

She turned again. Inside the cage the blanket had slipped back a little further and now she could make out more of the man's face. She saw folds of skin under the eyes, freckled blotches on the cheek, a moist, red-rimmed nostril.

'I want money, something on account.'

Madeleine had once been in the Hong Kong police. When she quit she'd retrained with Craike in commercial security intelligence. Now one of Ed's maxims came back to her. It was his lecture on how to run a nark. 'Always open with an earnest, Maddy. A large Scotch, a plate of oysters, whatever seems right.' She remembered how he'd laughed, that lecherous edge in his voice. 'But for Christ's sake don't pay everything up front. Don't drop your knickers first time. Cup their bollocks, tickle their nipples and promise *more*. That's the importance of an earnest.'

Swann was propped on one elbow now, still shadowed by the enveloping bedclothes, breathing heavily. She fished in her purse and found a couple of Hong Kong $100 notes. Folding them lengthways she slid them between the wire and into his waiting fingers.

'Just hang on here, Mr Swann. I'm sure we shall be doing business on this matter.'

\*

Out in the street the fumes of traffic and back-alley cooking smelled delicious to Madeleine. The district of Mong Kok, like an overturned anthill, seethed around her with its everyday lust for seedy profits. And yet, measured beside the human degradation of the Golden Fortune Boarding House, it all struck her as entirely wholesome.

She stopped at a doorway and reached inside her bag. Finding the button on the recorder she snapped it off, then pulled out a lipstick and small mirror. When she'd finished retouching her mouth she unclipped the chunky brooch, in which was embedded a sensitive radio-microphone, and dropped it in beside the recorder. Madeleine felt an inner glow, as if she'd drawn the Derby favourite in a big-money sweepstake. It was the most interesting information she'd had since she graduated from Craike's training course. It was almost as good as her first arrest as a WPC, when she had nailed a bent antique dealer from Hollywood Road. Yes, this felt good. A lot of Craike's clients would be interested in the news that the Chinese were gunning for one of the Hong Kong rich, not least the people in London. It was a fairly open secret that the British had their favourites among the businessmen in the territory. Some they would go to any lengths to protect, while others would quite cheerfully be left to die by Chinese firing squad.

Yes, this was a promising titbit. With a light heart she went off to find a cab.

# 3

The *South China Morning Post* carried the story on its front page.

### C. P. COTTON SUFFERS 'GRIEVOUS TRAGEDY'

The founder of the world's fastest-growing media empire, Hong Kong-based American billionaire Mr C. P. Cotton, has described the deaths of his daughter-in-law and grandson as a 'grievous personal tragedy'. The deaths occurred in the early hours of Sunday morning in a fire at an English country cottage where Mrs Elizabeth Cotton, 27, and her son Josh were spending the weekend.

The fifteenth-century thatched cottage was completely destroyed in the blaze and a senior fire brigade spokesman said that 'little in the way of recognizable human remains have been recovered'. The cause of the fire has not been determined although it is understood that kerosene heaters may have been in use.

Mr Cotton flew out of Kai Tak airport last night to visit the scene of the tragedy. Mrs Cotton's husband, Charles Cotton II, 30, who has been unwell, was with him. In a statement at the airport his father said they were both 'devastated by the occurrence'. Mr Cotton Senior added, 'My son has insisted on travelling against medical advice. You can judge my own feelings when I tell you I haven't seen my grandson since he was a baby. We're going to England to get to the root of this.'

Ed Craike folded the paper and sipped his coffee. He had not expected to be thinking about Madeleine's report of yesterday in such a very different light so soon. His assistant had been gushing with the news, and Craike had felt constrained to pour cold water on her enthusiasm, patiently explaining just how insubstantial Swann's titbit really was.

'We know sod all about him, Maddy. He walked in off the street with this, he could be anybody. Remember what I taught you? A new source is like a raw egg: until you've got it boiled, poached, scrambled or fried, the stuff slides off your fork. Get confirmation from another angle. Firm it up, *then* tuck in.'

Craike's life had tumbled about his ears once and it could happen again. Two years ago in London he'd just about reached Civil Service mandarin level before everything came down. He had been boss to a staff of twenty assorted gophers and grubbers. He'd attended cabinet committees, hobnobbed with the senior politicians and chiefs of staff. Then it had all ended. The truth was, Craike's reflexes were not those of a manager but a foot soldier, an action man. He had had bouts of acute desk-bound frustration, and in the throes of one of these he'd organized a scam too outrageous by far to share with his superiors. And it had ballsed up.

Had the thing come off, who knows? There might have been fanfares and gongs. As it was, he'd been hauled up to Whitehall to hear the Secretary of State for Defence vent his fury in a shower of saliva. Craike, in the minister's words, had displayed 'extreme irresponsibility, not to mention imperilling the entire substance and repute of Crown policy, you reckless bastard. Get out of my bloody sight!'

So, even before the ministerial spittle had dried on his face, Craike found himself disgraced, cashiered, humiliated. He had smarted. But someone had once told him that, in the Chinese lexicon, 'crisis' and 'opportunity' are the same word. This thought, whether true or not, had given Craike the idea of moving to Hong Kong. It was, he knew, an intelligence hotspot, and getting hotter as the 1997 transfer to Chinese administration came nearer. It seemed the perfect place to ply his trade, for government or commerce, and make a living from both. It would also get his feet back on the pavement, his finger on the trigger of action.

So, although his dismissal had felt awesomely terminal, Craike knew he had been shown a yellow, not a red, card. He believed, unknown to the minister (who would have been apoplectic if he *had* known), that he could stay in the game, although privatized now: his own man, a contractor paid only per item of service. So he did it. He was like an evicted dairy farmer who became the milkman.

It had meant a lot of pavement work – bloodhounding, placing bugs, taking snapshots. It was like his early days in the Service, in the 1970s, when he'd been young and didn't care what an untidy world it was. He had even gone as far as to invest every cent he had in the business. It had been touch and go, but there had been enough to get him started. Ever since, he had existed at the whim of an indulgent bank manager.

Then, last week, the bank had started to twitch at the rug. There were few worthwhile jobs coming his way in this recession and outgoings had to be contained. He had already decided to hand the brown envelope to Madeleine. The Swann job was to have been her Swann-song. It hadn't looked like much anyway – a try-on, if not actual flim-flam. Now, of course, he wished he'd sacked her before and done the work himself. He sighed with regret.

When she'd asked yesterday what to do next about Swann, he told her, 'Nothing, Maddy. Wait. If anything happens to one of our senior capitalists, we shall get back on the case. Until then, do nothing.'

At least, *you* do nothing, he had thought. And tomorrow you're out. Which was today, and today everything had changed. They had corroboration of Swann's story; they knew the name of the victim. Craike began to consider his next move. He must get back to Swann, get him under contract, then go and see Cotton with a package.

And by the way, who *was* Swann? Craike knew that a few European Maoists and American POWs had settled in China over the past thirty years. Many earned their living as translators and 'polishers' of official government papers, and some might thereby have had access to sensitive bits of information. Swann might just be a disillusioned example of the type. If he had really sold his soul in Beijing, then he wouldn't get back to the States too easily. Becoming an illegal, as he'd described himself, might have become his only option.

Craike took from his briefcase a piece of paper, a grubby leaf evidently torn from a cheap school exercise book and written on in pencil. It was the note he had received the previous Friday and it was signed 'J. Swann'.

I am told you are in the market for news that is not printed or broadcast. I have some such from across the Shamchun River. Don't miss this ideal trading opportunity.

I can receive visitors at 33C Golden Fortune Boarding Hse, 6th floor, 36 Fuk Tsun Street, on Sunday morning only.

It was a bald communication and Madeleine's first contact

had added only a little hair to it. Yet Craike might have guessed last night that Swann's information about a 'big shot' in trouble with the Chinese concerned C. P. Cotton. Beijing squandered no love on the Cotton Corporation. It was not among the established colonial 'Hong' companies – Swire or Jardine's – with whom the Communists had learned to live over the years. Nor was Cotton among the legion of indigenous Chinese new rich, with their pink fur coats and matching Rolls-Royces, who in the last two decades had thrived on Beijing's approval and its trade. C. P. Cotton was different. He was brash, he was American and he stood, above all, for a compound of Christ and capitalism, a brew which the Red Chinese found more deeply repellent than anything.

'You're talking to the Taipan of the Jesus Corporation,' he would say. 'The world's greatest trading commodity is faith, and we aim to corner the market.'

Previously Cotton had been based in Manila, under the patronage of his good friend Ferdinand Marcos. For ten years in the Philippines he steadily acquired publishing and broadcasting businesses around the world, all devoted to Christianity in its various forms, all evangelical and all increasingly profitable. With the collapse of the Marcos scam, Cotton needed a new home, and he came to Hong Kong. This bucked the trend that had already sent Jardine-Matheson scuttling off to Bermuda, with a bunch of Hong Kong companies in their wake, for fear of what the Chinese takeover would bring. Cotton, though, was not afraid. Hong Kong was the magic kitchen of capitalism. Where better to launch the last big ideological push?

'Now it beginneth,' he had told a press conference when he first came to Hong Kong, his face beaming righteousness. 'Where others have floundered, we shall flourish. Great is our goal: the conversion of China, no less. We're gonna bust through the Great Wall and build us a tabernacle in the Forbidden City, right?'

It was hardly surprising if Cotton had attracted the attentions of the Gonganju – Deng Xiaoping's Ministry of Public Security. That they would try to pull him down was predictable, and that they would do so in this indirect way was perfectly in character. The Chinese respect for family makes Mafia relationships look tepid. As their proverb observes, 'A man's two legs are his father and his son. Kick one and he limps; kick both and he falls.'

Craike drained the last of his coffee, folded the newspaper and signalled to a waiter. Yes, the discomfiture to Cotton might be the saving of Ed Craike's business. It certainly prolonged young Madeleine's employment prospects for at least a week. In fact, he was meeting her in four minutes; she needed her instructions.

'Where is the old man in 33C – the American?'

On her first visit the previous day Madeleine had noticed the pay window, but it had been shuttered. It was on the landing of the Golden Fortune Boarding House near the lift, a slot in the wall under a sign which read: ACCOUNTS OFFICE – PAY RENT OR SUFFER EVICTION. Now she stood peering through the scratched and yellow-tinged Perspex at a neat clerk who was rapidly thumbing a wad of paper money.

The boy acted as if he hadn't heard. He threaded the wad through the elastic band, released the band with a snap and punched some figures into a calculator. Then he picked up another heap of notes, meticulously squared it up and licked his thumb.

'I'm looking for –'

'OK. I heard.'

The youth looked up into Madeleine's eyes. An insolent stare.

'Well? Where is he? I visited him yesterday, but today his things are gone.'

The plastic bags, the greasy bedding, everything was gone. All she had seen in Swann's padlocked cage was a foam mattress in its stained polyester cover. She'd tried to question some of the old fools ranged listlessly in their bunks around stack 33, but they had looked at her with uniform amazement, tongueless or dumbstruck.

The clerk had worked through a quarter of the money, his lips moving as he counted. Madeleine rapped sharply on the window.

'Hey! Isn't there a supervisor or somebody I can talk to?'

The clerk pursed his lips as he doggedly counted to the end of the second pile of notes. When he had entered the total into his calculator he sighed, got up and moved out of her sight. A moment later a door beside the window opened and the youth leaned out.

'Come,' he said, now in English. 'The boss office in here.'

The boss sat behind a plastic desk in a room beyond the accounts office, a short, tubby man with greying hair and a silk-like blue suit which shimmered under the strip lighting. His watch was an expensive-looking chunk of steel mounted on a band like a tank's caterpillar track. Ostentatiously he slid it on and off his wrist – a gesture wasted on Madeleine, who did not know a Rolex from a Timex. In front of him on the desktop was a sign with his name, in characters and English: J. Lee.

Madeleine asked again for the old *gwailo* in 33C.

'He's an American. The bed has been cleared. Maybe he's moved?'

J. Lee spread his hands and parted his lips in a grin. Madeleine noticed that the teeth thus revealed were clamped together with unnecessary force.

'My time here, no American came far as I know.'

'But I saw him yesterday. I visited him.'

The clerk was loitering by the door and J. Lee dismissed him with a curt wave. Reluctantly the boy returned to counting the weekend takings.

'What apartment you say?'

'I'm sorry? Apartment?'

'What number?'

'Oh! 33C, a Mr Swann.'

J. Lee laid his watch down and turned to the computer at his elbow. Rapidly he typed an instruction on the keyboard. The screen unpeeled rows of green digits, which he studied, scrolling through the data. Then he turned back to Madeleine.

'Sorry. No name Swann in these records. 33C has not been rented two weeks. Last tenant was Mr Chen, and he died. He choke on his vomit.'

'Look, I don't understand. Didn't you hear me say? I saw Mr Swann here.'

'Sorry. You are mistaken. Another place maybe.'

Lee let out a sudden explosive laugh as he dropped his finger on to the keyboard. The emerald luminosity was swept from the screen as he directed his grin back towards Madeleine.

'No American has ever come here to live. This a Chinese

rooming house, everybody is very poor here. No Americans, no English, no Oz. Only Chinese in here.'

He laughed again, a high, double yelp. Madeleine knew she would get no further with J. Lee. That grin might as well have been a wall of stone teeth. Christ! Craike would be mad as a wet hen about this.

She turned and retreated through the accounts office. The clerk was hooking some poor deadbeat's dues through the vent in the Perspex window. He turned as he heard Madeleine move behind him.

'You take care now. Have a good day, we are glad to be of service.'

As she waited for the lift Madeleine remembered the boy's earlier insolence and wondered why he'd changed his tune. Then it struck her: the sentiments were lifted straight from the Canadian-American phrasebook. He was practising for the day he got his passport.

Opposite the entrance to the Golden Fortune Boarding House was a narrow opening. It gave access to one of the alleys that network the dense, decayed fabric of Kowloon's building stock like tunnels dug by urban moles. At a little more than head height, the bellies of rotten awnings hung down to catch jetsam from the windows above. The gloom beneath was almost subterranean.

A few feet within this entrance, stationed behind a stall selling English and Chinese books, was a barefoot man. He wore cut-off jeans and a T-shirt on which he claimed to ♥ Hong Kong. Held open in front of his face was a bestselling title, *Twisted Tits*, from the pornographer's stall. Ho had a taste for pornography and would have heartily enjoyed the book. However, as he had no idea at all of the English alphabet, he was not actually reading these pages of repetitive sexual encounter. Instead Ho Yu Ching was keeping a careful eye trained over the top of the book, waiting for the arrival of Madeleine Scott.

Then he saw her, but, shit!, she was already coming *out* of the boarding house, whereas he had been detailed to get to her before she went in. How could he have missed her – a *gwailo* with such flowing yellow hair? What's more, she had long, pinkly solid legs under a deliciously abbreviated black skirt. Even the very shortest glimpse of her, stepping into the bubbling stream of pedestrian traffic, had printed itself on his memory. It was a scrotum-tightening peek into forbidden ecstasy; tonight he would lie in his cot in the dark and think about it.

Ho Yu Ching plunged from the shadow of the alley and darted across the street. He caught up with Madeleine in less than half a minute, putting his hand forward tentatively to touch her arm, then more boldly grasping her round the bicep and pulling her to a halt. He saw her shoulders go up. She gasped and visibly shuddered before turning to face him. She was afraid. Yes. He found he liked that. But he had a commission to fulfil.

'Take this. It is from Mr Swann. He told me you maybe come today.'

Ho looked at her eyes as he pushed the sealed envelope into her hand. They were blue, and staring from a blanched face. *Wah!* This one was tense. He looked down at her knees. *Wah!* Perfection. One day, one day, he would fuck such a woman.

Then he ran off.

Ho's approach unnerved Madeleine only for a moment, and then she was ashamed of it. Mong Kok always made her nervous, though she hid such feelings from Craike. She had been a member of the Royal Hong Kong Police, after all, so no part of the territory should hold fears for her.

She looked at the envelope. It was clearly marked 'to Madeleine Scott'. She flipped it over and tore into the flap. The note, like Swann's previous one, was on paper torn from a school exercise book:

Don't bother to go into the Golden Fortune Boarding House. I'm no longer in residence. I guess you can guess by now the name of the 'big shot' that the Chinese don't like. The news screwed me by its timing – a day later or earlier and I might have reaped full benefit. But we can stay friends, because I have a name for you – the name of the guy who did the job on Mrs Cotton. This will be worth your payment. Just now, I am busy saving my ass but will be in touch to let you know where you can contact me.

Oh, I forgot to say. The guy lives here in Hong Kong. He will be returning from England any day I guess.

It was unsigned. Quickly Madeleine folded it again and

replaced it in the envelope. Craike would want to know this right away. She stuffed the note into her bag and ran to Mong Kok's metro station on Nathan Road.

# 4

After the white Rolls-Royce Corniche pulled up beside the garden gate, it stood closed and secret for several minutes. The engine idled in a dry whisper; the darkened windows offered no hint of activity within. The car presented a sleek contrast to the mounds of blackened, disintegrated, sodden ashes and debris that had once been a whitewashed, rose-entwined and thatch-capped cottage.

As soon as the car had turned into this side road, the waiting journalists chased forward, like players in a game of Rugby trying to get under the ball. The waiting hacks were a mixed zoo. Fresh-cheeked children from the local weekly papers and radio stations were yapping with excitement at this close encounter with celebrity. Older hands from the nationals, whose capacity to be thrilled had long since bunioned over, were grunting as they punched the keys on their porta-phones or hastened to get in position. There were even a few society columnists and one brisk woman from the business press.

Within a few hours the first wave of sensation caused by the fire had broken and died on the shore of public attention. By Sunday afternoon the journalists' numbers had dwindled to a skeleton crew, their task becoming predictable and dull. Mostly it was to pester officials – forensic people, officers of the fire service, at one point the chief constable – for a statement about the cause of the fire, and otherwise to argue over whatever visual clues presented themselves inside the magic ring of plastic police ribbon, a cordon which followed the boundary hedge of the garden.

For half of the first afternoon an ambulance was in attendance and some of the younger scribblers watched with uneasy stomachs as a series of plastic bin-bags were loaded. A woman, a man and a child, they'd been told: she the daughter-in-law of the media tycoon, the child his grandson, the man unknown. In the bags would be their mortal remains, raked from the ashes. These young newspeople had attended no wars. They were yet to cover any big civilian disasters, with corpses too numerous and far-flung for concealment. So, counting bags into the rear of the ambulance, the younger elements of the press were at a loss to grasp the frightfulness of fire and brimstone.

But among their experienced colleagues were those well able to visualize the bags' contents: those coked twigs of bone; the shreds of grilled flesh and human offal; embedded fragments of clothing; heat-mishapen rings, buttons and zip-fasteners; blackened, shrapnel-like teeth.

By nightfall a tip-off came from a police sergeant unable to contain the secret. Cotton himself was coming to inspect the scene of his only grandson's immolation.

'Sorry I can't tell you when, boys. Some time in the next twenty-four hours, that's all I've got.'

The hacks had groaned. This imprecision meant they must stay at their posts all night, or at least be back on the beat first thing. Now, fourteen hours later, the chief constable had returned, as had a second echelon of journalists. And then, at last, the great man who sometimes styled himself the Electronic St Paul was among them.

The limousine had already remained shut far longer than was reasonable. What was the fellow playing at? Had he been taken ill in there? Was he on the phone? Or asleep? After a further thirty minutes the cause of the delay appeared: a van festooned with aerials and with the initials CPC-TV emblazoned on its side came up fast and shuddered to a halt behind the Rolls. The film crew broke from the back of the van like marines out of a landing-craft and took up positions ready to capture events in sound and pictures. Only then did the rear door of the car click and swing open.

The knot of hacks craned forward. They caught a glimpse of the car's interior: green screens, handsets, a bank of keys and switches set in walnut and rich red leather. Then a brogue shoe in tan and white emerged, and the aperture was filled by the form of C. P. Cotton himself. He planted both feet on the ground, straightened and, for a moment, studied the group of journalists as they called out to him.

'Mr Cotton! Do you have any statement to make?'

'When was it you last saw your daughter-in-law?'
'Have you any information about what caused the tragedy here, Mr Cotton?'

But Cotton seemed not to hear. He was engaged in a meditation of his own, looking from face to face as if searching out a quality he required. The globes of his eyes seemed exaggerated in their roundness, and they gleamed with moisture. By contrast, the skin of his face was pallid, taut and dry, like the crust of a cheese.

He pushed the pack of journalists away and made room for his son to emerge from the car. Charles Cotton II was a head taller than his father, a large-framed athlete modelling an expensively fashionable suit. He posed with legs slightly straddled, arms loose at his sides, eyelids drooping, in a moody attitude that might have been acquired from a study of the glossy magazines. His father beside him was still scanning the crowd. Suddenly he shot out an arm, his index finger pointing.

'You!'

A rookie photographer standing diffidently at the back of the scrum tapped his chest and frowned.

'Me?'

'Yes, you.'

He jerked his thumb towards the embers of the cottage.

'You come in with us. The rest of you goddamn bloodsuckers can wait outside. Now, where's the fool police chief who's supposed to meet me here?'

He had already pushed his way to the edge of the group and stood by the wooden-slatted gate. With a traffic cop's gestures he waved the television crew through before him.

In a house fire oak beams and posts, if they're thick enough, don't usually reduce to ash. They burn inwards until a coating of charcoal is formed which chokes off the fire, leaving the wood emaciated but still of a piece.

Joe Harrington, Chief Constable of the Anglian Police, stood on what had once been the back lawn of the cottage with C. P. Cotton and Fire Brigade Superintendent Dick Darby. The ENG video-crew had been posted out of microphone range.

Harrington pointed to the two corner posts at the east gable-end of the cottage. Blackened and thinned in parts almost to breaking point, they nevertheless still stood, rearing starkly above the fire's grey detritus.

'It was a very intense fire, sir, but that was where it was least hot. At the other end, where it was really intense, you'll notice the posts fell. That was the end of the child's bedroom, I believe.'

C. P. Cotton seemed appalled by what he saw.

'Jesus, Chief. This place burned up like it was made of fucking toilet paper. I mean, there's nothing left here.'

Harrington had long ceased to be surprised by the famous. They never turned out to be like the papers painted them. A profane and foul-mouthed evangelist did not faze him.

'Just about the entire fabric of the house was either inflammable or insubstantial. It was wooden-framed, had a thatched roof and the walls were formed by nothing but wattle and daub. There was nothing to offer resistance.'

'Wattle and what?'

Harrington leaned over and caught the eye of Darby.

'Dick?'

The fireman cleared his throat.

'It's a lattice of thin laths, Mr Cotton, covered in clunch and whitewashed over.'

'*Clunch?*'

'A local clay. It doesn't burn but it falls off in lumps as the cottage frame buckles in the heat. Then the laths burn up like matchwood.'

In the centre of the cottage the chimney-stack had partially come down. What remained was a precarious steeple of bricks, like a detail from Coventry or the East End of London in 1941. The photographer was taking full advantage of this background to dramatize his pictures of the group of men, kneeling and letting the camera motor trip the shutter in rapid runs of four and five. For his benefit, the Cottons' faces were drawn and grave. The father made a gesture over the ash and char, like a Hindu casting incense on a burial pyre.

'But it must have been a holocaust in there. Why didn't they get out?'

'It was at night. They were asleep. They were overcome by smoke.'

'They suffocated before they burned?'

'That is almost always the case in incidents like this, yes, sir.'

'Where was the Fire Department?'

Darby, with gloved hands clenched behind his uniformed back, swivelled his body to right and left.

'Look around you, sir. There's no house for, what? Half a mile? There's a farm across there, just over the brow, but they were all asleep. The fire had burned for a good two to three hours before we even knew about it. By the time we did get here, there was nothing left to save.'

Turning to Harrington, Cotton's eyes seemed more protuberant than ever. He licked his lips before he spoke, as if it would make the words come easier.

'Chief, what, er, *remains* have you pulled out?'

'Well, I was coming to that, sir. Two bodies so far, one male and one female.'

'The child and his mother?'

'No, sir. Two adults.'

'I don't get it. Who was the man? My son Chuck is right here.'

He indicated Chuck, who hardly registered the attention. He seemed to be attending only to something inward, some narcissistic activity such as the tensing and relaxing of muscles beneath his clothes.

'You have no idea yourself, sir, who it might be? Or your son?'

'How could he? He wasn't here, was he? Don't *you* know?'

'We are making inquiries. Identification is almost impossible but we will probably find out through circumstantial evidence – someone who knew the man was here. So far, no one has volunteered any information.'

'What about the child? What about my grandson?'

'Well, I'm sorry to say we haven't found the child. We, er, don't think we will. We think there'll be nothing left of him.'

'Nothing left?'

'We've spoken to the cleaning lady, a Mrs Clarke, who comes in during the week from the village. As I said, young Josh's room was in that west end of the house. Below it was a wood and coal store and, according to Mrs Clarke, a drum of kerosene was kept in there too.'

'So the boy –'

29

Again Harrington looked across at Dick Darby, who picked up his cue more reluctantly this time.

'Nothing left to find, sir,' he said, finding, he hoped, just the right level of authoritative regret. Cotton's hand moved to scratch his cheek, as if verifying his own solidity.

'Dust to dust, right?'

'That's about it, sir.'

Slowly Cotton turned on his heel. His normally decisive, no-shit manner had left him for the moment. With his back to the fire scene, he pondered as the cameraman crouched, letting go a burst of shutter releases. Then he jerked up his head.

'You want us in the morgue? You want us to identify her?'

Harrington took a step towards Cotton and drew him away from Chuck. His voice was low, confidential and had a slight tremor.

'No, sir. There wouldn't be any point. The two bodies – I mean, it would take an expert just to sort them out into man and woman.'

'I see. Well, when you've got some kinda fix on the man, or if you find any part of the child, I want to know about it, OK? Now we've got to go.'

He strode back down the path, through the gate, through the suddenly baying, jostling newsmen and into the car, pushing Chuck in front of him impatiently. For an instant he sat forward in his seat, as if about to speak. The journalists fell silent. Cotton's eyes were wet. His lips parted. The journalists chafed shoulders and knocked elbows to catch the quote. Then Cotton reached out, pulled shut the door and the car was under way. It was pursued by the cries and curses of frustrated men.

Harrington stood with Darby looking after the Rolls as it dipped away down the lane.

'A charmer, eh, Dick?'

'Great men have their privileges, sir.'

'But that was bloody rude! Who does he think he is?'

Dick Darby considered for a moment.

'Citizen Kane, sir?'

In the back of the limo the Cottons each took their counter-measures against shock. C. P. Cotton lowered a walnut veneer panel and, lifting a decanter and a shot-glass from the cavity within, poured himself a brimming measure of bourbon. Chuck, meanwhile, placed a silver cigarette case on his knee and was sprinkling a 4-inch line of white powder across the lid. His father looked on, neither surprised nor approving. He just took a slug of Wild Turkey and rolled it around his mouth. He swallowed.

'Your wife was a bitch, son, for all her education.'

He looked out. The fields were all arable, and fuzzed in the middle distance by mist.

'To think she had that little kid in the house with her all the time she was being pronged by some piece of low-life. A goddamn slutting bitch.'

Chuck slid a gold tube from his kerchief pocket and hoovered the cocaine up his nose in a single toot. He lay back, blinked, and laughed in bitterness and melancholy.

'But she was my *life*, daddy.'

His fist closed on the slim golden cylinder. He squeezed and opened his hand again, revealing the object with mock surprise like a magician.

'We had no time, did we? We had no chance.'

'Forget that woman, son. It's the kid, Baby Josh, whose memory must not die. Not ever. So God-almighty innocent, he was.'

He took another slug of bourbon and set his jaw stiffly around it.

## 5

It was Sim Fielding's twenty-fifth birthday and for the first time in years he wanted a cigarette.

If he put his mind to it, he was still able to remember the exact tang of the tar, and the pulse-quickening jolt of nicotine that went with the day's first, deep drag. At the grammar school Sim had been known for smoking. He was a two-packets-a-day boy until, overnight, he changed. It was late one summer night, after he'd been to the pictures with Rosemary Melling. Rosemary's father discovered the two of them sprawled on top of a concrete bin-bunker at the side of the Mellings' house. Puffing round the corner with a Player's Weight drooping from his mouth and an overflowing wastepaper basket in his claw, Jack Melling was brought up sharp by the sight – his daughter with her tits hanging out and tights down to her knees struggling to part the zip of Sim's jeans and Sim sucking her earlobe with the ferocity of a newborn calf.

Jack had let the cigarette fall into the basket he was carrying, his face a mask of gobsmacked impotence. There may have been rage, too, but you couldn't see that. Just an old man who couldn't speak, let alone move or fight, whose scrawny shoulders jerked up with each desperate heave of his smoke-crippled lungs. Sim judged the parents of others all the more severely now that he had none of his own. He was tempted to go ahead and penetrate Rosemary right there in front of her dad, just to show his contempt.

But she'd told him Jack was only forty-six, and the sight of this man, a pulmonary pensioner before he was fifty, suddenly filled Sim with horror. In the next moment the wastepaper in the basket began to smoulder. Old man Melling could only stare at the rising smoke. He hadn't even the strength to put the thing down. So Sim bit Rosemary's ear one last, delicious time, climbed off her, took the basket of rubbish (now beginning to flame up) from Jack's frozen hand and emptied it into a puddle on the drive. Out of loathing and disgust he never smoked again.

But this morning, when he read his post, for a moment he could have done with a cigarette. There'd been quite a few birthday cards, for the village, as ever, had done him proud. But this, with its Manchester postmark, was the odd one out. It was a view of the city's rotund Central Library and read:

Dear Sim

The Pearl River Restaurant is a nice place to eat. You'll find it in Back George Street, Chinatown. Come Friday evening, 7.00.

LOVE Maurice.

The 'Dear Sim' was nothing but conventional. But what about the 'LOVE Maurice'? There was force, even bullying, in those capital letters. Why should Maurice now threaten him with love, when everything he'd ever done before had signalled the lack of it?

Breakfast coffee filtered noisily in the background as he stared out of his window. It had been his mother's cottage, a place standing apart, up on the high ground. Below him the road rose from the village of Moxon towards the fell top and now, on its verge, he could see an escaped sheep disconsolately cropping the grassy ditch. Occasionally she paused to broadcast to the flock that was similarly engaged on the other side of the drystone. Beyond them, the pasture land sloped away to the wooded furrow of the river, and then up again, more gently, towards the distant, portentous mass of Pendle Hill, upon which Lancashire witches had once held their sabbaths.

At the bottom of the road was a bridge where the valley tightened almost to a ravine, and it was in here that the village of Moxon was wedged. You could see, in the gaps between the roadside trees' rust-brown autumn foliage, the angled planes of roof slate, the industrially blackened stones and the shading of coal smoky air that always overhung the village in the morning. You could see also its three significant buildings, two of them ruins. Murthwaite's Mill roof was pitted with holes and its windows starred by children's stones. Moxon Abbey, dissolved by Thomas Cromwell four and a half centuries ago, was a tidier wreck – a few stone walls, with irregular, saw-tooth tops, surrounded by well-tended grass. Only St Matthew's Church, at the opposite end of the High Street from the Abbey, was in one piece.

Sim turned away from the window and poured himself a cup of coffee. The desire for a cigarette had left him now, like a temptation of the devil removed by prayer. He smiled, remembering his old reputation among his school friends, and the consternation when he told them he'd renounced the cigarette.

'It's for kids and crippled old fools,' he'd said self-importantly, after the Melling incident. 'I'm jacking it in. Anyone want to argue about it?'

No one did, for Sim was known by a second characteristic in the school playground: he never backed off from a confrontation with a stronger boy and could do a lot of damage before he was beaten.

He sat down at the kitchen table, read again the postcard and shut his eyes. He tried to visualize Maurice, but couldn't. It was – how long? Seventeen years since he'd seen him. Sim took a mouthful of coffee and knew he would go. He may have packed in smoking, but he was still unable to duck away from a scrap. He would go to the Pearl River. He would meet his father.

Sim walked into the Chinese restaurant wearing blue jeans, a leather flying-jacket and fur-lined biker's boots. He checked his helmet at the desk and looked around.

The tables were covered uniformly in postbox-red cloth. All those away from the walls were round, for the Chinese find angular tables inhibiting. Many were occupied by groups of Mancunians, most of them businessmen but with a leavening of couples and the odd family. The brittle chatter of the few children rose above the quiet, money-centred rumble of adult male conversation.

With his eyes Sim found the table he was looking for. It was one in a row of alcoves along the far wall, occupied by a man in a herringbone sports jacket and open-neck white shirt. The man's hair, a dirty fleece in thickness and colour, had gone unbarbered for months, and his chin winked with grey stubble. His frame was large, with a paunch creased by the table's edge and long legs splayed out uncomfortably beneath it. He was studying the evening paper.

Sim walked across and slid into the facing velour-upholstered bench seat. He was very calm, waiting for the other to react. When, slowly, the man looked up, Sim said, 'I think this place is meant for me, isn't it?'

He squared his shoulders, held the man's gaze and, for the first time in seventeen years, was looking into the face of his father.

Maurice Fielding took a drag at his cigarette. It was only half-smoked, but already was creased and bent out of shape. He crinkled his eyes beneath their spiny, grey brows, holding Sim's gaze for a second. Then he reverted to the sports page spread out on the table. He mumbled a few words which Sim took a moment to decode.

'I had a dirty weekend, double, good fuck-farm, I blued all my bloody *cash*!'

Sim sensed the faces of other diners turning towards them at the sound of the raised voice on that last word. He leaned a little towards Maurice.

'You had *what*?'

'Dirty weekend, a nag at Newbury. It ran like piss down my leg, won by twenty lengths. Only trouble was, I had it doubled with a spavined, broken-winded goat name of Good Luck Charmer.'

His face was lined and grey. It seemed bigger than Sim remembered, with pores that gaped as if the skin were struggling to stay alive. On his cheekbone, left side, rested the violet remains of a bruise.

Maurice's finger, stained mandarin orange by nicotine, jabbed down at the list of runners in the paper.

'What am I going to do, son? I invited you to dinner and I'm cleaned out. Can't even pay for the meal.'

He fetched a sigh, the endlessly repeated ten-minute hell of the mug punter down the ages, the gaps between the selection and adoption of losing fancies. Sim took out his wallet and placed it on the table.

'Why did you invite me?'

Maurice sat back and looked his son in the face again, smoking steadily. The eyes were relaxed and it was hard to read them. Sim hadn't seen Maurice since he was eight years old. He remembered the thump of his feet on the stairs, so early in the morning it was still not light. Sim had lain in bed thinking his father would be coming in to kiss him goodbye. Maurice often went away, and always he'd slip jauntily into the child's bedroom and kiss his boy, whispering, 'Your dad's got to go off and earn a crust. I'll be back in a couple of days, son.'

It was rarely as few as a couple of days, but in the past he always *had* returned. On a few memorable occasions he'd entered the house in triumph and there were presents, a new car, whole drawers full of clothes. But usually he'd returned crestfallen, the way Sim saw him now. He'd hear through the gappy floorboards of their stone terraced cottage his mother's reproaches.

'You said you wouldn't *do* that this time. You promised. I don't care about myself, but the boy! What about the boy? He's bright as a button. We could get him an education. He could be a doctor.'

Of his father he'd hear nothing except a low apologetic mumble. Later, though, in the room next to his own, the man would reassert himself. Sim would hear the savage, rhythmical creaking of the bed, the percussive expulsions of breath. In Sim's imagination it was identical to the sound of the large ratchet-jack he'd seen in operation at John Worsley's vehicle repair shop. Later in the night, ghosting in his dreams, he'd hear the jack in action again.

On that last occasion, though, the final going-away, Maurice had paused outside Sim's door but thought better of coming in. Then in an obscure way Sim knew. The usual promise of being away 'just a couple of days' may have been inaccurate, but it was always meant. This time there was no promise of return – and no return. Maurice simply disappeared from Sim's life.

So now Sim was wondering, how far could he forgive his father? He had travelled to Manchester in no mood for forgiveness. All he required was an explanation. But now, face to face, things seemed so much more complicated. Maurice and he were not complete strangers. A third of his life they'd spent together, and there was a whole history of games and laughter as well as tears to be dropped into the scales.

'Don't tell me,' said Sim, 'that you knew it was my birthday.'

Maurice took a while to react. Then he jerked his hand up and clapped his brow before moving it higher still to stroke the matted top of his head.

'Your birthday? By Christ, Sim boy, is it your birthday? What would you be, twenty –'

'Five.'

'*Twenty-five?* Christ, I remember your last one, I mean, the last one I was, er, in residence for, like. Your ma made a cake in the shape of a football pitch and I scoured every shop in Burnley for the men. They *had* to be Manchester City.'

'No. United.'

'United was it? I could've sworn it was City.'

'It was City you got me. I was a United supporter, but you got City.'

Maurice's eyes were moist as he took a pull from his cigarette and then, before exhaling, a mouthful of beer.

'I got a lot of things wrong, Sim. You must think I'm a terrible man.'

The smoke gushed out as he spoke. Sim wrinkled his nose.

'Do you want to know?' Sim asked icily. 'Do you want to know what I think?'

Infinitesimally Maurice's eyelids flickered.

'OK, son. Hit me.'

Sim held his father's gaze. Then Maurice sighed, shrugged, and looked away.

'To you I'm a shit. Unworthy of respect. But that is not true everywhere in my life. Elsewhere, where people's minds are different, I am more than that.'

'You're still broke, you still lose on horses. What's new?'

'No, I've built myself up. I'm a respected man now – in certain quarters.'

Sim felt the anger tightening in his chest.

'My mother is in her grave, and the man who put her there is telling me I've got to *respect* him.'

The flash of temper triggered another in Maurice and he snapped. 'Your mother? I won't talk about her. I won't discuss Eva.'

'Then there's nothing to discuss.'

Sim's mouth was dry and his muscles felt tense and tired. The man was pathetic and it was a mistake to have come. He was shifting sideways out of the seat when he saw the look of alarm crossing Maurice's face. It was the look of a salesman losing the day's one big-spending customer.

'I'm sorry, Simmie. Won't you stay?'

His use of the diminutive made Sim falter. Then a waiter appeared at his elbow. He looked as if he didn't want to lose a punter either.

'You want to order your food, sir?'

Sim looked from Maurice to the waiter and back again. Maurice was his father, after all, and he'd come to the meeting knowing nothing about him – how he earned his living, whether he had remarried. Perhaps Sim had brothers or sisters. The thought filled him with a new surge of curiosity. How could he leave without finding out what there was to know?

He sat down again.

'All right. Let's eat. Will you answer my questions?'

Maurice shrugged and pushed his lips out. Then he turned to the waiter and spoke to him rapidly. Immediately the waiter bustled away towards the kitchen. Sim was puzzled. Maurice had spoken quite audibly yet he hadn't understood a word of it.

'What was that you said?'

'Cantonese. I asked for *dim sum* and various other bits. They'll serve their specialities and best dishes because they know I'm not some Mancunian prat who picks his ears with the chopsticks.'

'You know Chinese?'

'Why not? I've been a long time out East, son. I'm a seasoned *gwailo*.'

'*Gwailo?* What's that when it's at home?'

'Cantonese term for the white man. It's also a fat insult, because literally it means we're devil-men. But that's no big deal. It only proves how much the Chinese have got to take us seriously. They're heavily superstitious, and ghosts, devils, genies, they may all be bad news, but they got to be dealt with. Dealing with the *gwailo* is what Hong Kong is all about – at least till 1997. When the boys from Beijing come marching home, Christ knows what-all's going to happen.'

Bottles of Tsing Tao beer arrived, and Maurice poured for his son. He had shed his diffidence and was starting to enjoy himself.

'So you're living out there now?'

Maurice seemed to hesitate, then he said, 'No. Obviously I'm where you see me.'

'Staying in Manchester?'

Maurice picked up the chopsticks, leaned forward and, selecting a dumpling, dipped it in soy sauce and deposited it in his mouth.

'As I said, I'm broke, Sim. As of now I need somewhere to stay. OK?'

Sim, too, ate a dumpling, handling the chopsticks awkwardly.

'No,' he said. 'The answer's an absolute no. You can't come back with me.'

Maurice leaned forward and stabbed the air with his sticks. His eyes were popping in emphasis.

'Well, what am I to do? No money, no prospects, no fixed abode.'

'Get a job. Find a hostel. Go to the police.'

Maurice jumped in mock horror.

'The *police*? Don't jest about matters you know nothing of. Me and the police don't mix, socially or professionally. OK, so I don't go with you to that small-minded village. Well, maybe you could let me have a small advance.'

His eyes rested on the wallet that lay in front of Sim, a hungry-dog look. Sim said, 'We can talk about it. Not now. You're not answering my questions. What have you been doing? What are these "certain quarters" you've been hanging out in?'

'You're very inquisitive. I shouldn't have mentioned that.'

A couple had risen from the next table, preparing to leave. The girl was blonde and she wore a short, dark skirt over black tights. She was in Sim's natural sightline, so Maurice had to turn to get a look. He did so, ostentatiously staring at the woman's legs and then her breasts as he spoke out of the corner of his mouth. 'Look at that! The melon-chested-schoolgirl look, Sim. Christ, I can hardly bear to view that.'

But view it he did. And as the girl arched her back to slip into a short jacket, those full breasts strained up against her silk shirt. Maurice took a hissing intake of breath.

'Jesus, look at *those*.'

He gave out a low but audible growl and the object of his attention shot a glance towards him, flushing red. By now the man she was with had registered Maurice's interest and he didn't like it. He stepped towards Maurice.

'Wha' you looking at, pal?'

Maurice winked. He cocked his thumb towards the girl, who had started to go towards the door.

'Not what – *her*. Your tart. Tasty. Tell you what, I'll take her off your hands. What d'you want for her?'

For the first time Sim heard the slur in Maurice's voice, and realized he was very drunk. Deliberately, the stranger leaned over the table, his face beginning to clock up all the stages between indignation and rage. His girl came back. She put a hand on his shoulder, bent and cooed nervously in his ear.

'Come on, Bill. It's not worth it.'

She plucked at the flap of his double-vented jacket. But Bill was a thick-set, thick-breathing Scot with a broken nose and he thought differently.

'Ye!' he snarled. 'Ye're lower than a ponce, ken?'

He reached out, took hold of Maurice's shirt by one end of the collar and jerked it.

'Come on out,' he said. 'Come out in the street. Ah'll learn you some fucking manners.'

Maurice raised his hands, fingers splayed, the gesture of innocence. His eyes were wide.

'Just complimenting you on a glorious piece of snatch, Billy boy. Just enviously looking on, OK?'

'*Not* OK, right? And don't call me by no name. I'd like to fucking kick your ass from here to London.'

'Jesus Christ, tell a bloke he's got A-1 taste in pussy, and he threatens you. Not that I wouldn't mind shafting her one, but since you're cock of the box, Billy boy, I'm not –'

Bill reached out and picked up Sim's beer glass. He smashed it downwards, breaking off the rim on the edge of the table. At the sound of the breakage, the whole room fell silent.

'Bill, don't,' the girl was saying. 'Please, Bill, come away.'

But Bill was already half-way through his punitive action. He took a handful of Maurice's sheepshag hair and, still with the jagged remains of the glass in his other hand, he punched it into the side of Maurice's head.

His girl gasped and put a hand to her mouth. Then someone behind her screamed as gouts of bright blood spurted from a ring of cuts around Maurice's ear. Bill dropped the remaining portion of glass in his hand. He threw a swift, jerking series of glances around the room, then turned and, pulling the object of Maurice's earlier lust behind him, ran from the restaurant. It was, more or less, a stage exit.

Just before bedlam broke over their heads Sim found himself considering his father.

'You know something?' he said. 'You had it coming.'

In spite of being decked out in white coat and stethoscope, the junior doctor on duty in Manchester Royal Infirmary A and E looked like a teenager. She was also so tired that she spoke and moved like a zombie.

'Your father's lucky to be all right. The glass missed the jugular by millimetres. Anyway, we've taken out most of the fragments and bandaged him up. You can cart him off now.'

Her voice was empty. It was right out of compassion. Nor was there any sympathy in her lacklustre, sleep-deprived eyes.

'Don't you think he should stay in, I mean for observation or whatever you call it?'

'Sorry, we're short of beds. There's been a pile-up on some motorway, so there's a pile-up in here. Make him see his GP in a couple of days.'

She moved off and Sim went to find Maurice.

He was sitting on the side of a bed with a thick crêpe bandage wrapped at an angle round his skull. He was dangling some car keys from his index finger and humming to himself gloomily. He held the keys out for his son to take.

'Here, you drive. I don't feel up to it.'

Sim was taken by surprise. They'd come to the hospital by ambulance.

'You've got a car?'

Maurice stood up and cautiously, with both hands, felt all around the bandage on his head.

'Course I have. How d'you think I get about? God, I must look an utter prat in this. Don't show me to a mirror, OK?'

'Is it yours, the car?'

Maurice raised his head and gave his son a teasing, half-finished smile.

'Auction somewhere in East London. Bit of a bargain, actually.'

Sim took the keys.

'So, where are we going?'

Maurice looked shocked, as if the question had already been settled.

'Your place, of course. You can't leave me here. They won't have me, for one thing. And there's nowhere else.'

Sim shook his head, but he knew he was beaten. Suddenly and inexorably, as the broken glass ground into the side of Maurice's face, the man had become his responsibility. He was wounded and flat broke, with nowhere to stay. And there was no one else, as far as Sim knew, who gave a bugger what happened to him.

*Shit!*

He would have to take Maurice to Moxon. He would have to keep an eye on him. The guy was his *father*, for Christ's sake!

*Shit!*

'Hey! Whoa! *Stop!*'

Five minutes earlier they had found the car in Chinatown, and Sim, abandoning his bike with reluctance, at least for the time being, was driving north along Deansgate. Maurice's shout brought his foot mashing down on the brake pedal and the car – a well-used red hatchback whose every bearing was as loose as a turkey's throat – slewed fractionally on the wet tarmac before its momentum ran out. Sim thought, at the very least, there must be a cat under the wheels.

'What is it?'

Maurice didn't reply. He was already fumbling with the door. As it swung open, he virtually fell into the gap between car and kerb.

'It's your birthday, and we need a wet, Sim boy. There's not much time before closing. Find somewhere to park and then find me in that place.'

Maurice pointed to a pub, 20 yards up a side street and bright with coachlamps and gilded lettering. Then he gripped the open door, swung himself to his feet and, aiming towards it, moved off with all the fluency of a novice skater on Largactil.

When Sim caught up with his father again it was in a narrow and crowded saloon bar. Indistinguishable rock music thrummed beneath the shouts and laughter of drinkers whose pitch of noise was now mounting towards the crescendo of closing time. A pall of yellow tobacco smoke clogged the air.

Maurice was engrossed in telling a joke to half a dozen young men. He broke off when Sim came towards them.

'Ah! Sim, good. Yours is that pint on the bar. Sup up, there's time for a couple more if you're quick.'

He turned back to his audience, a knot of men who wore the football colours of some out-of-town team.

'So, like I was saying, lads, the chambermaid looked up at the master of foxhounds like this, you know? "But squire," she says, "it hurts a bit", and he said to her "Oh, Christ, my dear, don't worry about that. I must've forgotten to take off my spurs."'

The punch-line was met with a roar of approval. Maurice was clapped on the back until he coughed, and his beer slopped on to the carpet. He came close to Sim and slung an arm round his son's neck, lifting his glass.

'Good health, and many of them.'

He drained the glass and pushed it into Sim's hand.

'Get me another one of these. Just going for a Jimmy Riddle.'

He wandered off through the crowd, his white-bandaged head bobbing as he jostled to get through and was jostled in turn. Sim settled with his back to the bar and sipped his beer.

He'd had one conversation about Maurice with his mother. It was when she was dying. Eva Fielding – now reduced to a few dry twists of skin around a skeleton – had lain in the public ward, struggling to find the words.

'He'll be back, one day. He'll come to you.'

She had sucked in a breath and gathered herself to speak some more. She seemed crushed by the weight of the sheet and blankets.

'He's a fool and untrustworthy. But he's not – really – evil. When he does come, try to forgive him. Will you?'

Around Sim drinkers were laughing, sweating, shaking their jowls, arguing, threatening, shouting for drinks, singing and, in the case of a woman beside the juke box in a worn coat trimmed with fur, crying. As a boy he had hardly ever cried, but he had been crying then, kneeling next to his mother's bed.

'All right, Ma,' he had said as she'd raised her bony, desiccated knuckles to his face and tried to flick away the tears. It was a promise.

He saw Maurice now, across the room; he was easily spotted by his turbaned head. Next to the door of the toilet was a payphone and Maurice was speaking into it, nodding his head for emphasis. Whoever he was speaking to was arguing back, and Sim lip-read his father shouting, 'Right, OK, bye.' Then he hung up and threaded his way back to the bar.

'Give us two tenners, old son.'

'What's it for?'

'Tell you later. Give.'

He snapped his fingers. Sim, hardly caring any more, almost laughed. This was a temporary holiday from reality. He picked two £10 notes from his wallet and handed them over. Maurice headed back through the herd and Sim, putting down his glass, went after him.

The corridor that led to the toilets was ill-lit and smelt of decay and disinfectant. Maurice was speaking to a greaser in full leathers, a giant who must have stood 6 foot 7. The money was being passed over. As soon as Sim came up the greaser turned away without a word and pushed past, zipping the £20 into a pocket of his jacket. His boots clumped with threatening force as he swung through the door and back into the bar. Sim spoke sharply.

'What are you doing with my money?'

Maurice hesitated, then opened his hand, disclosing a small foil-wrapped packet. He smiled lopsidedly, his eyes disappearing into the folds of surrounding skin.

'Just buying dope, old son. Hash, you know. Don't worry. All in a good cause.'

He pocketed the purchase, mock-punched Sim in the stomach, and strode past him into the bar.

'Come on, drink up. We got time for two or three more. Then we got a call to make before we blow out of town.'

An hour later, as they left the bar, Sim heard one of the football fans retelling Maurice's joke.

'Thing is, says the slag to the foxhunting geezer. It hurts a bit, right?'

Maurice reached the car first and stood on the driver's side, impatiently holding out a hand for the ignition key. Sim was in no state to drive. His brain was swimming pleasantly in his head and he viewed his father's antics with benign amusement. He tossed the key across the car roof.

Maurice handled the vehicle as if it were an unbroken horse needing ruthless subjugation. He wrenched the wheel and gears and punched the pedals to the floor, giving a wild, veering, surge-and-stop ride. Sim was grateful he hadn't eaten. Maurice swung left off Deansgate and, crossing the invisible river that lies between the two cities, hammered into Salford. He drove this way for five minutes, squealing through a number of corners before juddering to a halt outside a high block of council flats and switching off the engine. He pointed through the windscreen, angling his finger towards the upper storeys of the tower.

'I'm going up there. Be a few minutes, OK?'

'You want me to stay here?'

'You've got it. Just a few minutes, though.'

Maurice got out, trousering the ignition key. He dodged round the front of the car to the pavement with more bounce than Sim had yet seen. Then he waved genially at his son and headed towards the block's entrance. Maurice hesitated fractionally at the threshold, then, ducking his head as if afraid something might fall and hit him, he skipped inside and punched a button set in a stainless-steel panel on the wall. Sim watched his silhouette against the dim light – a big, paunchy figure in a bare lobby waiting for his lift. Then he disappeared from view.

After a while Sim, too, got out of the car. He looked the tower block carefully up and down. It was one of many in this neighbourhood, a dirty finger of stained concrete with peeling, pale-blue woodwork. Here and there, patches of sodden plywood covered the broken-glass windows of empty flats. Other windows, behind their rotten frames, were uncurtained and he saw the unshaded lightbulbs that illuminated ceilings and walls. In one room he could make out a poster-size photograph of Jimi Hendrix. It was a block waiting for the end, waiting to get empty enough for demolition.

What was Maurice up to? Getting high? Possibly. But Sim didn't think drugs were his father's particular problem. He was the wrong generation, too old even in the 1960s to have been much interested in anything except fags, pussy, booze and dog-racing. Besides, if it was a smoke he'd wanted, he could have rolled up in the car.

Sim smiled, thinking of all the fathers since the beginning of time who had stood around late at night, worrying about the activities of their sons. So how often were the roles reversed? He looked at his watch, aware of the alcohol making him sway slightly on his feet. Ten minutes had gone by. He strolled towards the tower-block entrance, one of whose doors hung drunkenly open, its upper hinge apparently ripped from the doorpost. Above it a painted sign gave the name of the block: Ena Sharples House. The glass on the other was smashed and boarded over. An unskilful graffitist had left his opinion on the plywood: MAN UTD UTTER SCUM.

Sim listened in the stairwell but heard nothing. The desolation seemed overwhelming. He went back out and walked round the block, looking up at the windows. But what was the point? He was not about to go up there and pull his father out by the collar. Then he noticed, away to his right, beyond the twin to this tower block, a parade of lacklustre shops all in darkness except for a garishly lit fish bar. Suddenly he felt hungry. He sidestepped dog droppings all the way across two sparse and gritty patches of grass, until he reached the place.

Later, back at the car, Sim began to feel sleepy. The midnight news on the radio had come to an end, lights had gone out, the fish bar's steel shutters had come down for the night.

He allowed his eyelids to do the same.

# 6

To reach the fish bar, buy his portion of chips and wander back had taken Sim about ten minutes and, in theory, the doors of the block that Maurice had entered remained in his view all the time. But he wasn't looking at it all the time. Some of the time he was glancing around, humming to himself. Then he was talking to the man in the chip shop, helping himself to salt and vinegar, counting his change. So he missed the three men who had come hurrying out of the place, the one in the middle protesting loudly as he was hustled along between the other two.

The one in the middle was Maurice. When not cursing the heavies whose hands were dug like grappling-hooks into his armpits, he was calling out Sim's name. But the appeals were muffled by a plate-glass door and drowned by the brassy voice of Tammy Wynette, belting out of the chip shop's sound system.

This is why he never saw his father pushed into an unmarked car and driven off at speed into the Salford night.

The lift had never come. After giving it a minute, and then another, Maurice had taken the stairs. They were dark, with lights that worked only on every third or fourth landing and a smell like a sewer without the chemicals – animal excrement, rotting food, stale cooking and piss. The stairwell, like all its kind, specialized in piss.

He climbed slowly, counting the landings under his breath, his tread feeling heavy, and sounding heavier in the hollow and damp of the concrete shaft. His head beneath the bandage throbbed. His indigestion was back, too, worse than any time since the night of the thatched cottage.

At the fifth, seventh and tenth floors he paused for rest. The stairwell was eerily silent, like a subterranean vault, an up-ended catacomb. Occasionally he passed doors – there were four to each landing – under which light shone or the growl of television could be heard. But most of the flats were vacant, padlocked and barred with security grilles against squatters. And now, as he climbed, he found the heaviness of his feet being balanced by a new light-headedness. He put it down to alcohol. It was not unpleasant.

On the twelfth floor he paused again and, holding the handrail, took in some deep breaths. The stench was less disgusting up here, and the extra oxygen steadied his head. He made the last four flights in good order and stood at last in front of the door he wanted.

There was no bell, so he hammered on it with the heel of his fist. He could hear speech from inside, male voices, but he couldn't tell if the men were there in person or merely part of a broadcast. *If that bitch –*

Then the door opened. The man was about thirty-five, stocky, with a moustache and prominent paunch forcing its way towards Maurice. The suit was blue and the tie had a pattern of small shields.

'Is Treeze in?'

The question sounded fatuous, like a child asking if his friend could come out to play. Maurice backed away slightly but the other man's meaty hand came after him, grasping forward until it clamped on to the back of his neck.

'Come in, dad, come in. You're very welcome indeed.'

The interview room was the usual thing. Cream gloss over brickwork, a window and a strip light, each protected by strong mesh, a couple of tube-framed chairs and a scarred, plastic-veneered table. The one recent fitting was a narrow metal shelf fixed on brackets to the wall above the table. This held the double tape-deck, whose spindles could be seen turning and whose sound was a light swish. Detective Sergeant Smallwood dragged on his cigarette and tossed the small cube wrapped in silver paper on to the table top. It came to rest by Maurice, with a corner of dark brown dope showing through.

'. . . and of course we found this in your pocket.'

Smallwood watched the evidence intently, as if it might suddenly sprout wings and require swatting. After a moment, he shifted his attention to the suspect and raised an eyebrow, a trick he had perfected after months of practice in front of the bathroom mirror.

'*Into* dope, are we?'

'No,' said Maurice. 'I did buy it, but I don't like it myself.'

'Oh. I see. Selling it, then?'

'No. A present. It was just a present.'

'Oh! A *present*, is it? How very generous. Sort of like bringing a bottle to a party, perhaps?'

'Something like that.'

Smallwood considered for a moment and his mind took a decisive turn. He spoke towards the recording-machine.

'"I am now terminating this, my first interview with the suspect, at 1.33 a.m." Switch the thing off, Bentley.'

DC Bentley, a raw-wristed, red-haired man, leant across and snapped the switches. Maurice noticed that he had a small, milky overgrowth on the ball of one eye. As he pulled the cassettes out of their slots and began laboriously to label and seal them, Smallwood brought his elbow down smartly on to the tabletop, making it judder. A little harder and it might have splintered. Smallwood's sleeve was rolled up, his arm was thickly muscled and hairy, and sported a tattoo: 'Wirral Squirrels RFC.' He jabbed his index finger into the air under Maurice's nose.

'I'm going out there, Fielding, and I'm going to verify what you've told me. We've got Treeze in another room. And when to my own satisfaction I've had the same story from *her* as I just got from *you*, I shall consider my next step. And if I find you've been telling me untruth, Fielding, I shall see you punished. I will bang and you will whimper, got it?'

He rose to his full height.

'In the meantime, I want you to think over what you've just said, and consider whether there's any little thing, or any *big* thing, that you would wish to add. Right, get him a cup of tea, Bentley.'

Maurice sipped his sweet tea and dragged ferociously on the first cigarette he'd had since being pulled in. He was doing what the policeman wanted, thinking about the lies he'd told.

They weren't outright lies. They were what the Christian Brothers had described to him at school so graphically: lies of omission. He remembered Brother Peter swinging his tawse for emphasis as he spoke,

'Lies of *o*mission, Fielding, are just as bad an offence against Our Blessed Lady as lies of *com*mission. They stain her spotless gown, Fielding. Remember that next time you give an outing to your vicious, lying tongue. *They stain her spotless gown!*'

There was always a better chance of getting away with these lies, because they could be made to approximate to the truth. Thus Maurice had told Smallwood he'd been living for a long time abroad, the Far East. He'd landed at Heathrow, then travelled to London and bought a car. He had journeyed north to Manchester where, having met Treeze Lee in Piccadilly Gardens, he had taken her for a drink. From there they had gone to her flat in Salford. This was all only a week ago. He'd slept with her maybe three times all told. Her pimp? Christ, course he wasn't! He'd only just *met* the girl. Know she was a tart? Do us a favour! He fancied her, that's all, she's a good-looking kid. It *does* happen, you know.

Him, a pimp? No, they couldn't make that one stick. Even so, Maurice was sweating. The dope, they could tie that up with the Far East bit and make out he was a courier. He couldn't really have denied he'd come from there. His passport was in his pocket, with its fresh Hong Kong stamp. They'd have opened it quicker than it took a sheep to shit.

But the amount of dope was only good for a charge of possession, and something told him this lot weren't interested in that. They were vice, not drugs, and they'd been sitting on Treeze as part of some sex-industry clean-up. They didn't give a bugger about him, if only – *if only* – they never put him together with a burned-out East Anglian house and its charred contents.

This was the big omission, the matter Maurice had already been erasing from his memory as best he could. It did not seem like an omission any more, just a shadow cast across his life, as if this was someone else's fault rather than his own.

Brother Peter, a relentless bully of a man with a gift for cliché, had a favourite phrase for it: 'The greatest lie is the one you tell yourself. You lie to yourself and you commit a kind of suicide. Which, as we all know, is the most grievous sin of all.'

Forget sin. What about Sim? Maurice hoped he'd left the vicinity of Ena Sharples House when he saw the peelers. Maurice hadn't mentioned Sim to the police. No sense in antagonizing the kid; he'd be needing Sim before very long, no doubt of it.

Smallwood came back after forty-five minutes and called Bentley out. After a whispered conversation the constable returned with a smirk on his face. He was chuffed to have something to do on his own account.

'Who's a lucky villain, then?' he observed, standing and rubbing his bony hands together. The patch of opacity on his eyeball gave him added malevolence – the one-eyed man in the country of the blind.

'The DS says I'm to throw you out, with the message that the cannabis can be considered as something that never happened. Slapped wrists. Don't do it again.'

Maurice kept po-faced, but inwardly he was smiling at the thought – the two policemen pulling their squad car into some quiet lay-by at the edge of the manor, rolling up the joint and passing it between them.

At the desk he was given back the items from his pocket. The last thing he received was his passport. Bentley withheld this for a moment, saying, 'You will be glad to see your son.'

For an instant Maurice was nonplussed. Sim? Had they found the car, arrested Sim too?

'Yes, but how did you –'

Bentley waggled the passport.

'It's all in here, isn't it, sir? Robert William. One year ten months.'

Only then did Maurice remember.

'Oh, you mean – yes, of course. Robert William.'

'Stays with his mummy, does he, while Daddy's over here on business?'

'Yes, of course he does. Now please, can I go?'

After a teasing hesitation, a further fraction of a second, Bentley slapped the passport into Maurice's outstretched hand.

'Right, just sign for this lot, and you can.'

Bentley turned from him and started a conversation with the the desk sergeant. Maurice scribbled his name on the flimsy police form that had been placed ready on the counter. As he handed back the pen, Maurice said, 'Just one thing. About Treeze – I mean, Miss Lee. You letting her go too?'

'No, she'll be our guest a little while yet, Mr Fielding. And look, I'd advise you to steer clear of the likes of her in future, OK? For little Robert's sake, if nothing else, eh?'

Bentley's face wore a patronizing sneer. As Maurice stumbled down the police-station steps into the very cold night, that sneer stayed, as if imprinted on his retina. It typified one of the reasons he had left England. He spat into the gutter and began to walk back to his car.

## 7

*Tap-tap-tap.*

Sim's sleep in Maurice's car had been dreamless, until the image of a chick tapping out of its egg presented itself. *Tap-tap-tap.* It was slimy inside the egg. He slopped around, his limbs restrained by viscid jellies and thick custards. *Tap-tap-tap.* He was drowning in goo. He must get out. And through the translucent eggshell came this warm, welcoming, incandescent light.

Sim opened his eyes. A torchbeam was shining in through the car window, and he could see the chromed epaulettes glinting above its dazzle. The policeman was rapping on the glass. Sim rolled the window down an inch.

'You all right, sir?'

'Oh, yes. Thanks. Long drive, stopped for a rest.'

He couldn't see the constable's face behind the torchlight.

'Funny place to stop, if you don't mind my saying so.'

Sim hoisted himself to a sitting position and blinked at his watch: 4.30. Where was Maurice?

'I got a bit lost in Manchester. Thought I'd better sleep.'

Why was he lying? Cobbling together a story for Mr Plod was a way of covering for his father, he supposed. But why *was* he covering for Maurice? He reached for the ignition, as if ready to drive on. The copper waited wordlessly. Sim's fingers groped, but of course the key wasn't there.

He got out of the car and stretched ostentatiously.

'Think I'll walk around the block before I'm on my way. Bit of fresh air, waken me up. Bye. And thanks for rousing me.'

He walked, aware of the policeman's eyes boring into his back. Then the guy's voice came after him.

'Hey! Hold it just a minute.'

Sim turned.

'Yes?'

The policeman, a fresh-faced boy, looked at Sim through narrow eyes.

'This is a rough neighbourhood, right?'

Sim smiled.

'Oh, I can look after myself, thanks.'

The copper nodded. He had noted Sim's height, and the breadth of his shoulders.

'But,' he said, 'the car can't, can it?'

Sim frowned.

'I don't get you.'

'You forgot to lock the car. However crappy that radio is, it'll be Bang and Olufson to somebody round here.'

Theatrically, Sim smacked his forehead and moved back towards the car. With no key, he had the presence of mind to go to the passenger side, from where he could lean in and lock all the doors internally, without needing a key. He did it, then slammed the passenger door and smiled. Producing the motorbike's ignition key from his pocket he dangled it briefly for the policeman to see.

'Don't look so worried. I'm not locked out.'

But he was. There was nothing for it but to walk back to the bike.

By 8 a.m. the next day Sim was working on Sammy Newton's Ford Fiesta, trying to make sense of the wiring. He enjoyed lying under a car; he could do it hour after hour, though he hated to drive one for more than five minutes. He objected to being trussed up with buckles and straps inside a box, like some humiliating bondage game. Besides, there was so much wasted roadspace. A motorbike was on the human scale, and it put you out there, on the tarmac, between the hedgerows, breathing the air. Even after years, the sense of exhilarating strength he took from a motorbike had hardly palled.

But last night, as he'd ridden the BMW back to Moxon, alone on the road for the last part of the journey, the usual exhilaration was missing. There was a feeling of something having changed inside him.

The BMW sped north through the cotton towns and villages where industrial mass-production had been given to the world. The people who once worked these vast slate-roofed weaving sheds had been the first symbols of the factory system and its soul-shrinking communality, living always on top of each other, always interdependent, never alone. But Richard Arkwright's legacy has passed to other economies far away, and the mills of Rawtenstall, Padiham and Accrington are demolished, or ruined, or partitioned as 'community workspaces', or converted into industrial museums. In the post-industrial age, people in these parts have reverted to the reserved individualism of their farming and out-working ancestors.

Yet occasionally they could still give a display of common decency, of joining together to help another human being in trouble. It was, after all, what they had done for young Sim.

Nominally Sim had been alone ever since his mother's death. He was then twelve and had no brother or sister, no known close relations except Maurice. But his father had been gone four years. He had disappeared from the map so totally it was as if he had never been. His mother never spoke of him, except for that one time in the hospital. After the funeral no one thought seriously about trying to contact him.

Sim might easily have felt utterly alone in the world, but he didn't. Eva Fielding had left him no money, but she had bequeathed a priceless legacy none the less – a stock of such goodwill in the village that no one would even consider letting Sim be sent away. 'She was a good person, your ma,' they had told her son in their sententious but purposeful way, and that purpose was to act collectively, when the crisis came, to see that Sim didn't fall hostage to the welfare state, becoming a child 'in care'. Communal support was offered – money, clothes. The cottage, Sim's only property, was let and the orphan was taken in by old Worsley, the garage owner, who had a rattling big house all to himself. But in reality Sim had been adopted by the village as a whole. There had been times when he felt like a regimental goat: he wasn't quite a free-standing individual; he was everybody's child.

He'd reached the cottage by 1.30. Getting his mother's old home back had been one of his ambitions ever since he could remember. It had finally fallen vacant when, at twenty-two, he was just starting back after college to work for Jack Worsley. The old man had generously offered him a salary over the odds, so he could afford to live on his own. Now, as he pushed open the door, he was aware of the smell of the place – polish, a touch of dampness perhaps. It reminded him of Eva in her last days, going around the house crabwise with a yellow duster and spraycan of Pledge.

On the mat beneath the letter-slot was a picture postcard, a view of The Ram and Heifer, Moxon's pub, with its thick pelt of ivy concealing the brickwork. The handwriting was Julia Singleton's.

I baked a cake for yr bthday. Where were you? I wouldn't want you to be twenty-five without me being there. Come down and blow yr candles out tonight at the pub? PLEASE!
Love J.

Julia!

His eyes rested on the writing, not reading but enjoying the flow of the penstrokes. Her handwriting was like her face, a beautiful, assured cursive. When you love someone, your body responds to every distinctive thing about them.

Julia always gave him some small present on his birthday. Although just ten years older than he was, she had seen the orphaning of the twelve-year-old Sim and appointed herself his surrogate godmother. She would come into Worsley's and mend clothes, take him on shopping trips or out to the pictures. She would also be there for him to cuddle when the sorrows overflowed. Never neglecting to find him a birthday present of some kind – model kits, book tokens, once a personal stereo – had been a point of honour with her. What would she come up with this time?

He climbed wearily into bed, smiling at the memory of his sixteenth birthday, when her present had been a packet of Durex, wrapped in gift paper and a pink ribbon and the message 'Now you can do it legally, you may as well be prepared.'

Julia had known instinctively that old Worsley would never tell him about sex, so she took on the job herself – sticky details and all. He'd known already, in the way school children do know – the sounds from the parents' bedroom, the dirty talk of the playground. But from Julia it made sense – ridiculous but impossible to deny.

Julia's presentation of condoms had made him angry. Sex? It was only her he loved, sex didn't come into it. Yet within a few months, all the rubbers were used up, as he'd screwed his way methodically through a generation of girls in his first year at Nelson Technical College.

In what remained of the night he was teased by dreams of conflict without resolution, and had come to work early, wanting to lose himself in the most intricate task available. Sammy Newton's Fiesta was certainly it. A flash previous owner – it couldn't have been Sammy – had apparently loaded the interior with every gizmo in the catalogue – from digital compass to an electronic screen flashing messages from the rear shelf. Only the cigar-lighter, big enough to ignite one of Fidel Castro's smokes, and a spaghetti of leads and cables survived. Now Sim was working his way through every piece of wire to see which of them he could safely strip out.

Once his father, in the money, had come home with a convertible Ford Zephyr. It was a beautiful anachronism, a collector's item, or icon from Maurice's own youth – two-tone paintwork of cream and emerald green, whitewall tyres, valve radio, a compass mounted in a chrome-domed binnacle on the dashboard. Where had the money come from? Crime, gambling, extortion? *By their fruits shall ye know them.* It wasn't true. The real question was, how have they come by those fruits?

He sat in Sammy Newton's driving seat and switched on the ignition. He tested the lights, indicators, wipers and, lastly, the cigar-lighter. It was an ugly, cheaply made attachment, but Sammy's instructions had been clear.

'No, don't rip it out, Sim. I can light my fags on it. Mend it for me, will you?'

He pushed the lighter into its socket and waited to see if it worked.

*By their fruits . . .*

Occasionally, during Maurice's absences, Eva would receive letters, and they were always on the same type of paper – cheap, lined stuff with bits of wood embedded in it. At the top was a box with a name and a number handwritten in it. When he'd asked her, she told him, 'Your dad's on official business. Now no more questions, all right?'

Sim's pulse had quickened at that. She made his father sound like a spy.

With a resonant twang, the cigar-lighter ejected. He picked it from its slot and peered at the glowing orange coil. He watched it as it cooled to a deeper and deeper red until, like a sunset, it faded to grey.

He was still gazing into the cooled spiral when Worsley came out of the office, steering his wheelchair round the shop with the same panache that he'd displayed in his motor-racing days at Brooklands and Aintree. His harsh voice barked out, the product of a larynx sized and stiffened by years of tobacco: 'Sim, we still haven't had that auto-choke for the VW. Have you finished this job?'

'Just about. Then I could start on Marcus Ball's Mini, the dynamo.'

'That's not come yet either. Why don't you get over to Preston and pick them both up?'

Ten minutes later, Sim was on his way. He took the bike down the High Street and past Moxon Field, the swathe of grass that was the village green. High Street was bordered on one side by a row of shops, including the pub and a Chinese take-away, and on the other by the Field. Beyond the grass was a 50-yard stretch of river, whose further bank rose steeply enough to display three terraces of small cottages teetering above the water. At one end of the Field, upstream, stood the old Mill. Here a wooden footbridge led across to the parish church, which was perched high above the far bank of the river. Downstream the Field ended with a stone bridge, where the road traversed the river.

As Sim passed he saw, in the middle of the Field, Moss Baker and the Sawleys unloading timber pallets from Moss's 3-ton truck. Later they would pile the pallets high, interspersing them with logs and old doors and tea chests – any old wood that would increase the bulk of the bonfire. It was the start of a week's preparation. Next Saturday was 5 November, the date of Moxon's annual Fawkes Fair. Later in the week awnings and tents would start to rise, and travelling rides would roll on to the grass. Sim felt a flutter of primitive excitement as he accelerated the bike past the head of the stone bridge and veered uphill, away from the river. At Fawkes Fair he'd had his first taste of life's most atavistic pleasures, for anything had been possible there: sin and risk, passion and pleasure. People used it as an excuse to rip away everyday constraints and do something dangerous. It was a mini *Bierfest*. Even now that he was grown up, the event provoked a rare mixture of hope and desire, a renewal of lost feelings.

The errand to Preston went badly. He had secured parts for the dynamo, but the automatic cold-start fitting was out of stock and he was recommended to try a supplier at Fleetwood. The Fleetwood man assured him on the phone that he had it, but when Sim got there the thing couldn't be found. At last he ran the accursed part to ground at a wholesaler in Lancaster, but by then the day was gone.

He was aware of hunger by the time he puttered into Moxon at 7 p.m. It would be best to lay a foundation. This was sure to be a drinking night.

In Moxon there are two choices if you want to eat out: nuts and crisps at the pub or – the more substantial alternative – a take-away from Jimmy Ho's. Jimmy had come to the village five years previously from Liverpool, a scouse Chinaman with a Liverpool-Irish wife. People had been sceptical, but the restaurant had been a success, due less to the cooking than to Jimmy's sunny temperament and Jackie Ho's financial skills. Sim opted for one of Jimmy's Chicken Chow Meins.

'I hear it's your birthday, Sim. So it's on the house,' said Jimmy, holding up a hand to prevent further discussion. Sim thanked him and went to sit at one of the laminated tables reserved for customers who preferred to take their food no further away.

Jackie came in from the back room.

'Hello, Sim. Giving you freebies, is he? I've told him not to throw away the profits on poxy bikers. He won't listen.'

'You never got near enough to know about poxy, Jackie.'

She laughed. Jackie concealed her underlying nature – a tense, bird-like nervousness – under a brand of familiarity which sometimes, to Sim, seemed forced.

The food was uniform in consistency and bland in taste, but it filled him up. He swallowed the last mouthful and was putting on his jacket when little Kevin Ho ran in. He stared at Sim, fascinated by the array of fasteners on the suit of leathers. He reached out and pulled at the zip for Sim's right boot. Sim showed him how to make it run up and down from knee to heel.

'How old is he now, Jackie?'

'Soon be two.'

'He'll be talking, then.'

She laughed. 'Oh, he doesn't need to talk. He's fluent in body language.'

She came over and crouched behind her son, pulling his pyjama bottoms high over his rounded stomach and smoothing his hair. Sim stood and stretched.

'Thanks, Jimmy. That was exactly what was required.'

'Happy birthday, Sim. Catch yer.'

The Ram and Heifer, like any good pub seen from outside and in darkness, gave out a mellow light of welcome and conviviality. When he'd killed the bike's engine, Sim sat astride the machine for a moment, savouring the Saturday night glow of the place. The murmur of voices was punctuated by the chink of glass and money, and laughter in two kinds: the females' rapid rising scales and the lower register of the males' chortling.

He went in. The bar was small and he was seen at once. A cheer went up. Slapped on the back by hands that sounded like rain on roofing felt, he ran a gauntlet of congratulations all the way to the bar.

'Happy birthday, Sim lad.'

'You can sell that bloody motorbike now. You're too old for that.'

'Come on, there's a pint on the bar for you. Get supping it.'

Half-way across the room he saw Denise Greenwood. Big-breasted Denise was a nurse of Nordic fairness. He put his arms about her waist and kissed her mouth. She laughed with delight and let her eyelids drop. Then at last he stood in front of the beer pumps. Julia Singleton leaned over the bar and wrapped her arms round his neck.

'Where've you been? We'd almost given you up. Give us a kiss.'

Her lips tasted of sherry. She slipped a small package into Sim's hand, which he dropped into his pocket. He whispered, 'Thanks, Julia. You're wonderful. Shall I open it later?'

They were all wonderful. Julia was wonderful. So was Denise Greenwood; and the Sawley brothers, who took him poaching as a teenager; and Mrs Benlow in the bakery, who for years gave him free sticky cakes after school; and old Worsley, sitting in his wheelchair beside the fire, smoking and coughing and reciting tags of poetry to anyone who'd listen. This man had taken him in, nurtured him, suffered with infinite patience through his puberty and his first sexual entanglements, given him a job.

Sim tried to stand his round but there was no chance. The collection of untouched drinks bought for him never seemed to diminish as the evening progressed. However hard he tried to pour them down his throat, they were always replenished. There were jokes and laughter. Marcus Ball was sick in the coal scuttle. He had a farm over the hill, but tonight he was riding back on his Fergusson.

'You've got my Mini in your place,' he told Sim lugubriously as he wiped his mouth.

'I know,' said Sim.

'Bugger's lost its electrics, so tonight I'm getting pissed as a prat and tractoring home cross-field.'

The noise level crept higher. Barry Sawley and Peter Taylor arm-wrestled and it seemed they would never stop. Trisha Pimlott tried to sing the Beatles' 'Yesterday', but she began to sob each time she reached the phrase 'I'm not half the girl I used to be' and had to give up. It wasn't long after that when Jim Gornal picked a quarrel with Jer Allard, accusing him of groping his Karen in the passage outside the pisser. Then half the bar traipsed outside to see the matter settled on the crown bowling green, only to groan with disappointment as Jer fell down trying to get his jacket off and lay helpless in the flowerbed, babbling nonsense.

Then they were all back in the bar. Barry Sawley, flush from his arm-wrestling triumph, was trying to get everyone to sing 'Yellow Submarine', but he shut up as Julia rang the brass bell hanging at the end of the bar. Then the lights went out.

In darkness Sim's birthday cake was brought from the kitchen. Twenty-five candles blazed over its white icing and as he bent to blow them out the moisture in his eyes glistened. He pulled back for a moment, drained his glass, bent again to the cake and took a deep breath.

At this moment a stranger pushed his way in and stood for a moment in the doorway of the bar. He wore a crêpe bandage wrapped around his head and was crumpling between his hands the greaseproof wrapping from a portion of Jimmy Ho's chips.

'Christ on a bike,' he observed to no one in particular, 'this looks like a good party.'

It was Neil Sawley, leaning by the wall next to the door, who replied.

'Yeah. Birthday. Feller called Sim. He's over there blowing his candles out.'

'Sim, is it? Well, I know Sim. It's him I've come to see. I'm his dad, I am. Good old Sim. Isn't this amazing?'

Pauline Fairbanks, standing right beside Neil, heard what the man in the head-bandage said, and instantly began passing the news on. It moved through the bar like a ripple on a pond.

'His dad. Sim's dad's here.'

'Where? Christ, that he is. Eva Lawson's Maurice. I remember him.'

'Who? Who's here?'

'Sim's *dad*. Over there, look.'

The bar fell silent. Julia turned on the lights. Sim's candles streamed smoke like mill chimneys in the heyday of cotton. Sim turned and saw Maurice moving through the people. He dropped the screw of chip paper in an ashtray and held out his hand.

'Sim lad. Happy birthday. Put it there.'

The hand, when Sim shook it, was still greasy from the chips.

# 8

Every Sunday morning, like the descent of starlings, a dense murmuration of female humans flocks into Hong Kong Central. Congregating in groups large and small, they occupy every rail, every step or patch of paving, every low wall. They dance and sing, picnic and gossip, read aloud their letters from home, laugh and flirt and lark around. They are the Filipino housemaids of Hong Kong, enticed together in their thousands to celebrate the one day of rest allowed them by their masters and mistresses.

Craike passed through the centre of this joyous weekly reunion on his way from Caro Jenks's place. He looked about him, remembering how Caro loved this gathering, calling it the most life-enhancing event in Hong Kong's entire week.

He thought of Caro herself, how she'd been sitting a few minutes ago, morning-fresh at the kitchen table, flapping a hand absent-mindedly as if to waft him from the flat. She was wearing only her ancient quilted dressing-gown and a rubber band to bunch her hair. The band pulled it back across her skull and formed a stubby, pointed, ash-grey brush at the nape of her slim neck. With a cup of coffee steaming in front of her and a smile of anticipated pleasure playing on her lips, she had been unscrolling a long computer print-out. Caro had a Sunday of number-crunching to look forward to.

That was Caro, the closest he came to a girlfriend, a straight-backed beauty with – when dressed – a ferociously expensive taste in clothes and a phenomenal facility with numbers. They'd met when he'd been called in by the Hong Kong and Shanghai Bank, where Caro earned her richly paid living, to run a security check on the Australian credits section. Without Caro he'd not have known where to begin – he was no expert in banking – and yet he had told himself at the time, *This is it, boy, your ticket to undreamed riches*. But it hadn't turned out that way.

The Hong Kong and Shanghai was the nearest thing in the

territory to a Central Bank, a straitlaced big brother to the younger tearaway banks in the family. If they had decided to employ Craike regularly, things might indeed have turned out as he had hoped, but he never was employed by them again. Craike claimed it was because there had been nothing at all amiss with the Australian Credits Section, which was hardly his fault.

Yet out of the job had come Caro herself – a friend, an unfailing source of financial gossip and an occasional lover.

'We lead such fulfilling busy lives, we two,' she'd told him once. 'We don't have time to be a couple. We just go to bed for the fun of it.'

'OK, Caro,' he'd replied. 'That's fine. Just think of me as your bit of rough.'

Caro was fun and she didn't want to get serious, and that is every man's favourite fantasy. When he'd been with her he could easily put her from his mind until they met again. Now, this Sunday morning, he did so, for there was business to see to. Ed Craike had an appointment.

Unlike the Filipino maids, Hong Kong's office workers like to have their workplace available to them on Sundays, and most of the big buildings in Central are equipped through the weekend with security guards and receptionists. After a few minutes' casting from one huge plate-glass door to another, Craike found the address he was looking for and entered an atrium whose corners were dense with potted miniature rain-forests. He read from an index of brass plates on the wall, and then rose by express lift to the seventeenth floor, home of Morrison Financial and Property Services plc.

Finch-Reynolds, Morrison's chairman, met him on the lift landing.

'Ah, Mr Craike,' he exclaimed, coming forward to shake hands vigorously, like a man working a rusty water pump. 'Good of you to make a meeting on the Sabbath. I wanted to see you when the office was, er, more or less empty.'

He stepped back and shot a glance behind him, as if there might nevertheless be watchers or listeners nearby. He adopted a conspiratorial tone, contorting his face and speaking through the left half of his mouth.

'I have to ensure confidentiality, you see. Come through, won't you.'

The man looked harassed. His eyes were popping and restless, darting up, down and around Craike as he ushered him into his office. And, when they sat opposite each other across a desk, Craike noticed the toast-coloured, half-moon stains between eyelid and cheekbone which said, *I wish I could sleep the night through*.

Finch-Reynolds gestured at his clothes with an embarrassed high-pitched laugh. He wore light-blue shorts and a polo shirt which stretched over his well-fed belly.

'Hope you don't mind the garb. I normally sail on Sundays.'

'What's it all about, Mr Finch-Reynolds?'

The Chairman took a deep breath.

'Well, it's about my finance director, that's Tommy Plummer. Thought he was the brightest appointment I ever made, you know? Blue-eyed boy, star in the firmament, all that. I left a lot of the day-to-day stuff to him. Now, he turns out to be a bloody crook.'

Craike was led quickly through the affairs of the company, a financial services and advice outfit like thousands of others, profitable until things started to go wrong, things that couldn't be attributed solely to the state of the market.

'Letters were apparently coming in, addressed to me mind, from some of our oldest clients – complaints about how their accounts were being manipulated and what-not. Tommy just had the letters shredded, I never even saw them. His banking arrangements were byzantine, to say the least, and the books were like 10 miles of tangled fishing line. I've had a go at unravelling them, but I can't make head or tail . . .'

He clicked his tongue and shook his head, making the jowls flap.

'Is Plummer still employed here?'

'Yes. I've got nothing to sack him with yet. He's got a bomb-proof contract which means I have to find something criminal or pay him off with a small fortune. That's where you come in.'

'Does he have any accomplices? In cases like this there are nearly always partners, probably on the outside – a co-conspirator at your bank, for example.'

Finch-Reynolds gave another, single shake to his head, as if to dislodge a twig caught in his hair.

'We use the one bank for most of our assets, and it's a pretty solid outfit. They give us incredibly good service, anyway.'

'Do you suspect anyone else in your own organization?'

'No, no one. But that's not to say there aren't others involved.'

Finch-Reynolds toyed with a glass paperweight on his desktop, pushing it from hand to hand. 'Plummer's very popular,' he added gloomily. 'Very popular indeed. Always buying the girls presents, remembers all their birthdays. Amazing, really.'

Craike got to his feet and strolled to the window. He looked down on the glistening harbour, and on a 747 lumbering through the world's most dicy landing pattern, the roof-scraping approach to Kai Tak airport.

'Mr Finch-Reynolds, you want me to investigate this man Plummer with the minimum of publicity, right? Well, I see no problem. I'll need to have my assistant go through your books, and I shall require an advance of 20,000 Hong Kong dollars.'

'An advance?'

Finch-Reynolds looked shocked. Craike leaned forward across the desk and lowered his voice.

'Well, if Plummer has really taken you to the cleaners, at least I don't lose out on my fee. OK?'

Finch-Reynolds drew a chequebook from his drawer, wrote the cheque and slid it across the desk. Craike picked it up.

'Coutts? Are they the pretty solid outfit that you mentioned?'

'Oh, no. They're my personal bankers. The business uses the Trans-Africa, but I can hardly write you a company cheque, can I? Plummer would find out.'

Wearily, he dragged his knuckles across his eyes and sighed.

'All I want is for this company to retrieve its good name. Do it for me, Mr Craike, won't you?'

Craike tucked the cheque into his wallet and grinned.

'Count on me, Mr Finch-Reynolds. It's just up my street.'

But as he left he was thinking it was just up *Madeleine*'s street. Apart from all that police rape work, there had been a stint in the anti-fraud squad, if he wasn't very much mistaken. And the Morrison case would be handy in keeping her out of the Swann business. Craike wanted to handle it himself, if possible.

Sim lifted his head from the pillow, then let it fall back. His skull was throbbing, his tongue more parched than the Sinai Desert. A searing sensation racked his vertebrae as he moved his neck.

He opened his eyes: muted morning sunlight through the window. Someone was singing. He knew this room. Christ! He was in the pub, in *his* room.

Julia Singleton didn't live at the pub. She had a small house on the other side of the river and slept at the Ram and Heifer only during the summer when there were bed and breakfast guests to see to. Now the season was over, the pub's bedrooms lay empty, and would do so all winter – a fact which hadn't gone unnoticed by Sim when, at eighteen, he had started helping out behind the bar. With Julia's approval he had acquired the use of one of the guestrooms as a place to study or simply to be alone. This was the room that he had taken over, hanging posters on the walls, putting up bookshelves and installing a secondhand music system. These personal fittings had long gone, but there was another association and it was brought back powerfully by the female voice humming in the bathroom. The room had been more than a perfect retreat. It served as a perfect place to bring his girlfriends.

She came in, towelling herself from the bath, and Sim smiled. Even that hurt a little, but he wanted her to see his pleasure. Denise Greenwood had a stupendous body. Then he shut his eyes, as if overwhelmed by the sight of her.

'What happened?' he whispered. 'I'm a little fuzzy.'

She sat down beside him and slipped a hand under the bedclothes to pat his stomach.

'Last night you weren't fuzzy. Pissed, yes. Pretty forceful, too. The night was interesting.'

'Was it?'

'You don't remember? I'd have thought you could work it out.'

Denise looked down at the bedclothes. It looked as if a dry typhoon had recently romped through them. Sim propped himself up on an elbow and surveyed the ruin of sheets and blankets.

'I remember all *that*. I meant before it, in the pub. It's a very long time since I was in this room like this. How did we get up here?'

'Your father's a very charming bloke, you know. Filthy jokes, he tells, but –'

'He's very devious, I think.'

'Yes, well. We all had a great night. You were well away, started singing Gilbert and Sullivan with Mr Worsley. Yes, you did! In the end you were falling all over the place and Julia told me to bring you up here for a bit of peace and quiet. You just went off to sleep.'

'And then?'

'I came back just on closing and found you, with all your clothes off, in bed. Well, I'm not a girl to let a good opportunity go to waste, so –'

He kissed her neck.

'It was quite a birthday party, Denise. And you made it even more quite.'

She laughed. Her voice had a deep tone, a hint of gruffness, which he found sexy. They had first slept together a couple of years back. It was an occasional, uncomplicated thing.

'It was a *family* celebration, Sim. It was great.'

'Tell me about him.'

'Your father?'

'Yes. What happened after I was bundled up here?'

'He was really good fun. Bought everyone drinks, told jokes. Mainly for the boys, it has to be said. At one point he was making up to me, trying to get in my knickers, so I told him I preferred you and he just laughed. After, he tried to sit Marge Blackledge on his knee, and you should have seen the look *she* gave him. But he went down a treat with the guys. Tales of oriental massage parlours, betting coups. God, they lapped it up. After Julia called time I gather a whole lot of them went over to the Sawley brothers' place for more beer.'

'And he bought drinks, you said?'

'Loads. Pints and pints, and masses of shorts too. Had a huge wad of notes.'

'Did he now? That's interesting, because he was flat broke when I saw him on Friday.'

She shrugged.

'Said he'd had a big win in the betting shop.'

'Oh.'

Sim didn't feel like talking about Maurice any more. He sat forward, snaking his arm around her back until the hand slid over her hipbone and on to her belly. His index finger began exploring her navel. Then he pushed his face into her side, nuzzling the ribcage with his nose and lips. Denise twisted over and bit him in the back of the neck.

'Stop it. I'm on duty in half an hour.'

'But it's Sunday.'

'Exactly. On Sunday us nurses are thin on the ground.'

But the contact with her fresh and faultless body was lifting his hangover. He nudged harder with his head and she toppled sideways, giggling. He slid on top of her.

'But we don't have to do it on the ground. We've got this bed.'

He tickled one of her breasts and the nipple popped out. Bending to close his mouth around it, he was reminded of Sammy Newton's cigar-lighter.

Neil and Barry Sawley lived together in their whitewashed terrace opposite the northern end of the bridge. The cramped dwelling had originally been tenanted by their grandmother, and the boys – thrown out of the family farm for their tearaway behaviour – had been taken in by that kindly but bewildered old lady, who died soon afterwards. As their residency in the cottage was established before the grandmother's death, the boys continued afterwards to rent the property. It was a disorderly but, they thought, successful arrangement.

Sim came to the door and rapped in a firm, taking-no-shit style.

'Hi, Sim,' said Neil Sawley. He had opened a crack and was peering through with his head turned sideways. 'Great party last night.'

'Is he here?'

'Who? Your dad?'

Neil pulled the door fully open. He ran a hand with fingers spread through his long but sparse strands of turnip-coloured hair. He looked jumpy.

'Come in. I'm doing breakfast.'

He stood aside and Sim stepped across the threshold. The sitting room was no bigger than a cell, and drastically over-furnished, with two armchairs, a sideboard and a table by the window covered with scarred oilcloth. The room reeked of Neil Sawley's frying from the kitchen beyond.

'Fancy some? I'm only doing a fry-up.'

'Did he sleep here?'

'Fried bread, bacon, sausage.'

'Did he?'

'Well, we came back after the pub. *Hell* of a party, Sim. You should have birthdays more often.'

Neil stood at the bottom of the stairs and yelled.

'BARRY! Your breakfast'll be ready. Five minutes.'

He turned back to Sim. 'We're off out after some game later. Remember *our* poaching days? Hey! Why not join us? Fell should be good for a bird or two.'

'Well, not today, thanks, Neil.'

They stood in the narrow, stone-flagged kitchen. It was one that had never known plastic lamination or medium-density fibreboard. The single tap was brass: worn, scarred and dangling loosely over the sink at the end of a bent lead pipe. The sink was stone and the drainer a sodden piece of grooved beech. The green-painted shelves had been hung by Neil Sawley's grandfather half a century ago. Dirty plates and mugs were piled everywhere.

A chocolate-coloured teapot stood on a white enamel unit. Neil rinsed a mug under the tap and poured for Sim.

'Well, where is he, then?'

'Hell of a good bloke, your dad. A right laugh. He had us up till 3.00 talking about Filipino prozzies and stuff like this. I wish *I'd* travelled.'

'Look, is he still here or not?'

Neil hesitated. He tore off a piece of kitchen paper, removed his metal-frame glasses and began to polish them. Suddenly from the sitting room Sim heard the front door slam. He looked back sharply but the room was empty.

Sim crossed the room and, leaning his hands on the oilclothed table, saw Maurice momentarily through the dirty panes of the window. He was making for the pub car park, but Sim wasn't going to go chasing his father in public all over the village. He returned to Neil, who was smiling sheepishly, showing his gappy teeth. Sim picked up his mug of tea.

'Why didn't you tell me he was here, you prat?'

'Thing is, he told us, if you came, not to say owt.'

Sim left Neil to his fry. As he kicked the bike's start-lever, he saw the scruffy red hatchback swing down from The Ram and Heifer and turn left across the bridge. Once on the other bank of the river, Maurice dropped down to second with a tearing gargle of gears, and took off up the hill past the church. It was the way he would be going if he'd decided to piss off back to Manchester.

'Well, fuck it,' said Sim, and went home.

On Monday he again showed up for work early.

'Morning, young Sim. I noticed you found the pace a little rough Saturday night. Had to retire from the fray, did you?'

However early you got to work, you never got there before Old Worsley. God knows what hour he got up, or if he went to bed at all. He was always there when Sim arrived, smoking his Full-Strength and doing the paperwork as he listened to the Morning Concert on BBC Radio Three.

Sim stood beside the wheelchair and flipped through the diary, which showed any jobs booked in for the day.

'It was my party. I could cry if I wanted to.'

Worsley nodded slowly and took a drag on his cigarette.

'I never talked to your dad.'

'No.'

'Is he stopping long?'

'I don't reckon so. Any priority jobs today?'

The old man let drop the subject of Maurice Fielding. He never pushed things.

'There's that cold-start to do, and the Mini's dynamo. You got the parts Saturday?'

Sim's reply was lost as the old man floundered into a paroxysm of coughing. By the time it stopped Sim had hefted his toolbox and gone through to start work on the Volkswagen.

He worked through the day and late into the evening, not finally knocking off until 8.00. When he finally reached home the red car was drawn up outside the cottage, the lights were blazing and Maurice was sitting in front of the teapot at the kitchen table. He held up a hand in greeting, like a Hollywood red Indian.

'Hi. Been waiting for you for hours. Got to go out now, matter of fact, so I'm not stopping.'

'How the hell did you get in?'

'I didn't break anything. Your place is laughably easy. Tea?'

Accepting a mug, Sim drew up a chair.

'Well, don't go yet, we need to talk.'

Maurice seemed to measure the weight of this.

'OK. What about?'

'What exactly are you doing here?'

Maurice raised his tea mug.

'As you see.'

'Let me rephrase this. What's going on in your life to bring you back in touch with me after all these years?'

Maurice shrugged.

'Fine thing when I can't come back and see my only son.'

'Fine thing walking out on him and his mum in the first place.'

Maurice had got up. He was looking at a picture on the wall, a photograph of Eva dressed in a straw hat, posing on the doorstep of the cottage.

'She was a pretty girl, your mum.'

'Oh, for Christ's sake. Is this the time to get sentimental?'

Irritated, Sim stood up. His father turned and grabbed Sim's wrist. His eyes were moist, he seemed to be struggling to speak.

'Do you believe in Face, Simmie?'

But Sim misheard him.

'Fate?'

'No, *Face*! It's the principle which rules all Chinese business relations, in fact all relationships outside the immediate family. Face means never being seen to lose, or back down, or cock up.'

'Or say you're sorry?'

Sim's question was meant to be snide, but Maurice seized on it.

'Exactly! That's it!'

He was looking intently into his son's eyes and his grip on Sim's wrist was rigid.

'I came over here to do a bit of business. When I go back I will get Face, if I do it right. That's important. Face is not just make-up. It's a matter of survival. Prosperity – just, well, *enjoying* life – depends on it. Face is like varnish on the planks of a junk: unless it's good and hard the timber splits, and then you sink.'

He released Sim's wrist and sat again, taking a swig of tea.

'I *am* going back, if that's your problem. I'm not about to settle down here. After Hong Kong this would be – Christ! This seems like living in a bloody Wendy House. I'm just waiting for the new varnish to dry, and then I'll be gone.'

'So what business did you come over here to do? Or should that be what *crime*?'

'There's no difference! Crime *is* business and the other way round. But if you don't agree with that idea, it might be better for you not to know any more.'

'You proposing to stay here tonight?'

Maurice chuckled, rubbing his hands.

'No thanks. And I'm not stopping with those Sawleys either – nice boys but a bit thick, aren't they? No, I'm fixing myself up. You'll only be judging me, if I stay with you.'

He looked at his watch.

'That the time? Christ, must be off. Glad we had this chat. We can finish it another time, yeah?'

Then he was gone.

Maurice Fielding found plenty of time for drinking in The Ram over the next day or two. Garage customers were full of enthusiasm for the new arrival in their midst. To Sim they talked of little else.

'Eh, Sim lad. Grand man that dad of yours. For telling stories,' said Marcus Ball when he came in to pick up his Mini. 'Brilliant, I reckon.'

This agreed with the views of Jer Allard, who came in on the Tuesday for a set of spark plugs, and of Karen Gornal, when she needed Sim to help her fill her car with petrol. It was from her that he learned just how Maurice had 'fixed himself up'.

'I think he's right nice, your dad. He says it's too crowded in the Sawley boys' place, so he's asked if he can book in to stop with us.'

The Gornals' was a small farm and, to make ends meet in tough times, Karen did farmhouse bed and breakfast.

Sim said, 'Are you sure that's a good idea, Karen? Have you told Jim?'

Sim would bet Jim Gornal hadn't been consulted, because Jim would have said no. Karen was not only very pretty, but she knew how to communicate it. Her body language was sometimes so explicit that, in public, it could reduce Jim to jealous gibbering. Jim Gornal was a man who knew pigs better than anyone within a 10-mile radius, but he didn't know his own strength, or the strength of his feelings. Once, in a frenzy at Karen's flirting, he'd gone out and smashed the head of his own boar with a clubhammer.

'It's not Jim decides who to have staying,' said Karen. 'It's me does all the bookings. And the work.'

Karen stood with one of her legs flexed, making a cursive S of her slim body. She rested one hand gracefully on the roof of her car, the other on her pushed-out hip. If Maurice was going to stay at the Gornals', he could have only one motive in mind, thought Sim, ramming the pump nozzle back in its slot.

In the office he took her money.

'When's he coming to you?'

'Tonight's his first night.'

'Did he say how long he's in the area for?'

'No, and I didn't ask. Don't *you* know? He's your dad.'

Sim merely handed her the change, plus five vouchers towards the current incentive offer – three months' free supply of paper handkerchiefs. Appropriate. This was certain to end in tears.

In the afternoon Maurice came to the garage. He nodded at old Worsley and then stood awkwardly in the middle of the repair shop while Sim wriggled out from under a Ford Fiesta. Maurice had dispensed with the bandage now. He looked fresher and more healthy than Sim would have thought possible.

'Simmie, sorry I had to run off the other night.'

'Come on, let's walk,' said Sim. He looked at the old man. 'Back in a minute, boss.'

They walked without speaking as far as the Field. There were already a few arrivals, the first of the articulated trucks, pick-ups and caravans of the fairground people, who would be providing much of the hoopla for Fawkes Fair. Towards the end of the Field nearest the stone bridge, and at some distance from where the fairgrounders were forming their wagon-circle, the completed bonfire stood, monolithic and massive.

Maurice stopped in front of a van belonging to *Lady Rose Lee – Your Fortune in your Palm*.

'"Luck be a Lady." I must come down and try her.'

He rotated on his heel beside Sim, taking in all the preparations.

'Oh, look. There's the guy who has the Chinese chippie! Never thought I'd find one of those here, though I should've known better. Is there anywhere left without one?'

He pointed to Jimmy Ho out on the green, beyond the caravans and just opposite his shop. He was playing ball with little Kevin. Maurice started towards them.

'Come on over, I want to talk to that man.'

Sim stayed on the asphalt path while Maurice jogged over to Jimmy and the child. Maurice called out something in Cantonese, smiling and waving, but Jimmy took no notice. He reached the pair and spoke again. This time Sim saw Jimmy laugh and shake his head. Maurice knelt on one knee and chucked Kevin on the chin. Maurice picked up the ball and tossed it to Jimmy, laughing. He jogged back to the path. The little exercise left him seriously out of breath.

'Guess what.'

He was drawing in wheezing lungfuls of air and rubbing his chest with the flat of his hand.

'The guy doesn't know a word of Chinese, not any dialect. Born and brought up in Liverpool, so he says.'

Maurice was still looking across at the Chinese father and his half-caste son. He waved and turned away. They began to walk again.

'Cute kid, isn't he? Look, Sim, I'm sorry if we got off on the wrong foot. I can explain what happened in Manchester. You probably saw the police. Is that what made you scram?'

Sim stopped.

'What are you talking about, the police?'

'Well, when I got up to that flat, they were there. Now I hardly knew the girl. I was just going up for a swift leg-over – you know? Before we fucked off out of town.'

He sighed. It was the sigh he'd use when telling of a losing bet.

'Anyway, that wasn't to be. They took me straight down to the copshop.'

'The police did?'

'Yes. I didn't mention you, I'm entitled to some credit for that, by the way.'

'When did they let you go?'

'Couple of hours later. They'd got nothing to hold me on. It was the girl. She's a tart, a professional, so it turns out. They thought I was her ponce or something. It was the vice squad. Honest to God. I didn't even *know*.'

As they walked, Maurice tried to take his son's arm, but Sim shrugged free.

'And what about the dope? They must have found it.'

'They couldn't have cared less. They kept it to smoke themselves, that's all. No charge. So there was nothing to get excited about. It was just a present for the slag, anyway.'

'So why do I get the feeling you tried to use me? I don't really like that.'

'I don't quite know what you mean, Sim boy. Don't know *what* you mean. Look, I'd better be off. See you around.'

The policeman at the cottage door was a uniformed sergeant. He walked towards Sim with that air of gravity studied by members of the force and looked the machine over from front to back while Sim removed his helmet. The intricacies of chrome and alloy around the bike's belly seemed to absorb him. Finally he spoke.

'Wondering if you can help us, sir.'

'Oh?' said Sim. 'What's the problem?'

'Well, we've got a missing person, you see, and it's been linked to your father. That's, er, Maurice Fielding, isn't it, sir?'

'That's his name, yes.'

'Would you know where he might be?'

'He was staying at Gornals' Farm, out on the Chipping Road, last I heard.'

'Well, that's just it. Mr Gornal has reported his wife Karen Gornal gone, last night. And at the same time your father left the farm. We believe they went together.'

'That sounds like a fair assumption.'

'And she hasn't been in touch with her husband, you see. No one knows where she is.'

Sim slung his helmet from the bike's handgrip and moved towards the house.

'Don't you think my – don't you think Maurice Fielding knows?'

'Well, yes, but we don't know where *he* is. Mr Gornal is rather distressed. He seems to think Karen wouldn't go off of her own free will.'

'Karen? Wouldn't she just.'

'How do you mean, sir?'

How he meant was, Karen's relationship with Jim Gornal was based on a double excitement. *She* flirted outrageously with other men, *he* was pathologically jealous. They both liked it that way, but it made for an unstable partnership.

'Karen was a bit like a firework, sergeant.'

'She was?'

'Just waiting for someone to light her fuse.'

'Another man?'

'Probably not a pig, a cow or a sheep, anyway. What's it to do with me, by the way?'

'You're his son.'

'And not his keeper. He may need a keeper, I happen to think he does. But I'm not it.'

'He hasn't been in touch?'

'No.'

'And you've got no ideas where he might be?'

'No. I saw him yesterday, briefly. That's all.'

Sergeant Caldwell scratched his squat, almost boneless nose and fetched a sigh. Sometimes he felt as if all the loony families in Ribble Valley were on his back.

Caldwell returned to the squad car and plucked open the door.

'Well, if you *do* hear from your father, Mr Fielding, we'd be grateful to be let know. It'll be a weight off Mr Gornal's mind to know she's all right.'

'Of course, Sergeant. I will.'

With the Sergeant gone, Sim considered the weight on poor Jim Gornal's mind. It was not the kind of burden Jim was well equipped to bear. And, to go by past form, his boar if not his entire farm stock was in immediate danger of violent assault.

# 9

On Wednesday it had started to rain, a drenching, continuous fall that quickly made impatient torrents of the hundreds of streams and ditches that drained the Fell. These fattened the river until, in places, it lapped grossly over its banks. At Moxon the Field was partially inundated, and there was talk of moving Fawkes Fair to higher ground. Even the massive piers of the stone bridge seemed threatened by the current's obesity.

The farmers, unable or unwilling to go into the fields, took to the pub. The disappearance of Karen Gornal remained a prize talking-point. To the looser-tongued, younger men Karen had been a notorious prick-tease and, if her choice of a middle-aged man was a slightly sore point, there was a general feeling that, in most respects, Maurice was the very fellow to tame the bitch.

'I reckon he's poking her pubes off,' whispered Pete Sawley to a group round the fire on Tuesday. 'He's experienced, see? Old Jim isn't much cop at it. She told me that, once.'

'Get away,' put in Jer Allard. 'He's normal, is Jim. It were that bitch. She were near a nymphomaniac.'

'Well, Maurice has been around and about,' observed Pete sagely. 'Been with a lot of prozzies, Thailand and that. He knows what they want doing them.'

Jim Gornal stayed away from The Ram and Heifer. He skulked in his farmhouse, nursing the ego that Karen had bruised to the bone. He drank heavily by himself and, some villagers were saying, could be heard out, at night and in the downpour, baying abuse at the night, the weather and his stock, all the time revving a chain-saw. They all waited expectantly for more violent news from that quarter.

The other hot topic in the public bar was the Owleg. Owleg was a rucking game played each year at Fawkes Fair between This and Tuther, the teams drawn from men living either side of the river. For the last three years Tuther side had carried the day. But the drinkers in The Ram and Heifer, where This side had its stronghold, were plotting to end Tuther's recent run. The contest, staged just before the torching of the great bonfire, and on a pitch rimmed by straw bales, principally generated betting, dirty tricks and torn ears. The nearest thing to Owleg would be Rugby, except for one significant difference. Instead of a ball the players were required to chase and handle a live pig, greased with bacon dripping.

By the Friday afternoon, after two days of continuous rainfall, the weather changed again. Now a drying wind blew from the south-west, saving Fawkes Fair from being ignobly decamped from its traditional site. The Field would certainly be boggy, the Owleg pitch a quagmire and the marginal flooding on the riverside remained. But, to everyone's relief, the celebrations and ceremonies of contest and fire would be held this year on the spot where they had continued for centuries.

On Saturday morning old Worsley – always keen to bring on anyone's knowledge of local lore – had motored out into the repair shop in his wheelchair while Sim wrestled with a line of intractable nuts in the engine of an Escort. He shook a newspaper at Sim.

'Have you read this thing in the *Advertiser* about the origins of Fawkes Fair, Sim? Load of crap. Only talks about Guy Fawkes and the Gunpowder Plot.'

'Isn't that it – the origin of it?'

'It's far more ancient.'

'I thought it was to celebrate the discovery of the Plot.'

'No, it was the old Celtic New Year, this. Early November. The Christian took it over and called it Hallowtide, but truthfully it was a pagan do. *Folk*'s Fair they called it. They held a Wake for the old year, and a bonfire to burn off the bad spirits.'

There was pleasure in the old man's creased and yellow face. This wasn't book-learning to Worsley. It seemed like something he might once have witnessed, even himself capered half-naked round the flames, in his days of youth and usable legs.

'At the start they burned the odd witch – or imagined witch. Then Guy Fawkes and friends came along and tried to blow up the king and parliament. So they put him in the witch's place and Folk's Fair became Fawkes Fair, see? In Lancashire speech there's no difference anyway.'

The nuts Sim was working on had fused in a corrosive embrace with the engine-casing. He threw down the spanner, swore under his breath and straightened his back, hearing the wowing sound of open-air pop music coming on the wind up from Moxon Field. He strolled out to the forecourt, from where he could look down on the roofs of Moxon, the river and the Field. The Fair was getting under way – the big wheel was turning and the stalls were open for business. He felt now the tug of the thing. It was time to go down.

'I think I'll pack it in for today, boss. All right? Those nuts need drilling out: it'll do Monday morning.'

'All right, lad, off you go. Enjoy yourself. You in Owleg?'

'Yes. Every year I say it'll be my last, but they talked me round again. Coming down to watch?'

'Joking. I'll need this chair fitted with caterpillar tracks before I go on the Field today.'

What it had been for the Celts, Fawkes Fair was still – a splurge of social energy, a sexual spree before the long doze of winter. The women and girls, dressed defiantly of autumn weather in loud, flimsy dresses and delicate shoes, would be warm only where their cheeks were encrusted with facepaint. The men and boys jostled and joked, manoeuvring for precedence, showing off their skills through contests and strong-arm displays.

Sim took his turn at these, malleting the wooden pommel on the 'Muscle-o-meter' to make its bell ring, sparring a round in the boxing tent with Guy, the Gloved Gorilla, shooting clay pigeon off the bridge.

By late afternoon he was in Julia's beer tent, talking to Sammy Newton and charging his bloodstream with alcohol in readiness for the Owleg. Julia had never been so busy all afternoon. The tent's canvas was actually bulging in places, and the fuggy atmosphere was filled with loud boasts and counter-boasts, the ritual pre-match posturing of the Thisses and the Tuthers. A quarter of an hour before the pig was due to be outed, the rowdiness was reaching a beery climax. Then, without warning, a shock of silence pulsed through the tent – the effect of a bucket of freezing water on a dog fight. Heads turned. Beer glasses stopped between hand and mouth. Maurice Fielding had walked in.

He had a secretive smirk on his face, though his skin was greased with sweat and its colour was overall grey, with bluish highlights in the sagging flesh around his eyes, and yellow streaks in the eyeballs. He did not look healthy. The first to approach him was Barry Sawley, who lurched forward with raised arm.

'Eh, Maurice. You back, then?'

Maurice sidestepped Barry's scything attempt to clap him on the back and continued towards the makeshift bar – an uneven line of trestle tables. Ordering a pint, he waited without speaking while Julia drew it. She put it in front of him and stood while he took a long draught. Julia's fists were bunched pugnaciously on her hips. She looked ready to do three rounds with the Gloved Gorilla herself.

'Where's Karen, Maurice?' Julia asked.

Maurice removed the glass from his lips. He spoke, looking into the half-finished pint.

'Took her back home. We've been to Blackpool.'

He raised his eyes and looked swiftly around. He saw Sim and the lips and eyes smiled again, but it was a cagy, defensive acknowledgement. He began to drink again.

'What do you think's been going through poor Jim Gornal's mind?' Julia's blood was up now, and she wasn't going to let Maurice off lightly. 'Did you consider *him* at all, when you went flit without a word?'

Maurice finished his pint and planted the empty glass down.

'Jim's a grown-up. Another please.'

Julia looked as if she might spit.

'No. I'm not serving you. Go on. Take yourself off.'

Sim didn't want to witness the sequel. He slipped away before his father could catch his eye once more, and walked rapidly towards the Owleg pitch. He found Jimmy Ho, with little Kevin hoisted on his shoulders, standing on the straw-bale perimeter. They were watching a troupe of cloggies from Bacup doing their stuff.

'Hi, Jimmy. So what do you and Kevin reckon to this?'

The dancers, serious-faced and with front teeth winking through their beards, were most of them young accountants, dentists and the like. They hopped and clumped through their measures with unskilful relish.

'It shouldn't be done in public, Sim. It's worse than a school play.'

'That's what I think – consenting adults only. But they've got young Kevin mesmerized all right.'

At that moment, there was a yell from beyond the beer tent and two or three people came running, shouting Jimmy's name. A column of smoke was rising from a small pavilion near the fortune-teller's van: Jimmy's fish and chips booth was on fire.

'Oh my God, Sim. The stall. I knew I shouldn't have left that bloody get in charge. He's my nephew and he doesn't know custard from snot.'

He hauled Kevin down and pushed him into Sim's arms.

'I'll be back.'

Jimmy went running off and Sim lifted Kevin and jiggled him up and down. The boy seemed contented, easy. He pointed at the cloggies and laughed. As Sim was hefting the child on to his shoulders, Maurice appeared beside them. He was breathing heavily as he stuck a finger into Kevin's small fist and shook it.

'Hello, my young friend. Hey, Sim, Julia Singleton's been taking it on herself to lecture me. Tells me I shouldn't have gone away with Karen Gornal. Bloody bitch. What's it to do with her?'

'Everything's to do with everyone here. That's the contract if you live in a place like this.'

'Well, I'm not signing it. In fact, I'm off. Soon as possible.'

'Things not work out, then – with Karen, I mean?'

'Oh, yes. Very much so, they did. Very lively girl. Too lively, though I hate to admit it. Your dad's getting a bit old for forty-eight hours non-stop in the Norbreck Castle Hotel. We did everything a man and woman *can* do, several times over. It was like that thing students get up to, trying to visit every station in the London tube in a day. I think we surfaced for a burst of sea air once. Jesus! But it was nice having a big, brassy woman again. Not that I don't like the Chinese girls, I do. In fact that's the attraction of the East – delicate, submissive flowers, Sim lad, that's what they are. But, still, just for a change –'

His sigh was nearly a groan.

'What's more, she loves me. I mean, if you listen to her. *Crazy* about me. So, you see, I *got* to get away.'

The cloggies were packing away their staves and unlatching

their knee bells, while into the middle of the pitch old Ned Salmon was dragging a battered wicker basket with a hinged lid. The basket was rocking and squeaking, for it contained a sucking pig, carefully selected for speed and agility, and ready to be let loose at the start of the first out. Meanwhile, the teams were assembling and several of the Thisses were calling to Sim.

'Come on, Sim lad. Team talk.'

Maurice laughed when he saw it and turned to Sim.

'Are *you* in this? Here, I better take the child. His dad coming back for him, is he? Go on, give him me. I'd like it.'

Maurice held out his hands, his face suddenly sparkling with eagerness. Sim hesitated. Jer and Neil were beckoning to him, shouting his name. OK, it wasn't much to ask. Maurice only had to stand here and wait for Jimmy to return.

'But for Christ's sake don't wander off, or his parents won't find you.'

He placed Kevin on Maurice's shoulders, gave the boy a pat on the head and went to join the game.

Owleg was never less than muddy, but this year the mire was calf-deep. At times the pig was swimming through it as players clawed and kneed and thrashed each other to get to her. At each end of the pitch was an enamel bath filled with water, and a goal consisted in dumping the pig in the bath at your opponent's end. The Tuthers managed the first of these when Carl, a monstrous boy from Bashall, emerged from the argument brandishing the pig above his boulder head while Barry Sawley, whose finger was caught in the loop on Carl's boot heel, was trawled in his wake 10 yards through the mire.

With a change of ends, and of pig, This side fought back and it was Jer Allard who restored the balance. Sim, with a mighty, side-straining effort, forward-passed the pig to him over a squelching octopus of rucking players and Jer timed his run to the goal exquisitely. As he skidded up to the scoreline the slippery porker popped out of his arms, hung in the air for a moment above the bath and plopped into the water like a lump of wet soap. One – one. Then Ned Salmon emptied his lungs through his silver whistle and the match was over.

At some point during the contest, and for no apparent reason, a name travelled through Maurice Fielding's mind, like a blip on a cardiac monitor. *Erskin*. It passed, and then came again – *Erskin, Erskin* – passing and repassing until Maurice had fully grasped its meaning. It was the answer. It repaired the hole in his life. *Erskin*.

As he walked away from Moxon Field, which he did immediately, Maurice was still mentally repeating the name like a talisman. *Erskin. Erskin.*

Plastered from their hair to their toes with mud, they limped across the Field to the beer tent, like a battle-sore detachment of chocolate soldiers. Once fixed up with pints of beer they compared their bites, rents and bruises, bragged about their feats of strength and courage. But most of all they laughed at the foolishness of it all. It was the echo of identical laughter that must have been heard from every generation of their forefathers for hundreds of years. Owleg was daft and it always had been. It was the daftest tradition anyone had ever heard of. By next year, of course, they would all again attend the preparatory meeting organized by Ned Salmon, select pigs to be played for from Ned's stock, draw up lists of players and reserves, weigh form, try to better the opposition in pre-match hype. But for now they were all united in laughter, and their sores and injuries were soothed by it.

It was nearly time for the lighting of the bonfire and the launch of the first rockets of the firework display when a cry was heard near the entrance of the tent. It was an unnatural, meaningless sound. Glancing up, they saw it was Jimmy Ho, owner of their Chinese chippie. Jimmy had been running. He stood for a moment, panting, waiting till he could gather the breath for a silencing yell. Then he found some words.

'HEY! HEY! EVERYONE!'

The drinkers looked up. Some stopped in mid-sentence, others completed their remarks and then quiet settled. It was a surprise in itself to see Jimmy Ho in the beer tent. Although his shop was only a few doors from The Ram and Heifer, Jimmy didn't go there. He probably never took anything stronger than tea. They watched him, the way a herd of cows will watch an intruder in their field. There was something charged about Jimmy. He seemed to gather himself, like a candidate speaking to a hostile meeting. He stood on a folding chair, his chest heaving with effort and emotion. The words had some difficulty in coming out.

'I can't find my little boy, right? Has anyone seen him? Little Kevin? See, he was at the Owleg game when my chip stall went on fire. I left him with Sim Fielding. Sim? You here? You gave him to your father when you went on the pitch to play, that right?'

Sim nodded. The drinkers looked about them, at those they were sitting or standing with and then around the tent in general. Somebody spoke.

'Hasn't Jackie got him, Jimmy?'

'That's what I thought,' said Jimmy. 'And Jackie was over in the shop, thinking he was with me. I've looked all over.'

'Well, where's old Maurice?' somebody asked. 'He'll have Kevin, or he'll know where he is.'

'That's just it. Maurice's car was parked just across from the shop. Jackie saw him driving away. He left our kid. He just put him down and walked away. That bastard!'

Jimmy's voice trembled.

'And I'll kill him for it! I'll kill him if there's harm to our kid!'

He was speaking almost under his breath, as if performing a ritual act of will, holding himself together only by single-minded concentration.

'He might be out on the Field, Jimmy. Have you looked on the Field?'

'Yes, I've looked. I've been to every stallholder in the fairground. No one's seen him. And my Jackie's out there looking now. Someone *must* have seen him!'

'He could be in some house. He's likely been taken in.'

There was a pause and a silence, and then, in an unspoken collective decision, the tent emptied. Even Julia abandoned the bar and ran outside.

It was beginning to get dark, but they could see the scene well enough. At the stone bridge end of the Field the travelling fairground was going strong, though the amateur, villagers' stalls had closed down. If they turned to the riverbank, they could see the encroachment of shallow, fast-flowing water which had spilled a little way up on to the grass. This had seemed fairly innocuous on its first appearance. Now it carried such a dark implication that nobody wanted to think about it. Yet they were forced to by the figure of Jackie Ho, turning this way and that on the margin of the spate with her hands cupped to her mouth, shouting words that the wind whipped away.

Some of the Owleg players went from house to house, asking after Kevin. Others walked to the stone bridge and looked down at the current. The river level was so high, closer to them than most could remember from the vantage point, that they all realized the essential truth: down there Kevin Ho would not have a chance.

They were shortly joined by additional volunteers, men and women in boots and quilted jackets, tweed hats and headscarves. Downstream they moved, flashing powerful torches across the water-race, poking sticks into the deeper pools, combing the river bank and the ruins of Moxon Abbey. They pursued the search along the anglers' path, slipping and skidding in the slick mud, and clutching each other to avoid tumbles into the water. Some drove to strategic points lower down. Sim, on the BMW, was among these, nauseous with dread. If the child had died it was his fault, he knew it. He was given charge of Kevin Ho and he'd abdicated the responsibility. Sim stood on the edge of the river looking intently at a shingle bank out in mid-stream. Normally at this point the pebbles would be exposed, although now several inches of water flowed across them. Yet it was shallow enough so that, if he was in the water, Kevin might easily be recovered from such a place. Alternatively his sodden body would be snagged on the branches of an overhanging bush, or jammed into a clog of flotsam at some crook in the bank. Tired of scanning the roaring water Sim rested his eyes on the dark sky, where high white cloud was being busied along by the wind. If he'd had any idea of prayer, or anything to pray to, he might have said something.

What had Maurice been thinking of? He *can't* have been thinking. He put the child down and walked away. He was leaving Moxon, and no doubt didn't want another brush with the Gornals. But why hadn't he given Kevin to someone he knew?

On the other hand, perhaps he had. Not everyone on the Field that day was local. Kevin might have fallen innocently into the hands of any pervert. But the permutations were too unsettling.

Sim climbed on to his bike and rode down to the next shingle bank.

The night passed with no news of the child. There were appeals on the television and, next day, a search of the wider area – the fields and hedgerows, lines of police interspersed with the same volunteers, dogs. Every villager, every member of the travelling funfair was questioned. Other visitors to Fawkes Fair were interviewed. But it had been dusky when the Owleg game was coming to its end. No one had seen anything.

It was the next day, too, that an untidily dressed, middle-aged man walked into a police station in Burnley, 10 miles to the south of Moxon. It was lunchtime.

'I'm Maurice Fielding. I saw the news, OK? That kid who disappeared up at Moxon.'

He was taken to the office of a grizzled chief inspector.

'What exactly happened, Mr Fielding?'

'I was holding the boy, watching that daft game. I put him down. Then I left. That's all.'

Maurice leaned forward on the policeman's desk, his elbow propped on it, smoking.

'You put him down, just like that?'

'Yes. He was wriggling so much I couldn't keep hold of him.'

'What did he do? Run off?'

'I didn't see where he went to. It was getting a bit dark, you know? He seemed to run to someone he'd spotted, so I reckoned it was all right.'

'Who was it he ran to?'

'A tall, bearded bloke, red hair maybe, with glasses. That's all I can tell you about him. I didn't really see him properly.'

'You didn't bother to check who he was?'

'Well, no, I didn't. I reckoned the kid must have found his uncle or whatever. What do they think happened?'

'Could be he fell into the water.'

'Oh, my God. Drowned, was he?'

The sergeant doing the questioning was large, bursting out of his nylon shirt. He leaned nearer to Maurice, straining the shirt buttons to the limit of their tolerance. He spoke in a low murmur.

'We don't know. We haven't found a body. The alternative

theory is that someone abducted him. Was that you, Mr Fielding?'

'*Me?* Do me a favour! Look, I know I've got form, but that's ridiculous. That wasn't my game, and you know it.'

They did know it. And they never got round to formally questioning him, never even began the rigmarole with tape-recorders and typed-up statements. For six hours they kept him, and did everything to turn up some hint of the missing child. They sent a squad-car screaming round to the bed and breakfast where he'd stayed the night. They took his luggage and his car to pieces. They talked to people he'd talked to. They found nothing.

'Your car's very clean, isn't it?'

'Course it is. I'm selling it. I had one of those pricy in-and-out car washes, make it look better, you know. They swarm all over the thing with vacuum cleaners and carpet shampoos. It's quite amazing.'

In the end they let him go. There was no evidence that Maurice Fielding had abducted the child. He was guilty of nothing more than wanton carelessness.

The CID team was despondent. The chief inspector tried to chivvy his boys along.

'We'll just have to try to find this tall, bearded redhead, won't we, lads?'

There was a collective groan. None of them could believe in this individual and, in fact, no such person was ever traced. The cloggies, bearded to a fault, were followed up. Every bearded man in Moxon was given a second chance to remember something. The police poured constable-power into the investigation. The hunt was national news, but it led nowhere.

None of this was much comfort to Jimmy and Jackie Ho. Their shop was shuttered, and the curtains of the upstairs windows were drawn.

His mama had told the child about Big Bad Men. If you weren't good they came and took you away in cars and gave you sweets. And however much you wanted to eat the sweets, you mustn't.

In the car the Big Bad Man had indeed given him all kinds of things: Jelly Babies, Smarties, licorice and crisps. The child had sat looking at these gifts for a long time and cried for his mama.

But then he got hungry and pulled open the bag of crisps. They had scattered all over his knee and the car seat. The Big Bad Man was angry about that.

They left the car at a place like a train station, except he couldn't see any trains. The Big Bad Man didn't talk to him. He was still angry with him, hurrying him along. Later they sat in a long room with a lot of chairs and people, like a bus, though he knew it wasn't because the windows were different. These were like the windows on washing machines at the Launderette. He wasn't allowed to look out but he started to feel the room shaking. Suddenly his stomach lifted as his head was filled with a terrible roaring noise, like the giant in the story who shouted '*Fee-fo-fi-fum*' from the middle of a burning mountain. He shut his eyes tight.

When he opened them he turned to the Big Bad Man next to him and was sick all over his lap.

## 10

Sim had felt the village atmosphere go cold towards him, like a bath he'd lain in too long. When he bought a loaf of bread, Mrs Benlow had no smile. At the garage, the customers avoided contact. In the pub he started all his conversations, and they died within seconds as people turned away, finding they needed a piss or a refill. He rang Denise for a date, and her string of excuses covered an indefinite period in the future.

Even Julia, whom he loved like a mother, was bitterly reproachful when he complained about Denise. She pulled him into the passage that led from the bar to the kitchen.

'What the *hell* do you expect? You handed that child to a stranger.'

She shut her eyes and her fingers impatiently tinkled an imaginary keyboard.

'All right, all right. He's your father. But he's a stranger all the same, and he's trouble. We all know *that* from the episode with Karen Gornal. So I hope you realize what those people are going through. Christ, lad, I thought you'd bloody started to grow up in the past year or two. But you haven't. You're the same spoiled, pampered, thoughtless boy.'

He listened to music, alone in his cottage, and brooded on the peculiar sense of fault that had been hitched to him. It was an accident, wasn't it? He couldn't have known. But was that any excuse? He remembered an old school teacher, a man of over fifty, who had railed at Sim's class in tones of withering sarcasm on the subject of excuses.

'God, you're so lucky, you kids, your generation of kids. You've had no war, you've had no hardship, you don't believe in old-style absolutes like good and evil. There's no precision about you, it's all just *moods* and *feelings*. You're always saying, "know what I mean?" because you *don't* know what you mean. With you mood is an excuse for everything, and the only absolute you have is appetite. How convenient.'

After two weeks he had heard nothing from Maurice, and Kevin Ho was still missing. If anything, Sim's isolation was deepening. He did nothing to end it. He withdrew entirely, staying away from the pub and doing his shopping out of the village. By his action he was signalling his next move. It would be a move away from Moxon. The answer to all this lay not in the village but in the meaning of Maurice Fielding's movements. And he wanted to find the answer.

'Boss, I'm no longer the favourite son.'

They were in the garage office. It was the end of the working day, and the room was almost dark.

'You've noticed, then.'

'It's like I'm a plague-carrier. The papershop empties when I go in there.'

Worsley considered, fiddling with one of the controls on his wheelchair.

'That father of yours. Do you think he was just careless, or was it – well, worse?'

'You mean, did he kill the kid? I don't think he did – I don't think he could have. But then, I can't think anyone could have, deliberately.'

'It happens.'

Worsley's rasping breaths, and the clunking tick of the tin alarm clock on his desk, were the loudest noises in the room as Sim said, 'I don't *think* he's a pervert.'

'But you shan't know what he really did till you look him in the eye and ask him yourself.'

Sim blushed, invisibly in the dusk. The canny old man.

'Well, I'll not get the chance. He'll have gone back to Hong Kong. He's made his smell and now he's walked out of the room.'

'You've got a passport, haven't you, lad?'

Worsley reached into a drawer, pulled out a chequebook and pulled the top off his pen. It seemed to take him minutes to write that cheque, the pen moving so slowly along the printed lines, poised while he pondered the amount and tried to recall the date. But at last he ripped it from its stub and put it in Sim's hand.

'That's a contribution. If you need more, you can ask. Your job'll be here when you come back. I'd expect you to sell that bike, mind. That'll be your contribution.'

Sim folded the cheque and slid it into the pocket of his jeans. He touched the old man on the shoulder.

'Thanks, boss,' he said, almost in a whisper.

Sim got no reply at the house, so he recrossed the cobbled yard and made his way between the Gornals' barn and the tractor shed. An ammoniac reek stung his nostrils as he passed near the sileage. This was placed at 30 yards' distance from the buildings on the other side – a miniature black plastic Himalayas cooking beneath its weight of rubber tyres. All around was the rusted evidence of a farmer's inability to be rid of redundant tools: discarded feed hoppers, old baths, a spike harrow, the corroded chassis of a trailer, an engine-casing capsized in a stodge of oil and mud.

The yard, the outbuildings and the fields beyond seemed deserted, though not derelict. A stillness possessed them, yet he expected at any moment someone to cross, whistling from threshold to threshold, from milking parlour to dairy, humping a churn, from back garden to chicken run with a bucket of millet. All farmyards at mid-morning are pregnant like this.

Sim thought of the paradox of Karen Gornal. She was Jim's partner in business as much as in sex. She was expected to get up at dawn, as he did, take a stiff brush to cow shit, operate the milking parlour, drive a tractor at haymaking, boil pig swill. And these things she did, or she would not have lasted the six years of her marriage to Jim. The role, so traditional, so spartan, was hard to reconcile with the sexy, bum-wriggling, short-skirted bimbo who frequently caused such havoc in The Ram and Heifer.

The stillness broke in a volley of barks from a wooden kennel under the garden wall. The collie-cross shot out and checked at the end off his chain, yelping. It seemed bent on choking itself. Sim skirted the dog's limited arc of freedom and approached the piggery.

The piggery was a recently built, breeze-block shed with corrugated-iron roof surmounted by three airvents like little bellcotes. It contained two ranks of stalls. Open sluices ran the length of it, with an aisle of ribbed white concrete between. He walked in. Some of the animals were observing him curiously. Their small, malicious eyes gazed as they twitched the dirt-mottled flaps of their ears. Others took no notice, but rooted in their litters, snuffling and giving out little yips, or merely sleeping in obese contentment.

At the end of the building was the closed door of a storeroom. It was made of steel and Sim tried the handle. The door did not move, and as he released his grip and turned to go back, the handle's springback made an audible *tock*. It was then he heard the voice.

'Jim?'

It was a woman's, high and tentative, and it was on the other side of the door.

'Jim?'

Sim tried the handle again, giving the door a sharp tug. It didn't move.

'Karen? That you in there?'

Suddenly the voice was shriller, more panicky.

'Who is it? That's not Jim. Who's there?'

'It's Sim, Sim Fielding. I came up to talk to you. It's about my dad.'

There was a silence as he waited for a response, which did not come. Sim waggled the door handle again.

'Karen, have you locked yourself in? Are you afraid of Jim? He's not around, you know. You can come out quite safely.'

No reply. He pressed his head to the door and listened. Behind him was the gentle obbligato of pig noises; through the door he could hear her breathing.

'Karen? Karen, unlock the door. You'll be safe, I guarantee. There's no sense in hiding in there.'

He hammered on the iron.

'Don't, Sim! Just go away, OK?'

Her voice shook.

'Why don't you come out, Karen? There's nothing to hide from. There's nobody here, only me.'

'Leave me alone. Don't interfere in what you don't understand. Please.'

And it came to him. She wasn't in hiding at all.

'Karen. He locked you in here, didn't he?'

'Sim, go, will you?'

'No, I won't go. Did he lock you in here?'

It was a solid steel door. The hinges were firmly anchored. The lock was integral.

'*Didn't* he?'

She spoke, but he didn't catch her word.

'What, Karen? What did you say?'

'YES! He locked me in here. It's none of your business. Now go away.'

'How long, Karen?'

'It doesn't concern you – you, of all people. You should leave me be.'

'How *long*, Karen?'

'Just this morning. He's gone down to clear some ditches in the bottom field.'

'I'm breaking the door down, Karen. I'll just go and find something to do it with, then I'll be back.'

'No!'

She was immediately behind the door now, but lower down. Sitting, or on her knees, perhaps with her head pressed to the door.

'I'm getting you out, Karen. I want to talk, and I'm not doing it through a quarter–inch of steel. I'm breaking open this door.'

'NO!'

The scream signalled the capitulation. When her voice came again, it was lower, more reasonable.

'He hangs the key on a nail to your right.'

Sim looked there. An old army beret was hanging on the wall. He lifted it and found the key underneath. It slipped easily into the lock.

Karen wore only underwear. She was on the floor and the storeroom was dark, illuminated by miniature roof-lights. For a woman of such physical presence she looked here almost two-dimensional, like a pale moth against the dark ground. The strap of her slip had fallen to one side, off a bare shoulder.

She struggled into a crouch and then eased to her feet. Sim noted the black eye, the bruises on the arms, the nervous, apologetic smile. She lifted her spread hands away from her sides and let them fall back with a light slap.

'He locks me in now, when he goes anywhere. He doesn't trust me not to go off again, you see?'

Sim nodded. Jim Gornal had always been verbally inarticulate, and, rather than expect him to try to talk a problem away, you would back him to swing a fist. Or else slam a door on it, pretend it wasn't there. In the case of his wife, he had evidently done both.

Karen stood back and extended a hand, like an usherette.

'Come in, please.'

'You know what they're saying, don't you?'

They were seated on 2-litre paint cans, Karen wrapped in Sim's jacket. She frowned.

'No, what *are* they saying? I've not been anywhere, have I?'

'They're saying he took little Kevin Ho.'

'Maurice?'

'Abducted him.'

'Who's saying that? Police?'

'No, people. Moxon.'

'But why would he?'

Sim held her eyes intently, refusing her question. Her eyes looked fierce, affronted. She shook her head.

'Bollocks. He wouldn't.'

'When you were with him, was there anything about Maurice – what he was doing – that worried you?'

Karen had begun to recover her spirit now. She gave him a lop-sided smile.

'No, I *liked* what he was doing, Sim. It was tremendous. God, where did he get that from? Did he pass it on to you?'

'Karen, what I meant was, did he meet anyone, telephone anyone, make any contacts?'

'No, don't think so. Nothing.'

'Were you with him all the time?'

'Course I was.'

'Did he talk about Hong Kong at all, what he does and what he's doing over here?'

'Well, I knew he lived in the East, like. But we didn't do much talking. Mainly drinking and screwing is what we were into. You know.' She shrugged. 'I'm sorry, but there it is. Or was.'

'What did you use for money?'

'My money.'

'He didn't have any?'

'No. He was temporarily embarrassed.'

She laughed, embarrassed herself. 'That's what he told me.'

'Did you see his luggage?'

'How do you mean?'

'Was there anything there that seemed out of the usual?'

'He's your dad, Sim. Why don't you ask him?'

'I can't. He's gone. *Did* you look in his case?'

'I saw in his wallet. He had these photos.'

'What kind?'

'Photos of a kid. Chinese kid.'

'Not Kevin Ho?'

Again she shook her head.

'No, I don't think so, but about that age. Dark hair, spiky-like. I guessed it was a kid he had out there. You know, Chinese wife and that.'

'Did you ask him about that?'

'Yeah, but he told me not to pry. He was dead touchy about it.'

'What sort of pictures were they? Snapshots?'

'Yes, that sort of thing. Red eyes one of them had – flash.'

'Anyone else in them?'

'No. Just the kid.'

'Any background on them, any clues about where they might have been taken?'

'No, they were indoors, that's all.'

Sim went on, shooting questions. He was doing it like some policeman, but there wasn't so much time and he didn't know a better way. So, while he was with Karen, had Maurice talked about his boss, his work, his home? Had they talked about Moxon, about the Ho family, about Sim?

No, no, nothing. They had gone to Blackpool, they'd torn each other's clothes off, they'd dirty-talked and fucked and ordered champagne and dirty-talked and fucked some more. They went out for a walk on the sand once. Maurice had said he wanted to have her under the pier like the teenagers on holiday did, once upon a time. But it was too cold. So they'd gone back to bed.

There was nothing more, Sim was sure of it. Anyway it was time he left. Jim would be back and there was no point in provoking any incident.

They stood awkwardly beside the door which stood a crack open. Karen pushed it slightly, hooked a hand round and extracted the key from the outside of the lock. She gave Sim back his jacket and then she gave him the key.

'Christ, Karen, are you sure –'

'Yes, I deserve it. It won't go on for long anyway, then we'll be back to normal. Jim needs me to work, and anyway, he loves me.'

Sim gestured to the surrounding storeroom, Karen's jailhouse.

'Oh yeah?'

He closed the door on her and, carefully, turned the key until bolt plopped into mortise with lubricated ease. He replaced the key on its nail and walked away from her.

It was the fourth door he had knocked on. Of the others, only one had opened at all, and then just a crack. He'd heard the security chain clink and go taut as the door stopped against it. There was a vertical blind of light and the panting of a big dog, its paws rattling on a linoleum floor. The dog's nose appeared in the narrow aperture as the owner, still unseen beyond, asked who was there. Sim framed his question and the answer came back sharply.

'Never heard of him.'

And the door slammed.

Now at the fourth flat he could again hear someone moving around inside, a shuffle of feet. The door opened with a simple turn of a Yale lock. The outdraught carried with it a waft of cannabis smoke.

She was tiny. Black hair wrapped in a towel, dressing-gown, pompomed slippers. Her face was scrubbed clean of any make-up. She had recently bathed or showered. She was Chinese.

'I hope I'm not disturbing you. It's about a man called Maurice Fielding. Do you know him?'

He knew already that she did. Her eyes were dilated, a little watery and glazed, but they registered the name as soon as he mentioned it. She stood looking at him and swayed. Clasped in her hands was a scarred and battered tin of rolling-tobacco.

Sim said, 'I'm his son.'

'His son?'

She squinted and ducked her head forward, peering at him in the gloom of the landing.

'He didn't mention me?'

'Yer, he mentioned you all right.'

Sim hadn't expected the raw, nasal Salford accent.

'Can I come in?'

'Come on, then.'

She stepped back and he crossed the threshold.

In the hallway was nothing but a telephone on the floor. Through one door, slightly ajar to the right, he glimpsed tumbled bedding, a heap of household detritus, a hair-drier on the floor, some cardboard boxes, a plastic potty. Through another was the kitchen, with a stacked draining-board, liquor bottles on the fridge-top, an ironing-board. A third door, wide open, revealed most of the bathroom – dripping tap, rust-stained bath, the shelf a packed terrace of bottles, jars, tubes and pots.

She showed him into the sitting room. It was scarcely furnished at all. On the wall was a tattered Manchester United team poster, the Sellotape yellowed as if it had been there for years. Another, more recent, showed a Chinese pop- or film-star in a tasselled, gleaming-white suit and cowboy hat. There was a grey cord carpet, the nap worn to the backing in several places. The sofa, wood-framed, had uncovered and rat-chewed cushions made of foam. The picture windows – misted thickly with condensation – were uncurtained. A convection heater stood in the middle of the room and on a glass-topped table was a television showing tonight's game show.

Sim said yes to the offer of tea and she left the room to make it.

He thought of the neighbour with his Rottweiler and toughened-steel doorchain. Such was this locality, and yet the girl had accepted him without question. Why?

*Har-har-har. Lays and gennermen, give a good hand for a grey sport, a grey-grey sporting compeddita. Thank you, thank you.*

The television audience dutifully clapped and hooted as a

losing player was led from the stage. Sim could hear a phone ring, and then the woman talking somewhere in another room.

When she brought in a tin tray with a teabowl and straw-handled pot, he said, 'What's your name?'

'Teresa. They call me Treeze.'

'Makes you sound like a nice Irish girl.'

He smiled, but the remark did nothing to put her at her ease. She poured tea for him.

'You shoulda told me when you were coming. What if I hadn't a been here?'

'Well, I didn't really know –'

'Will you watch television? I'll be back again in a moment.'

She left him and he sipped his tea. It was like a mouthful of liquid smoke.

Treeze was out of the room for about five minutes, but the change, when she returned, might have been the work of an hour. The turban-towel was off her head and she wore a red velour dress fitting as close as a surgeon's glove. It was slashed vertically up one of the seams from hem to hip. She hovered in the doorway, smiling automatically.

'What do you want to do?'

Weighing down her right arm was a large, shiny ghettoblaster. She put it on the floor and punched the cassette-play button. A slow, caterwauling Chinese pop tune meandered from it, competing with the tides of induced laughter from the television.

'You want to dance for a bit, yeah?'

She came to him and started to sway slightly from side to side, her head canted. The blue-black hair was gathered asymmetrically to the left of her head and flowed down over the shoulder. The lips glistened with sticky crimson, the eyes were outlined with a thick kohl pencil, with lashes weighed down by slabs of mascara. Sim smiled again. It wasn't a surprise that Maurice's girl in Salford was a Chinese whore. He just hadn't been ready to be treated like her fare.

'I only wanted to talk.'

'Talk, then.' She spoke flatly, seeming barely interested. 'Talk, dance, talk. Whatever you want, it's your party. I'll blow you after, if you like. Or if you want a tongue bath, I'm supposed to be good at that. Whatever.' She shrugged. 'You're paying.'

'Am I?'

'Yeah. He said so, £100. Told me to look out for you, he'd give you the money for your birthday. Give you a good time.'

This time he laughed openly. She stopped swaying and looked at him in reproach. He was fighting against the atmosphere she needed to create. He was a spoiler.

The spoiler showed her the palms of his hands.

'Look, Treeze, I'm sorry to disappoint you. I'm not here for a birthday treat from my dad. He was talking bullshit, as usual.'

With a short sigh she broke away from him and sat on the sofa, breaking open her tobacco tin with a practised thumb. She took out three papers and began to stick them together. She scowled as she worked.

'Well, fuck it. I fucking wasted this make-up, didn't I? Special lipstick, this is, and it's dear.'

'Oh? What's it do for you?'

She looked at him pityingly.

'It doesn't do nothing for me. Gives *you* extra thrills.'

'Oh. Look, I'll pay all the same, if you like. *If* you really will talk about Maurice. You see, I need to find him.'

Sim sat down on the carpet opposite her, watching her assemble the cannabis joint.

She laid the trinity of papers on her knee and arranged a line of tobacco along it. Then, heating the small cube of hash with a butane lighter, she crumbled it in and rolled the spliff in a single forward-and-backward action of the fingers. Finally her tongue came out between the crimson lips and delicately, like a cat, licked the gummed edge.

Sim extracted two £50 notes and smoothed them on the carpet until they lay flat and she could see them. It would buy her quite a lot more dope.

'My father came up here, what, two weeks ago late at night and the police were here. He got arrested. Can you tell me about that?'

'Not much. It was vice squad, man called Smallwood, another man called – oh, I forget. They came in here about 10 p.m., said they wanted to wait. When *he* turned up they nicked him, and me too. Thought he was my pimp! That's a joke.'

But it was a snort, not a laugh, that she gave.

'So who really is –?'

'Pimping me? No one. Well, there's a bloke I pay squeeze to

in Chinatown. You got to have some insurance really. I make my own way, you know? I'm not some wanker, me.'

'How long had you known Maurice?'

She flicked the wheel on her lighter and touched the flame to the toffee-paper-twist at the end of the reefer. It flared momentarily and then she drew the fire into the cigarette itself, inhaling and holding her breath. She spoke with a wheeze of cough as she exhaled again.

''Bout a week. He picked me up in Piccadilly Garden. I was walking my –'

She darted a look at Sim, and he saw she was suddenly wondering why she was doing this. He saw her eyes fall to the £50 notes on the floor between them and then she went on.

'I was walking my dog, he approached me and said how he liked talking to Chinese chicks, so we came back here.'

'Was that the only time – apart from when you were arrested, I mean?'

'Christ, no. He was back the next day. Said he wanted exclusive rights, said I was the greatest fuck he'd ever had in his life.'

This time her laugh was more genuine. Some of the sheer effrontery of Maurice Fielding had returned to her mind.

'He made out he was terribly rich and he'd pay me by the week. I told him he looked more like a dosser and he said he was doing some secret work, under –, undercover or underground. Something like that.'

She was holding the joint close to the knuckle and inhaling through her closed fist. It was her good manners, in case he wanted to share with her. She held it out to him now, and he took it. He inhaled the same way.

'Do you live here with anyone?'

'No.'

'I heard you talking just now. Who's out there?'

He made as if to get up. Treeze said, a shade too quickly perhaps, 'No! There's no one. Just my little dog.'

Sim handed her back the spliff.

'Did Maurice ever talk about this undercover work?'

'No. He said it was something to do with the government. I thought it was crap and I still do. It didn't stop me letting him bonk on credit, though, fool that I am.'

'Did you know he lives in Hong Kong?'

'Yes, he said. Speaks better Cantonese than me.'

'You liked him?'

'Yeah, I *liked* him. He was funny. At first he was interesting – '

'And then?'

'Boring. He got boring. Asking for money so he could bet. Losing. Asking for more.'

Her head was tilted back, the chin raised, remembering. Gently she was stroking the hank of luxuriant hair which now rested sleek as the body of an anaconda between her breasts.

'When he came back that night I thought, I mean I hoped, it was to pay what he owed me.'

They had smoked the joint down to the roach now, and she stubbed it out on the lid of the tobacco tin. He had watched her movements becoming slower and more deliberate. She must have been smoking for some hours.

Was it why Maurice'd bought the cannabis – to mollify her? Not payment in full, but enough so she wouldn't slam the door in his face when he came back.

But did he come back?

'Did he come back after the arrest?'

Her head rested back on the chewed-out foam cushion, her mascara-choked lids dropping so he could see only thin crescents of dark moisture where her eyeballs were.

'No. He didn't come back.'

She jerked her head, coming awake, and looked at him with a thin, ironic smile.

'They never come back, do they?'

*She was lying. But why?*

'He didn't even come back to collect anything, anything he'd left?'

'No. I told you. They never do!'

'It's just that I don't think –'

'You don't think, eh? Look, I'm tired, OK? I don't want to talk any more.'

'Why are you lying to me?'

'Just leave me OUT, OK!'

She had shouted. She seemed to shock herself, because she slumped back into her former position. Then there was a noise from the door.

'Treeze, you all righ'?'

It was impossible to tell whether the newcomer had come from the bedroom or the street. He looked like a trainee accountant, in a blue Burtons suit, white shirt and tie. The difference was he carried two short lengths of broomhandle coupled by a lavatory chain.

Sim's reactions were slowed by the smoke he'd had. Before he could rise, the flail was around his neck and the handles were being twisted around each other. The accountant tugged him like this to his feet.

'Get up. What you say these bad things to Treeze for? She's only trying to help you.'

Sim swayed from side to side as the guy tugged this way and that. He heard a voice from the television, strangely amplified in his ear, braying. *Well, how about that? One hun-dred pounds!* Sim coughed. The air rasped down his constricted airway. He felt the blood in his head swell, its outflow held up by pressure on the jugular vein. The strangulation was not enough to make him lose consciousness. But it put him completely in this maniac's power. If he didn't act now, he would shortly be too weak to act at all. He lunged backwards.

They staggered together, in reverse and in step like a couple of top-hat-and-tails hoofers losing control. When they hit the wall the impact of Sim's larger mass kicked the air from his attacker's lungs with a percussive *oof*. The chain round Sim's neck went slack and he found the strength to drive an elbow backwards into the other's chest. Then he ducked out of the chain, turned and punched the man's face once, twice, and if the hits pained his hand, he knew they must hurt the other man more – especially because his head, taking the impact, snapped back on to the wall. Sim switched to work on the body, three blows hard to the chest and then three more to the ribcage. He shouted to Treeze.

'Who is this? Your insurance man? Your pimp?'

Behind him he could hear the woman, her voice quavering.

'Hit him. Go on, hit him. Hit him. Smash him.'

It wasn't till later, when Sim recollected this, that he identified the *him* in these cries.

Now the pimp was doubled over. Sim ripped the flail from his unresisting fingers and jabbed the bunched handles into his stomach. With a groan he slid to the ground.

Sim stepped back and turned his head to look at Treeze, who was watching the engagement with her mouth open, a waxwork pose. But he shouldn't have allowed his concentration to wander, for the pimp reared upwards and rammed two clasped fists into Sim's solar plexus. As Sim's head dropped reflexively, the pimp reached forward and clapped both hands on the crown of his head, helping it on to his upspringing knee. The bang on his forehead scattered Sim's thoughts like a starburst and he wobbled backwards on rubber legs. The pimp was breathing hard as he followed up. Had he been fresh, the next blow would have been decisive, but it merely glanced off the side of Sim's cheek. Paradoxically, this woke Sim up again and he kicked – getting a hard contact in the sponge of the pimp's groin. As the pimp groaned and doubled, Sim leapt on his back.

The two men rolled together to the floor. They went on rolling, stupidly, trying to gouge, punch, claw at each other's face. Sim, on top of the pimp now, noticed with some half-engaged background sense Treeze flitting past. But his fingers were in the pimp's mouth and nostrils, fighting the jaw open to prevent a bite. His other hand, meanwhile, was reaching out, stretching for the flail. But it lay just out of reach on the floor.

A moment later he thought he could get it. He grasped but the flail was gone. He didn't see at once what happened; it seemed to fly up of its own accord. In surprise he relaxed his grip on the mouth and felt the other's teeth instantly sinking into his flesh to the bone. A double, wooden crack resounded. Both flail handles bounced on the pimp's head. The pimp tensed for a second, then lay still.

Treeze was standing over them. She held the flail by the chain; it swung down by her knees. The breath sobbing in his trachea, Sim hauled himself to his feet. The tiny woman, still in her strumpet's regalia, looked at him fiercely.

'Get out! Get the fuck out! He won't know who hit him. He'll think it was you. Go on. *Now!*'

In the hall she closed the sitting-room door and stood with her back to it, defensively. She was still gripping her tobacco tin. Then she seemed to think of something.

'No. Wait one moment.'

She slipped into the other room and began rummaging through a handbag on the bed. He stood in the doorway. She came back with a roughly torn scrap of newsprint and held it out towards him.

'I should've told you. Maurice *was* here, two days ago. Telephoned someone in Hong Kong, arranging to meet. After he'd gone I found this. I don't know what it means, I just know he had it.'

She was trembling, looking over her shoulder at the closed sitting-room door.

Sim said, 'Was he alone? When he came here, I mean?'

'Alone. Yes, alone. I don't know anything. I don't know anything else.'

She was still proffering the scrap of paper. He took it, opening it up. It was from a poor-quality newsprint, but the photograph was in colour. He could see the back of a man. Beyond and above him stood charred beams around a blackened chimney stack. In front of his feet stood mounds of grey and black ash.

Treeze opened the door for him, holding it wide. Her hand went to his shoulder and he felt the pressure of the fingers urging him through. He yielded, allowing himself to be pushed out on to the bare concrete landing. Before Treeze closed the door on him she whispered through tensed lips.

'Bring him back. Oh please. Bring him back.'

She gestured backwards into the flat.

'He made me, but he doesn't understand. I just wish I . . .'

Suddenly there was a bump behind her and in panic she slammed the door shut in Sim's face.

He stood there, squinting again at the crumpled piece of paper. There was no story to accompany the picture, only a caption. In the near-darkness he could hardly read it: 'God's TV tycoon C. P. Cotton mourns beside the burnt-out cottage of his daughter-in-law.'

He refolded the sheet and slid it inside his wallet.

## 11

C. P. Cotton's errand boy looked Ed Craike up and down.

'We have a few house rules, sir. I'm sure you won't mind. First off, Mr Cotton would not like you to wear your shades when you are with him.'

The smooth-cheeked young man in the silk suit was *designed* to be unsettling, thought Craike. Somewhere up on the fortieth floor of this corporate steeple of mirror glass, stored on a computer hard disk, were his specifications. Under twenty-five, dress stylish, looks like an *Esquire* clothes horse, probably went to Harvard Business School and, above all, cocky.

'He also has the preference that you do not use a handkerchief – I mean to blow your nose, of course. And, if I may say so, it *is* a pity you chose not to put on a tie today, sir. Still, we can fix that.'

Craike allowed himself to be ushered back towards the great circular reception desk, from which he had strayed during his ten-minute wait. They were in the lobby of the CPCC building on Des Voeux Road, Hong Kong Central District, the hub of the biggest religious media operation in the history of the world. Craike had an appointment with the honcho himself: the pugnacious, unpredictable Charles Pilsbury Cotton.

The errand boy had a security pass on his jacket labelling him as a Jonathan Pappingay. He murmured briefly to the Eurasian girl of stunning beauty who sat within the ring of marble, then hovered while she delved beneath and produced a blue bow-tie with yellow dots, attached to a circlet of elastic. With a smile of orthodontic perfection, Pappingay presented the tie to Craike.

'Mr Cotton does insist on a tie, as he can't stand the sight of the male Adam's apple. Mr Cotton has a particular thing about that.'

Craike had heard all about Cotton's eccentricity. He tucked the sunglasses away in the breast pocket of his tropical jacket, closed the collar button of his shirt and inserted his head into the tie's elastic. It was all part of the softening-up process. If you find no crack, kick the paintwork.

Pappingay led him across the cavernous atrium and up the widest flight of moving stairs Craike had ever seen. On the first deck they entered a glass elevator labelled TO PENTHOUSE ONLY. Launched towards the top of the building, it delivered enough *g* to cause Craike to stagger. Its walls displayed a multitude of instructions to visitors: SMOKING CIGARETTES OR PIPES NOT PERMITTED IN SUITE; LEAVE YOUR GUM IN A RECEPTACLE; PLEASE ACCEDE TO SECURITY ADJUSTMENTS; FOR YOUR CONVENIENCE, AUTO-SHOESHINE IS AVAILABLE.

They stepped out into a luxuriously carpeted anteroom, on whose walls were several small Impressionist canvases. While acceding to security adjustments, Craike looked one of these over – it was a balletdancer by Degas, a delicate, bending form within a starburst of white tulle. He smiled at the beefy Chinese security guard who had completed the body frisk, indicating the picture. The guard's eyes moved suspiciously to the wall. He grunted.

Craike checked his watch. He was punctual to the minute, but it took another fifty-nine before the summons came. The time-lag was standard in Craike's experience. Important people make lesser mortals wait, and the larger the importance gap, the longer you wait. You own a TV company back home in Austin, Texas? That's fifteen minutes. Control a string of Filipino holy-knick-knack franchises? Thirty minutes. Have a shoestring security consultancy in your backroom? Why, you're lucky to get inside an hour later.

Craike had learned patience as a soldier. He passed the time looking at Cotton's artworks, shining his shoes and flicking through the stiff-paged magazines and auction catalogues provided for the purpose. Finally Pappingay came bustling back.

'Mr Cotton will see you now. This way.'

The office had a wide, curved sweep of plate-glass window and was very light. This was useful, because the room would have been dark, as its floor and walls were of polished jet-black marble. The famed publisher and broadcaster was reclining on a divan. A jockey cap, in his personal racing colours, was set on his head and he wore black-silk pyjamas. In a gruff voice he was issuing directions to a white-coated chiropodist who crouched over his naked feet.

'And make goddamn sure the edge of the nail winds up blunt, mister. You know what I pay for socks? $30 which I'll deduct from your fee if you leave sharp edges.'

There were six others in the room, all men, standing around waiting, like courtiers, to step in with a suggestion or a point of detail as the foot-carpenter rasped away at Cotton's big toenail. Craike was brought into the ring.

'Publisher, Mr Craike is here,' said Pappingay.

Cotton looked up.

'Ah, Craike. Where were you? You were due at a quarter of.'

He shook his foot, as if to dislodge a crab, and rose, removing the jockey cap to reveal a hairless head. Cotton was a bulky man with thin legs and long feet. He walked like a duck, but his face was far from inviting ridicule. It was lean and sharp, and the tight skin shone where it stretched over the cheekbones. Pushing his aides back like they were undergrowth, he waddled barefoot to his desk, a huge marble slab as big as a snooker table. It had three telephones, an intercom console, and a rank of heavyweight reference books. Cotton tossed the silk cap down and picked up a VHS video cassette.

'Hey, Pappingay! Close the drapes. I want our guest to look at my video. You –' He pointed to the podologist, who was sitting with emery board still poised over the place where Cotton's foot had been. 'You can see this too. Siddown. Craike, this is a vision of the future.'

He shook his index finger once.

'Watch and learn, OK?'

A television monitor was wheeled into place, the lights were dimmed and the music swelled – Gounod's *Ave Maria*. Craike could hear Cotton in his great winged leather chair humming along with it, moving his hand like a conductor. The screen showed a model of the earth with a number of satellites wheeling around it. Gradually the shot faded to one of Cotton himself, seen from slightly above and sitting where he was now, at his desk with the panorama of Hong Kong harbour laid out beyond his egg-like head. On the desk in front of him was a thick leatherbound book with silk placefinders and a gilt cross on the cover. His hands were laced together on the blotter. His smile, as the slightly protruding lips parted around it, was pure plastic. He wore a dark preacher's suit and sober silk tie.

'Hi. My name is Charles Cotton, and I want to share a few thoughts with you today. How many of you realize that, in less than half a lifetime, the benefits of space technology have reached all around the globe? Military endeavour, entertainment and that questing after secular knowledge which we call science have all been enriched by a magnificent sequence of achievements. But hold on. Isn't there something *missing*?'

The music swelled and the screen changed to a fast-cut sequence of images. Black and yellow faces, Indian and white. National costumes, tribal dances, figures in prayer, faces in chanting. Monks, bridal couples, gravestone crosses, the Virgin by Raphael, the Christ of El Greco.

'Yes. God is missing. In all the exciting space developments we have seen, is it not shameful that the first man to orbit the earth should be an atheist?'

Grainy black-and-white shot of Yuri Gagarin with Khrushchev.

'That the space probes sent out to orbit the planets and go questing into outer space should carry equations and the figure of man, but nothing, *nothing* about God?'

A shot of the *Pioneer* spacecraft. On its side a brass plaque containing clues about the nature of Man – binary mathematical directions to earth and a sketch of the male and female proportions.

'Now CPCC – the world's largest religious communications corporation – is gonna do something about that.'

A montage of Cotton himself followed, the Cotton who hobnobbed with the world's religious leaders – shaking hands with the Dalai Lama, chatting up Desmond Tutu, posing with the Ayatollah Khomeini. The sequence faded into an aerial shot slowly orbiting the building Craike was in now, a pencil of glass embedded in the architectural chaos of Central District Hong Kong. Cotton's voice began to swell with pride – a bullfrog's swell. As the screen dissolved once again to show the big cheese himself, now standing beside the window, looking up at the sky.

'On my personal initiative we have brought together a

consortium of scientists, space technologists, theologians, evangelists and broadcasters to plan the greatest religious enterprise maybe since the creation itself, codenamed Operation Pentecost. They are working on a unique space probe, the St Paul, which is designed to carry the word of God outward into other galaxies, as far as human beings will endeavour. For surely if the Lord indeed *has* created other worlds, he has fitted us with the audacity to evangelize them.'

Cut back to the orbiting satellites. This time each was surrounded by an orange-red nimbus, pulsing. Craike smiled when he saw their significance. These were haloes.

'And, back towards earth, a quartet of CPCC satellites – Matthew, Mark, Luke and John – will create a truly global church, an electronic world chapel, a home pulpit that can be seen literally planet-wide.'

The sainted satellites began putting out rays towards the earth, which splashed on to the planet's surface and radiated outwards like ripples.

'By means of these four linked telecommunications satellites hanging in geostationary orbit 15,000 miles above the earth, the word of God can be communicated to His people as with one voice. Among great religious leaders who have put their seal to this work are the Holy Father the Pope, the Archbishop of Canterbury, Mr Billy Graham and Mother Teresa of Calcutta. Join us in this great work of the Lord. Your donation can also be an investment.'

The screen went dark. And then a motto, like a needlepoint sampler, was faded up: In the beginning was the Word – and then came the spaceship.

There was a scatter of obsequious applause from the entourage. Curtains were drawn back and Cotton, who had meanwhile dressed himself in jeans and a Dodgers T-shirt, dismissed his acolytes with a curt wave. When they had whispered out of the room, Cotton sat behind the desk and gestured at the TV screen.

'Whaddya think of Operation Pentecost, Craike?'

Craike opened his lips to speak, but before he could utter Cotton was talking again.

'It don't come cheap, right? *Plentycost*, I call it.'

He laughed without humour – it was a well-worn crack.

'No, Craike, this project's set to put my bankers in the funny farm. I got a fistful of investors nervous as rabbits.'

'Who's going to shoot all this hardware into space for you?'

'I still got some talking to do on that.'

There was a silence. Cotton remained in his chair, slightly slumped, the lips set forward, the cunning small eyes fixed on the Englishman.

'It's a big project,' observed Craike. He touched the bow-tie Pappingay had forced on him. Damn silly chin-wings. Made him feel awkward, talk like the fool that Cotton wanted him to feel. Cotton slapped the desk.

'It's gonna make a billion. I could do even more out of satellite pornography, but I'd get a lot of liquid shit from a lot of governments if I took that road.'

He sighed and nuzzled the back of his hand to remove an itch on his nose.

'No, religion sure's the next best, and no one, but *no one*, can mount an objection to it. Go ahead, they tell me. Make as much money as you like, just as long as you're pushing the word of God out there. Opium of the masses? Yeah! I *like* that.'

'You're being extremely frank with me, Mr Cotton. You're telling me you don't do this work solely out of commitment.'

Suddenly Cotton's face reddened and he growled at Craike.

'Don't get smart with me, Craike. Don't forget there's a couple reasons why I should kick your ass outa here.'

Craike said nothing while Cotton splayed his hand and indicated the index finger.

'First off, you're a Brit. I hate Brits. I hate *Great* Britain, as it still stupidly calls itself. Country lets itself be controlled for ten years by a *pair* of women. Jesus! Not democracy, *hyp*ocrisy. Tinpot, deluded, sneaking. They tried to bring us down in the Civil War, and they bin trying ever since. I hated that shit country ever since I was in grade school.'

He jabbed the air between himself and Craike.

'Second off, you're a spook. That's what I call a dirty trade. Digging out coal's clean to that way of life. So. You're a Brit spook: two reasons why I should haul your butt into the street.'

'I used to be what you call a spook, Mr Cotton. I'm retired from intelligence now. I run a small personal security consultancy here in Hong Kong. It's all above board.'

Without warning, Cotton changed the line of questioning.

'You got a religion, Craike?'

'Well, not exactly. Though where I come from you're not allowed *not* to have a religion. Unless you specify, they stick you down as C of E – Episcopalian, I think you call it. That goes for hospital, the army, prison.'

A secretary of extraordinary beauty stalked in, put a letter down in front of Cotton and dangled a fountain pen. Cotton absently took the pen, signed his name. She picked up the letter and replaced it with a neat cardboard folder. Cotton opened the folder and waved her away without speaking. For a few moments he perused the documents inside.

'You ever been in prison, Craike?'

'No. But I did fifteen years in the Paras. Then more than ten in government service. Alternatives to prison.'

Cotton was turning over a page of closely typed A4. It looked like a report. He flicked a glance up at Craike.

'I have been there.'

'Oh?'

Cotton laughed.

'No, it's not what you think. Prison *camp*. Korea.'

The American read on, turning a page, and then another before looking up again. He tapped the file.

'I got a dossier prepared on you, Craike. Someone asks to come and see me personally, someone I don't know, about something particular, I always get a dossier made.'

'What have you learned?'

'You fouled up in England and they fired your ass. You came out here. Now you got a little freelance business selling intelligence to the highest bidder. How'm I doing so far?'

Craike simply nodded, pretending admiration.

'You maintain pretty good contact with the Brit government and my guess is that a lot of your trade is still with them. Otherwise you are dealing with the banks, the insurance houses, the entrepreneurs. You work to contract and you also sell information on. I guess you're a two-faced bastard, and why should I trust you? Please enlighten me now, Mr Craike.'

In a few terse sentences Craike summarized the meeting with Swann. He did not mention Madeleine's second contact through the ragged fellow in the street. As Cotton listened his lips were

112

wet and in a pursed position, pushed outwards and a little upwards, as if to sip from some invisible tulip glass.

'So, Mr Cotton, I thought, in view of what happened in England, you should hear about this and perhaps I could continue to provide you with a service through to this man Swann. A channel of communication.'

Cotton sniffed. Craike pressed on.

'We would have a contract. Call it some extra security if you like. 10,000 US dollars, payable monthly in advance, in return for me keeping in touch with Swann and telling you everything he tells me.'

Cotton rose from his chair and trotted barefoot across the carpet to the divan, where he had lately been reclining. He picked up one of the $30 socks, sat and slipped it on his foot.

'Why should I be interested in doing that, Craike? I could merely call in the police.'

Craike smiled sardonically.

'The police, here in Hong Kong?'

'Well, OK, but I got my own security people.'

'I'm sure you have. But Swann's knowledge could be life or death to you. I'm in touch with him and your people are not. Besides,' he added, taking a calculated risk on Cotton's indulgence, 'half your guys are apes, night-club bouncers. The other half are nerds. You need someone with the right pedigree for this job. In short, me.'

To his relief Cotton laughed.

'Apes and nerds, huh? OK, you're probably right.'

Down on his hands and knees, groping under the divan, Cotton was looking for the second sock.

Craike said, 'I can do more for you. I can cross-check this stuff about China, about the secret service. I have other sources I can dial up. Would you like that?'

Cotton found the sock and sat on the divan. Breathing heavily he netted his toe, drew the sock up to the ankle, picked up his shoes and carried them back to the desk. He sat down heavily in the studded armchair.

'Awright, Craike.'

He raised one of the shoes and pointed it.

'I'll hire you, but on one condition –'

There was a knock and Pappingay put his head around the pine-panelled door.

'Publisher, there's a call from Cardinal Polanski at the Vatican Bank. You want me to –'

Before Pappingay could complete the sentence C. P. Cotton's shoe was spinning accurately across the room towards him.

'Get the fuck OUTA here!'

Pappingay pulled his head back smartly to avoid being struck and the shoe bounced off the edge of the closing door. Cotton waited fifteen seconds and pressed a key on his intercom.

'Send that dumb-ass Pappingay back in here.'

Pappingay came back, his face flushed.

'I'm sorry, Publisher. I just thought –'

'Like hell you did.'

He pointed at the floor to his young aide's right.

'My shoe. Bring me my goddamn shoe.'

Pappingay found the shoe and brought it across to Cotton, who snatched it back.

'And don't come in here till I call you.'

Cotton smiled across the desk at Craike, who thought if a fish could smile – a piranha, maybe – it would look like that.

'Nerd is too good for him. He thinks brains is an entrée at a fancy French restaurant.'

Blushing like a peach, Pappingay let himself out.

'What was I saying?'

'One condition.'

'Oh yeah. You report only to me. I don't want to hear you're blowing into the ear of MI6 or the CIA. To me only, right?'

Craike again fingered the bow-tie at his throat. It was make or break time. $10,000 a month pulled him out of the bank manager's pocket but it put him in Cotton's. He swallowed hard. It would mean he'd have to find Swann again, make the bluff good. And he'd have to deliver on the Chinese connection.

He found himself saying, 'I think we have a deal, Mr Cotton.'

'C. P. Call me C. P. We're associates now.'

He pressed the intercom key.

'Mr Craike is leaving. Have them make out a cheque for $10,000 US, then bring it in here for me to sign. And meantime get me Polanski in Rome.'

The truth was, Craike couldn't afford to turn the job down. He had been slowly going bust for a year and more, his bank had been nagging at him for over three months to pay off his overdraft or produce some collateral. But he had no way to secure the loan and his Service pension was derisory.

He turned east out of the Cotton Building. Struggling through the pack of shoppers, messengers, porters and loiterers that surged along the pavement in both directions, he made it as far as the Mandarin Hotel. Time for an early evening jigger of malt.

In the Captain's Bar he ordered a Bowmore and sipped, inhaling as he did so the dense vapour of the whisky. Hong Kong had $5\frac{3}{4}$ million souls. Where would he begin to look for Swann?

Craike sighed. He reached into his pocket, took out and unfolded Cotton's cheque. It was drawn on the Trans-Africa Finance Bank and signed in a rather childish, back-sloping hand. He needed this, and how. So he'd just have to deliver the goods, wouldn't he?

Cotton was terminating his phone conversation.

'Your Eminence is most kind, most kind... No, I wouldn't have dared to suggest that. The Vatican's money *would* be safe in Operation Pentecost, but I quite understand that you can't come to a decision just yet... Exactly. Well, we meet in Rome, day or two. Yeah. Great talking to ya!'

He dropped the phone into its cradle.

'Your eminent piss-ant.' Then his finger was on the intercom key. 'Pappingay! Get in here.'

The factotum reappeared.

'Send in Lee Hung.'

A thin, intense man wearing wire-rim glasses and a well-cut business suit came hesitantly through.

'Lee, that *gwailo* who was in here, did you get a man on his tail when he left, like I told you?'

'Yes, Mr Cotton. I've entrusted my two sons Adam and Michael with the organization. They are efficient boys.'

'They better be. I want Craike watched in relays, round the clock. Just remember, he's smart.'

'My sons are intelligent also.'

'Good, then they'll get me what I wanna know.'

Cotton spread his fingers and counted off his desires.

'I want to know who he sees, what he does, where he goes –

church, whorehouse, public toilet. Right? Can they look after that?'

'They can look after that, sir. You can count on them, as I do, implicitly.'

'Your fatherly pride commends you, Lee Hung. Just keep me informed, every second night, wherever I may be – Tokyo, Bangkok, the Apple, *wherever* I may be.'

The skinny man nodded and smiled, a disarming show of the whitest possible teeth.

'We shall keep you fully informed, Mr Cotton, sir.'

Lee Hung's Mercedes had an impressive array of communications – fax machine, cell-phone, microcomputer, even the ability to receive satellite television, which he had installed in deference to his very productive association with C. P. Cotton. While the car travelled two blocks, he checked the Hang Seng index and called the property company that was next on his list of appointments. A further three went by while he tried to contact a series of numbers in Kowloon. Eventually one of them answered.

'I have just left him. All is satisfactory. Put Michael on the phone . . . Yes, Michael. Anything to tell me?'

He listened to the fuzzy voice laconically and answered Michael's questions in monosyllables, except for the last. This required more detail.

'No, you don't need to. I already have a man in mind for the job. He is a most foolish fellow, but he likes to be useful and he is of no consequence. In case of anything accidental, no one will burn much paper for his ghost.'

He put the phone down, rubbing his hands together slowly and meditatively. The car picked up speed with a surge as it entered the gullet of the Harbour Tunnel.

## 12

Maurice Fielding sat on the floor with his legs bent and a two-thirds-empty bottle of Long John whisky between his thighs. His chin was cupped in his hands, his elbows were braced on the raised knees. Every now and then he removed the hands to tip some liquor before resuming the pose. A telephone waited on the carpet beside him.

The room was clean and smelled of fresh paint – white-glossed skirtings, eggshell walls. The oatmeal carpeting had a thick rustic weave.

'Very good office building,' the agent had told him a few hours earlier. 'Very cheap.'

He was right, it was cheap. Too cheap.

'If it's such a good building, why have none of the offices on this floor been let?'

'You are the first. Others will come after you, I guess.'

But Maurice guessed otherwise. He'd been told the building had been rehabbed more than two months ago, with the other floors being let even before the work was done. Yet these three rooms stood idle. In Hong Kong it was unheard of for space to go begging without good reason.

Bad *feng shui* it must be. The geomantic auspices – the position of windows, the arrangement of doors, the orientation of stairs, who knows what ill-omened concatenation? – would be unfavourable to good business. In such a case the Chinese would avoid it as they would downtown Chernobyl. Then the suite would be good only for the use of Europeans, and *gwailo* small businesses were not a growth industry in Hong Kong these days.

'I'll take it.'

The agent's face had flipped from gravity to delight, as if at the touch of a switch. He'd come towards Maurice with hand outstretched, ready to seal the contract. In this moment Maurice saw that he was desperate to make the letting. Perhaps it was a question of face. He'd promised the owners he would fill the rooms this week, yes, the *very* week, on the ashes of his mother's eyes. He was desperate enough to accept what in other circumstances would be a pretty humiliating deal.

'What if I take the other two as well? All three rooms, at a 30 per cent discount, yeah?'

Maurice had calculated right. The smile split wider and developed into a high-pitched laugh.

'OK, mister, 25 per cent reduction. Then they are yours.'

So it was done. In the scales of face, Maurice had done well out of the agent; he had come through as a big spender, prepared to take risks. But in return he had given the agent face in the eyes of his property-owning client. That made it a highly acceptable type of deal all round. They shook hands with, on the agent's part, a kind of passion. Face is almost sexual to some people. In the face stakes, the fear of failure is a debility, but success comes with a rush of joy. Face makes the world go round.

And what the hell, there'll be plenty of money if *this* comes off, Maurice thought as he peeled off a month's rent, cash in advance, from his wad. Having the whole floor would make security much easier, and besides, it was a bargain.

There was nothing to move in, no furniture, no clothes. At this moment he had only the phone, the key and the bottle. It was so delightfully clean and simple.

Groping for a folded scrap of paper in one of his trouser pockets he opened the paper with deliberation, like a poker player examining his hand. Then he pulled the phone towards him, raised the receiver and entered a number with many digits. A moment later he was speaking.

'All all right? Yeah. Come tomorrow. This is the address. Got a pen?'

He dictated briefly, then hung up. He took a long pull of whisky and looked around. The place looked a mite bare, but at least it was spacious. Not like a prison at all. And, for tonight at least, he had it to himself. He tipped the bottle to 45 degrees, letting the last of the whisky flow into his mouth. He moved it around from gum to gum, enjoying the sting in his tastebuds. Then he pulled a roll of money from his other pocket.

He counted it, slowly. It was a source of some amazement to

him. He had arrived in Bangkok insolvent once more, but a phone call to his friend Jimmy Cheng, the jockey, followed by a visit to the Royal Bangkok Sports Club, where he had laid six bets in rapid succession, all Jimmy's suggestions, had presented him suddenly with enough cash to last several days.

He spread the money in a fan on the floor next to him. He must make sure he didn't lose it on the gee-gees here in Hong Kong, but he thought he *would* have a bet tonight, just tonight, before they arrived from Bangkok. A spot of racing would be a justified small indulgence, because soon the world of responsibility would close again around his head. He felt good, like a husband who travels in advance of his family and is now waiting for them to join him in a new posting, a new life. The accommodation was secured but still empty. The future lay before them like a virgin betting-slip.

Remembering his earlier resolution, however, he divided the money and placed half of it under the carpet, ripping out the tacks to make space for the wad to go in. Then he went to the washroom and urinated, splashed his face and welsh-combed his tangled hair. The track was called Happy Valley and they had evening racing tonight. He would bet on only single horses, no long shots, no combinations. He would be careful. Really.

He stood outside the suite, in the lobby in front of the single elevator, ready to bang the door shut behind him. But he hesitated. His hand went to the pocket with his folded cash float. He drew it out and studied it, peeling back the edge of one or two notes as if curious as to their composition. He pocketed the wad again and went back into the room. Shit, if he got on a roll he might require *more* than half the cash. Crouching, he groped beneath the carpet and withdrew the stash.

His remaining concession to thrift was to place it in a different pocket from the rest of the money. He patted both his pockets and looked around him once more. He grinned. No, not like a prison, not in any way. Just to prove it he'd follow custom: after he'd been to the track, win or lose, he always bought himself a girl; he always kept enough back for that.

He went out, slamming the door with a bang that echoed down all seven floors to the ground. He went away to Happy Valley.

★

The water at Aberdeen, on the south of Hong Kong Island, is darkened by the shadows of the densely packed boats, and by the human turds and garbage which drop from their sterns. These are houseboats, a great paralysed flotilla, a rafted town of 20,000 souls. Many of the junks have been long lost to seafaring through the rot and depredation of decades, although among and alongside them, thwart to thwart, are moored the licensed 'three planks' – the diesel-engined sampans. These scud around, carrying cargo to the seagoing junks that lie removed in their self-importance. Or else they go out to lay fishing lines, pick up floating consignments of refugees or illegals or any other transportable contraband. Between the territory of Hong Kong and the long, round, fat-paunch coastline of the People's Republic is a constant traffic, both legitimate and furtive. The sampans are the tug-boats and bum-boats of this trade.

In the end it was Swann who contacted them, telling Madeleine to bring money in a brightly coloured child's lunchbox. She went to Watson's and chose one in fluorescent pink. Carrying this in the brightness of the day, Madeleine felt conspicuous, but then, that was the idea.

It was a strong, wrinkle-faced woman in purple pyjamas who approached her at last. She took Madeleine's hand and, as if leading the blind, led her down and over the side of a junk tied to the embankment. They clambered awkwardly from junk to junk until they were more than half-way along the floating pier which the lashed-together boats formed. The junks, all of the same pattern, with high sterns and square deckhouses, were hung with awnings and strings of washing. Families squatted on deck, the men smoking, the women's hands never idle – paring vegetables, cleaning fish – while their eyes followed with cool curiosity the progress of the old woman and the *gwailo* giantess from boat to boat. Some of the children crawled about with lines around their waists which, at the other ends, were secured to the mast or to cleats in the deck. Madeleine had been told that boys, more often than girls, were secured by these safety lines, in token of their greater worth. If it were true, it might just be to the girls' advantage. It might instil self-reliance from an earlier age, a confidence that the umbilical boys would discover only later, if at all. She wished she could have a greater share of that type of confidence right now.

They reached perhaps the twentieth boat out from shore when the woman yanked Madeleine towards a hatch that led below. Madeleine pulled back for a moment, looking towards shore. Somewhere back there in one of the bars, or standing relaxed in a doorway, was Craike. It would be impossible for him to follow her any closer and not be seen, but he would note the junk she was on. She thought, I must not quail, he would only laugh and be confirmed in his opinion of me. Swallowing hard, trying to make the saliva flow again, she ducked her head and followed the woman below.

The cabin stretched across the whole beam of the vessel, walls curving and bellying outwards. An oil lamp smoked on the table, creating only a dim, polluted light which hardly illuminated the extremes of the compartment. The air was greasy with the smoke. Only tiny wisps of light penetrated from the outside, through the two horizontal slits in the boat's sides level with the ceiling.

Yet there was enough light to see the sparseness of the furnishing: a low table, a few miniaturized chairs, little else.

'Take a seat, Miss.'

The voice came from the gloom beyond the table lamp. It was his voice all right. In spite of her nerves, she smiled. How he loved shadow and concealment. It was more than just security, she was sure. Swann *enjoyed* it.

He said something sharply to the woman and she disappeared. Madeleine perched on one of the child-sized chairs, saying nothing. It was for him to make the running.

'I guess I'm sorry I disappeared like that – from the boarding house, I mean. Obviously living there I was standing out like a pig in a chicken house. It wasn't healthy to stick around.'

'That's OK. I'm glad you contacted us again.'

Now that she had stopped moving she became acutely aware of the boat's movement. Madeleine did not like boats, but this one was the worst she'd known because of the smell. Lampblack, fish and faeces.

'We're really very interested in maintaining contact with you.'

'I don't know how possible that will be. Have you brought money?'

Madeleine put the lunchbox on the table.

'15,000 Hong Kong. In hundreds and fifties.'

'Good. That is good.'

'What is the information you have for us? You said you could give us a name.'

A hand flapped conductor-like out of the shadow, slowing her down.

'Ease down, will you? It ain't too often I get to talk to a beautiful English gal. I'm in no hurry.'

The woman returned with tea. A teapot, a steaming jug of water, two cups wider, but scarcely bigger, than eggcups. She held a bunch of tea in her hand and this she thrust into the pot before pouring the water. She was already backing out of the room as Swann reached forward into the light and grasped the tray. Madeleine could make out his thickly veined and mottled claw, sliding the tea to his end of the table and out of Madeleine's reach.

'Why don't you come round and sit by me?'

She could see now that he sat on a low divan wide enough for two, but only just. He was patting it in invitation. She straightened her back.

'I prefer to sit here.'

'It's a long time since I was near to a – Caucasian woman. Forty years is a long time.'

'Forty years?'

'Yup, 'bout as long as that. Now why don't you come sit by me?'

He was leering now and it made the hair on the back of her neck stiffen.

'We are very private here, you savvy? Nothing to fear from peeping Toms.'

'I still prefer it this side of the table.'

His face fell. He did not give up entirely, but he seemed to be murmuring as much to himself as to her.

'One learns a lot, living in China. Officially they hate sex because it is a passion that cannot be controlled politically. But in reality, in private, you know, they are the best lovers. Truly, the best.'

He poured tea and pushed her cup around the smoking lamp. She said, 'But you are not Chinese.'

'True. But, like I said, one learns. One learns a lot.'

Madeleine picked up her tea and drank from it as assertively as she knew how.

'Look, Mr Swann, why don't you get yourself to America, like you say you want to, and do your philandering over there? You'll have no problem, I promise you. The Western world had changed a good deal since you were – since you lost touch.'

Swann sighed and gave up.

'I'm afraid it's rather *dark* in here. They have electricity, you know, but just at the moment it's kaput. And these things don't have what we know as portholes, do they? So we must put up with the incompetent illumination of this lamp. Now –'

He slurped his tea – a sound like a plughole.

'Would you be so good as to slide that case across to me?'

She watched as he unclipped the lid and examined the money. He fingered it uncertainly, as if unsure what he was looking at. When he spoke again his voice trembled, 'I don't believe I've ever handled such a very large sum. I was really so young. Oh well, strike that. What shall we talk about?'

'The name. The one you promised me.'

She found herself listening to his old man's breathing. She wanted to make her voice soothing, even seductive. Christ, how her friends would laugh.

He said, uncertainly, 'Yes, well. You don't want it already, do you? You just got here.'

His anxiety to prolong the meeting was nothing to her own burning desire to get off and away. He held his breath a moment and then let it out in a sigh. She knew she'd won.

'Tell me.'

'OK, OK. It was – it was Fielding. A man called Fielding killed C. P. Cotton's daughter-in-law.'

'And he lives here? Here in Hong Kong?'

'Yes.'

'Where does he live?'

'I don't just know. Here, I guess. Or Bangkok, Manila, Taiwan. Who knows? But the guy's a Chinese agent. Chinese shitface agent.'

Madeleine got up. She felt the first signs of nausea leaking into her stomach. She was shaking.

'How do you know this, Mr Swann?'

He shrugged. She went on.

'I may need to find you again. I may need to pursue that question.'

Right now she just wanted to get out. The place was pressing in on her. Swann looked alarmed.

'Look, don't go. There's more to all this. There's more I can tell you. He didn't *just* kill. He did more. You might think, worse. What the hell, I'll tell you the whole thing. It doesn't matter to me now.'

She cursed inwardly. The whole thing – it could take hours. The adrenalin was like snow falling inside her. She sat down once more.

'Shoot then.'

But before he could speak there came some disturbance from behind her. Through the hatch which gave on to the junk's deckhouse she could hear the woman speaking. She knew nothing of this dialect, but could tell the matter was urgent.

She felt on her neck the slightest movement of air and half turned, looking up at the curtained hatch behind her. A figure stood there in front of the curtain, a figure she vaguely recognized. The man's voice barked out.

'Hey! *Gwailo!*'

'Yes?'

She spoke in reflex but the intruder had not meant her.

'Stand, American. Stand up!'

Swann rose. His face could not be seen but the area of his stomach, covered by a rumpled shirt, and his waistband were clearly visible. Above, in the near-dark, floated the white ghost of his face.

'What do you want?'

In a momentary standstill of time Madeleine was seized with the knowledge of what was coming next. And, in the same moment that she thought it, the sounds came – thuds like fists in dough, each followed by an impossibly rapid, in-drawn breath: *one-two-three*.

Swann fell. He made no more dramatic sound than a grunt. The bullets had struck somewhere just above the illuminated part of his body. She watched him slip out of sight, out of the circle of light, and knew he'd died before even hitting the ground. The main impact of his body was light and it made only a slight sigh and a bounce, but the last part of him to strike the wood cracked audibly. It was his head.

She went down on her knees, and then her haunches. She was

vaguely aware of cringing away from the shadow by the hatch curtain, yet contemptuously aware that it would do her no good. She might as well stand and face it as crawl down here. *One-two-three.* She felt her lip curling in horror, she heard sounds issuing from her mouth like the cries of a hurt kitten and the blood doing a tattoo in her brain. *One-two-three. One-two-three.*

Was it only Swann they wanted, not her? She looked round and found the gunman's shadow gone. Now there were others in the cabin, she didn't know how many, but three or four men. They heaved something across the cabin floor – in her foggy state she only half understood what they were doing. But it was clumsy, heavy work.

'Come on, move, you. *Diu!* The fucker's heavier than he looks. Got that sack ready?'

They bundled him out of the companionway. Madeleine sat as if paralysed. They would come back for her. *Surely* they would come back for her now. She waited through seconds that stretched themselves into impossible longevity, as the last moments of a life are said to. There was nothing, and then still nothing. She heard some muffled bumps, like a boat alongside the junk. Then a few words spoken low and a footstep outside. The shadow came into the room again, it was the same shadow she was sure. Madeleine stiffened, she could not look. She made a vague and muddled attempt to prepare herself. *Shit! What a way for it to end. Stupid, stupid, stupid.*

The man stepped forward. In the corner of her eye Madeleine could see the table edge and the light that fell on it from above. She saw the plastic lunchbox clearing the table, drawn by the man's gloved hand. Then she was alone again.

She continued to lie there, afraid that any movement might bring the killer back. So it stayed for an indeterminate length of time until the old woman returned, hesitantly, as a wren to a birdtable, to pluck at Madeleine's sleeve.

'Why didn't they kill me, Ed?'

Craike was brisk with his assistant. It was better than giving her illusions.

'They didn't think it was worth while. You're a woman. There's a saying: To prune a man's balls is a better bet than to kill his wife.'

Madeleine made a face.

'Whose balls would those be?'

'Cotton's, maybe.' He shrugged. 'Or mine.'

'But they know he gave me a name, the murderer's name.'

'Maybe they don't mind you knowing it. It's interesting, I suppose, but I don't know yet what it stacks up to. Swann wasn't going to give you the name at first, was he?'

'Yes, but he was playing a game then and I had the feeling it lacked conviction. It was like a comedian who knows he's lost his touch, isn't funny any more. He gave up really fast. He was always going to give me the name, I think, in the end.'

She lit up, inhaled and stubbed out. One cigarette, one drag, that was her rule.

'He tried to make a pass at me, you know. Then he dropped it, no great pressure. He might have been doing it out of politeness. Matter of fact, I think he's gay.'

She frowned and corrected herself.

'*Was* gay.'

'Well, gay or straight, we've lost our golden tongue. But he died pointing handily in the direction we've got to look now.'

'Fielding?'

'Yes, though we have to consider the possibility we've been set up. We try to find him, but until we are sure, we treat Fielding with caution. This information cost me 15,000 Hong Kong that I can't afford. We are *not* going to let it go to waste.'

'I don't know how the hell we can even find him.'

Craike got up.

'Not we, you. I'm going to a meeting. You're going to the airport.'

They sat in the deepest leather chairs while a white-coated steward with drinks on a silver tray swung into their orbit. Craike took the Mortlach. Vanteel had chosen a Pimms, having formed the idea that only this was a proper match for the ambience. He looked meaningfully at Craike.

'Things are not going too well, are they? Personally, I mean.'

'I'm getting by.'

'Not according to our information. How much is C. P. Cotton paying you?'

*Money*. In Britain we're reticent to the point of coyness about it; abroad we return to the subject like dogs to a lamp-post. For Vanteel, Craike halved the figure.

'Five K Hong Kong. A month.'

'And that's . . . what? Remind me.'

'That's about £400. Or, put it another way, it's nothing, a retainer.'

'Of course, of course.'

Vanteel's tone was edged with scepticism. Bloody *git*. When he heard they were sending Vanteel, Craike thought, Jesus, not that barrow boy. Gets to his mid-thirties and starts behaving like he's short-listed to take over the cabinet office. Vanteel had been nothing in the department when Craike was there. Now he thinks he's flying the plane solo.

'I'm not his property, Vanteel. I'm running a business which requires turnover. I sell in the open market. So, what's *your* offer?'

As Vanteel sipped his drink, the flotsam of fruit bumped his upper lip. He had filled out since Craike had last seen him, with the kind of face-fat that makes a man appear to be wearing cheek pads.

'If – *if*, mind you – this stands up, we can offer you a K.'

'A *knighthood*? Oh, you're much too generous, my friend.'

Vanteel tutted at the frivolity.

'A grand, a thousand.'

Craike looked offended.

'You can't buy much with that. Not in this town. A cream tea and a pair of socks would stretch a budget like that.'

'*Pounds*, Craike.'

'Yes, pounds, I know.'

'And for that we'd expect to be fully plugged in. We'd know what Cotton knows, know what *you* know.'

'How will you pay?'

'Triple three now, same in two weeks, same when we wrap it up.'

Craike shook his head in wonderment.

'God, London never changes. Everything on the cheap.'

Vanteel arched his eyebrows and made sure Craike saw.

'You can't afford to turn us down, Craike. You're trapped in a barrel with this and you need us. Because whatever you say, if *we* don't buy shares Cotton will own you. Who else can you go to? Who else can spirit you away if and when the plop hits the prayer wheel? So don't get too cute, OK?'

He raised his forefinger and dotted the air.

'We commissioned a report. We *know* you're in, shall we say, difficulties.'

He shot his wrist out of its sleeve and looked at the time.

'Anyway, look, I've got to get along. Shall we summarize? You claim the Chinks are harassing C. P. Cotton for political reasons – either as part of an unsettling procedure to make us all jumpy or deliberately to get *him* out of Hong Kong. You say they killed his daughter-in-law and grandson in England and that an agent posing as an American named Swann is, or was, involved. Am I OK so far?'

Craike drained his drink and stood.

'Yes, that's about it, Vanteel. And I'll accept your paltry offer.'

'After all, it's a fairly far-fetched story, Craike. Is it one of your scams?'

'Where are you staying? This place?'

'Good God no. Kowloon. The Park Hotel. It's OK.'

'I'll be in touch, then. Thanks for the wet.'

Vanteel called him back.

'Don't be too long, Craike. I'm on a two-week excursion ticket. I would like to leave here knowing you are not giving us the run-around.'

An *excursion* ticket. Craike was laughing again as he walked away along Chater Road.

The silver-framed photo portrait spun across the room. Its corner struck a dent in the plaster wall, the glass shattering and the whole assembly falling in shards to the silk carpet. But Chuck wasn't satisfied. He looked around. The next object to hand was an engraved brass tray on a stand. He seized it, shook off the few small objects placed there, and swung it away from him like an outsize frisbee. Clumsily it scythed through the cut-glass chandelier. As the bulbs popped, strings of crystal droppers snapped and cascaded to the floor in front of him like monstrous artificial hail.

The door opened and he saw the Jap butler standing there, face contorted as he tried to reconcile fury with deference.

'Mr Chuck, you shouldn't have done this. Why you do this?'

Chuck strode up to the servant.

'I *trained* to be an attorney. Did you know that? A lawyer, who uses reasoned argument to make his points. And just *look* what your stupidity made me do.'

He brushed past the man and went to his own bedroom, returning with a silver-lidded box. He held it bottom-up so that the hinged lid hung open. A very few tiny motes of white dust fell out.

'You didn't fill this, did you? You were supposed to fill this today. You didn't. What happened?'

The butler's hand went to his mouth.

'Oh, sir, I forgot. I'm very sorry, Mr Chuck.'

He began to bow and, taking the box, shuffled backwards.

'I will do it right away. No problem, no problem at all.'

But Chuck had already left him. He was feeling tearful and he didn't want the little man to see him in case he cried.

# 13

Sim sat on his canvas travelling-bag watching the traffic – the dust, heat, noise and fumes. He had been in Hong Kong seven hours, and already he was broke.

To his back was the wall of Kowloon Park, where alongside beds of dusty-petalled flowers old men performed their Tai Chi exercises while young boys and girls jogged in circles. Before him was Nathan Road. Northbound movement had seized up completely a few minutes ago and now a motor horn raised a long wail of mechanical frustration. Then another took up the cry, passing the cue to six more. Soon fifty cars, vans and taxis, on the main drag or backed up the side streets, were punishing the air, all because a truck had dumped its load of scaffolding. The heap of bamboo poles straddled the carriageway like a Pick-a-Sticks game.

The city models a future for the crowded planet. It is a matrix of congestion. Overhead painted and electrical signs are stacked like trash, their letters, characters and logos jamming the space between buildings: SINCERE SAUNA; HAPPY DRAGON JEWELRY; LOVE EATING HOUSE. The messages lock together, struggling like battler crabs: COME IN! LUCKY MASSAGE; WELCOME LOANS COMPANY; SEX BOOK EXCHANGE; TOPLESS GIRLIES – ENTRANCE FREE.

The scramble for space goes on everywhere, outside and inside walls. It's in the heaving ticket halls and carriages of the Mass Transit Railway; in hugger-mugger shopping precincts and department stores and street markets; in the desperation of scraggy beggars, baring their stumpy amputations; in the snake-pit innards of the middle-aged, tormented by money; in the clean, ambitious young, springing about everywhere in trainers, freshly clean.

And somewhere in all this was the father he had come to find and punish. That punishment was not a problem. The punches and blows, the broken bones, the cuts and bruises – the worst that Sim could imagine, that bastard deserved, not just for this crime, but for himself, for everything he was. There was none worse than Maurice in all his son's experience, and none better than his son to ram it down his throat.

So, he could imagine the punishment. But, now that he saw Hong Kong, it was the *finding* he had trouble with. He had prepared himself for a crowded city, but not the scale of this pullulation: people massed and on the make, their tortuous and infinite complications of movement and exchange. In backstreet restaurants, dim hallways, tawdry foyers and sparkly shops they hurried to enter and exit, to buy and sell. They touted racks of garments, trays of fake Rolexes, boxes of jade and ivory, platters of hot rice, scoured and blood-dripping pig carcasses. It was a massed yet differentiated crowd; a cursing, bullying, arguing, eating, bargaining crowd; a chaos of deal-doing, tea-drinking, shoulder-barging, belly-scratching, hand-shaking, gob-spitting. And all in a language of which Sim knew not a word. In this town, he was tongueless.

And now, broke too. *Christ!* How could he have let it happen?

At the airport he had asked a taxi driver to find him a cheap hotel, and they had come to Yaumatei. Yaumatei is half-way up Nathan Road, half-way between Boundary Road, the line beyond which the leased New Territories begin, and the Peninsula Hotel, sitting in luxurious state on the tip of Kowloon's round nose. To the immediate south of Yaumatei is the shopping Shangri-La of Tsimshatsui; to the north the low-town stew of Mong Kok.

The hotel they came to had no English name. Its door lay in a back street, under a red neon column of characters, pinched between a jeweller's shop and a dusty outlet for dental appliances. The driver pointed to the sign and translated.

'Pearl Dragon Hotel, very good place. It's very cheap. You go there OK? You stay.'

He went there OK. The owner was standing at the door smoking a cigarette as long as a toothbrush. He was big – for a Chinese he was a giant – the head a crew-cut rock, the body that of a superannuated wrestler with a pumped-up belly. A leather pouch – the case, Sim saw, for a cell-phone – swung by its loop from his wrist. The taxi driver leaned over to the passenger side and sang out a greeting. The owner smiled and waved. Good friends, good mutual business. Sim was ushered inside.

The owner, too big to be neat, was nevertheless clean. He wore a shirt and black trousers of a crispness that might have shamed staff at the Peninsula Hotel itself. Sim gave up his bag, encouraged. There were no check-in formalities. They simply entered a lift and rose three floors to a dim corridor. Had the passage been any narrower, Sim would have found himself going crabwise. The owner walked with both shoulders brushing along the walls, which were of yellow plaster. The paper had long ago been stripped from them and never replaced.

With a proud flourish the owner threw open a door. It crashed back against the wall and Sim entered. His spirits sagged. The colour scheme was predominantly brown and grey, the colours of dust. It could not have been decorated for thirty years; whatever could be cracked, and whatever could be stained, was. The chest of drawers was staved-in and beetle-chewed. The carpet belonged on a dumpster. The word 'dingy' was too genteel for the space. The room was a shithole.

Sim's nostrils retracted in involuntary disgust. He pulled back the bedding, and reached down to test the mattress. Before his fingers could make contact, tiny black motes were jumping off the grey-washed sheets.

The hotel owner was watching intently as Sim moved to the window and pulled at the sooty nylon net. It tore, brittle in his fingers. The window glass was coated with deposits of polluted air. It gave on to a blackened air shaft in which circulated the odour of cooking fats and steams.

The owner lingered in the doorway, his face holding a complacent smile. His gut ballooned out from his pelvis in a hard mass, ramming the waistband of his immaculate trousers. Then he began swinging the door shut. It closed with a thud, making Sim turn, expecting to be alone. But the man was still inside the room, and now he was unzipping Sim's bag.

'Hey! What are you doing? Hey!'

But the contents of the bag had already been tipped on to the floor and the owner was stirring the tangle of clothes with his foot. Quickly he concluded there was nothing worth his trouble. He shambled towards Sim, who backed and circled until the bed was behind him. The owner produced a small black truncheon from a trouser pocket and raised it in his left hand. He spoke a single syllable in Cantonese, a word which came over to Sim as a threatening grunt. The man made as if to strike.

Sim's arms went up to ward off a head slap. It left exposed his midriff, ribs and solar plexus – still sore enough from the fight in Salford. The man's left fist came hammering in towards his ribcage and, flinching to protect his bruises, he dropped his arms. But the punch, too, was a feint. The man saw that Sim was off-balance and he seemed to leap forward, almost as if tripping, and butted Sim with his stomach. The stomach was rock hard. Sim bounced off the blow, and careered out of control backwards on to the bed. The owner followed and simply lay on top of Sim.

He was winded, trapped, wedged under the weight of the hard stomach like a cat cinched under a truck's wheel. The owner was groping him. He shut his eyes, grimaced and heaved, trying to roll the man off, first to the right and then to the left. It didn't work. He felt the chubby hands on his shirt, under his jacket. The man's breath reached Sim's nostrils: mint mixed with sour smoke. He was actually grunting now, as his hands wandered around Sim's body, searching, groping.

Sim had gone straight from the Pearl Dragon Hotel to the District Police Headquarters, just a few blocks south along Nathan. The duty officer, keying details into his computer, had been extremely polite and not particularly sympathetic.

'This was robbery, was it?'

'Well, at first I thought I was getting sexually assaulted.'

The sergeant looked up sharply. 'You been raped, sir?'

'No. I *thought* that's what he wanted to do. No, but he took my credit card, passport, most of my money.'

'OK, robbery. It's your passport he wanted. Valuable item in Hong Kong these days.'

The deskman let fly a high-pitched discharge of laughter and took the rest of Sim's statement.

Later the victim had returned to the scene of his humiliation with a constable, but there was little to be discovered. The true hotel owner turned out to be another man, older and dirtier. He knew nothing of the incident, he said, as he was drinking tea in a restaurant along the next street. The taxi-driver? Sim could only vaguely remember him, and certainly not the licence number. Yes, he *had* talked on his radio during their journey into town, or was it a car-phone? Yes, it could have been a car-phone. And his attacker had had a portable phone. A neat set-up, then, a well-sprung trap.

The real hotelier was more in keeping with the condition of his property. He looked like a starved bird and his pyjamas were shiny with wear and grease. Yet he was all concern. The policeman translated: Mister must have the room anyway. He stay free until he gets more money, OK?

Sim said to the constable, 'Tell him I'm grateful. Nice thought. But sorry, this place is too high-class for me.'

He shook the hotel man's hand and smiled.

'Besides, the room's full. There's a family of sub-miniature guests already in it.'

Sim had left them puzzling over this remark, and over the inscrutability of Occidentals. Now, an hour later, he felt as stuck as the line of vehicles trying to go north on Nathan. Perhaps he shouldn't have passed up the offer of the free room, in spite of the bugs. He watched the truck driver and his mate over on the northbound carriageway, manhandling bamboo scaffolding back on to the loader. They did it with a kind of cheerful desperation. He was trying out a similar frame of mind himself.

It wasn't just the money and the passport that he'd lost. The newspaper photograph of the burnt-out cottage had been in his stolen wallet. Suddenly, as he mulled over his situation, Sim desperately wanted to look at it again. He had tried to shut the idea out, but he already knew that the fire must have been Maurice's work, the business he'd travelled to England to complete. Well, Sim could remember the news coverage at the time. He knew that people had died in that fire. In which case, his father *was* a murderer after all, and where did that leave young Kevin Ho?

There had been another piece of paper in his wallet. At Ringway Airport, standing on the concourse beside old Worsley's wheelchair, Sim had felt a note pressed into his palm.

'There's a name on that paper. Might be useful. Person I knew once in Wanchai.' Worsley laughed, an embarrased guffaw. 'A girl.'

The public-address speakers chimed: 'This is the third call for

Flight CX 146 to Hong Kong. Would passengers proceed to gate ten.'

'Where's Wanchai?'

'Hong Kong, of course. You mean you haven't heard of Wanchai? Red-light area. All bars and tarts. Dead seedy.'

'. . . Passengers on Flight CX 146 to Gate Ten, please . . .'

'And you still remember this girl you met there?'

'Thought I'd found my Susie Wong, actually.'

That embarrassed laugh again.

'Yes, but when was it you were at sea – thirty years ago?'

'Yeh, must be. Before you were born, lad. Well anyway, I give it you. Use it if you can. If she's still anywhere around, she'll be worth contacting.'

He unfolded the paper and read the name. *Nancy Lo*.

'Who was she?'

'A bar girl, a kind of a singer. Nothing special, not exactly Shirley Bassey, I mean. But a beautiful girl. I remember the name of the club, too. The Morocco, it was called.'

'You keep in touch after?'

'What, a bar girl keeping in touch with a seaman?' He snorted. 'You're joking, lad. I only knew her for a few hours.'

'So why her in particular? Why d'you give me her name?'

'This is the last call for Flight CX 146 to Hong Kong. This flight is now closing at Gate Ten, please.'

'Come on, that's you. You've got to go through.'

Old Worsley pressed the control on the wheelchair and whirred forward across the glassy marble-slab floor. For a moment he was on course to breast the rubber-ribbon barrier, erected to funnel travellers into the departure lounge. But stylishly he spun the chair at the last minute to face Sim.

He gestured towards passport control. 'Go on.'

Sim took no notice. He held the piece of paper in front of old Worsley's eyes.

'Yes, but if you only knew her for a few hours – I mean, there's no *chance* she'll remember you. So what's the point.'

'She'll remember me.'

'She was a prostitute, wasn't she?'

He looked up at Sim, as if he didn't understand the word at first. Then he said, 'Yes. I suppose you'd have to call her that, yes.'

'They see hundreds of men. She will have known literally hundreds, even thousands. She won't know you from the King of Sicily, not at this distance in time.'

The old man wore that stolid, stubbornly offended look that Sim knew well in him.

'She'll remember me, OK? She won't have forgotten. Now go on through, or you'll miss it.'

He'd folded the paper into his wallet and was gone.

But there was no need to read it again; he remembered the details. Nancy Lo. The Morocco. If in doubt, he thought, ask a policeman.

The desk sergeant at the police station seemed unsurprised to see him again. A filename was keyed into the desk-top terminal, then the names offered by Sim. After a pause while the digits churned in the Hong Kong computer system, data began spilling on to the screen. The officer studied it and scribbled something on a scratchpad.

'No place called Morocco in this town, sorry. But Miss Nancy Lo, yes. We have a police listing for this lady. She owns a bar.'

'In Wanchai?'

'Yes, Wanchai.'

'Is that near here?'

The policeman had looked at him with pity for his ignorance.

'This is Kowloonside. Wanchai is Hong Kongside.'

He ripped the top page of the pad and presented it to Sim ostentatiously, as if he'd won a cheque.

'This is the address.'

'How do I know if it's the same Nancy Lo?'

The sergeant shrugged and smiled.

'Ask her.'

Madeleine was struggling to keep Robert out of her clothes when the phone rang. In the grip of his usual after-lunch lust, he was trying to get on top of her, kiss her along the jawline, bite her earlobe, run his fingers under her skirt, pinch the whiteness of her thighs.

'Get *off*, Robert. Bloody pest. This is probably work.'

'But you're at home, it's lunch-hour. Tell them to take a flying fuck.'

She reached for the receiver and got it to her ear.

'Yes?'

'Miss Scott? Madeleine Scott?'

'Hello? Yes, speaking. *Robert!*'

'This is Au, Sergeant Au. Tsimshatsui District Police HQ.'

'Hello, Sergeant Au.'

'Maddy, you're so sexy.'

There was a pause while Sergeant Au translated.

'Sorry about that, Sergeant. Take no notice. How can I help you?'

Straightening up, Robert giggled. '*Au* can I help you?'

There was a glass half-full of wine in his hand and he tipped it down his throat.

'No, I'm helping you, Miss Scott. You put the word out for a man, name Fielding. Is that right?'

'Yes. Have you got him?'

'We have had someone with this name come in, yes.'

Robert had casually dropped the drained wineglass on the carpet. Now his hands were around Madeleine's body, stroking downward from ribcage to hips, the thumbs smoothing her belly through the cotton of her shirt.

'Christ, Maddy, I can't stand this.'

Starting at the waistband of her skirt he began opening the shirt, button by button. When he came to her navel he stopped and inserted a finger, tickling it gently from side to side.

'We haven't *got* him,' Sergeant Au was saying. 'But he came in. Robbery victim in Yaumatei. A tourist, I guess.'

Robert bent his head and Madeleine felt him tonguing her navel with a circular motion. She ignored it, trying to concentrate on Au's voice.

'The man's first name is Simon. Simon Fielding. Tourist. Arrived this morning. Got robbed in a hotel trying to check in.'

A naïve tourist? It didn't sound too promising.

'Where did he come from?'

Robert's face had come back up to rest on the rim of the sofa, beside her ear. His fingers had resumed their crab-crawl up her shirt front and meanwhile his breath was annoying her. He held it in, then, as each button came free, expelled it. The sound was like a hot iron releasing bursts of steam.

'He told us, Manchester. Gives an address in a place called Moxon, Lancashire.'

Au gave her the spelling.

'And where is Fielding now? Where's he staying?'

'We don't know. But he's around. He's got no money, no passport, seemed a bit lost, you know? But he had one contact in Hong Kong, a bar owner, Wanchai.'

'Can you give me the bar's name?'

The unbuttoning had finally reached her throat and now the shirt came open. Robert's hands grasped her neck, the fingers sliding round to dabble in the silky hair at the nape. She hammered on his shoulder until he released her and she could stretch as far as the table for a pad and pencil. She slapped it down on the sofa beside her and wrote at Sergeant Au's dictation.

As she was writing, Robert's fingers crept behind her back and released the hooks on her brassière. Holding it pincerwise in thumb and finger he delicately peeled it back, as if removing a fish skin. He tossed the bra away.

As she was thanking Au and hanging up, Robert's mouth went down on her left breast. When drunk, he liked to slobber on her tits. She lay back and let her hand rest on his head. It would occupy him for at least the next ten minutes: time to do some thinking.

Wanchai. 'All bars and tarts. Dead seedy.'

Old Worsley's memory didn't match the Wanchai Sim was seeing as he moved down Lockhart Road. This was a place of designer-clothes shops, antique-carpet dealers, picture-framers, even a children's shoeshop. There were food stalls of exemplary cleanliness. There were modern banks, dried-flower sellers, rattan dealers, pottery shops, a kitchenware boutique. In the thirty-five years since Old Worsley was a roaring seadog, spilling his wild oats like typhoon rain, Wanchai had found respectability.

In the side alleys aftertastes of the old squalor still lingered. Sim entered one of these, trying to visualize the young Worsley stumbling along it with his shipmates, half blinded by rum and Chinese beer, past the tarts who posed in the doorways. The girls' thighs would be peeping through slits in their dresses, their alizarin lips giving glossy kisses to the hot night air, their fingers crooking and straightening and saying, 'Come on, come in, I am whatever you want, I have whatever you want . . .'

But it was still daylight, mid-afternoon, and the images were too diluted to be real for him. He quickened his pace along the alley, counting the doorways until he came to that of Nancy Lo's place. A violet-magenta sign advertised the bar's name: The Mama-Bunny.

The door's plate-glass was darkened so that, going in, Sim passed from coruscating brightness into shade. At the same time air-conditioning enveloped him in a cold rush. He had entered a small, black-carpeted lobby in which another darkened-glass door faced him. Beside it was a pot plant on a steel-framed table; beside that a coat-check window. He handed his canvas bag to the wizened attendant, who looked at him curiously. The man's facial expression carried a message, but Sim could not decide between two interpretations. Was it, *You don't belong here, so why not skip it?* Or, *You don't belong here, so this could be interesting?*

Without a word he pushed on into the bar, whose floor was an opulent skating-surface of black marble. The space was not wide, but it extended deep towards the back of the building, the bar running along the side wall, until it ended half-way down the room. The atmosphere was dusky, stroked with the music of violins. For fittings Nancy favoured stainless steel and black leather. The place seemed expensive, although Sim didn't know what it took to *be* expensive in this world. He hoped he had enough change in his pocket to pay for an exploratory drink.

The barstools were elegant – shiny black-hide mushroom-tops on flared cones of steel. A single customer in a business suit, Japanese possibly, sat nursing a Scotch while the white-jacketed barman looked on and polished glasses. Sim ordered a Chinese beer and glanced into the area beyond the bar's end. Here the room broke up into enclosures for two or four people which – to allow for intimate conversation – were segregated by the high bench-backs. Of the six visible from this angle, only one was occupied. It contained a man and a woman who sat engrossed in their bottle of champagne. Above them the muzak began to churn synthetically through a Lennon-McCartney number.

'Is the toilet down there and to the right?'

The barman nodded. Sim left his stool and walked through the room. He felt he was surfing dreamlike on a wave of James Last music. Going by, he saw that two more of the stalls were occupied by couples not unlike the first – the men in business suits, each talking urgently into the cleavage of a woman. The figures of the women strained the seams of their satin dresses.

The toilets were indistinguishable from an executive washroom, so clean that a piss felt like an act of vandalism almost equal to writing *Sim wozzere* on the wall. An attendant was here too, standing beside a small table on which rested a brass collection-plate. As he left Sim flipped the smallest coin from his inadequate hoard into it, and he saw again that look in the servant's face: *What the hell are you doing here?*

Returning, he passed the Japanese who had been at the bar. He was escorting an elegant but overweight woman, a good twenty years his senior, to one of the enclosed tables. At the bar a newly arrived customer was leaning forward, bending the barman's ear.

'Hey, I see no chicks. Where's the topless women?'

A tourist, he wore baggy T-shirt, bermuda shorts with dayglo zigzags, straw homburg, easy-for-idiots camera, sandals. He was Australian.

'This is Wanchai, ain't it? So where's Susie Wong?'

He looked around as if he suspected they were deliberately hiding the lady. The barman said nothing, just placed a beer in front of him. The tourist drank and tried to bring Sim into the discussion.

'You see any loose pairs of tits hanging out in here, mate? 'Cause I sure as hell don't.'

Sim said nothing. The tourist rose from his stool and came over to perch next to Sim. His eye-whites were small roadmaps, his head swayed slightly, his distended lips hung open like orchid petals in decay.

'I've been in The Bottoms Up. You been there? It's tame. I'm looking for a bit more action.'

Sim said to the barman, 'And I'm looking for Miss Nancy Lo. Is she around?'

The tourist heard him. He crowed, and plucked at Sim's sleeve.

'Nancy, Nancy, tickle my fancy. Got it, tell us where she is, bar *person*? I wouldn't fight shy of a piece of that.'

The barman was frowning now. He raised both his hands showing the tourist his palms before turning to Sim.

'No, sir. Miss Lo isn't here right now. She was here this morning. She will come in later tonight, I guess.'

'Where does she live? Can I go and find her?'

The tourist was breathing hard after taking a long suck at his beer. But he took up Sim's question and ran with it.

'Yes, *where* does she live? And how can she live without us? Tell you what, hey!'

He slapped Sim's shoulder with a light backhand.

'We'll go there together, you and me. We'll take a cab, which we'll share, and when we get there we can go on sharing. What's it called? Three in the bed?'

Sim laughed.

'Sorry to disappoint you, but I'm not into it.'

This bozo's presence was making him feel a little better. To the barman he said, 'You can't give me her address?'

'No, sir. Sorry, sir.'

The tourist seemed not to be following any more. His face had acquired a faraway look.

'When they hang their tits out in these bars, that's only good business practice.'

He might have been addressing a sales conference in some English south-coast hotel.

'It's a way of supercharging the sales curve. Now my line of business is fruit, right? Tinned fruit. We put a luscious girl on the label with Himalayan knockers to her, we get rid of a lot more pears in syrup, because of course pears are breast-shaped anyway –'

Briefly he seemed to run out of forward momentum as he examined the middle distance, his brain flooding with mammary images. Then he trip-started again.

'Course, that's what our tame company shrink calls vendor-prompted association. It's dicy in a way. Here it's more of a cert, as it's straight cause and effect. Swing a lot of dinkie-di boobs out over the bar and you're bound to shift more drinks. It stimulates the auton – the autonomic thingie. Makes you thirsty looking at them, see? It's the same as giving the punters free salted peanuts.'

He sighed, as if his knowledge of the secret cogs and wheels of behavioural psychology burdened him. He added, 'But I know which I like the better of the two, and it's not peanuts.'

Sim slapped the bar. He finished his beer, getting bored now.

'All right. What say the two of us go on somewhere? Find the action?'

The fruit merchant's face came alert and bright at the invitation.

'Now you're talking. Action's the name of the game here in Hong Kong, so I've been told.'

The man's amply stuffed wallet was on the bar. Sim picked it up, took out $50, replaced the wallet in his jacket and pulled him firmly from his stool. He handed the fifty to the bartender.

'I'll come back later.'

The barman raised his hand to mark their leaving, but did not smile.

# 14

A noise like a buzz-saw from the next room bothered Maurice's ear, a fluctuating high-pitched whine. It didn't sound human, which was OK. The less human the sounds, the better he felt about them.

And where the fuck was Swann?

Maurice had used the phone until his forefinger hurt, but the line Swann had given him for contact was deaf to his furious dialling. Now he lay at full stretch on the carpet and considered. Swann had entered his life from nowhere, and without explanation, that was the bugger of it. There was no certainty he even lived in the Territory.

'Don't worry about me, or who I am,' Swann had told Maurice. 'Just consider the offer. We need you because you have the passport. What we want we can write into the passport, because you got no dependants on it, that so? So all you do, you get paid a half, you go to England. You make the hit, come back with the valuable goods, we pay the balance.'

He'd snapped his fingers.

'Cinch, right?'

Maurice had been inclined to go along with that. He was being asked to steal some valuable item. Fine. He'd done that before. He didn't need to know the guy he was stealing from, any more than he wanted to be able to name the client at the end of the line – the one behind Swann or, maybe, the one beyond *him*. The less he knew, the easier he could shut his eyes.

The circular saw had given way to an amplified pepper mill accompanied by baboon hoots. Maurice shut the sounds out. He wanted to go on thinking, dragging at the threads of this entanglement. If he couldn't find Swann, Swann couldn't get the rest of the money to him. That had been the deal. Swann to set up the rout home as far as Bangkok, fix short-term accommodation there, fix an amah to meet him there. But Maurice had wanted to run the last stage of the operation himself – find the Hong Kong living-quarters, then contact Swann when he was in place. It made for security. It gave him a measure of control, and Swann had reluctantly agreed.

But if he couldn't *find* Swann, what then? What was he to do about the valuable item in the next room? How was he to collect his pay-off? He would have to start taking the initiatives himself. He knew what to do, all right. But the thought made him flush hot and cold.

By agreeing to remain in the dark about the players in this game, not to mention their motives, he had acted like a novice chess player failing to look ahead, anticipate trouble and juggle possibilities. How different the distribution of pieces looked already, just a few moves further into the game. Much of the change was Maurice's own doing. First with the cock-up back in England, then with the remedy, and now with the idea that was creeping insidiously into his brain.

The cock-up he had left behind him, somewhere in a scooped-out hole in the high Pennines. He would not be able to find the place even if he tried; anyway, it was unimaginable from this distance, wreathed in amnesiac fog. Yet the cock-up had been explosive. Like a charge on the tramlines, it had seemed to blow the entire enterprise off track. It had scared him witless for a time, almost sending him on the first plane to South America. But pretty soon he'd squandered all the money in betting shops and, even if he cashed his Hong Kong ticket, he'd only be penniless when he got to his destination. No. He had gone not to Valparaiso but to Moxon and to Sim, buying time while he thought of a way to repair the cock-up.

*Erskin.* It had come, just like that, when the child was up on his shoulders during that stupid game, the pig game. He *could* have made the connection before – in Chinatown maybe, certainly in Salford when he was hanging around that tart Treeze. And how he had failed to see it that afternoon in bed at the Norbreck Castle he would never know. Maybe it took the boy, up there like a jockey, to uncover the key to the lock he was struggling with: *Erskin.*

The fact was, he'd lain alongside that beautiful, over-heated bitch Karen and actually talked about Erskin. He'd told her the story of how, a long time ago, a hangover and a mistaken identity had caused Erskin to be castrated instead of Johnny the Junkie. And he did it.

'You did *what*?' She propped herself up on one elbow, her hair plastered by sweat to her forehead.

'I didn't do it personally, Karen. But it was because of me.'

She made come-on movements with her fingers.

'Tell, Maurice. Tell all.'

'That was my first-ever paid job, a stable lad. God, my pious Catholic mother was beside herself at the thought. She only let me go after Dessane the trainer wrote to say he'd spotted potential talent in me. No one else had ever done that, I can tell you.'

'What sort of talent?'

'It was crap. He only said it to get me to go. Being a stable lad is a kind of slavery which should be notified to the United Nations. Trouble is, the slaves collaborate in it, because they all have the illusion they're going to be the next Lester Piggott. Anyway, I was dead flattered and so, in a way, was my mum, so I went.'

She giggled.

'And was this Erskin guy who lost his nuts one of the other stable lads?'

'No, sugar. Erskin was a *horse*. All would have gone to plan if it hadn't been for old Erskin; perhaps I would have been the next Lester after all. Erskin and his nuts changed my life.'

He had rolled up and was now lighting a cigarette.

'Stable lads did *two* in those days – two horses that you looked after exclusively. Well, Erskin was one of my two, and the other was Johnny the Junkie. They were in next-door boxes, two colts of the same age and very much alike to look at, so much so in fact that the whole stable knew them as the twins. Not in racing ability, though. Erskin was a decent handicapper with a few good prizes under his girth. Johnny was a stroppy bastard, lazy on the gallops, but out on the course he pulled like the Flying Scot before running out of legs by the 3-furlong mark. So the chop was for Johnny, a last chance like, to teach him how to settle in a race, quieten down, maybe send him jumping. But on that particular morning when the vet came, it was Erskin who got it.'

'Go on. I'm agog.'

'I was half-blinded with the aforesaid hangover and, without thinking, I led the wrong twin across the yard. The vet was a locum. *He* didn't know any better, he simply did the job. By the time Dessane found out it was too late: Erskin's balls were in the bucket.'

She pulled a face and was about to speak. Maurice stopped her.

'But that's not all. The *point* was, only the week before Erskin had been sold to an Australian paper millionaire for stud duties in New South Wales.'

'Oh dear.'

She wrinkled her nose and he bent over and kissed the corrugations. She borrowed his cigarette and took a drag.

'So what did your boss do?'

'Dessane? To me he simply said, "Your cards, Fielding. I never want to see you again." Pompous voice, like that. I just packed my bag and left.'

'But what did he say to the Australian paper guy?'

'I didn't hear about it till later. I hung around Newmarket for a while, you know, spending what little money I had in the pubs, winning a little in the betting shops. Anyway, in the end I heard just how easily Dessane had solved the problem.'

'And?'

'He asked himself two questions. Had this Australian ever clapped eyes on Erskin? He certainly had not, at least in the flesh. So why would he know the difference between Erskin and Johnny the Junkie, his "twin"? He wouldn't. Therefore they didn't hang around or wait for second thoughts. Johnny simply became Erskin. He was bandaged and boxed up and air-freighted to Bendigo, along with Erskin's papers and a letter from Dessane saying he hoped he'd get lots of winners. And the weird part is, according to gossip in the tap room of The Coach, he really was quite a success out there. He even got a colt who was placed in the Melbourne Cup.'

He laughed.

'And to cap it all the *real* Erskin fulfilled Johnny the Junkie's destiny and became a lousy steeplechaser.'

But even then, he'd not seen the answer. They'd tipped wine down each other's throats and rolled over and eventually got round to humping again. Jesus, that woman! Anyway, it wasn't till the next day, when that kid was sitting up on his shoulders like a jockey, that he'd seen it. *Johnny the Junkie simply became Erskin.* Of course. *So* simple that a two-year-old could have understood.

From the news on the day after he'd torched that cottage Maurice knew the target for Swann's operation. C. P. Cotton was such a very plausible mark. Everyone in Hong Kong knew about him, his brazen business style, his vow to the Chinese government that he would ram Tienanmen down their lousy heathen throats as soon as his satellite TV station was on-line. Cotton's big public ego made him difficult to attack publicly. On the other hand, it made him all the more vulnerable in private and through his family.

But what gave Maurice power over C. P. Cotton was something in addition, something Cotton had said to the press about the grandson. *I haven't seen him since he was a baby.* Maurice lifted the remark and kept it inside himself like the working part of a confidential and deadly device.

Maurice rolled over and crouched, his knuckles on the floor like an ape. With a grunt he pushed himself to his feet and crossed into the next room. He liked his new base, the spaciousness of it, the fact that it was commercial premises. A flat was always a flat, but a suite of virgin offices could be an operations centre, a headquarters, a command bunker.

The adjoining room, unlike the one he had left, was furnished after a fashion. It had a mattress for the amah, a playpen, a barred cot, an ironing-board. A packet of disposable nappies stood beside two suitcases propped open against a wall. They were spilling the clothes of the amah and a few items from what looked to Maurice like a doll's wardrobe. He'd arrived in Bangkok with not so much as a change of clothes for *it*, so the amah had been sent out to buy things while it slept. Letting her go out was a risk, of course, but he knew he would feel out of place in such a shop, like a butcher in a ballet class. She had come back, thank Christ. He had been angry with her for spending so much – clothes and *toys*, for Christ's sake! He had no money for toys, but she had bought a whole stack of them anyway. He had raised his hand to her, and enjoyed it as she flinched away. But he hadn't struck her. What was it Ma used to say? *A man who strikes a woman is no better than a brute.*

The amah was in the narrow, windowless kitchen. A microwave oven whirred and the faint, corrupt smell of stewed meat was finding its way into Maurice's nostrils. *It* was sitting in the playpen, giving out noises that would not have disgraced a crack-crazed blues singer. He walked past, trying not to look, yet looking with the corner of his eye. He thought of the nightmare journey from the UK to Bangkok, when he'd tried to keep it quiet with sweets and crisps until it was sick repeatedly all over his shirt and lap.

He refused to give it a name. He tried to think of it only as an animal, being shipped between zoos.

In the kitchen he flipped open the fridge and took out a beer. The amah turned to him. She was pretty and young but, like so many Filipinas, a prude. He'd tried to fuck her the first night but she'd fought like a cat and, for the moment, he'd given up. Now she said, 'We need more food. *He* needs fresh fruit, vegetables. I can't just give him this tin stuff all the time, this shit!'

Maurice was already moving out. He turned and looked at her.

'Make a list, I'll get it.'

She took a step towards him.

'Let me go. I'd like to. I can't stay locked here all the time. I can't.'

'Yes you can, sugar. That was the deal. So I'll get the stuff. You stay here with – with, you know.'

He could see the tension and fear in her face. Shit, if he let her out, she might not come back at all. She might tell somebody. But worse, if she didn't return, she would be leaving him alone with it. He thought a judicious warning was in order. He raised a finger to her.

'You're being well paid for this. You've had some money and you will get more from Mr Swann. But if you ask a lot of questions, or fuck up in any way, you won't get more. Also, I shall have great pleasure in hurting you. Now shut your mouth, OK?'

He strolled back into the bare room with the telephone and lay back down on the floor. Now, where was he? Oh yes, Swann. Where the fuck *was* Swann? He spilled beer down his chin, trying to drink and think at the same time.

★

Craike looked at Madeleine critically, as if she were wearing clashing colours or a crooked wig.

'You still seeing that pillock Robert Dowling?'

She said yes with her eyelids. What business was it of Craike's, anyway?

'He's a security risk, you know? You mustn't tell him anything.'

'He's OK. I never discuss work with him. And anyway, he'll do anything I tell him.'

She was furious with Craike, but she laughed, wanting to show him the right level of carelessness. 'Robert's putty in my hands.'

'Slaves can be dangerous. If they turn against their betters they do an awful lot of mischief.'

'Like Spartacus, you mean? But *he* cared about people as well as being clever – at least, that's what I've always been led to believe. Robert may be a brilliant property lawyer but he has the emotional detachment of a baby. He won't be raising the flag for a slave's revolt and meantime I'm finding him pretty useful. It's an arrangement we both like.'

'All right. Just be careful with him. Now, any luck with Fielding?'

'I've been to this Mama-Bunny place. He wasn't there, but a canvas grip in the cloakroom had British Airways tags all over it. The barman said the owner was coming back to see Nancy Lo later this evening.'

'What's it like?'

'The bar? It's a very strange place, I can't work it out. Looks like the usual girlie bar, but no girlies. Nancy's well past the topless stage, as we know. But *all* women in the place seem to be of her vintage, give or take a decade.'

'All Mama-Bunnys, in fact?'

'Well, is that it? A hang-out for people who like their hookers drawing a pension?'

'You'd better go back, take a look at this guy with the bag, see if it's Fielding, see where he's staying. Don't talk to him. We don't want you to get your fingers blown off prematurely.'

'Prematurely? It's all right if I get them blown off in due course, is it?'

Craike laughed and laid his hand on her bare arm. She

shuddered minutely and shrugged him off. He said, 'You'll need them to write your report, won't you?'

Vanteel, on the home territory of his own hotel room, seemed just a little more at ease. Craike set out to re-establish superiority.

'How's the trip? Have you been round the night-spots yet?'

Vanteel was huffy.

'I'm here to work, Craike.'

'I thought you said you were on a fortnight's bargain-price package tour.'

'We can't afford to throw money around, like you people in the private sector. I didn't come out here to go to night-clubs.'

'Can't think what else you'd be doing.'

Vanteel bristled with indignation.

'You are not the only bloody pebble on this beach, Craike, you ought to know that. We've got 1997 coming up. It's an awful lot of work for the Service, making sure we're ready for when the slit-eyes arrive. And in the meantime we've got a bloody great garrison here. I've got to go to Stonecutter's Island to report on some apes the Gurkhas are supposed to have shot up. The Gurkhas are saying they weren't apes, but bloody Chink spies.'

Craike laughed.

'On Stonecutter's? What were they spying on, punishment runs? Squaddy fatigues?'

Vanteel said, 'The island happens to feature very largely in our plans, Craike, as you well know.'

He did. Stonecutter's Island, for so long an army camping-ground, was the site for a relocated Royal Navy base. He just said, 'Crazy plan, anyway, Vanteel. Bit late in the day for the Empire to be planning new naval bases.'

'Shut up about that, Craike. This is a public place! What have you got for me, anyway? What's your decision?'

'Well, you're in, though I don't like your terms much.'

He took from his pocket a manila envelope and tossed it on the coffee table between them.

'That's two reports: one on Cotton, another on James Swann. Cotton's is my own, Swann's is from my assistant, Madeleine Scott. She doesn't know I'm feeding it to you.'

'Who's Swann?'

'Swann is our source. I should say, *was*. Madeleine saw Swann killed yesterday.'

'Killed? My God!'

'It's all in there. We don't know who killed him yet. He was living like an illegal here, probably had no official identity. The Chinese must have done it to shut him up.'

'Does Cotton know that he's dead?'

'Not from us – but of course *they* may have killed him.'

Craike rose.

'Now, Vanteel, I believe the banks are still open. There's a little matter of the transfer of some funds, OK?'

In the Captain's Bar, Craike sat alone. Last thing at night he liked a Laphroaig, or maybe a Talisker. The Lowland malts were inclined to seem bland at the end of the day, and then what he craved was the strong reek of seaweed and bog water from the Western Isles.

His pocket contained the stamped counterfoil of Vanteel's remittance, a transfer through an untraceable account with a small Middle Eastern bank. The amount had been paltry, it hardly made a dent in what he'd already shelled out for Fielding's name. But the start had been made. Next time he would be upping the stakes, for only when London were paying out real money would they start to take him seriously. Then it would be easy to make them appreciate that this attack on Cotton was just for openers. 1997 might be five years away, but as far as the PRC was concerned, Hong Kong was already wide open. There were plenty of officials in Beijing itching to move in on the big Hong Kong operators – scare them off or cut them down one way or another. This shit about Beijing wanting to take over Hong Kong as a thriving and prosperous concern! They loathed the spirit of the place. They wanted it begging and on its knees; they wanted to ride into the city like warriors, past heaps of smouldering financial rubble.

London, of course, was blinkered as usual and couldn't see it. That was because they depended on fucking new guys like Vanteel to tell them what was going on. Vanteel, who went around looking for spies dressed up as monkeys. God. It would make you weep.

Yet Craike was feeling happier than he had for months. At *last*, he was beginning to fight back. Why should all these half-educated rookies in their tracksuits and flop-sided haircuts always push him into the shade? Craike was fluent in four languages, had been involved in three wars and had killed many men with his bare hands and, once, a woman.

He looked down at the lights of Kowloon across the harbour, a fantastic display of static fireworks in the night. Somewhere down there was a man called Fielding. When Craike found him he would have power in the palm of his hand.

He snapped his fingers for another shot of whisky.

At the round table a group of eight men dealt and played their cards, silent but for the occasional sigh of disappointment. When they won they showed no emotion. The scarcely lit room in which they sat had a low, sagging, damp-tainted ceiling. The furniture was decayed beyond repair, the floormat held in its webbing the odour of decrepitude and rat shit. Illumination, such as it was, came from a pre-war desk-lamp, attached to a junction box that was hooked illegally on to a main several floors overhead. The hooded lamp stood upright at the centre of the table, its kinked, flexible steel stalk rearing from the base to give the appearance of a petrified cobra watching the game. A dust-clogged electric fan, hooked up in the same dangerous fashion, whirred and ticked on the floor. The brightest articles in the room were the coloured plastic chips with which the players gambled.

They were drably dressed and of various ages. Two were in extreme old age, with long beards like unravelled lengths of baling-twine hanging thinly from their chins. Of these two old men, one was winning heavily. He had won chips from all of the others, but most of all from his fellow geriatric, who was being taken ruthlessly to the cleaners.

Among the remaining players was Ho Yu Ching. He too was losing, because his mind was only half on the game. With the other half he was thinking about women. Ho Yu Ching was known as Fuck-mad Ho. He was so obsessive about sex that he could never keep a job unless every worker was male. No woman, not even an old and shrivelled one, was safe from assault, because Ho had absolutely no sexual restraint. It made him an object of general pity among men, who regarded him as they would a simpleton or a man with a twisted foot. Women, if they were wise, had learned simply to avoid him.

A knock was heard on the door and, with creaking hinges, it opened. A boy of thirteen or so, posted outside as watcher and alarm-raiser, pushed the door back to admit the bespectacled Lee Hung. Closing up again, the boy withdrew to his post and Lee stood there politely, smiling into the thin splash of light. As the players drew, studied and cast their cards on the table in silent rotation, Lee picked out Fuck-mad Ho within the circle. Across the fan of his hand Ho frowned a question. Lee Hung nodded and made a slight movement of his hand in front of his chest. Then, as the men started to slap down their cards and call for a new deal, he said, 'Come, Ho. I want you.'

As Ho left the game Lee Hung greeted the other players with handshakes, going round the table from elders to lessers. Then he bowed his way out, followed by Ho Yu Ching.

Threading their way through the stinking warren of alleyways, Lee could sense Ho's excitement. Whenever Lee Hung came for him it meant a job for Ho, which in turn meant payment, which, as spring followed winter, meant the chance for him to buy a good whore.

'What you got for me, Lee Hung? Another letter to deliver, like that one I gave to the *gwailo* woman in Mong Kok that time?'

'No, it's something more than that, Ho Yu Ching. It's more difficult, and more dangerous. It is a job for a lot of money.'

A lot of money. *Wah!* Ho followed the great Lee like a dog who knew he would soon be given a bleeding chunk of steak.

## 15

Sim decided he would not leave the tinned-fruit man – Duggie was his name – lying under a table in the Tsimshatsui hostess club. For three hours Duggie had been in prime form, buying beers, brandies and champagne for anyone coming within range. There seemed no shortage of cash as he splashed about. It was the perfect distillation of the good time he felt Hong Kong owed him: drink, loud sexual cross-talk and low-intensity voyeurism, the bread and butter of the topless-hostess bars.

Only gradually had Duggie slowed, but now he was nearly immobile. Resting the back of his head in the lap of a silk-gowned, bare-breasted, tart-mouthed hostess, the only part of him left with any vitality was his tongue. In extreme drink, Duggie had discovered an affable, almost poetic eloquence.

'Young Sim, at this point you may leave me, if you so wish. You have led me most manfully into heaven. I'm as tight as a turd in a trouser leg. My only desire now is to lie here and gaze at the stars.'

Above his face the hostess's nipples swung tantalizingly close, but he had trouble focusing. He fanned his hand, as if to disperse fog.

'I am most deliciously lost. I can't remember my wife's name. I can't remember the nature of my job, the number of my house. Are these a Hong Kong houri's tits I see above me?'

A few minutes later he slipped altogether beneath the surface of consciousness, and then beneath the table. The hostess was no help. She had gone already to a nearby table, where she was ruthlessly insisting on its occupant placing an order for champagne while she placed her thighs for his comfort.

Left to deal with his comatose companion, Sim rifled Duggie's pockets. In the jacket he found a courtesy street-plan. He woke Duggie and supported him to the street, where they entered a red and grey taxi. They sped together to the hotel on

Kowloonside, whose name Duggie had forgotten but which was printed on the courtesy map. Sim paid the taxi from Duggie's wallet and got him to his room. Then he walked the six blocks to the Kowloon Star Ferry pier, on his way back to the Mama-Bunny.

The ferry boat across the Fragrant Harbour has two classes on separate decks. Above, you pay a dollar for a superior view of the Hong Kong seafront, whose glass and concrete towers pack so solidly together along the level apron which separates water from mountain range. Even during the day the peaks are enveloped by a peculiarly local mixture of low cloud and misty pollution, with Victoria Peak to the west, Mount Parker to the east, and the bumps of Gough, Cameron and Butler strung along the saddle in between. But Hong Kong is not its mountains. The soul of the place, if it has one, resides in the brilliantly lit buildings that hang above the waterfront at night like a gigantic, shimmering, mile-long stage curtain.

Sim chose the upper deck, and stood at the boat's rail. As they neared Blake Pier the towers reared above him, their reflection taken into the water and played with to form a liquid mosaic of coloured light. The strangeness of the place suddenly hit him with a frisson. Here the land is reclaimed, the light is electric, the sounds are mechanical. It squared with nothing he had ever known. That was so much the better. Here he was free to act, unknown and unjudged by whatever surrounded him.

He landed and hurried down to Wanchai. Outside the bar, he stopped and put on his sunglasses, though it had been dark for hours. He did it to add a touch of Robert Mitchum to his entrance.

The watcher, unseen in a specially constructed hide, had tracked Madeleine Scott from the door to the bar and watched her choose a place nearest to the wall. A defensive move, the watcher thought. The girl ordered a vodka-tomato juice and sipped delicately, as if meaning to make the drink last. She was incongruous and realized it, but she was here with a purpose. That much was clear.

The man came soon afterwards, a big young man in jeans and a loose jacket who hadn't shaved for a day or so. He came in untidily, bumping the furniture. Light in the bar was a rationed commodity and those heavy shades gave his eyes no chance. The clumsiness was just a little endearing, the watcher thought. But he, too, was out of place here. He must be the boy whom Jackie, the barman, had mentioned, the one who'd been making inquiries earlier in the day.

They pretended not to be together, but the watcher thought otherwise. Why else was the girl so coyly looking at him every half-minute? She was no hooker, that was for sure. And wasn't he trying to get their eyes to meet? If he was, she didn't want to. She wanted to go on pretending. In a moment the watcher would go through and find out what this was all about.

The stool Sim had chosen was half-way along the bar. There were four empty ones between it and the good-looking girl in the corner. His awkward, stumbling entrance had reminded Madeleine of the men in her family – brothers and father, all oversized for the village terraced house in which some of them still lived. Like the watcher, she would have found it endearing, if she hadn't had a different preconception to overrule the feeling.

Sim, as he groped his way on to a stool, hadn't noticed Madeleine except as a wraith in the corner. Then he took off the glasses to dispel the Stygian gloom he'd imposed on himself. Now he did see her: a strong-looking girl sitting with what could have been a Bloody Mary. She was by two decades the youngest female in the place.

Her eyes constantly swept the room in case he thought her curiosity was pointed only at him. She got in the occasional longer look by raising her glass and sipping slowly. Then she could train her eyes, apparently unfocused, over the glass's rim and in his direction. She guessed it was Fielding, of course: he was the only round-eye in the place for a start, and he was certainly a Brit.

He started to throw quick glances at her, because he sensed she was doing the same. He was hoping their eyes would meet, but they continually missed each other. To him she looked a North European, not American, because there was something too careful about her clothes. They were just a shade older than her real age, which is not something North Americans do. This woman he put at twenty-five, but she dressed thirty.

Not that *thirty* would be old enough to enable her to fit in here. What the fuck was she doing on a beat where all the other women were grannies? Maybe she lived upstairs, and used this as her local bar. Perhaps she liked the compliment of being juxtaposed with an older generation, being unchallenged in the joint for wrinkle-free skin and unknotted veins.

She looked for the killer in him and didn't find it. That was OK. She had been around a fair slate of murderers in her time with the police, and had never seen the killer in any of *them* either. The idea that a murderer carries the mark of the beast on him, and that the trained and initiated can thereby pick him out, was crap. Killers look like the rest of us, only more so. And the *more so* wasn't something you noticed until you already knew they were killers.

When he'd taken off the glasses she saw his eyes were blue and peculiarly clear. Guileless. It confirmed her thesis: the more innocent you look, the more guilty you look.

'Has Miss Lo come in yet?'

It was a light northern accent, but not high pitched or nasal. Not George Formby. He spoke to the barman with unnatural loudness, as if not wishing to appear a conspirator. She knew he was Fielding for sure then – the fire-setter, the near psychopath, the homicide and, according to the late Swann, the perpetrator of even more frightful acts. Her forehead felt warm and the sweatglands at her temples began to prickle infinitesimally.

'Yes, sir,' said the barman. 'She is in back. She will come out into the bar right away and I show you to her.'

'Right. Good.'

He asked for a beer, and shortly after it was poured he noticed the young woman's fractional movement of the fingers, discreet and momentary as a bidder at Sotheby's. The barman jumped to refill her glass, yes, a Bloody Mary. Why did that trick never work when *he* tried it?

She didn't look like a whore, but then, what did he know? In Manchester he'd seen whores. They'd been grossly obvious figures, their bodies an advertising space for their wares. This woman's linen jacket and skirt, dark stockings and white-silk shirt were ordinary business uniform. She wore hardly any make-up. She looked so good that she had no need to beautify herself, but maybe that was just another style of whoredom. This place was so weird already, nothing would surprise him.

Madeleine really needed the second drink as a fillip. In the bar she felt comprehensively out of place. During the half-hour in which she had been here, several Japanese men had come in. These were of any age from twenty-five upwards, all in their business suits, all having checked their briefcases in at the hall. Invariably they were solo and wore the furrowed foreheads of men on whom the world placed impossible burdens. None of them took the slightest interest in her, thank God. Each was taken in hand by a determined middle-aged lady who emerged from the back room beyond the bead curtain. In the main, she thought, these women were Japanese. Madeleine recognized just one Cantonese, and she was fluent in Jap. Among these women there were no round-eyes.

From their different vantage points both Madeleine and Sim looked at the hostesses and asked themselves, what are they? Whores? It seemed unlikely. Typing pool supervisor would be nearer the mark for some. Others were soft, mumsy types, although they all wore low-cut dresses which showed the fleshy upside of their chests. They did not disappear with their clients through the bead curtain to romp on feather beds, but merely slipped into the booths with them, drank lightly while the men drank heavily, held their hands, patted their cheeks, laughed at their jokes, tut-tutted over their problems.

Madeleine thought, it doesn't matter. Fielding was her concern. She tried to concentrate on him.

Sim thought, Nancy Lo would tell him. He tried to think out what he was going to say to *her*.

A woman of perhaps sixty swished out from behind the beads. She had a strong head of shiny black hair pulled round by a comb fixed at the back. Her shoulders were bare over a dress brilliant with sequins. Her shoes were high but not steepling. Her calves were sinewy. By the way she walked, looking from side to side into the booths, you could see she was the boss.

She stopped at the bar. The barman gestured at Sim and she turned to him.

'Are you the young man who's been asking for me?'

Sim nodded and said, 'I wondered if we could have a few words.'

She took his arm above the elbow. Although her fingers were not long enough to close the circle, it was a decisive gesture that reminded Madeleine of the way Hong Kong's poulterers grasp a live chicken's neck before they jam it down on to the block. Sim was being led away towards the nearest empty booth.

Sim looked back at her. His mouth was small but the lips were full. They twitched. His eyes said to her, shit, what have I started, help. She thought, what a bastard, a cold and shameless murderer, a spy – and joking with me.

'So. Tell me who you are.'

Nancy Lo had manoeuvred him into the booth first and settled herself. She looked a little grim, like a teacher who suspects some pupil is about to waste her time.

'My name's Sim Fielding. I'm from England. I got here this morning.'

'You a tourist, Mr Fielding?'

'No, not a tourist.'

'Business?'

'Of a kind. I'm looking for someone.'

'I see. Looking for someone.'

She repeated the words as if testing them for soundness.

'Yes. My father. I'm looking for my father.'

Nancy Lo smiled. Something amused her.

'Good, that's very good. Did he get lost?'

Sim decided to keep it simple.

'He left my mother a long time ago, when I was a kid. Then she died. I recently discovered he came here.'

Nancy Lo liked this, she liked it very much. The suspicions lifted from her a little and she became attentive, concerned.

'And do you think *I* know your father?'

'Well, no. I mean, that's not why I came to see you.'

'What's his name, your father?'

'Fielding.'

She smiled. 'Obviously. But his *first* name?'

'Maurice.'

She considered and Sim felt an irrational surge of hope. What if she did know Maurice? It would be an incredible coincidence, a stroke of real luck. But Nancy shook her head.

'No, I can't recall the name Maurice Fielding.'

She registered Sim's disappointment and touched his arm.

'That doesn't mean I don't know him, it means I can't remember him. I see a lot people, you know?'

'It would have been too much like luck if you did know him.'

Nancy Lo was shaking her head.

'There's no such thing as luck, as any Chinese person will tell you. Everything is directed. I could easily have known him and for that reason you would have been sent to me. Why did you come, please tell me?'

'My boss. He was a seaman. He said he'd known you a long time ago, so when I told him I was coming here he mentioned your name.'

'What you mean by a long time ago?'

Sim shrugged.

'Thirty years maybe. He said you worked in the Morocco night-club.'

Nancy Lo raised her chin and laughed. The cords in her neck tightened visibly.

'Thirty years *is* a long time ago. A previous life of mine, actually.'

She became serious again, harder and more emphatic.

'I was a streetwalker then, you know. Probably I must have met 500 to 1,000 sailors every year and you want me to remember just one of them?'

'He remembers you. He said you were kind to him and you would be kind to me too.'

'Ah, I see!'

She was grim-faced again. She got up and, gesturing for him to stay where he was, clipped back to the bar. There was impatience in her movement. She snapped her fingers at the barman.

'Give me that message pad next to the phone. And a pencil.'

While she waited she looked at Madeleine. Nancy Lo was no fool. Close up the girl looked like a cop. Why was she in here – for herself or for Fielding? There was something going on.

She went back to Sim's table and, without sitting down, wrote on the pad. She ripped off the top copy and passed the small piece of paper to Sim.

'Look, you want to get laid and you don't mind if they make you wear a condom, this place is clean and the girls are more like your own age. It has good medical inspection, fair prices. Don't pay more than 750.'

'Hey, did I say something? What's the matter?'

'Nothing at all. Just I've got business to look after. You won't get what you want here. This is a very different type joint.'

'Look, you're getting me wrong. I didn't come looking for sex. I was robbed this morning. When I was at the police station I asked about you. They had your name on the computer.'

'It doesn't mean anything. I'm legal. They just list all the bars, that's all.'

'I meant, if I hadn't been in the police station I wouldn't have known you would be listed. I would never have found you.'

She fixed him with a glower.

'Tell me what you *really* want, Mr Fielding.'

His mouth was dry and his glass was empty. He felt intimidated by this small, fierce woman skewering him with her eyes.

'Somewhere to stay, just until I get money from England. I've been robbed. The guy who knew you in England, he's kind of my godfather and he'll send me some in a day or two.'

'I don't believe in this man. What does he call himself?'

'Worsley. His name is John Worsley. I told him there was no chance you would remember him, but he really insisted –'

'John Worsley?'

An extraordinary change had taken place in Nancy Lo. She looked as if someone had suddenly called her name. She was looking around in confusion.

'John Worsley? It's impossible. John Worsley died.'

'You *do* know him?'

'Knew him. I knew John Worsley, yes, of course I did.'

Sim watched as she gathered her scattered wits.

'Why *of course*?'

'John Worsley did something I can never forget. Look, Mr Fielding.'

Her mouth was set and twitching slightly. She gripped his wrist and repeated herself, as if translating into another language.

'Look, Mr Fielding, I need a few minutes. Get yourself

another drink, it's on the house. Talk to that nice-looking girl you brought with you. I'll come back in a very few minutes and I'll tell you the whole story.'

Through the bead curtains Nancy Lo kept a bathroom. It was hers alone, never used by *les pouliches*, as she sometimes called the team of middle-aged ladies who worked for her. This bathroom knew of no dismal secrets but her own.

Was it so long? She had not kept count and thirty years had gone by like a weekend. And she had thought John Worsley was dead.

She examined in the mirror the lines and puckers encircling her neck like tiger stripes, and the corrugation of little vertical fissures that shrivelled her upper lip. With a savage pinch she took up the sag of flesh around the jawline and turned her head this way and that to see again what had been. Beneath her eyes were loose, crescent bibs of skin. She pressed the crown of her cheeks sideways and down, smoothing them momentarily away. The eyes stared back at her, frightened and exposed.

But now eyes caught hands. In this cold, too-honest strip light, she found them grotesque. All the kind, young, palpable flesh had gone from them and their skin was stretched drily across string-like tendons and distorted joints, joints as knobbly as the opal and emerald rings that she wore alongside them. Her beautiful fingers, which had made men so compliant with desire, had become crayfish claws.

John Worsley. If she closed her eyes she could form a ghostly image of him, sitting with two shipmates in a dark corner of the Morocco. She had registered their presence as men who had been in before. It was still early in the evening as she began running through her limited repertoire of songs.

> The minute you walk in the joint, I can see
> That you're a man of distinction ...

Later business would liven up. There would be loud conversation, jokes and arguments to drown out the limitations of her voice. Later still the round-eye sailors would begin bidding for her favours, with Joao, the club's Macanese owner, as the dispassionate auctioneer. After much goading and chivvying, and praise for her skilful mouth and dexterous hands, he would at last award her – with a flourish and a free drink – to the highest bidder. Later still, on a sagging, iron-frame bed in a small upstairs room, airless and full of dust, the man would collect his prize.

But now, with only half a dozen customers in front of her, she sang with even less lustre. Joao told her it didn't matter. Sure, her voice was ugly. But she had a beautiful body and men found the contrast sexy. Then he would place a hand on the back of her neck and, with the other, flick one of her earrings so she felt it swing. She was his most valuable possession. Never must she leave him, or even think of it.

> Hey big spender! Spend a little time with me.

As she sang a slim young man was arguing with Joao over the bar. Both men kept looking at her, gesturing. The slim guy was Chu, called Snakeface from the small size of his eyes and the general shape of his head. It fitted his character too. He was a *Hung Kwan*, a redpole who worked for the famous Triad gangster Limpy Ho, and he came through every Thursday night to collect squeeze. Nancy knew what they were arguing about, because they had the same disagreement every week. Joao, when asked to pay his dues, always opened with a point-blank refusal. Snakeface Chu would respond by observing what a pity for such and such an item of decor to be stolen, or broken. Joao then bared his teeth and told him what he would do to any club-jumpers who came here to make mischief and what a Holy Mary mess was made by his old wartime gun. He had got it from a Japanese soldier during the liberation and (as God was his witness) he kept it loaded and ready under the counter.

In reality Joao had little enough to defend. The club was seedy and ill-furnished and, as he himself was so fond of pointing out, its most valuable assets were its stock of alcohol and its beautiful, sexually available singer. So these weekly arguments with Snakeface Chu usually degenerated into threats against Nancy. In the end, of course, Joao capitulated and paid Chu straight from the till.

But tonight seemed different. Joao had finally reached the point of obdurate refusal. He shook his head in woeful disbelief as Chu told him the squeeze was henceforth subject to a 30 per cent increase. His palms massaged his face, he groaned, hammered the bar and finally yelled obscenities and defiance at Chu's face.

Chu stepped back and turned away from Joao. He moved towards Nancy. He drew out a thin blade mounted on an ivory handle. Nancy's song faltered and Charles the fat pianist twisted away from his keys to see what was wrong. Chu snarled at Charles, sweeping the air in an arc with the knife, and Charles leapt so fast that his stool went clattering and bouncing across the dancefloor. Charles blundered away to the furthest wall.

Chu had reached Nancy now. He put a finger under her chin and showed her the blade.

'Tell Mr Joao that he must pay squeeze. If not, I will cut his pretty little whore's nose off.'

In a redpole there is no anger, just cruelty. Among Triad societies the redpole was traditionally the enforcer, the expert in martial arts, whose job was to punish dissidents as much as enemies. More recently, the skilled use of knives and flails had replaced some of the old hand-and-foot disciplines, making the *Hung Kwan* even more dangerous. Nancy looked into Chu's eyes and reckoned he would carry out his threat literally and without emotion.

Chu's fingers were forcing up her chin, tightening the vocal cords and making it impossible to speak. She tried to look down and past Chu's shoulder to where Joao had been, but she could not see him. But over the other shoulder a shadow flitted and a voice spoke in English.

'Leave her be. I *say*, leave the girl be.'

The interrupter took another step nearer. The man was in front of Nancy now, and she could see his young face – pink like raw meat from deckwork under the sun, the brown hair partially bleached, and the expression skewed by concern.

'You all right, Miss?'

He didn't seem to realize what a ludicrous remark this seemed, or what peril it put him in. A burning cigarette was held almost casually between his fingers.

Chu swung and ducked to the side, his foot whipping upwards, catching the *gwailo* glancingly on the ribcage though without properly repelling him. The seaman dropped his cigarette and raised his arms with balled fists, in clumsy readiness. The redpole shouted in his own barbarous Swatonese dialect.

'Back! You stupid motherfucking bastard.'

He feinted with the knife and the seaman dodged sideways. At that moment Joao chose to fire. He held the Jap revolver in both fists, arms at full stretch, but the weapon was inaccurate and he was without any skill. The explosion was thunderous, and it was not Snakeface Chu but the interfering *gwailo* who fell. Chu froze for a moment, then gave a cry and, before Joao could loose off any more shots, ran out.

The *gwailo*'s name she learned, from his shipmates who came back and told her the next day, was John Worsley. This Worsley was in hospital, they said, and as their ship sailed the next day, they would have to leave him. Anyway, he was badly hurt and would die for sure. He was like that, impulsive. Live, die. Risk all. Used to be a racing driver. They'd tried to stop him, but you couldn't, not with Johnny Worsley. By the way, would you kindly drop in and pay him a visit some time? If he's still alive. He likes you, you know.

She went to the hospital and sat by his bed whenever she could. For five days there was little sign of life, and then he would come to consciousness for short periods, sensible consciousness in which they talked or rather she talked and he listened with the amused tolerance of those who can't comfortably frame replies. Then he had needed an operation. Afterwards she telephoned for news.

An English sailor, the shooting case? they said. Oh yes, very sorry to say, he died on the operating table, never actually woke up.

She put no more questions, simply replaced the telephone. She was quite able to accept it. How could he have survived? She had seen the body bleeding all over the dancefloor. How could any person lose so much blood and live?

Now, looking at herself in the mirror, she realized it must have been another seaman, another shooting case who died, because John Worsley, her saviour, was alive in England. He had been all these years. If he had known all that he had given her, he might have been proud: this business, this freedom. Without John Worsley there would be no Mama-Bunny, no *pouliches* and no comfortable apartment above Causeway Bay.

The shooting which had freed her from Macanese Joao for ever had made Nancy her own woman. She had everything to thank John Worsley for.

She left the mirror, after refreshing her make-up, and went to the little room that she kept locked. It stood exactly behind the bar, behind the mirror-glass wall on which the optic bottles hung upended and the glass shelves hung too, with the tumblers, champagne flutes and whisky miniatures, the cocktail cherries, the salted almonds, the Worcestershire Sauce. Seen from this side, from this very private room, that mirror was a window.

She saw the girl, as she had seen her earlier when she came in, but now finishing her second Bloody Mary. Fielding had not joined her. He continued to sit where she had left him.

She locked the hide and went directly to the hostesses' room. A group of half a dozen women were sitting and smoking over a game of cards.

'Lily, the young Englishman alone out there, the one I was talking to. Go and get him in here, to my sitting room, will you, please?'

# 16

When Nancy Lo left through the bead curtain Madeleine saw a woman angry, moving with sudden resolve. What had Fielding told her? She wondered about the connection between this place and Fielding's world of violence and spooking. Was it a safe house, a drop zone? Fielding seemed somehow uncertain, as if he were making contact for the first time. Perhaps this was the start of some new phase in the action against C. P. Cotton. Or maybe it had nothing to do with Cotton. Fielding was probably freelance, Craike had told her. He would work for anyone, anywhere, as long as the fee was right.

She considered her own predicament. Craike would skin her if he knew she had gone into the bar without back-up. She was certainly conspicuous. Playing the tourist who dropped in to slake her thirst had seemed the best ploy, but she could hardly keep it up all night. This was too obviously not that kind of place.

What kind of place it was still puzzled her. She had expected to see couples, however sexually ill-assorted, leaving the bar together. They would go, she thought, either through to the rear or the upstairs of the building, or otherwise to some convenient privacy outside. It hadn't happened. Customers lingered with their professional companions, drinking a lot of whisky, talking long and with emphasis and, as time went on, filling the bar with an energetic hubbub.

Several of the men she saw in tears. One was sobbing uncontrollably, howling like a four-year-old above the noise of the bar, while his hostess dabbed solicitously at his tears with a linen handkerchief. Another cried quietly and morosely, without ostentation, muttering his woes through a mouth distorted by emotion. A third hung weeping around the neck of the hostess. She wore a low-cut dress and his head was sunk in her bosom, the tears trickling down her cleavage.

Then, five minutes after Nancy Lo had left him, one of the hostesses approached Sim's table and bowed low to his ear. He followed her into the rear, pushing through the beads with new assurance so that they swung briskly. Madeleine finished her drink. It was time to go and contact Craike.

Sim was shown upstairs by a smiling, heavily rouged Lily and into a room immediately above the bar's front entrance. This was a large sitting room with gilded furniture, deep-pile rugs and silk-covered walls. Nancy Lo stood at the window, velvet drapes slightly parted, looking into the street.

'Your girlfriend has left, you know. Did you send her away?'

'If you mean the woman at the bar, I don't know who she is.'

'Well, she's very interested in you. I was watching her. You seemed interested too, I thought. For what reason I didn't know, but you both seemed to me to pretend to be apart while actually being together.'

'No. I really don't know her.'

Nancy shrugged.

'Oh well, it doesn't matter, does it?'

She moved to the fireplace and sat in a throne-like chair upholstered in damask. It was the sort which might have been a French antique. She indicated that Sim should sit too. Then she began to tell him about John Worsley.

When she had finished Sim sat for a while without speaking. He knew the old man had been paralysed in the Merchant Navy, but he'd always thought he was hit by a loose block or a falling piece of freight; never that he stepped in front of a crazed barman's bullet.

'He reckoned you were kind to him, Nancy. But he didn't get a chance to know you, did he?'

'He must have been thinking of the times I went to him in the hospital, sat by his bed so long. Three days in succession. I told him my name, I think.'

'That explains it OK. He's never forgotten you, that's for sure.'

'How is he? I mean, did he get well again in the end?'

'Oh, he's in a chair, he's a cripple. But otherwise he's OK. Smokes too much, but he's got a constitution like an ox. Got his own business, a garage. I work for him, in fact.'

It seemed so far away, as if he was describing the life-cycle of the polar bear. Nancy seemed pleased, though. She sat up and smiled, like a person who has confessed and gained a blessing. Then she brought both her hands down on her knees with a light slap.

'So now, Mr Sim Fielding. What is it I can do for you *exactly*? You were sent by the man who saved – well, if not my life, then certainly my nose. If what you want is in my power, I'll give it. Are you really looking for your father?'

'Yes, I am. I think he committed a crime back in England. I think he kidnapped a child. I want to get the child back to his rightful parents.'

'Tell me. I must know a little more about you, I think. About England and you, your papa and Hong Kong, everything. Tell.'

She sat back in her chair languorously to listen, and Sim told.

He finished his story, satisfied Nancy's curiosity for a little more detail, and then Lily was called again.

'Lily, this is Mr Fielding. He's going to be staying with us, room six I think. He will have a key and come and go as he pleases, like any of the other tenants. But he pays no rent, OK? He is my guest.'

She turned to Sim.

'Lily is housekeeper here. She looks after the tenants – we have quite a few in the house. Some of my ladies, and then several others, you know. Now, before you go see your quarters –'

She withdrew a sheaf of new banknotes from her wallet. Lily's eyes widened as she watched her mistress counting out twenty $100 notes.

'That should be enough for you in the next few days. Go on now with Lily, she'll show you up. Come to me if there's anything more you want.'

Sim wasn't quite ready to go.

'There's one thing, Nancy. It's a matter of curiosity more than anything. What *is* the Mama-Bunny? At first I thought it was about sex, but it doesn't seem to fit the theory, at least not from what I've seen.'

Nancy Lo laughed, a tinkling run down half a scale.

'No, it doesn't. And it's not sex we're selling, my friend, it's babyhood. My girls are all mothers. They lend an ear, they soothe, they are so, *so* sympathetic. But these are strictly *short-time* mothers. You got it? They're rented by the hour. Now, off you go.'

She laughed again as Sim went on his way with Lily.

'You did *what*?'

Craike was half-way through his kendo workout when Madeleine found him. The *dojo* was thinly attended so late at night. Only one other pair of fighters were going through the exhausting training routine, their grunts and cries ringing through the high gymnasium as they advanced and retreated, bamboo *shinai* swords clacking together. Craike, sweating profusely under his cloth armour, removed the protective helmet and scowled at Madeleine.

'You let him *see* you? Don't you think that was a little fuckwitted of you?'

Madeleine wished Craike wouldn't be so irascible when his kendo was interrupted. He was scarcely an attractive advertisement for Zen Buddhism, supposedly the philosophical basis for the sport.

'Look, I *am* sorry I had to trouble you, Ed. But don't you think you'd better come with me to the bar? I mean, Fielding's in there, and I'm sure he's our man. This is a perfect opportunity to interview him.'

'Was. He's probably gone now, and you blew the chance to follow him and find out where he's staying.'

'Anyway, you'd like the place, you know. It's full of your kind of people – Japanese.'

'What was the place called?'

'Mama-Bunny.'

'Really, and it's full of Japs is it? Interesting.'

He brought himself up to his full height in front of the kendo master, who had stood politely aside during the exchange. They swapped formal bows. Then Craike started to unstrap the padding which covered his torso and shoulders. He said, 'Right. Give me ten minutes and I'm on my way.'

'Jap men never get over their mothers, poor bastards.'

They had bought tea from an outdoor stall a few yards up from the Mama-Bunny and were watching the door in case

Fielding emerged. Craike had been inside to check the place and came back with the diagnostic confirmation.

'It's a mother-bar all right. Absolute clone of the real thing in the Ginza. Can't see your boyfriend, though.'

Now he was expounding the social significance of the Japanese mother-bars.

'These fellows spend the first six years of their life entirely in female company, swathed in adoration, praised for everything, incapable of doing wrong. Then, suddenly, they get the complete breeze. Chucked into the ball-shrinking cold water of a man's life. Aggression, criticism, backbiting, competition – first it's in school, then college and ultimately, of course, business. It's not surprising they'll pay good money for a bit of recreational regression.'

'You mean that's what this place is for? Regression to childhood?'

He nodded.

'That's it. The name gives it away. There are hundreds of bars like this in Tokyo, always called Mama-something or other. They're like girlie-bars, except these girlies are solid, maternal types. Punters choose one slightly like their own mother – or like their ideal of a mother, maybe. They take her off to a booth with a bottle of Suntory and they're away.'

She laughed and shook her head.

'What do they do? Just talk? No sex?'

'God, no. Certainly no sex. They talk, but it's no trivial thing, I can tell you. It's like those sandbags in Japanese factories painted to resemble the bosses. You bash the sandbag and you're less likely to bash the boss. These ladies get their ears bashed.'

'Haven't the men all got wives?'

'You don't shit on your own doorstep, Maddy. These guys are unloading shit and poison. All the fear and hatred, the anxieties and moral viruses that build up in their lives, things so vile that no one except Mama-san will listen to them. It's got to be fuelled by alcohol, of course, that's why these places are bars. The men are so fucking emotionally repressed it's the only way they can get the poison out.'

'Well, they certainly do that. I think I saw four men crying like babies in there. But this is China, not Japan. What's the Mama-Bunny doing here?'

'Japan is Hong Kong's biggest trading partner these days. The Japs were shits during the war. They beheaded people on the open beach at Stanley to make examples. But all that's been forgotten in the euphoria of mutual profits. There are 10,000 Japs living here now, and whoever thought of starting that place over there is a very clever person indeed.'

'Her name is Nancy Lo.'

'So she's Chinese, is she? She's certainly doing well. Cleaning up, I'd say. That place is absolutely stuffed with Japs, and she can afford to import the girls.'

'Women,' pointed out Madeleine.

'Rent-mothers,' suggested Craike. 'Anyway they're the genuine article, *from* the motherland. And our Nancy has to pay them pretty well, I'd say. It takes a special type to do that sort of work. Selling your body must be easy by comparison.'

Madeleine struck him sharply on the arm.

'Ed! That's a man's point of view. Remember, I worked on vice for two years.'

But he only laughed.

And yet it may even be true, she thought later as she hailed a taxi. They'd given up on thoughts of locating Fielding by now and she was looking forward to a night on her own. Robert was in Bangkok on business.

She smiled, thinking of Robert's long monologues about Jack Blessington, who always put him down at partners' meetings, or 'that promiscuous bitch' Naomi Silvers, who (he claimed) tried unsuccessfully to seduce him at the office Christmas party, and now constantly passed hurtful remarks about his clothing and general appearance whenever they came into contact.

Sometimes Madeleine had to put up with Robert's piteous squawking on these subjects for an entire evening; sometimes she reached screaming point trying to stiffen up his ego. On the other hand, to make him come was the work of a couple of minutes.

Back in the flat, Madeleine poured a glass of wine and pulled the telephone book from the shelf. She dialled the number of the Mama-Bunny.

'Hello? Is that the Mama-Bunny bar? . . . Yes, I'm trying to reach a Mr Fielding. Is he there please? . . . Yes, an Englishman . . . Oh, is this Miss Lo? *Is* he? Well, perhaps you could give him a message? ... Well, I'm the young woman who was sitting at the bar earlier this evening, and I wonder if Mr Fielding could possibly come and meet me ... Tomorrow morning, in the lobby of the Regent Hotel, OK? I'll be there at 11 and I'll give my name in at the desk. Thanks. Thanks very much ... I'm sorry? Oh! My name, yes. It's Mary Playfair. Got that?'

She spelled the name and then put down the phone.

She smiled. *Fuck you, Ed Craike, I've got* him!

## 17

Maurice had waited for the cover of darkness before venturing out. After locking the door firmly on the amah and her charge, he came by a roundabout route to the Star Ferry, chose for security the lower deck, and paid his fare of 60 cents. Like the trams that ply up and down Hennessy Road, these ferries are reversible, and so are their passenger seats. Maurice slammed the hinged seat into the forward position and sat waiting for the short journey to begin.

An old man took the place next to him. He was thin and brittle. His eyes watered and his bones protruded alarmingly, tautly stretching the shined-up, dried-out skin of his face. He wore an utterly incongruous jacket of herringbone tweed with patch pockets and a stitched-in belt around the back: a Norfolk jacket. From the cuffs of his grey trousers, striped pyjamas poked out. From the too-large collar of his shirt reared a mottled tortoise neck. He sat perfectly still alongside Maurice, staring straight ahead, his hands neatly crossed over his fly. Incessantly and tunelessly he hummed to himself.

The older-generation Chinese act like they've mastered all their emotions, all their curiosity and capacity to startle. They seem to possess inner tranquillity and self-absorption, even when they live in the eye of a maelstrom of commercial greed such as Hong Kong. Maurice recognized this quality in the old man and quite admirable it would have been to him, had it not felt so unsettling.

The problem was he couldn't tell if the old guy was interested in him or not. Even if he was following Maurice, or eavesdropping on him, Maurice wouldn't know it from his behaviour. The elderly Chinese wear total emotional camouflage. Their intentions are invisible, their body language is silent.

At the Hong Kong Central pier he sat on for a moment while the old man rose and shuffled across the deck, his legs slightly bent, his feet nudging forward. Maurice rose then and walked quickly past him up the ramp, looking about for more watchers and dangers. Then he began to fumble a path through the crowd.

In spite of the hour, the bus to Aberdeen was full of men and women returning from work. Maurice had flopped into one of the last seats, but passengers continued to pile aboard, ignoring the printed notice in old pidgin which said NO STANDEE.

Maurice was wishing he hadn't come out. He felt he'd not had enough to drink; he lacked fortification and was not sufficiently dulled to the possible attentions of others. And there were so many others: shop girls, students with clipboards, office workers with briefcases, shoppers burdened by their bulging plastic bags. They all seemed to have businesses and lives of their own, but any one of them could in reality be concerned with *his* business.

Surrounded as he was by these unknown quantities, Maurice was quaking. But it was when he saw the old man, the one in the herringbone Norfolk, heave himself up like a novice rock-climber into the bus that he cried out.

The old man, shuffling into the bus now, gave no sign of hearing the cry. It came out like an over-amplified hiccup, which Maurice tried to convert into a cough. Passengers in the immediate area turned to him with impassive faces, noticing him as they might notice a macaque running along the roadside. Maurice wiped his mouth and looked with concentration at his knees.

After a few moments he had to look up again. A seat near the front had been given up for the old fellow. Maurice kept his eyes fixed on the back of the rigid, short-cropped, grey head. In spite of the violently lurching bus, the man maintained his upright posture doggedly, as if following some private discipline.

They passed through the Aberdeen tunnel and drew up at last by the waterfront. Maurice made immediately for the rear door of the bus and jumped to the ground. He took up position under a stone portico which fronted a rare survival, a row of pre-war shops. He watched the passengers come down from the bus.

The last to do so was the old man. Could he know where Maurice was? Impossible. He wasn't following him, then. To celebrate the fact Maurice took a drink from his hip flask of vodka.

He stood on the edge of the quay, looking down at a sampan

bobbing on the water. Its owner, bent low, was doing something to the engine. Maurice knew he could have walked boat to boat until he got to Swann's junk, but he reckoned the sampan would be safer and easier. Fewer people would see him go past. He called down the registration number of the boat he wanted to visit, and where it was. The sampan owner nodded and gestured for Maurice to come down.

Half-way across they motored past another sampan. Looking into it Maurice saw the old man from the Star Ferry and bus perched on the transom. He was not looking towards Maurice. Even on a bobbing, pitching boat he maintained the demeanour of a waxwork – detached, meditating on the foolishness of it all. His pose was precarious but he held it without anxiety.

Maurice asked the sampan boy if he knew the old man.

'I know him,' said the boy. 'A rich old grandad.'

'Rich?' said Maurice. 'He doesn't look rich to me.'

'Can't you see it?' asked the boy. 'But he has the true mark of prosperity.' He spat into the water. 'He hasn't much use for his money. He will die soon. He wants to be with his ancestors and doesn't care for the company that is around here.'

Maurice laughed, and the release of tension felt good. If the old man was rich and about to die, then he had nothing to fear from him.

When they had travelled about 100 yards they came alongside a junk, moored in the middle of a long chain of houseboats which stretched to the shore. The sampan boy turned a rope around a cleat on the transom of the junk. Maurice remembered her all right. She had a peculiarly clean smell about her, as if she'd been recently revarnished. It was here he'd met Swann for the first time, here that he'd received his briefing for the English job, and had the first instalment of his money. He had, of course, been warned that he must never come to this boat again. But what choice had he? He stood up.

There was no one in the cockpit. He started to climb up, but the sampan boy tugged at his jacket, demanding payment. Maurice handed over a $10 note.

'You stay here. Wait for me.'

Then, balancing for a moment on the gunwale of the sampan, Maurice heaved himself up and floundered on to the junk's deck. He stood and called out.

'Swann!'

It was a warm night and much of the neighbourhood was up on-deck, sitting around lanterns, eating, talking. He could hear the multiple clack of mah-jong tiles and the babel of a dozen ghettoblasters and televisions – competing channels, battling tunes.

But from this boat there was darkness and silence. He moved across into the cover of the wheelhouse, which was open on the cockpit side. He hammered on the hatch which led below.

'Swann? Are you there? Swann!'

Somewhere inside the boat his knock had a response, for someone moved. There was a shifting sound. Then, through the forward-looking deckhouse windows he saw the hatch slide open. A wrinkled head appeared. The eyes peered through the low windows of the deckhouse towards him. It was a woman. She called back to him, a cracked, frightened voice using dialect until she saw Maurice's silhouette. Immediately she switched to English.

'You go way here. *Gwailo* gone. Gone dead. Go way here.'

Before he could get in a question she had disappeared again.

Gone? Gone dead? Jesus H. Gone *dead*?

In spite of the hot night he went suddenly cold in the stomach. His balls contracted in sudden fear. He turned and looked down to the water, expecting to see his lifeline, his sampan. It was not there. He cast around, as if for a scent, and saw that the boy had pushed off and was adrift some feet from the junk. He too had heard the woman speak of danger and death. Maurice felt the rising nausea of panic.

'Come back! Come back here!'

But the sampan boy had been paid once, and he knew better than to risk his boat only for the sake of another $10. He shook his head, bent and started his engine. Maurice saw a puff of blue smoke and the sampan going on its way, without him.

He began scrambling to the shore across the bridge of boats. There must have been more than twenty of them, joined gunwale to gunwale. It was his only escape path, but a slow and laborious one, and he travelled it under the mounting stress of his fear. The old woman had been unmistakably warning him off. It meant at any moment there might be gunmen. A flash of flame, a searing pain and then the report in the ears.

Maurice knew something of what it would be like. Maurice had been shot before.

But guns were still a comparative rarity among Hong Kong criminals. So if not gunmen, some guy in the dark with a blade, or a length of picture wire taut between hands, going up and over the head, and drawing in a jerk around the neck. It made a terrible mess, picture wire. It burst through the skin so that blood spurted out as you strangled. Some of these people liked to throttle their victims half-conscious, and then saw the wire back and forth across the gizzard until the windpipe ruptured.

He would have been sick into the sea had he not kept moving.

He had crossed only five boats. If some young Triad killer came after him, or was waiting to meet him, he was dead, like easy meat. The shore appeared so damned toytown-comforting to him. He looked and saw it as a dying man might do: warm lights and pin-small people going about their pin-small lives. Without fear they were, or noticeable excitement; impervious to the drama that made his stomach turn.

His legs ached from the effort of climbing and dropping and climbing again, but he kept on. He dropped into the tenth boat with a loud thud and stood up, panting to get more oxygen into his painful lungs. The cockpit contained nothing but an aluminium folding-chair and, in it, the emaciated figure of a crop-haired ancient, smoking a cigarette through a silver-banded holder. By the low light of an oil lamp Maurice could see the pyjamas which protruded from the cuffs of his grey trousers, and a jacket in some kind of tweed hanging from the back of the chair. The old man looked at Maurice with no surprise, or even curiosity. It was a shrewd look, with just the faintest aura of a smile in the vicinity of the thinned-out lips. The guy was halfway to a husk, but you couldn't miss the amused, detached superiority in his watered eyes.

Maurice stalked across the cockpit. His neck hairs were pricking. He did not look again. He hoisted himself on to the thwart of the next boat, and then the next, and the next. A few minutes later he stood on the quayside, his shoulders heaving like an asthmatic; he could not trap enough breath inside his overtaxed lungs.

Swann was dead.

If this was true – and why wouldn't it be? – he was alone with the kid and its amah. In this city of millions, he was alone with *them*. And what was he to do? What was he to *do* with them? He made his way back to the terminus and found a bus bound for Central getting ready to leave. He ran and leapt. He was the second last to board.

The last to board was Ho Yu Ching, inches behind. He found a seat near the back where he could watch the head of the *gwailo*. Ho was so excited his heart battered the inside of his chest. It had been a vigil, but at last it had paid off. Now Lee Hung would be pleased. He remembered Lee Hung's instructions so well. *Watch the boat. Anyone comes, follow them, find where I can find them.* Yes, Lee Hung would give such an excellent present to Ho, if only he did not lose the *gwailo* in the crowd. If only he could find out where the *gwailo* was staying. He must remain vigilant and agile in pursuit and, then, what a payday! He wrapped his arms round himself and squeezed. *What a payday!*

'Kidnapped, Mr Cotton?'

'C.P. I told ya to call me C.P., Craike.'

Cotton was staring out of the floor-to-ceiling plate-glass window into the depth of the Hong Kong night. The cordless phone was cinched by an upraised shoulder against his ear.

'Anyway, yeah, that's what I believe. Kidnapped. My grandson.'

'Do the police know?'

Craike's voice, though flattened by the telephone compression, sounded sceptical.

'Cops think the child's dead – died in the fire with his mother. Mother's dead right enough, but I know the kid didn't fry. They didn't find a body. Said the fire burned so hot he disappeared in the ashes, which I don't believe.'

'Was your daughter-in-law murdered deliberately?'

'Can't say, wasn't there.'

'Has any one or any group approached you with claims or demands?'

'No.'

'And you think the fire wasn't accidental?'

'Doesn't look that way to me.'

'Why not? It's a pretty big thing, to burn a house deliberately, kill your daughter-in-law and take a child, all to put pressure on you, Mr Cotton.'

Cotton leaned forward to rest his forehead against the cool glass, his lips jutting at full stretch.

'Hey. You're making like you don't believe me, Craike.'

'I'm only saying, if no one's been in contact, you don't have any evidence that the child's been snatched. Maybe he *is* dead.'

'Maybe the Pope's a Jew. I'm a big guy, Craike. Things like this happen to big guys. Heard of the Kennedys, the Gettys? The people who took him are here in Hong Kong. Your job's gonna be to find them. Call me when you got something.'

He disconnected and strode to the desk, pressing his person-to-person console.

'Have Pappingay haul his ass in here right away. And I want the chopper standing by to take me home.'

He went back to the window. From the highest floor of the Cotton Building, the diamonds-on-velvet night view of the colony usually soothed him, but not tonight. Tonight C. P. Cotton felt a stirring of emotions that were strange to him. His whole life had been a carefully balanced structure of always getting his cheese, but now for the first time he wondered if the edifice were teetering. His nerve wasn't in question. He could take heat. But he felt the recurrent impotence of a great schemer, bound by the limits of his own design. Leonardo, maybe. The Wright Brothers. It riled him so, being in the hands of others – bankers, bishops and now some crum-ass English jerk-off standing between him and what he wanted.

*They* were out there, and he could do nothing. What in Christ's name was Craike up to? He didn't need to be Sherlock Holmes on this; it was a cinch, wasn't it? Find Fielding, get the kid, bingo! A mortal lock. So what was taking him so long?

'You wanted me, Publisher?'

Cotton swung around. Pappingay stood in the doorway, his weight on his forward foot like an athlete waiting for the gun. Cotton turned back to the window and growled.

'Is Lee Hung in the building?'

'Yes, Publisher, he's right outside.'

'Before you go get him, something I been meaning to raise with you, Pappingay. This "Publisher" garbage. You been calling me Publisher ever since you fuckin' came on board here.

Where d'ya get the idea for that? That some pinky-crooking East Coast business-school talk?'

'No, sir, it was your own idea, sir.'

Cotton faced his assistant again. He moved towards him, brought their faces close together. He sniffed. His eyes strained like boils, the wings of his nose flared and contracted in suspicion.

'You dicking me around, Pappingay?'

'No, Pub – Mr Cotton. You directed that I call you by that title, don't you recall?'

'Recall? I recall jack-shit.'

'It was in my letter of appointment, I think. You were referred to as the Publisher, so I figured –'

Cotton raised a finger in menace.

'Now see here, Pappingay. You call me by that faggoty name again, so help me, I'll fire your ass from here to Shitkicker, Ohio. I don't like it, OK? Now get that snoop in here, willya?'

Lee Hung took off his glasses and polished them.

'From our observation of Mr Craike, he seems to be doing comparatively little, Mr Cotton. He has been very interested tonight in a club or bar, the Mama-Bunny, in Wanchai. It's a Japanese bar.'

'Japanese?'

'He was there with his assistant, Miss Madeleine Scott. They stood outside and drank tea. They talked a lot, stayed an hour, then they went away. The club is owned by a former prostitute, name of Nancy Lo. She was once a singer in Wanchai, a long time ago. Later she went to Tokyo. When she came back she started this bar, and it seems very successfully.'

'What kind of inquiries has Craike been making?'

Lee Hung shrugged.

'I haven't used a bug. But he has met one British official twice in the last week, a man called Vanteel. He stays at the Park Hotel, that's a businessman hotel Kowloonside, also plenty of Australian tourists stay there. I put this in my reports. I tried to check this guy Vanteel out but I got nothing much. He recently came from London and he goes back in the next few days.'

'Vanteel? I never heard of him. It may be nothing, but I'll keep it in mind. Now listen up, I got a new job for you. Forget about Craike for the moment. He ain't up to snuff as far as I can see. What I did want from him, I now want from you – to locate this man.'

He unlocked a drawer in his desk, picked out a file and selected from it a photograph of Maurice Fielding. It was a fairly recent shot, Maurice leaving a Tsimshatsui gambling club. His hand was inside his coat, placing something in the pocket, or taking something out. The eyes were careful, almost furtive. You couldn't tell from them if he had won or lost.

Lee Hung put on his glasses and studied the picture.

'Yes, I know him. This is Fielding, Maurice Fielding.'

He looked up and smiled. Cotton too was suddenly very happy.

'Exactly right, it is Fielding. You're good, Lee Hung, I'll say that. What do you know about him?'

'Fielding is a small-time crook. He was sometimes used by the British secret service as an errand boy, until four, five years ago. Then he got shot, probably by PRC gangsters running drugs in from the mainland. After that he was in the newspapers and therefore he wasn't useful to the British for a while. Since then I don't know what he's doing.'

'Well, I'll clue you in. He's been to England and he's come back with something I want. I don't know exactly where he is. I do know he's somewhere in the Territory, probably in town. Think you can find him?'

Lee Hung shrugged.

'Eventually, sure. No problem, Mr Cotton.'

He didn't ask what it was that Cotton wanted. Lee Hung knew better than to ask questions. Curiosity is a dilution of face.

'Then do it,' said Cotton. 'Do nothing else. Tell me where the schmuck's living, that's all.'

All the servants in C. P. Cotton's house, where he now went by helicopter, were male: a French chef, a couple of houseboys and a Japanese butler to boss the place. Occasionally, there was a firm of psychiatric nursing contractors which sent in a male attendant during daylight hours, to care for his son through his periodic breakdowns. The staff reckoned they could cope with him at such times in the hours of darkness, which Chuck largely spent drugged and sleeping.

C. P. Cotton was proud of the fact that his household had no women. None of his marriages had lasted more than eighteen months, and he was thankful he'd never sired a daughter. In recent years women had become loathsome to him – not necessarily in their bodies, for he wasn't queer, but in their minds, in the attitudes they struck. He could not even think the word 'feminism' without his bile rising. This was why he had come to the Orient in the first place, hoping to get shot of that. But now, goddamn it, the thing was spreading here too, like a vile plague infecting them all – even though they didn't know it, even when they tried to fight it.

Elizabeth, his daughter-in-law, had not even tried to do that. She was the worst type, a mushhead Chinese lawyer, with a mouth he could get pissed with after fifteen seconds. *Women have the right to their own bodies, C.P. We women are tired of this media mind-rape. The female nation is on the march, so don't stand in the way or you'll be crushed.*

In fact, he did all he could to steer clear of organized womanhood, but tele-evangelism must sometimes suck the money-tits of the female nation, and Cotton, in the fund-raising cause, had to do some light apple-polishing with wealthy widows occasionally. Also, from time to time, he'd obey the tug of his dick and have sex with a woman. But live with one? He couldn't.

There'd always been zip-all chance he could live with Chuck's wife. The thought of her alive and yapping her slogans could bring him out in a sweat. The thought of her dead was what calmed him. Chuck was safe from her now. And Josh was safe.

Tonight C. P. Cotton came home late. He took off his coat and hung it on the breakfast-room chair. Wandering into his study, he found the two houseboys sweeping up fragments of glass and china. They looked up at him, their faces aghast, as if caught out in a crime. Cotton wearily scanned the room. It had been trashed again – pictures askew, books pulled from the shelves and kicked about the place, a vase hurled to the floor. Cotton grunted,

'This happen tonight?'

The houseboys, kneeling to their work, looked like supplicants.

'Where is he? In his room?'

They nodded in synchrony. Cotton found Chuck on his bed

listening to his music, wearing headphones, his body jerking with light spasms.

Cotton sat alongside his son and put a hand on the crown of his shoulder. Chuck had not acknowledged his father's coming in, and now he showed no sign that he felt the caress. Cotton was suddenly tender towards Chuck. He drew his hand down along the upper arm, feeling the boy's strong muscle, grown hard by fanatical work-outs in the gymnasium which Cotton had specially built for him. He always thought of Chuck as a boy, though in years he was a man of thirty. Yet boy was right, for he was a man who couldn't *be* a man, a boy trapped in a man's body. This was why he broke furniture and wrecked rooms. Goddamn frustration.

Chuck had not always been this way. As a teenager he was difficult, moody, but what teenager isn't? The first breakdown – *fit* his father called it – had come around his eighteenth birthday, after his mother killed herself. The bitch. That had started it. Chuck had lengthy good periods after that. He even went off to study law at a smart East Coast college, where he discovered cocaine at some point and C.P., noticing that this seemed to stabilize him, tried to ensure that his son got only the best pharmaceutical grade.

In his mid-twenties Chuck had met Elizabeth Yip, who convinced everyone she could make their marriage into an idyll. The *arrogance* of that ball-buster. Chuck was strong and handsome and she met him on heat. She had no idea of what his real nature was like. Cotton had pleaded with her to leave him be. He might as well have tried to talk down a typhoon.

They married and she conceived. For a while Chuck stopped taking his dope but the birth of young Josh released all hell. Chuck was suddenly insanely jealous of Elizabeth, accused her of having affairs, which maybe she was. Cotton wouldn't have put it past the woman. Chuck started smashing the place up, raved, he bit a hunk of flesh out of his own arm once. Or he would sit on the carpet with his chin on his knees staring at nothing, hour by hour. She laughed about it at first. Then she tried to kid him out of it, but he only went back on coke. Elizabeth had told him she would leave him if ever he did that – which was the reason his father had got it for him.

And, thank God, she did quit. But Cotton left the kid out of his calculations, even his own feelings about the boy. When Elizabeth took baby Josh to England, Cotton learned what he felt – a kind of raw, bloody feeling, as if some part of himself had been physically torn loose. But he never figured out his son's feelings about his losing the boy. He *seemed* to mourn only for Elizabeth.

He went on stroking his son's strong arm. The music in the headset rustled and rattled, like locusts stripping a distant cornfield.

After his father had left him, Chuck removed his headphones and laid them carefully on the bedside table beside the pictures of his mother, son and wife. He smiled. Dad felt sorry for him, thought he was crazy. Good. Chuck did everything to encourage that idea.

It meant freedom, of a kind. He could break things any time he wanted and his coke habit was tolerated, in a way it had never been when Elizabeth was with them. He drummed his knee with his fingers. He could do with a toot right now. The randomness of his emotions told him it was time, and the dragging tiredness in his head. Chuck had never cried so much as after he'd gotten the coke habit – that is, when he couldn't get the stuff. After he'd taken it he felt a refreshment of his feelings that was like nothing on earth. The only thing that surpassed it in his entire life had been the night he first made love to Elizabeth on the yacht. They bathed naked in the early morning, and then fucked on the breakfast table like a pair of polecats.

He took out his slim 24-carat snorting tube and examined it. He tried an experimental sniff in case there was some residual white dust clinging to the inside. He felt nothing. He got up and flipped open the Georgian silver sugar-basin that contained his supply. It was empty. That goddamn butler had forgotten again; he was supposed to get it refilled *every* Monday morning.

He rose and picked up his house keys. He went through to the breakfast room, where his father nearly always hung his jacket on a chair. As usual the wallet was stuffed with cash and Chuck helped himself to a few thousand. He left the apartment quietly.

The night-club had a stripper who thought she was Marcel Marceau. She did her act to weird electronic music, sibilant hoots, sandstorm winds, metallic clanks. At the moment she was acting a slave caught and tied in a cage. She held her arms stiffly behind her back, wrists clamped together, and writhed her shoulders and hips. Her mouth came open sexily and she mimed her bondage, throwing herself back and bouncing off unseen bars, her tits lifting fetchingly with each imaginary impact.

Chuck had to admit she was good, but the business in hand was more pressing and he turned back to face the two guys who sat across the table from him. Their names were Adam and Michael. He had met them at a party, where they had given him business cards and informed him they always had fresh supplies of the best Colombian nose-candy in town.

Customers at neighbouring tables – if they were regulars – would know the one in glasses. His name was Michael and he ran the dive. If they were a hair more in-crowd, they would recognize Adam, too. He was Michael's brother and looked after the stud-poker game that was staged most nights in a remote back room. Adam held the bank, dealt the cards and called the variations – five-card, seven-card, roll-em, anaconda. People who joined the game liked to keep the right side of Adam. Crossing him could be expensive; pleasing him meant you could sometimes get him to call your favourite variety of stud.

The pair were said to be the adopted sons of some Triad big shot.

On this particular night, a sufficiently interested observer might have seen the three men huddled in intense conversation. If he were sharp-eyed, he might notice something sliding across the table from the Chinese boys to the American under a cupped palm as the conspiratorial conversation continued. Then, suddenly, the Yank clubbed the tabletop with a fist and raised his voice to make it just audible above the music.

'He's *dead*, Mister!'

And the two young Chinese men were smiling as they shook their heads and begged to differ.

# 18

As he swung out through the revolving doors of his apartment block Craike saw an empty taxi loitering in the road. He pounced on it like an early blackbird yanking a worm from the lawn.

'Harbour Police Station,' he said.

He was conveyed through the tense, frustrated crawl of early morning traffic to a government office somewhere west of Central. The Harbour Police superintendent, who yesterday had agreed to see him, was opening his morning mail. His name was Dunsop.

Dunsop was young for the job. He was sharp-eyed and wary, though he pretended, at this early hour, to be some way short of peak efficiency.

'God, it's too early, Ed. I don't normally see anybody till 10. Can't you go away like a good chap, get yourself a coffee and croissant, and come back in an hour?'

This was normal office role-playing: to be one of the lads you must not be a machine. You have to start the day with a hangover, very black coffee and a tab of soluble paracetamol. Craike took no notice of what had just been said.

'Have you got the name I asked for? I called in yesterday. Here's a photocopy of the request I put in.'

He pushed a sheet of A4 across Dunsop's fantastically tidy desk. Dunsop looked at it and placed it in a file which lay ready on his blotter. He must have pulled the file as soon as they told him Craike was coming in.

'Yes, no problem about getting the information, Ed. But I'll need you to tell me *why* you want to know.'

The 'Ed' was an irritant. True, they had met once or twice socially, but back in Craike's old job in London these blokes had jumped to attention when Major Craike showed up.

'I think a man may have been killed on this boat, that's why.'

'And you've reported this?'

'I said, I *think*. I don't report theories; I try and prove them first. I mentioned it to your muckers in CID, and they say they've not tripped over any bodies. That doesn't mean there wasn't a killing, though, does it? It just indicates that nobody else has an inkling of it except me – and the people who did it, of course.'

Craike had thought of mentioning Madeleine, but it seemed more judicious all round to keep her out of this. Dunsop filled his lungs long and luxuriously through the nose and held the air in for a moment. Then he inclined his body slightly on his chair and thoughtfully let the air slip out again, as if he were easing a fart. When he considered he'd made his visitor wait long enough he said, 'Well, I'm sorry. I can't release information from police records on the basis of an unsubstantiated theory. You'll have to give me something or other of substance.'

Craike smiled, without humour.

'Look, Dunsop, let's get back to the basics. This boat in Aberdeen may have been used as a control centre, a safe house, or a relay station. We don't know.'

He didn't elaborate on the collective pronoun. He wanted to keep Dunsop guessing.

'The point is, it played a part in an operation which we believe was initiated by the PRC intelligence services and aimed at a prominent Hong Kong resident. This isn't simply a matter of Hong Kong jurisdiction. Crimes were committed in Britain as well as here. I'm trying to establish the truth, and you're obstructing me.'

Dunsop let out a monosyllabic laugh.

'I'm the policeman, Craike. I can't obstruct *you*. Who are you working for?'

'I don't have to tell you that.'

'You do, unless you're in government service, which I think you are not. Not directly, anyway. You *could* be in the pay of the PRC yourself, for all I know. Or the Japs, the CIA, the Sandinistas and Fred Karno's Army.'

'Well, OK, you got me. I'm a general in Fred Karno's.'

Dunsop smiled with a little more warmth.

'If I'm going to give you the information you want I have to have some very compelling reason. Oh, come on, Craike, who is it you're working for really? Tell, and I'll tell.'

An American would have been incredulous. Over there information like this would have been on a public register. But British secrecy has to be experienced to be believed. Under British law, to impart the brand of toilet paper used in Downing Street is a chargeable offence. Craike decided to move to his next position.

'Well, OK, if I must. It's Vanteel, Ministry of Defence. He's in Hong Kong at the moment, staying at the Park Hotel, Kowloon. Would you care to call him and check?'

'Vanteel, is it? From London? Well, why didn't you *tell* me, Craike? No, I expect there'll be no need to check directly, but if you'll be good enough to give me just a few moments to myself, I think I may have some good news for you later.'

As Craike withdrew from the office, Dunsop was reaching for the telephone.

In the outer office Craike sat down on a plastic moulded chair opposite a young secretary. She was working with concentration at her desk-top computer, a pencil gripped in her mouth like a horse's bit. Her teeth were bared around the pencil, and they were startlingly white. Her hands, the nails painted carmine, scuttered feverishly over the keyboard and, upon making a typing mistake, she gave a little cry, allowing the pencil to fall. It bounced off the keyboard and, before she could stop it, dropped and rolled up to Craike's shoe. Retrieving it, he noticed the deep bite marks made in the wood by her flawless molars. Working for Dunsop was not a breeze.

As he handed the pencil back to her, he picked up Dunsop's voice from the other side of the door. 'Yes, I know he's a freelance, but sometimes they can be damned helpful. OK, OK, I'll make that clear.'

Seconds later Dunsop was at the door, sweeping past Craike and the secretary imperiously and without a word. Craike exchanged a smile with the woman.

'Bit of a young tearaway, isn't he?'

She ducked her head in a momentary, silent, cowed giggle.

Dunsop returned a few minutes later with a length of computer print-out rustling in his hand.

'Come back in, would you?'

Craike followed sullenly. He hated this role: the applicant, the one who waited. Dunsop studied the faint, dot-matrix print in the window's sunlight.

'Right, this is it. The boat in question's owner is an interesting gentleman. He's got just a few fishing boats, a couple of junks and three or four sampans. But he's not really a fisherman, he's something a bit more surprising.'

'What is he?'

'He's a security consultant, Craike. A private dick, like yourself.'

Dunsop had calculated the *dick* nicely. Its tone fell a millimetre short of being offensive.

'What's his name, Dunsop?'

Dunsop held up a hand. He was enjoying himself too much to be hurried.

'What d'you think he is, Craike? Brit or Yank or Jap? Round- or slit-eye?'

'What's the *name*?'

'All right, the name's Lee Hung. Mean anything?'

'If it did, I wouldn't share it with you. What's his company?'

'The Perfectly Secure Company, it says here. The address is in Jardine's Bazaar. Oh! Are you going? Is that all you wanted to know?'

'Yes, that's all, Dunsop. A lead, nothing more.'

Smiling thinly, Craike had got up to leave. He made no effort to thank Dunsop, who was clearly a prat. Craike had a tendency to wear his abrasiveness like a badge. It was enough to prevent him getting rich out here. His enemies were already far too numerous for the effect to be reversible if he were suddenly to discover politeness, however.

'Ed, I must warn you to use this information discreetly, and not to divulge its source.'

He sounded like he was reading from a card.

'Right, Dunsop. I will, and I won't. Bye.'

Dunsop was typical of the middle echelons among whom Craike found it particularly hard to kiss ass. He knew it was a career blunder. In Hong Kong, from now until 1997, these middle ranks would count for most. The head honchos were gone, or making their plans. The ones at the bottom of the shitheap would still be at the bottom for ever. The middle-weight jobsworth was the main man now. He was the element of continuity. Stodgy and uninspired though he was, he had temporarily inherited the Fragrant Harbour.

'May I know just a little more?' asked Dunsop. His tone had become a tad plaintive. 'Who is this, er, prominent resident?'

With some enjoyment, Craike quashed the appeal.

'Sorry, Dunsop, you're probably not cleared to know.'

Dunsop's mouth turned down, sulkily.

'Well, screw *you*,' he said.

The public areas of the Regent Hotel are like a marble airport concourse without the mass anxiety. The hotel is the territory's newest luxury model, sited on concrete piers driven into the water on the very tip of Kowloon. The lobby is also a vast bar and coffee shop, patrolled by gliding waiters.

Madeleine wondered how she should act towards Fielding when he arrived. He was a criminal and, in spite of appearances, dangerous. He had killed, whether deliberately or not she didn't know. But a child and his mother had been two of the victims. That was horrible. She would like to turn him in, but she knew what Craike would say. The man was a small fish with useful information about a bunch of sharks and piranhas. He *might* be allowed to trade this for his freedom – that was the sort of pond they all swam in.

'Are you Mary Playfair?'

She swivelled round. She was miffed at having let Fielding come up on her blind side.

'Oh! Yes, I – I am. I'm Mary Playfair.'

Madeleine, a bad liar, did not sound as if she believed this herself. She had been caught way off balance.

'Hi. I'm Sim Fielding. Shall I sit here?'

As Sim took the seat a waiter materialized.

'You want something to drink, Mary?'

Now here was a poser. Accept a drink from a murderer or insist on buying *him* one? She allowed her usual practice to prevail.

'No, I'm getting these. What do you want?'

'A beer, please.'

He knew exactly what he wanted and this was the first surprise: he was so composed. He even seemed amused by Madeleine. Ordering his beer, and a coffee for herself, she was unable to think of a line with which to start the conversation. It was Sim Fielding who supplied one.

'Tell me. You're not really called that?'

'What?'

'Mary Playfair. That's a fictional name, right? From a nursery rhyme, or something?'

'No, no. Of course not. It's a real name.'

'But is it *your* real name?'

She hesitated, and then owned up.

'Well no, it's not my real name.'

'Then whose name is it?'

'I don't know. Somebody's probably. Does it matter?'

'No. I like it. Can I go on calling you that?'

His smile was very good. Warm and confident. Sexy, it might have been, in another context. She didn't answer his last question. She was wondering how to get to the point. He took the decision out of her hands.

'So you saw me in the Mama-Bunny?'

'Yes, I did.'

'Funny type of place.'

'Isn't it?'

'Apparently Japanese men have this need every now and then to hire the services of surrogate mothers.'

'Yes, I know. By the hour.'

'At first I thought it was something else.'

'I know.'

'How?'

'I'm sorry?'

'How do you know I thought it was something else?'

'Well, I did too. At first.'

'You mean, sex?'

'Yes. I thought it was some kind of kinky young guys going for older women thing. A specialist club.'

'Well, it is a specialist club.'

There was a silence. Both of them were waiting for the other to broach the topic on each of their minds. The drinks arrived: espresso, San Miguel. They each looked into their drinks. They sipped. It was he who cracked first.

'So why did you ask me to come here?'

She took a deep breath and looked around. There were people everywhere, she was quite safe. He could hardly murder her here.

'I know about you. I know what you're doing, what you've done. I work for a –'

*A what? How best to put this?*

'A *detective* agency.'

He looked at her in amazement, his glass suspended half-way between beermat and mouth.

'Are you serious? You're a private detective?'

She nodded.

His eyes were marvellous, wide and fascinated. She had to suppress an impulse to touch him. What was the matter with her? Was it the fatal attraction of the criminal psychopath – Dr Crippen, Nevile Heath, Charles Manson? She shuddered.

She expected him to jump up now, to leap from the trap he must, surely, suspect had been laid for him. He *must* take himself off, and she wished to God he would. Craike would be bloody furious with her but it couldn't be helped. All she wanted was to be shot of this smiling charm-bag. She felt hot and oppressed, although the room was well cooled by air-conditioning.

Fielding's actual response demolished her expectation.

'Well, look, if you're part of a detective agency you might be very useful to me.'

'I'm sorry?'

'I'm trying to reach my old man. I know he's somewhere in Hong Kong, but I haven't got an address. Maybe with your expertise you can help me track him down.'

She groped for her coffee in a fog of confusion.

'Your old man?'

'Yes, my father.'

Madeleine shook her head.

'I don't understand this.'

'I'll explain it, shall I, Mary Playfair?'

He was smiling at her expectantly, with his mouth and his eyes. He looked like a terrier awaiting the thrown stick.

'Yes, please. Explain.'

'OK. I've just come from England searching for him, OK? His name's Maurice Fielding. He left me and my mum when I was a kid. He came out here. He's completely bent, by the way, been mixed up in something pretty bad. I can't tell you about that, not just yet anyhow. But I really do need to find the bastard, and if you really are some kind of private detective, perhaps you could help. You know, point me in the right direction at least – if you haven't got too many cases on. I don't actually have any money, but I reckon I could arrange for someone to pay your fee.'

Suddenly and without warning the mists cleared. Madeleine flopped back into her deep chair and found herself laughing.

Sim Fielding's features slackened a little.

'Why are you laughing, Mary Playfair?'

'Because, oh –'

Madeleine wiped her eyes with the back of her hand. She sniffed her face straight.

'Because, Sim Fielding, we both happen to want the same thing.'

'What do you mean?'

'Well, I didn't know it till now, but both of us want to find your father. And together we might do it.'

'Craike, you've been a big goddamn let-down to me.'

Craike was surprised to be seeing C. P. Cotton so soon after phoning for the appointment. Furthermore, when Pappingay came down to the lobby to get him, there was no nonsense about putting on a tie or waiting around. He was shown straight in to the black marble office, to find Cotton looking up at him from his telephone conference.

'Siddown. I *may* tear your face off.'

He returned to the phone.

'Like I said, there must be some other way to do this, Copperfield.'

Craike didn't sit; he prowled. Over by the far wall was a Perspex model mounted on a steel support – a quarter-scale satellite for Operation Pentecost, one of the four Evangelists. Someone was getting very steamed up about this – the Chinese, maybe. If they didn't like the idea of Cotton beaming Christianity and game shows – his favourite formula mix – into every home in the PRC, then they really might think of killing him, or at least of frightening him off.

Craike touched the model and found that it rotated. He made it spin round slowly on its axis, smiling. But for Cotton, there were one or two problems, weren't there? Money, for example.

'OK, Copperfield, why not issue some stock, call in some

debts? . . . Whaddya mean by that? Look, people owe me money way round the world, don't they? What about the Ethiopian government? Well, screw the drought. I want the money. We got a research programme to pay for. Now, Craike, you lousy jerk-off, I paid you ten grand and you been doing diddly shit, right?'

He had slammed down the receiver and switched subjects without a pause. The guy's neurones must be wired along some highly unusual pathways. Craike returned to the desk and sat down.

'Well, no, I've been pretty busy, Mr Cotton, I –'

Craike had expected to make a report. Instead he found himself on the defensive. He hesitated and Cotton jumped back in.

'Busy? Sure you've been busy. But doing what? I could even be ahead of you, and I ain't paying myself ten grand. First off, I know there's a guy called Fielding mixed up in this. Second, I know Swann is dead. Third, I know you're doing the tango with some creep called Vanteel from London.'

His mouth worked behind shut lips.

'And I got *none* of this news from you. So, open it up, *if* you can. I figured you for some brains, Craike.'

Miyamoto Musashi, in the Bible of kendo strategy, describes two ways of dealing with a sudden ferocious attack: launch a counter immediately and with equal ferocity, or feign weakness. In the latter strategy, says Musashi, you will see the enemy relax; *that* is when you let him have it.

Craike looked at his fingernails and said nothing. Froth was beginning to form on Cotton's lips.

'I shoulda known better'n to trust your ass, Craike. Our contract is cancelled. Get the fuck outa here.'

He was bluffing, Craike was sure. He must want to know why the cottage was torched, why his daughter-in-law and grandson died. Craike stood up and buttoned his jacket.

'Mr Cotton, I knew about Fielding, and I came here today to tell you about him. As for the death of Swann, I didn't inform you straight away because first I wanted to be sure who killed him. It may, in fact, have been Fielding himself, and he may be getting ready to kill you. I have a line on Fielding and soon hope to be getting close to him. Then we will know what happened.'

He moved up a gear, stiffening his posture.

'I'm very angry that you put another investigating team on *my* tail, Mr Cotton. You say you shouldn't have trusted me, but of course you didn't, did you? I really don't like not being trusted. You must appreciate how dangerous these times are for you personally and we all partake in this danger to a greater or lesser extent. We can't have rival teams working against each other. *Have* you employed another firm?'

'Sure as heck I have, because –'

'What is its name, Mr Cotton?'

'I won't tell you that, damn you.'

'Do you want me to continue to act for you in this or do you not?'

Cotton suddenly became reflective and emollient.

'Well, you got to get me some results, you know. You said you'd be a contact between me and Swann, if I remember aright.'

He spread his hands, suddenly the reasonable man.

'Now Swann's dead and we're no further on.'

'But we are. We've got the name Fielding. I believe I've found him. Just let me finish the job, Mr Cotton.'

Cotton sighed and pressed his intercom.

'Mr Craike's leaving. Draw a check for ten grand right away. OK, Craike, one more ten grand, one more week, before I fire your ass.'

'Can I meet the other team, the guys who told you about Swann, Fielding and Vanteel?'

Cotton shook his head and wafted the air with his hand.

'Sorry, Craike. Now, goodbye. I got to call the Pope.'

Standing beside the lifts with Jonathan Pappingay, Craike said quietly, 'How would you like to see your boss behind bars?'

Pappingay looked at him, alarmed. He glanced around but there was nobody near them, nobody to hear. Craike offered further reassurance.

'No danger to you, Pappingay, *if* you know how and when to take the right action.'

He studied the young secretary's face. He'd judged him correctly: Pappingay was tempted. He hated C. P. Cotton to a depth which, if plumbed, could be of considerable use.

Craike said, 'Meet me at 6 p.m., the Tiger Bar, d'Aguilar Street. I'll tell you how.'

Pappingay stood there, mildly stunned, wondering if he dare. Then the lift came.

## 19

The Tiger Bar was beginning to fill up with shoppers and office workers who had all finished their busy days and were in acute need of alcohol. Most were expatriates and young.

They stood or sat in occupational groups, chewing over the day's work that was behind them. Bankers told of dodgy positions and fast-footwork in the bond market. Brokers spoke of call and put, Dow-Jones and Footsie. Solicitors swapped tales of the Bangkok property market, barristers of the ignorance of the bench, computer programmers of viruses and logic traps. Shippers considered reflagging or the defeat of piracy in the Gulf of Tonkin. Shoppers compared bargains and regretted those they had turned down.

Ed Craike settled himself early, at a relatively quiet booth in the corner. He watched the door as best he could through the crush, sipping occasionally at an indifferent vatted malt and thinking about the problem of Madeleine. Where was she? She'd said something yesterday about an appointment this morning – the dentist, was it? Or hair? Anyway, she'd not appeared in the office since, and he was hoping she'd make some progress on the Morrison case, just for a change.

Madeleine was a puzzle. She went off and did crazy things, like chasing Fielding into that bar last night, and yet sometimes she seemed to have only half her mind on the job. She certainly had good contacts around town, especially in the police, and finding Fielding was a real coup. And yet, Craike suspected, she was more of a liability than an asset, and if he ever discovered the underlying ground for this suspicion he'd have to sack her. Pity. A nice girl, in her way.

Only a few minutes after 6.00 Pappingay was there, swivelling on his heels inside the door to locate Craike. Doing so, he looked across without smiling, his face showing only a grim nervousness, shading into fear. Craike thought, if he's *this* afraid of C. P.

Cotton, his loathing must be phenomenal, or he wouldn't be here at all.

Pappingay pushed his way to the bar, ordered and came over with a large vodka and tonic. Craike held up his own empty glass and said, 'Thanks, Pappingay, I'll have a Glenfiddich this time.'

Without a word Pappingay made the return journey to the bar.

'Now,' said Craike, when they were both seated. 'What do you know about your boss's activities?'

But Pappingay was sipping. He held up his free hand while he lowered the glass.

'Now hold it just a minute, Mr Craike. Maybe you'll tell me what it is you want, and what *exactly* is in it for me.'

'What do I want? Well, the embarrassment of Mr C. P. Cotton, Pappingay, that's what I want primarily. There are some subsidiary matters, but that is the principal one. As to what's in it for you – well, revenge is pretty sweet, isn't it?'

'Revenge? Why should I –'

'Cotton treats you like dirt, that's why. He treats everybody like dirt, of course. He probably treats the Pope like dirt. But the Pope's on an outside track compared to you, Pappingay. You know what's going on in the Cotton Corporation. You can spill a whole mountain range of beans, I'm sure.'

'Yeah, and put myself out of a job.'

Craike tried a shot in the dark.

'Well, consider this. Suppose Cotton is ever convicted of crimes, and his company is dragged in. You'd be dragged in, then, wouldn't you? Cotton is clever enough to spread his dirty work around. I mean, how many of his dodgy business arrangements are channelled through the private office, through you? You're an accessory, Pappingay. You can save your skin only by telling what you know, before the toothpaste tube splits and squirts all over your hand.'

Pappingay gazed at the slice of lemon floating in his drink. Then he looked up with a rueful smile.

'You're government, right?'

Craike's eyes, looking into the American's, were still as stones.

'Shit, man. I thought you were a civilian. How come you're involved in this?'

'It's thanks to the vision of our late great leader, Pappingay.

We can't see a public service without shoving it out to tender, and now the practice has spread to the *secret* service. In fact, they've had no choice. The staff's so pared down they have to use freelance idiots like me or lose precious ground to *your* people, or even, God forbid, the French. It's the donkeywork mostly.'

Pappingay leaned back in his seat for the first time since he'd joined Craike. He still looked scared, but he'd reached a decision.

'I'll give you what I can, but I want an assurance.'

'Which is?'

'You warn me before the toothpaste bursts.'

'OK. Fair enough. First, I want to know about Operation Pentecost. It's in trouble, isn't it?'

'Pentecost? It's been in the shit since the start. Nobody takes the idea of the Jesus probe in any way seriously. Cotton's really pissed about that. He thought of it as a great marketing and PR tool to bring investors flooding in. It's had the opposite effect. The bankers said from day one that they would only consider financing the TV sats. They didn't want to know about that space-probe.'

'Does it matter? It's in the satellites that Cotton's going to get his profit, isn't it?'

'Sure, but Cotton's going into it all wrong. Of course, he won't listen. He wants to put up the China transponder first. He makes a lot of noise about taking Jesus to the Commies, but it's a lot more complicated than that.'

'Like persuading the Commies to let their people have receiving dishes.'

'Right! You can't do that. That was the original flaw, and it will probably wreck the whole scheme. With no dishes, there would be no viewers. Over in China personal television *sets* are still high-profile property. Private dishes are completely unknown, and the government can keep it that way as long as the present political system continues.'

'So how do you plan to get around it?'

'Cotton's got hold of some Japanese invention that could enable satellites to disseminate their signal in some new way. It might then be picked up with a conventional aerial, or if not, then by some easily home-made receiving gear. Don't ask me how it works. In fact, so far I don't believe it does. Cotton's pumping millions of dollars he hasn't got into financing the research and it's going nowhere. The PRC must think it's a goddamn joke.'

'OK. Well, this leads on to the other thing: the PRC. Have they any motive to pressure Cotton? By killing members of his family, for instance?'

Pappingay shrugged.

'You mean the fire in England? I can't say they would have. Like I say, Pentecost isn't working out too well at the moment. Cotton's got a lot of big names on board, but he's not got the answers yet, and he's running out of the mazuma he needs to keep chasing them. Bankers are pulling plugs. Recession's hit his Stateside stations, publishing's near rock-bottom. On top of *that*, Cotton had a lot of cash wound up in Mid-Eastern banks – BCCI, Kuwait. The Gulf War nearly killed him. He survived the BCCI crash only because he was tipped off with minutes to spare. The only real money he can lay his hands on now is from one source. He's finding the going real tough.'

'Which source is that?'

Pappingay lowered his voice and leaned forward.

'He's heavily committed with a Nigerian outfit called Trans-Africa Finance – head office in the Bahamas, main bulk of its business done through Hong Kong. It's very glossy on the surface, very impressive offices, brilliant customer relations. But the honest truth is, they don't come much more tacky than Trans-Africa. If anyone happened to be looking for a BCCI Two, I'd tell them to look no further.'

Pappingay smiled, but without humour. He was inching out on to a limb, and he knew it. Craike moved quickly on.

'OK, Cotton's finances are a little ropy. But that doesn't tell us why his family's been hit, and by whom? Triads?'

The American made an American face, a movie actor's face, mouth pushed out and turned down at the corners. He hunched his shoulders.

'Could be, but I don't think so. For a couple of years Cotton's been palling up to a guy named Lee Hung –'

'*Who?* Say that name again.'

'Lee Hung. He's a big dome in one of the larger Triad

societies, I guess. He's got a security business as his front. Cotton uses him for consultancy work.'

'Christ! Sounds like the Triads – or this Lee Hung's Triad – might have the bite on Cotton.'

'In a kind of a way. Except the societies are genuinely useful to us. I mean they buffalo *for* us. It's saved a fortune on groundrent for that high-riser since the Triads paid the landlord a visit.'

'But maybe Cotton's falling out with Lee Hung – got behind on his instalments, or something. He's in financial trouble, anyway. That might provoke Lee into moving against Cotton's family.'

'I don't think so. I see our contingency bank account. That, incidentally, is with Trans-Africa Finance. Lee gets paid out of it, same as you do – and he *does* get paid, 25,000 bucks every month. I can't see Lee has a motive to do anything but keep Cotton sweet on him. Myself, I think that fire was just an accident.'

'What was Cotton's relationship with his family, his son's family? I mean, I don't really know much about the son's role in his father's life?'

'Chuck's the cross he has to bear. Chuck's a basketcase these days, if you want to know. I mean, he's always been a fruitcake, but he wigged out completely like six months back. That's why Elizabeth, the wife, took off to England. She could see it coming. more. Cotton always hated her, and of course he blames her for the breakdown.'

'He hated her? So, damaging her isn't quite the thing to do if you want to damage him. Could even be the reverse effect.'

'Yes, could be. But you're forgetting one detail – the grandson. The kid fried with his mom.'

'And?'

Pappingay leaned forward and rapped the tabletop.

'C.P. worshipped the kid.' He laughed. 'You know, all that Christianity? He made a fortune out of it, but he thinks it's all crap. We've all got to subscribe on the surface, but underneath we don't give diddly-shit. Cotton's real religion is himself, and his own genes. His son, Chuck, is a lamebrain, so the one ray of hope in C. P. Cotton's universe is his grandson. Attack the grandson and you hit Cotton right where it hurts most.'

'So it could still be the Triads.'

Pappingay drained his glass and glanced at his watch.

'Look, the Triads *like* Cotton, or at least respect him. Far as their opinion goes he's one *gwailo* with real face in this town.'

He stood up and straightened his suit.

'They're not going to go out after him, specially when he's making all these anti-PRC noises. I don't know who would. Hey, I got to roll now, Craike. I got a date.'

'OK, Pappingay. It's been interesting.'

Pappingay raised a finger at Craike.

'You remember your promise, Craike. I get *warned*, right?'

'Yes, Pappingay. You get warned,' lied Craike.

Nancy met Sim as he came in through the side door of the Mama-Bunny. Her voice was serious, even severe.

'I want to talk to you about this father of yours.'

He followed her up to her sitting room, feeling like a boy following behind his headmistress. She shut the door. They both remained standing.

'I want you to understand that this business may be dangerous.'

'Oh, well, I'm not going to –'

'Does anyone in Hong Kong know you are here, looking for your father?'

'One person does.'

'Who?'

'A girl.'

'That one in the bar last night?'

'Yes. I met her again today, to *talk* to, I mean. She's – look, I know it sounds silly, but she's an inquiry agent, I mean a kind of detective. Used to be in the police.'

'I see.'

'And her company's actually been hired by someone to find my father. They got the name through the Kowloon police when I went in to report the thieving bastard who ripped me off in the hotel. Naturally she thought I was my father and followed me in here.'

'How do you know she is what she says she is?'

He shrugged.

'I trust her.'

'Never trust anybody. It does not pay in Hong Kong. The only people in whom there is trust are the Triad gangs, and that is because they get chopped if they break trust. Believe me. Next question. Who was it that hired her company?'

'I don't think I should –'

'Yes, you should. I need to know this stuff, and I need to know what your father has done in England to make so many people look for him here.'

'He – I think he set fire to a house and some people were killed. They were family of C. P. Cotton. It's Cotton who wants to find my father.'

She nodded and walked three steps to the window. She looked out.

'Thank you, Sim. I must think about this. I read about the C. P. Cotton business in the papers, of course, and there are quite a few rumours going around about it.'

'Rumours?'

'Yes. But I won't tell you until I have asked a few people. Wait for old Nancy, Sim. I got my ear to the road, OK?'

He left her and went to his room.

Sim's room, on the third floor, was as basic as a room can get. The floorboards, plaster walls and ceiling bulb were bare. The furniture was a bed and two wooden chairs. The basin was plumbed to cold only, the window blinded by a roll of canvas in sun-faded blue whose cord was a string of knots. The view across the alley revealed a dusty elevation of windows, in which could be seen a hair salon, offices, a few bedrooms.

He lay on his bed. He had intended to think what to do next in his search for Maurice, but the whole thing suddenly seemed less urgent. The crime, if it was one, had taken place on the opposite side of the earth. Moxon's rejection of Sim, which in the first place had seemed to be such a monstrous injustice, crying out to be revenged, now appeared unimportant, as the village itself appeared trivial against the immense backdrop of Hong Kong and the stewpot of people it barely contained. He felt vaguely, uneasily conscious that this was a betrayal, but he could not concentrate on the hunt that had begun when old Worsley handed him that cheque. He wondered if he would mind never seeing Maurice again.

*Wait for old Nancy.*
Perhaps he would.

He found that he was thinking more about Madeleine than about Maurice. He'd mind all right if he didn't see *her* again. He liked her. He liked her straight back, her feathering golden hair, the strength you could see in her limbs and face. But if he was honest, it was because he fancied her sexually.

The two of them had agreed to combine in searching for Sim's father. Madeleine wanted to prove to her boss that she could get somewhere in this investigation without him, that she was no bimbo. Sim could see she wasn't and thought the boss must be blind not to know it too. The compliment had been a little laboured, but Madeleine had not responded, choosing instead to treat the remark as a truism.

'Lots of men are blind,' she pointed out, when they had walked out of the Regent Hotel and on to the new concrete walkway which abuts the Kowloon waterfront. 'Maybe all men.'

'Not women?'

'Not as many women. Not all of us.'

There was a primness in her formulation. She demanded to know why he had laughed.

'Because you are so definite, and I don't feel definite about anything. Not any more.'

'And that's funny?'

'It's because I used to be a know-all, blabbermouth, cocksure smart-arse. Until yesterday morning.'

He told her how he'd been robbed, and that made *her* laugh.

Sim dug some fresh clothes out of his bag and left the room, looking for a shower. Along the corridor some 5 yards was a door that looked possible and he opened it. It was not the bathroom; it was somebody's bedroom and she was at home.

'Hallo! Who are you?' she inquired.

She was tiny, a child, he thought at first. She was wearing a silk dressing-gown and standing in front of a long mirror doing something to her hair. There was not much she *could* do to it, since it was cut short and straight, in the way that was still the approved norm in the People's Republic.

'My name's Sim. I was looking for the shower room.'

'It is the next door.'

She was obviously not a child, since she had perfectly mature breasts and hips. Her voice was very clear and very distinctly modulated, as if she was doing an elocution exercise. But, Sim discovered, this was her natural mode of speech, at least in English.

He said, 'We're neighbours. I've just moved in next door.'

She marched across to him and extended an extraordinarily small hand. When he put out his own hand she made no attempt to grasp it. She simply let hers lie inert in his.

'I have decided I shall be called Madonna. Madonna Lee. It's my new name.'

'What happened to your old one?'

'That belonged to another portion of my life. I have moved on now.'

'I see.'

Madonna Lee laughed.

'I can see that you don't. It's good to have lots of different names to mark the different movements in your life. All the Chinese like to choose new names when they make a change.'

'Ah.'

'You are obviously new here.'

'Is it that obvious?'

Madonna smiled.

'I am new here too. We shall be friends, I think.'

'OK, then. I'll get on with my shower now. See you.'

He shut the door behind him. He was depressed: low and serious. Even the hot, torrential shower could not disperse the feeling.

Three-quarters of an hour later he was again lying on the bed. There was a lurking sense of anticlimax, as if he were a firework that had shot, sparkling and crackling with energy, into the night and had spent itself too soon. The fear was of irrelevance, the skyrocket's stick falling unremarked to earth while the heavens dazzled with other people's brilliance. Why had he come here? To find his father, to be sure. It was a gesture out of the myth and legend books he'd read as a child, but gestures couldn't sustain him. He must remember the basic facts of the business. At the start, back in Lancashire, a wrong had been done him, and the only place he could regard as home had turned against him. The idea of coming to Hong Kong, to root out the man who had been responsible for his misfortunes, had been a real and urgent one. The fact that it was his dad gave the quest a dramatic tinge, sure. But he had travelled half-way round the world to do something *real*, and he still hadn't done it. For all he knew the bloody man wasn't even in Hong Kong, and if he was, then Madeleine and her crew would get to Maurice first and rob Sim of his prize.

The doorcatch snapped, and Sim turned in sudden panic towards the threat. It was Madonna Lee, bearing a tray. 'Teatime in England,' she said. Her tone had a child's simplicity. 'But I will not give you that English drink, with milk in it.' She made a face. 'So rich, and it spoils the taste.'

She crossed the room and laid the tray on the low table beside Sim's bed. As she settled herself with easy grace on the floor, he sat up, swinging his legs to the ground.

'I like it strong, me. Stiff.'

'Perhaps that's the English way. For the Chinese, also in Japan, tea is an artform. It must be taken delicately, never – what did you say? – *stiff*.'

She laughed, a girlish giggle.

'The word makes it sound male, whereas tea is in fact female.'

She showed him a little of what must be done, the first infusion, different in character from the second and third, the importance of scent, and of savouring the tea before swallowing.

'You must never gulp it. You see? Like this.'

She took a sip and held her lips tight and budded around the small mouthful.

'We take tea as seriously as you take wine and motor cars.'

'Bikes – in my case, beer and motorbikes. But I do follow you. I feel this way about tappets. It's a cultural chasm. I doubt I shall ever bridge it.'

She looked at him inquiringly.

'Tappets? What are those?'

He was about to explain, and then he thought better of it.

# 20

Maurice had thought about who he could trust to deliver the letter. The amah was out of the question. Was there anyone else – from his previous life here in Hong Kong perhaps? He hadn't seen any of his former acquaintances since arriving from Bangkok; he hadn't wanted to.

There had never been any *friends* as such. Maurice had never had any trouble being liked by other men, but for him it was a performance. It was so transparently easy that he couldn't in any way like the men he attracted. He simply got what he wanted and avoided them thereafter. Equally, he couldn't think of a woman as a friend. She was a mother, a fuck, a meal ticket, a banker; she was a sounding-board for his plans, opinions and jokes. In the short term he could always charm and then dominate a woman, but over any length of time she always buggered off.

Except Ma, of course. But that was different.

Since there was no other solution, it would have to be a complete stranger, and the conditions would have to be researched. That is why he had spent most of yesterday sitting outside the Cotton Building, watching the arrivals and departures. He had seen C. P. Cotton himself emerge from a black Mercedes limousine and bustle into the building. Satisfied, Maurice had started back, buying on the way notepaper, pen, envelopes, rubber kitchen gloves, the *South China Morning Post*. He had gone to Watson's and bought a Polaroid camera. At the same time a bright-yellow child's school-case in light plastic caught his eye, and he bought this too.

Now wearing the rubber gloves, he fingered the envelope he had addressed to C. P. Cotton. The moment had an intensity about it, of fate impending. Soon the storm of action and anxiety would break about his head, but for now there were a few moments of stillness and anticipation. In the next room he could hear the amah talking, a cooing, sing-song voice that women use when they soothe young children. He remembered Ma, rubber-gloved too in her narrow Liverpool kitchen. She must have sometimes talked to him like that, although the fragments he now remembered were harsher exhortations, usually extracts from her own unofficial catechism of superstition.

*Maurice, every blasphemy against Our Blessed Lady is like a twist of torture on her soul. When the donkey brays that is her soul crying out from the pain, did you know that?*

And *Hell is full of men with their tongues split down to the root. When liars go there they have it done to them by the Devil using a rusty razor blade, and that's true.*

The letter in his hands was still unsealed. He slipped the twice-folded sheet of paper out and read the message again. Would it do?

The problem in composing it had been how to set up a line of communication with Cotton without revealing where he was. He needed some way to receive the money that would reveal nothing and leave no scope for negotiations. It would be all or nothing. Maurice knew there were specialists at kidnap recoveries, men who came feet first through windows and shot on sight. He didn't want any of that.

He had eventually solved the problem without recourse to anything traceable such as telephones or fixed dead-letter drops. It was quite elegant, though he did think so himself.

Maurice shuddered at the thought of Cotton calling in a professional. He had no weapon to defend himself. If he had still had money, he might have been able to get a shooter of some kind, but that was impossible now. The cash was shrinking. He'd had a run of three or four losers at the racetrack the night before last. And they had been large bets, because he had panicked. He had done what you should never do when you badly need a win – come down with big stakes on long-price runners. All of them had been beaten.

If Maurice was going to secure a way out of Hong Kong, he'd have to do it after Cotton made the pay-out. A boat would be the best thing, but boats cost a lot.

So the ransom note *had* to do. It had been as carefully composed as any poem or love letter, the words weighed for what could and couldn't be read into them, for any ambiguities, for the force with which they conveyed the resolution of the kidnapper to do what he threatened to do if . . . The writing of it too had been laborious, in rubber gloves and with his left hand, the letters coming out shaky and badly aligned, like the efforts of someone partially paralysed. Quickly he refolded the letter, pushed it back into the envelope and licked the flap.

Shit, he shouldn't have done that. There was genetic fingerprinting now, which meant that even his spit could give him away. He took another envelope from the packet he'd bought, picked up the pen and, gripping it tight, wrote in crooked southpaw, 'To C. P. Cotton. Absolutely Private and Confidential (for his eyes alone)'. Then he ripped open the other envelope, restuffed the new one and wet the flap with beer from the tin beside him.

He went to the door of the next room and, without opening it, shouted, 'I'm going out.'

He heard a scramble and a voice pursuing him, but he was already closing and locking the door of the office suite before he heard anything distinct.

'Mister! Mister! Please!'

No one would hear her behind the locked door. The office suite had a small lobby before you reached the lifts and this acted as an effective sound-lock. In addition, there was no stairwell to carry her voice either up or down. Oh yes, there *was* a fire escape, but there was a locked room between her and that. His prisoners were safe enough.

He took the Mass Transit Railway, getting off at Central, and made his way to the Cotton Building.

It was a clear blue morning. Above the grind and rattle of the traffic he could hear a higher-pitched juddering and looked up: a helicopter. It came in at a sharp angle of descent from the area of the Peak, disappearing over the perimeter of the building and no doubt plumping down on the chopper pad on the roof. Maurice set his teeth and cursed silently. This was, of course, Cotton arriving for work. And he had been counting on the limousine.

For an hour he walked around in circles, nerving himself to go into the building. A dog picked up his trail, a coal-black Labrador, the tongue lolling and the eyes reproachful as if at the neglect suffered at the hands of the human race.

The dog tried to insert his head under Maurice's hand to be stroked. Maurice flinched away. He had a horror of dogs. That too was Ma's fault. Ma had hated dogs. She used to point to them in the park and regale him with her own catechistic version of the *Just So Stories*.

*That black dog is a descendant of a dog owned by Judas Iscariot. And the other one is spotty because there was a white one of the breed owned by Pontius Pilate. And when he washed his hands he shook the drops off his fingers on to the dog's coat, and that's why he's spotted to this very day.*

At last, as much to get rid of the dog as anything else, he approached the doors of the CPCC headquarters. As soon as he was inside, it was no longer such a big deal. It was like a railway station concourse, with a river of people streaming through the vast atrium, using it as a route from one street to the next, or standing around in groups, passing the time of day, holding impromptu meetings. He was as anonymous here as he had been in the street.

He noted the great circular reception desk in the centre of the place. He could go there and make an inquiry, just to test the temperature. But he was afraid to do so. Once done, such an action couldn't be undone. He would have announced himself and then, he felt, the fatal process would have begun, unstoppably, with no cancellation or going back. He wanted to remain as anonymous as possible for as long as possible.

He joined a group going up the moving staircase to the mezzanine floor. He toured it, and found the lift labelled TO PENTHOUSE ONLY. He hovered in front of the doors, wondering what to do next. He felt almost sick with anxiety.

He heard a chime and the light above the elevator door lit up. Maurice immediately began to retreat. He was already standing on the down escalator, looking back, as a small knot of besuited men emerged from the lift. At their centre, talking in a loud, abrasive voice, chucking words into the air as he moved like a combine harvester, was C. P. Cotton. Maurice plunged on, down into the atrium and then towards the main doors, which he knew Cotton would head for. Outside, the limousine was already waiting, a uniformed chauffeur wiping the windscreen. Quickly Maurice glanced around. Bounding up to him came the black dog, its tongue lolling. Chasing after it a boy in ragged clothes.

The boy grabbed the dog's collar, yanking at it but hardly strong enough to restrain its desire to get back to Maurice's side.

Maurice hunkered down and, with some effort, fondled the dog's ears. He said to the boy, 'See that door over there?'

He pointed towards the Cotton Building. The boy nodded.

'See this letter?'

Maurice opened his jacket, showing the white envelope projecting from the pocket. He didn't touch it.

'Take this, give it to a man coming out of that place there and then come to me around that corner there.'

He indicated in succession the Cotton Building and the corner of the neighbouring block.

'Then I'll give you $20.'

Maurice held up the banknote. The boy's eyes widened in disbelief. He took out the envelope and looked at the, to him, incomprehensible scrawl.

'There! That man, the one talking, waving his arms.'

The group of suits had come through the door and was advancing across the wide pavement towards the car. Cotton could be easily identified from Maurice's words. He gave the boy a push.

'Go on, run!'

The lift machinery clicked as it passed the second and third floors. Well, the first stage was over. Cotton had received the letter and now it was just a question of sitting tight.

He had been rather proud of the final text of the ransom demand. Maurice imagined Cotton reading, and rereading it. Maurice believed it struck just the right uncompromising note.

This is not negotiable. Your grandson, Josh, survived the fire in England. He was kidnapped and is now in Hong Kong. Here is his picture with today's paper.

A man named Swann commissioned this. To get the boy back alive do this. Go to the stationery section of Watson's Department Store. Buy a yellow child's school-case, brand-name Watson's Economy School-case at $15. It must be this type or the deal is off.

Put Hong Kong $1m in used $1,000 notes into the school-case.

Between 12 and 2 a.m. go to the New Territories. Have a Mercedes limo driven up and down the old road between Sham Tsen and Pearl Island. At one place a red warning triangle will be placed in the road, and the first time this is seen have the yellow case thrown out. Do not stop, drive on. Do not be followed by any other car. Do not come back for fifteen minutes. When the money has been received you will hear how to get the child.

The note was signed 'A Friend' – he liked that touch.

He smiled at the thought of it, leaving the lift, crossing the small landing, inserting the key in his door. He swung the door open, took a step inside and swept the door closed behind his back, without looking at it. And without looking *behind* it.

If he *had* looked behind it, he would have seen the amah. She was crouching just like a cat that was about to jump on to a wall or a tree branch. She had been there a long time, so that the backs of her knees ached; her spine too ached. But her head was clear, because she knew what she was doing. She had been waiting for Maurice to return.

Her name was Rosa and she had had it all precisely planned out since the early hours of the morning. She waits until that man goes out, that shit, that thoughtless, heartless bastard. After that *eunuch* has gone, her actions are swift. She settles the child in his cot in the other room, giving him a few toys and a drink of juice in a teated bottle to keep him happy before he sleeps. Then she draws the curtains, goes to the kitchen and takes the knife with the stainless-steel blade. The stupid man! Fancy leaving this knife in the kitchen drawer and not seeing what use she might put it to. Thank God he is such an ass as well as such a cruel bastard!

She would hold the knife projecting out from her fist sword-style. It is short and sharp, 4 or 5 inches. She must hold her position behind the door for as long as it takes, even if it's hours, listening through the locked door all the time for the sound of the lift opening. She must keep her station without wavering or weakening, in case he comes back without warning, without sound. She has to stay still and ready. And when the time comes, Rosa must not hesitate.

She didn't. She sprang at Maurice's back and got an arm around his neck. Maurice gave out a great roar, a bellow like a bull in the ring. He had ducked down and then stood up, trying to dislodge her. She was riding him like one of those cow-riders she'd seen in American cowboy movies, bounced and shaken in the fury of his attempts to dislodge her. Then her one-arm grasp began to lose purchase, her body was slipping, lurching off his back sideways. It was now or not at all. Now she must do it. Now.

She drove the knife into his back. God, it went in so easily. It went in up to the hilt, somewhere below the lowest rib-bones. The flesh was so soft and yielding just there, it was like putting a spoon into a custard.

The man's roaring was cut off, as if a switch had been thrown. He gave a cough or a hiccup, which shuddered his body. His writhing, twisting attempts to dislodge her ceased with a shocked suddenness and he stood there, breath held, bent under her weight, like a hod-carrier pausing beneath the weight of his bricks before going on his way up the ladder. She withdrew the knife and plunged again. This time it did not go in, not all the way. She had encountered the bunch of muscles running up each side of the spine, strong, tough muscles which repelled the blade. The knife penetrated the resistant fibres by only half an inch, giving out an audible *tiss*. Then Rosa fell off.

The thing had gone far beyond any premeditation now. She could not have foreseen how the knife, which had entered the son of a bitch's body so willingly one time, and refused to enter it another, would now feel so slippery in her fingers. Whether it was blood or sweat or a mixture of the two, her fingers were surprised by the slickness. They were losing their grip on the handle and, try as she might to grasp the knife more firmly, she actually squeezed its handle out of her fist like a bar of wet soap. It fell from her grasp to the floor, just as she herself was falling.

The fall knocked the wind out of her. It knocked the back of her head on the carpet and, for an instant, she was both winded and dazed and looking up into his grotesque, downturned, gargoyle of a face. His skin had become grey-white, like steamed fish. Gouts of sweat, held in place by their own surface tension, had sprung from its pores. His eyes were wide and staring; his nostrils flared and contracted spasmodically; his slug-coloured lips had parted and they twitched. It was as if they were trying to form words independently of the soundbox and the tongue.

Maurice shook his head and liberated the sweatdrops, which flew away from his face. It was amazement more than anything, his expression. Somewhere in his back was, not quite pain, but a disseminated throbbing, like a bruise coming up or a bang in the eye. Another, sharper, more localized sensation probed at the flesh near his spine. He focused on the feelings, trying to put them together into something coherent. Then his eyes found the knife, still glistening with his blood, and he knew.

He stood immobile, legs straddled, as if he had achieved an equilibrium and was reluctant to sacrifice it. But the person lying on the floor under and to one side of him, was struggling on to her elbows now, trying to move sideways. He heard, as if magnified, the effort in her breathing. She was reaching towards the knife. She must not be allowed to get the knife. The knife in her hand meant his death, he saw this in a flash of understanding. He must prevent it. He fell on her.

His whole weight just slumped on to her, slamming her back to the floor, pinning her torso with his chest and paunch. Their heads lay side by side, and he was groaning in rhythm with his breathing. It hurt to breathe now, hot rasps of pain drilling into his kidneys with each pull of the diaphragm. He would like to speak, to shout, 'You fucking bitch, you cunt, you murdering cunt.' But it was as if his mouth had a plug of wet paper impregnated with foul chemicals. Not that it mattered. If his mouth wasn't clear, his brain was being goaded now by pain and the desperation to survive into a sort of clarity. Speech would come after action, or it would never come again.

She was wriggling under him, stretching her arm out. He could feel her whole body straining and stretching with desire for the knife. It lay just a few inches from her fingertips. He saw his two options. He could try to beat her to the knife, which would mean himself stretching, trusting he could coordinate hand and eye in spite of scorching pain and her fighting him. Or he could go for *her*.

He planted his palms flat on the floor and jerked himself into the press-up position. *Christ!* The pain sliced through his entire body, cutting him into two screaming halves, each side of his wound. He saw her twitch as he released his weight. He pictured what he must do. A flash of memory came to him, an exercise he used to be made to perform at school by the Brothers: press-ups with a clap at the apex of the press. It had been a punishment, of course. He'd have to do something like that now.

She was moving, writhing with sudden freedom towards her objective. He gathered himself, feeling the pain pulse with increasing surges, and with one almighty release of effort he pushed himself up. He reared, jacking his upper body backwards, and brought his hands off the floor. He bent the arms as he felt himself falling back again and he brought them together smartly with a clap. They were around her throat.

Rosa had fought hard to clear the fog from her head and to regain the knife. Its blade meant life to her. There had been a moment, as he had lifted his horrifying weight, when she believed salvation was being given to her. But then she felt the terrible circle of fingers closing around her neck and she knew the gift was illusory. The fog began to return, denser and colder.

She resisted still. Her face stared up at his as she felt across the floor to her left, blindly twisting under him in the hope of chancing on the object that could save her. All the time she looked into his face, the muscles ricked with effort, the blobs of his sweat splashing on her. Her windpipe was under his thumbs, tight-pressed. What little air got through gave out a long, wet creaking noise. The veins which released blood from her brain and face were also constricted and she felt it pumping into her head, up, up to a peak of unbearable pressure. Her eyeballs were popping; her thoughts raced. Pictures of unconnected things flipped over each other: a pet dog she once owned, her father driving in a nail, a teacher writing on the blackboard, her brothers swimming naked in the river. The images came faster and blurred. Flashes of colour. Flashes of red and white light. Flashes. Two flashes. One more. Then nothing.

Maurice panted. The pain in his back was like a huge, malign parasite, swelling and diminishing as it breathed inside him. He held his position for as long as he could bear, the hands clamped around the woman's throat. But the back of his shirt was becoming heavy, wet, and he released his grip at last to feel the sticky blood. Crumpling his legs, he rolled off her with a yell of pain and was on his back, sliding on some hard objects that were under him. The amah had been wearing a bobbly red necklace and the bobbles had come unstrung in the struggle. Now they were scattered all across the carpet as if a game of marbles was in progress.

Maurice knew he could not stay like this. He had to roll again, then somehow move. Gingerly, he turned himself over, trying to avoid the red plastic beads that popped from under his arms and knees when he put his weight on them. He raised himself to all fours and began a long, tortured progress across the room, the blood smacking the carpet as it fell beneath him.

# 21

The mid-Levels on Hong Kong island is a geographical location; it is also a social status, a European enclave still preserving the same professional, upwards-aspiring, upper-middle-class population as at the Empire's zenith. Less snobbish than the Peak, but always more salubrious than the sweaty, coolie-packed waterfront, this sloping tract, rearing up behind Central District, is as well stocked with round-eyes as it is with trees. Among them, occupying separate apartments of the same block, lived Madeleine Scott and her lover, the lawyer Robert Dowling.

Craike fumed as he stood outside Madeleine's flat at 8.30, his thumb on the bell. There'd been no reply from her number last night, so he'd come over this morning to root the damned child out. What did she think she was playing at? The Morrison case was getting urgent. The clients had delivered the documents that needed going through a week ago. If she didn't show up for work today, he, Craike himself, would have to spend the morning on them.

There was no reply, no sound from within. He pressed again, another thirty seconds, then gave up. Ignoring the lift, he took the stairs, two at a time, up half a dozen floors to Dowling's place. She must be there.

Robert Dowling came to the door in shirtsleeves and without shoes. A yet-to-be-knotted silk tie dangled from his neck.

'Yes? Oh, Ed. Hi. Come in.'

Craike went in, and immediately regretted it. Robert's spacious flat was in a state of maximum disorder. A half-eaten meal, last night's dinner rather than this morning's breakfast, lay on the table. Case papers, legal documents, computer print-outs, dictaphone tapes, newspapers and magazines were strewn around on chairs, sideboard, coffee table, a desk and the parquet floor. Mixed in was an assortment of shoes and items of clothing. Craike noticed that a rack of compact discs had been knocked over and the CDs scattered in a wide arc, and on every surface there were empty bottles, sticky glasses and overloaded ashtrays. The place smelt sourly of old wine, old smoke and unwashed feet. Unable to block the surge of disgust, he wrinkled his nose.

'Robert, I'm sorry to trouble you so early. Is Madeleine around at all?'

'No, afraid not. Haven't seen her since the day before yesterday, actually. She said she'd got some big case on. Coffee?'

There was a pot of the stuff boiling in the kitchen, or rather burning. Dowling went off to retrieve it. Having declined the offer, Craike watched the man's shaking hand pour himself an acrid cup. He looked, quite simply, terrible. He was haggardly unshaven and the skin around his eyes was stained blue-brown. A twitch kept visiting his left cheek, jerking fitfully at the nostril and the corner of the mouth. Craike recognized all the signs: it was 8.30 a.m. and Robert Dowling needed either a drink or a toot – or both.

'Have you talked to her on the phone at all?'

'No.' Robert massaged his face warily, as if his fingers might accidentally detonate a small land-mine under the skin. 'What's the problem? The old girl's not gone missing, I hope?'

From his nose came a wild, disproportionate snort, as if he had said something funny. Realizing too late that he hadn't, he tried to turn it into a sneeze and, in so doing, jerked his coffee, which spilled over the rim of the cup. The coffee burned his hand.

'Shit!'

He ran into the bathroom and came back with a wet flannel covering the scorched area.

Craike said, 'She didn't come into work yesterday, and her flat's not answering. I wondered if she was ill or something.'

'Right as rain on Monday. But, as I said, I didn't see her yesterday.'

He was dabbing at his knuckles with the cloth. His body visibly sagged, as if the effort towards the vertical was a constant struggle, like the punishment of Sisyphus.

'Well, look, Robert. If she should get in touch, tell her I was here with a big stick, will you?'

'Sure thing, Ed. No problem.'

Craike let himself out. That spineless reject belonged in a

Salvation Army doss house. Instead, he enjoyed an executive position in one of the foremost firms in the Territory.

On his way down, Craike paused once again to thumb Madeleine's bellpush, with the same negative result. He turned and continued on his way out.

Was he awake? Sim's sensations largely fitted the hypothesis: daylight, thirst, a certain scratchiness between the eyeball and its socket. His bladder was full and his mouth felt like a plankton farm. Yes, this seemed to be awake, except for one detail: the girl, the slim and naked Chinese girl who was in bed beside him.

He shut his eyes. Reds and purples raced through his optic nerve like molten marbles. Then he remembered the whole episode. Madonna Lee. He had offered Madonna Lee dinner.

'Steak,' she had said unhesitatingly. 'American steak with French fries. But please –' she had held up a hand as if to prevent him falling into impetuosity – 'no hamburger. We don't like it, you know. Damp *bread*, oh!' She made a face and stuck her tongue out through rounded lips. It was that – seeing her tongue's little purplish tip – that gave him the first small, unmistakable prod of desire. It was that which decided him.

For Sim, desire had never been a difficult problem to deal with. He simply followed it, as a dog follows a scent, closely and persistently and without deviation, until he came to the inevitable moment of decision. Sometimes a door swung open; sometimes he was told to go and fuck himself; either way he was cheerful. His desire would not usually survive rejection anyway, and soon enough there would be a new scent to pick up.

He took Madonna Lee to the Regent Hotel. He had seen its unintimidating restaurant earlier, when he and Madeleine had looked down on it from the lobby bar. It was just the place for American steaks, and in any event, the only one he knew of. They had a table next to the harbourside window.

So far they had enjoyed inconsequential conversation but now he began to feel a new lust. He already wanted her physically but this physical desire, as often happens, had had offspring. It was intense curiosity to know everything about her. He began to ask his questions.

'Where are you from?'

'Singapore,' she replied. 'I work for a Chinese insurance

company with branches in Malaysia and Indonesia. We're just setting up shop here.'

'How come you're staying at Nancy Lo's place?'

Madonna Lee lifted her slender shoulders.

'I heard about it from a Japanese guy at work. He said she always has rooms to let for ladies. I was surprised to find *you* there, actually.'

'You said you were starting a new life?'

'Right, new life because I came here with a promotion. Last year, by selling life assurance and pensions, I earned 1,000 bonus points in the company's emolument-enhancement programme. Now I am a department deputy head – corporate retirement annuities department. It is very responsible work.'

'So you gave yourself a new name?'

'Right, a new name for a new life. I very much admire Madonna, you know. I would love to meet her so much, but I wouldn't know what to say to her, of course.'

'You could have a crack at selling her a personal pension.'

'I'm sorry?'

'Oh, just an English joke. Aren't you going to ask how I came to be staying at the Mama-Bunny?'

'Oh, I already know that. You're looking for your father. He's a kind of a rogue, a black sheep.'

The details of Sim's quest had spread throughout the Mama-Bunny building like a smell. A nice smell, she insisted, as of cooking, for instance. All the older ladies, whom Nancy Lo employed in the bar as hostesses, thought it very romantic because it fitted so well with the view of the world they adopted professionally. They themselves provided lonely, emotionally frustrated men with surrogate mothers. But a boy needs his father, too, and should be prepared to travel around the world to find him.

They laughed together at this. Then they ate, and in due course found themselves strolling on the same waterside walkway that Sim had trodden beside Madeleine a few hours earlier. He and Madonna Lee propped their elbows on a parapet and looked across the glittering water, pointing out unusual sights – strangers pooling their impressions of a strange place. Suddenly, Madonna Lee delved into her bag and pulled out an orange. She handed the fruit to Sim, taking another for herself. Feeling a dryness in his mouth as he looked at Madonna Lee, the orange was an aphrodisiac to Sim. He took the fruit, removing its skin thirstily with his teeth and fingers and segmenting the flesh with quick expertise. She did the same, showing her flawless teeth as she gouged out the first morsel of peel. Smiling, she closed her lips over the tart mouthful and cupped her hand to spit it out. But afterwards her lips kept the tease of her smile as she held his eye and watched just how he devoured and savoured the juice-filled fibres.

Back at the Mama-Bunny Madonna Lee went ahead of Sim along the corridor and straight into his room. Her undressing had been as natural and fluent as her removal of skin from the orange. She stood there, her arms straight and held slightly away from her sides, saying, 'You want to know why I gave you that orange?'

He moved close and folded his arms around her.

'To please me?'

'No. A small superstition of mine. I always do it. Because I always like to know in advance how it will be.'

He laughed.

'And?'

She had pulled back from the embrace and looked seriously into his face.

'Just – would you kindly get on with it?'

Now he turned in bed and looked at Madonna Lee's serene, sleeping face. The straight black hair was a miracle of darkness and shine on the pillow. He put his fingers down on it.

But what, he thought, just *what* had he got himself into?

Behind the door of her flat Madeleine had stood in a dressing-gown, smiling. She had seen Craike's face in the spy hole, and could hear the impatience in his sharp triple-rap. Well, perhaps she would ring him up later. But Madeleine knew what she wanted to do today, and working through the purchase ledger of Morrison Financial and Property Services plc from 1985 to 1991 was not it. From her talk yesterday with Sim Fielding, she already considered herself ahead of Craike in this investigation, and she intended to keep it that way. If he sacked her, fuck him. She'd be able to set up on her own if she cracked this one.

Madeleine opened her wardrobe. What should she wear for

Sim? She chose loose cotton trousers and jacket. She thought it the right combination of formality and ease – enough to make Sim Fielding see her as a collaborator, while glimpsing the tantalizing possibility of her as a lover. Madeleine knew her body and its effect, and she was not above letting it play its part in her career.

## 22

*It will be advisable to employ fictitious nomenclature in facilitating illegitimate remittances.*

The rotund words were from a note in the hand of Tommy Plummer, the finance director of Morrison Financial and Property Services plc, the individual whom Craike had been hired to investigate. It was addressed to some unknown co-conspirator, and had been intercepted by the company chairman. He had passed it to Craike.

At the British Army's expense, Craike had once attended a summer school in basic accountancy. The knowledge he had picked up was hardly sufficient to follow all Plummer's dodges and finagling, yet he could clearly see the thick smokescreen of unnecessary financial activity – bank accounts in numerous locations and an incessant, unexplained traffic of funds between them – behind which he had no doubt amply rewarded himself, and others too, out of the company's coffers. Craike could see the recipients' names clearly enough, of course. Some of them would be legitimately connected with the business. Others must be the false names recommended in the pencilled note. Craike noted down all the names as they cropped up. He would have them checked later. But the general picture was clarity itself. Patiently, drip by drip, Plummer was bleeding his employer white.

Wearily he ejected a mini-disk from the micro-computer and inserted another. He loathed the work. Many more of these jobs and he would have to employ someone with letters after their name. He was waiting for a menu to appear on screen when the door behind him squeaked.

'What the *fuck*? I had this crazy idea *I* was employing you.'

Craike swung round to find C. P. Cotton in the door of his office. Not for the first time, he wished he could afford a receptionist.

The evangelical tycoon stood there alone, spindly legs planted apart in support of his vaguely spherical body. One of his hands held a baseball cap over a yellow plastic briefcase, of the type Craike had seen Hong Kong school children carrying. His other hand, with an unlit cigar wedged into it, was rubbing a white handkerchief impatiently across his hot, bald pate. Craike groped for a response.

'Ah, Mr Cotton. I'm, er, waiting for my assistant to report in. She's following up a really promising lead.'

Cotton lurched into the room, almost tottering.

'That *girl*? Beats me why you use a girl, for Christ's sake.'

He sat down heavily in Craike's wobbly-legged cane armchair, with the yellow case planted on his knees. His breath took time to return to normal. When it had almost settled he reached into his jacket and pulled out a crumpled piece of paper.

'I figured you better see this.'

Craike took the paper and read Fielding's ransom note. Then he read it again. He looked up.

'I suppose with hindsight the kidnap isn't such an unlikely development. But it says here *Swann* commissioned the kidnap.'

'Right. It was Swann.'

'It was Swann?'

Craike was feeling obtuse.

'But hang on a minute. Swann tipped us off.'

He thought for another moment and the obtuseness cleared.

'Of *course*. He wanted us to be the go-betweens. Negotiate the ransom.'

'Not negotiate, Craike. You see the terms of the note – not negotiable. Even if Swann didn't write this note, I guess the sentiment would have been his. Nevertheless, he *did* want you. He wanted you to locate Fielding, do the drop, pick up my grandson, all that shit. Swann was playing a very clever hand. He was keeping way in the backfield; Fielding was there to run the ball.'

'But Swann's been dead since last week, so this must be from –'

'Fielding, yeah. Acting on his own account. He musta got greedy. Whatever Swann was paying him musta seemed like small change once he had the kid in his hands, once he'd *killed*

225

to get him, for Christ's sake. It's not so easy to do that. He figured he deserved more of the ransom – *all* of it.'

Craike blew air through his pursed lips.

'So Fielding then killed Swann.'

'Looks like it.'

Craike extended his hand.

'Can I see the photograph?'

Cotton reached the Polaroid from the same inner pocket and handed it across. Craike peered at it and asked, 'Is this your grandson?'

'Think I don't know my own flesh and blood?'

'How did the letter get to you?'

'Little kid handed it to me this morning on the sidewalk outside of my office. Street kid, bribed to do it, I guess. Ran off before I understood the importance of the thing.'

'And you haven't told the police?'

'Hell, no. I want to get my grandson back, I don't want him shot by cops in some crazy siege thing.'

'So, do you want me to do the drop?'

Cotton jutted his lower lips and nodded.

'I surely do. That was your intended role, and I mean to see you play it, Mr Craike.'

'It doesn't say when the drop is for.'

'Tonight. Tomorrow night. Every night until the money's picked up.'

Craike nodded.

'OK, Mr Cotton. I'm your man.'

Cotton placed the yellow plastic case on Craike's desk.

'There's the money. I'll have my car pick you up at 11.30.' He looked at his watch. 'Now, you got plenty of time to work out a way to put surveillance on that road so we follow this rat to his hole and get this little stash right back.'

'That would be extremely risky. I wouldn't advise –'

'I'm not about to let some cheap-ass punk get away with my money, Craike.'

'He's killed three people, Mr Cotton, and he's got your grandson. What about the child?'

Cotton tapped his stomach and leaned forward.

'I tell you something, Craike. I feel it in here that this shit-face who's got my grandson doesn't have the balls to do that. I *know*, that's all. So what we do, we watch, we follow, we find out where the child is, we get him back, then we get the money back. Is that clear?'

It was clear, but Craike knew the kidnapper's plans for the drop to be a very good one. Without involving a lot of manpower – the sort the police could afford – you simply couldn't watch the whole stretch of road. And if you could, it was just too easy for Fielding himself to find out in advance if there *was* surveillance and abort the whole thing.

Craike sat at his desk a long time while the idle micro's screensaver program created its slow-motion whorls, through which fish and ghosts swam with serene indifference. This case was not just a remote matter of governments trying to do down corporations or vice versa. A child had been kidnapped, a mother had been murdered. Somewhere in the city were the killer and the kidnapper, and Craike had much to gain from being in there at the rescue. He went to his tape deck and put on his most often played cassette, Allegri's *Miserere*. It always helped him to think.

He closed his eyes as the notes soared on their sublime way to a plane far above the level of mere music. This composition had once been regarded as so sacred that it was kept as a papal secret. Performances outside the Sistine Chapel had been forbidden on pain of torture followed by excommunication, and the score was jealously guarded in the vaults of the Vatican. But secrecy could not outlast a visit of the young Mozart, coming to Rome at the age of fourteen. Having attended a performance, he afterwards copied the entire piece out from memory. How could any human mind hold such a complex and extended code long enough to write it all down?

Thinking of this tangled business of Cotton, Swann and Fielding, Craike let out an involuntary laugh. No, the case was complex all right, but he would resist the comparison with Allegri and Mozart.

And yet there *was* something to tease out here. How had Mozart worked his piece of copyright piracy? There could have been only one way: to memorize the changes – key, theme, tempo. In music, the changes are the connections between the various fundamental elements – the tunes, you might say. Tunes lodged easily in Mozart's mind, but he would then have had to identify and commit to memory the connections between them.

It occurred to Craike that he had to do the same thing. The case had its three subjects or themes – Cotton, Swann and Fielding. What was the connection between them? Between Fielding and Cotton the link – well, the present link was the grandson, but this had come about only because of a prior link, which was Swann. He couldn't take this case apart without knowing a good deal more about Swann.

It seemed to Craike that they had all tended to take Swann on trust, just because he was dead. This could be a costly error. What exactly had Swann stood to gain by tipping off Craike's agency? Why didn't he simply deal direct with Cotton's own people? Who exactly *was* Swann, anyway? Craike knew, or thought he knew, what Swann *said* he was. But just suppose the fellow was really something more, or something *else*.

He rose, moved across to a filing cabinet and rifled the drawer in which he kept the field recordings. Somewhere among them was the cassette Madeleine had used at the Golden Fortune Boarding House. She'd done a transcript for Craike, but he wanted to hear the voice itself, to listen for its nuances.

He found the tape, turned off Allegri and slotted it into the machine. Then he hit the fast forward. After a couple of false stabs, he found the moment he was looking for. Madeleine's voice was heard first.

'What brings you to this awful place?'
'It's not so awful if you ever lived in an army billet or a POW camp. Anyways, I'm broke. I'm sick. I got no relations. I came here from the PRC with nothing.'
'You mean you come from China – from the mainland?'
'You got me. I shouldn't *be* here. I'm illegal.'
'What on earth were you doing there?'
'Look, my health is fucked, I got no time for this. Figure it out. I got some information which I guess is valuable. I'm offering.'
'What price tag is on it?'
'One you can afford. You bus me out of here: money, passport, ticket to the States. I'm being hunted. Got to keep out of sight. You could cover my ass for me.'
'I can't *promise* any of that. But if the information's good, we might be able to swing something. We're a private organization, you know.'

'Not what I heard. You have friends in very influential places. You can trade on at a nice profit.'

'Where did you get our name?'

'From a guy in a bar. Policeman.'

'Well, I can't make any promises. Not without some idea of what you've got for us.'

'*Will* you trade it on?'

'It's possible, yes. We sometimes – we have had dealings with official sources.'

'Well, OK then. Makes no odds to me either way. I can give you the detail when I know you're gonna do something for me. The bones of it is this. It concerns one of the big shots in Hong Kong business.'

'What's his name?'

'For the moment I forget the name. One of the *biggest* shots, OK? And it's like this. He's being targeted by the Chinks' secret service. They don't like his plans, they don't like his methods. They don't like him period. Come 1997 they don't want to take over this dump and find him still in a position of influence.'

'What are they going to do with him?'

'They'd like to bust his ass open. But he's too rich to be screwed financially.'

Craike found a pad of paper and a pencil and spooled back to run the sequence again. He began to write down everything he knew about Swann, from the tape and from Maddy's report. First, his background, age and appearance: American, apparently broke, about sixty, unwell, possibly chronically ill. Second, the fact that he mentioned the army and a POW camp. Army service would have been normal for a man his age, but POW imprisonment must surely mean Korea. At sixty he would be too young for the Second World War, too old for Vietnam. It had to be Korea.

The fact that Swann claimed to have come from the PRC was of course loaded with significance. He had made a point of saying it – that he was *illegal*. But he wouldn't tell her what he'd been doing in China. And, if he was really a US citizen, why would he describe himself as an illegal? Then there was this business of being *hunted*. Who was hunting him? The Chinese secret services, the Hong Kong authorities, the Triads? These were the three most likely persecutors of Swann, if persecution was really going on. He must find out.

He had read something about Korean prisoners of war, that

some of them had never returned and were thought to be in China. So was Swann one of these? A lost Korean War POW who, forty years later, was trying to make his way out of China?

He spent the rest of the morning on the phone and found an official at the US Consulate with some precious information.

'You want to know about Korean POWs? Well, you're in the right town, sir. There's a lady up in Happy Valley, she thinks about near nothin' else. You want the phone number?'

Madeleine knocked on the door she had been told was Sim's. His voice called her to come in.

He was wearing a towel around his waist and using a red telephone which stood on the bedside table. His hair was still wet from the bath or shower. As she came in he hung the receiver up.

'Hi, I was calling England, but there seems to be no one at home.'

He did not seem particularly disappointed, and of this she was glad. Gross disappointment would have meant love with a girlfriend or, worse, a fond wife. Madeleine looked around the room. His few clothes, out of the canvas travelling bag, were scattered about the room. She liked chaotic men. Affectionately she counted her way round his wardrobe: blue jeans, red socks, wide leather belt with dull steel buckle, battered and cracked trainers, logo-free T-shirt, boxer shorts, brassière. *Brassière!*

Madeleine strode across and picked it up. Small size – small tits then. Chinese?

'Who is she?'

Sim had been combing his hair in the mirror. He looked round.

'Who?'

Madeleine showed him the white lacy bra, hung by a strap from her outstretched thumb.

'Oh, that. The girl next door.'

He caught sight of her incredulous expression and laughed.

'Next-door *room*.'

Madeleine laughed too.

'Oh, I see. What's her name?'

'She calls herself Madonna Lee.'

He held up a warning hand.

'And don't say anything against her. I like her. You don't even know her, OK?'

Madeleine said nothing on the subject. Feeling a little tightness in her throat, she offered only, 'Why don't you get dressed? I'll survey the passing scene from this window. We've got some work to do, or have you forgotten?'

He dressed and they left together to get his breakfast. They went to the coffee shop of an American-style hotel on Lockhart Road.

'Sim,' said Madeleine. 'What do you think your dad has been up to?'

'No good.'

'Yes, but what no good?'

'Well, if you really want my entirely amateur assessment, it is this. I think he went in with this guy Swann, burned that house in England and the people in it, and then they got it into their heads that if they picked up some half-Chinese kid like Cotton's grandson, he could bring him back here to waft under Cotton's nose and pick up a large ransom. They'd then be away before the truth was discovered. What do *you* think he's been up to?'

'I'm thinking the same. It's a terrible charge, Sim. Don't you lose sleep over it?'

'Not over *him*.'

'The child, then?'

'Well, I do want to get the child back.'

'Wouldn't you like to see your father put away for a very long time?'

He didn't answer, but sipped coffee and took a mouthful of brioche.

She said, 'OK, next question. Why did they involve us – Craike and me?'

Sim was still chewing and Madeleine was left to provide her own answer.

'Obviously because we could do the negotiating, pay the money, transfer the kid to Cotton. It would slow up any chance of the kid being recognized as *not* Cotton's grandson.'

Sim swallowed.

'One thing,' he said. 'I don't think it was necessarily a spur of the moment thing, taking the kid from my village. I think they meant to kidnap the real grandson but something went wrong.

They wouldn't have gambled that the kid's body would be destroyed in the fire. The kid must have been removed before the fire, dead or alive.'

'But if alive, why bother with the Moxon child?'

'Something else happened to Josh Cotton. He is dead, I'm certain. His remains have got to be somewhere in England, and my father knows where.'

Madeleine shivered. 'Look, we've *got* to find him, Sim. Now, today.'

So they tried to figure out ways to find Maurice Fielding. Madeleine worked through all the usual methods of searching for a missing person.

'We could try the police again. I've already asked them to keep me informed of anything, of course, but they're busy and this sort of thing doesn't get much priority, doing favours for an old copper.'

'Not so old,' he said.

'An *ex*-copper, then. Otherwise we could go round the hotels, trying to get squints at the hotel registers, but of course they wouldn't be there, would they? It would be too conspicuous.'

'So where would they stay?'

She shrugged.

'Get a room somewhere, rent a room.'

'What sort of a room, do you think?'

'Well, a secure room. A flat.'

'OK, how do you get a flat?'

'You answer an advertisement, you go to agencies ... *That's it!* Agencies. We could go round them. We might come up with something.'

'Take a long time, and it's a bit of a longshot anyway. He'd probably set himself up privately. Don't forget, he's an oddity, a single bloke with a very young child in tow.'

'He may be with someone else, a woman. Make them look like a family.'

Sim shook his head, not because he didn't believe in this but because it was all too probable.

'It doesn't help us, though, does it? If only there was something you have to do when you sign a lease – you know, like register with a government department.'

Madeleine sighed, drooping her head down towards the table.

'There's nothing, just the phone company, if you've got a phone.'

A pause, and she raised her head. Their eyes looked down the same beam of light, one from each end and he was conscious of her for the first time. She was actually a woman. Not a girl, not a sister, or a smiling friend like Julia back in Moxon, or a matronly aunt-substitute like Mrs Benlow in the bakery. Nor was she a casual pick-up, a girl at a club, a girl in his class at the tech, a girl next door.

Momentarily, at the thought, he shrank inside. He screwed up his eyes.

'No! I mean it's too obvious.'

She smiled, her eyes wide. His were squinting, not believing her.

'Well, it's worth a try, isn't it? He might consider he had to have a phone, and if he rented a place *that* is the one thing no landlord puts in for free. He'd have to arrange it himself and he'd have to give his name, probably with proof of identity so they'd be able to trust him. That means he may appear as M. Fielding. It's just worth a look.'

'No, it isn't. It would be too easy.'

But she had already got up.

'Let's go back to your place and try the exchange. We'll dial every M. Fielding they give us.'

Still he hesitated, his face trying to tell her it seemed a foolish, naïve contrivance. But she was already on her way.

Sim drained his cup and followed her. He did not want to waste the insight he had just had into her. Desire, again. The tug like a thread attached to his nerves.

No, no, he said to himself. It was absurd. It was too bloody *obvious*.

## 23

After a while the gouting of blood slowed to a sticky ooze. Clotting, he supposed.

He had returned, pressed by some primitive urge, to the position beside the telephone that he had got into the habit of occupying. It took a long time to manoeuvre himself into place, his legs splayed and his back – the uninjured right side – propped against the wall. Looking across the room he could see much red on the carpet – the scattered necklace-beads and the snail-trail of gore whose smears mapped the route he had taken.

*You dirty! Filthy! Dragging all that mud in on your shoes that way when your poor Ma's been on her hands and knees all morning.*

One way or another Ma had spent most of her time on her knees. He remembered the tattered rubber kneeler she used to drag around the house to save her kneecaps. The rubber was so perished that unless you picked it up in two hands, bits would split off it. When she told him to 'bring that rubber kneemat here to me', he had to force himself to pick it up at all. It was shiny and yet rough to the touch, like a reptile's skin. It was so dark with grime that you couldn't imagine what colour it might have been when new. Of course he did it. In her own house Ma was an empress. It was only on the outside of that two-up-and-down palace that Maurice got into the habit of raising Cain.

He lifted his buttocks to find more comfort, and at once pain shot through him. Otherwise there was a heaviness, a throbbing in the lumbar area which he knew would be developing into real pain pretty soon.

Ma's undeviating routine when Maurice cut himself relied heavily on an antiseptic called TCP, which she imbued with mystical healing properties. So when he ran in after falling off his bike or from a tree, he would be sent limping up to the bathroom and told to bring down the TCP. This would be unscrewed with a kind of awed piety, sloshed on to a wad of cotton before being used to scour his cuts and grazes with a fierce and faithful abandon. He yelled and struggled as the astringent liquid seared his broken flesh, but Ma was unrelenting.

*It only stings because it heals, Maurice, and it cannot heal unless it stings. What's the use of medicine if it mollycoddles? Why do you think the Magnesia tastes so nasty, eh? Because it's good for you, that's why.*

This was her other elixir, Milk of Magnesia. It took its place proudly alongside the TCP in the enamel bathroom cabinet and, during the period of Maurice's childhood when he most often came running in to her, bawling out his pain, the family must have got through TCP and Magnesia the way many alcoholics get through gin.

The Magnesia would be for internal pain and presumably, if Ma were here now, having splashed him with TCP, she would at once begin pouring the cold, chalky spoonfuls of Magnesia down his throat every ten minutes. He shuddered, and this movement created a fresh rending sensation in his wound. There was another warm trickle of blood into his already sopping shirt and he felt, too, a slight intensification of the throbbing deep within his back. It was in fact only a small increment, like a shift up to a marginally higher gear, but now it was happening every few minutes.

*Don't feel so sorry for yourself. D'you think you're the only person in the world to suffer? It's what we're here on this earth for, so don't you be complaining.*

He was breathing faster now and for the first time noticed a moist, bubbling sensation in his lungs, reminding him of a hookah. His brain seemed light and evanescent, in contrast to the leaden balloon slowly inflating itself around his guts. In front of his eyes floated strands of red, yellow and grey gauze. He shook his head and tried to focus on something. There, at the far end of the room, by the door, lay sprawled his attacker's body, a shapeless, insubstantial form to him now. He tried to think. Who *was* it, anyway? It was a woman, yes, he remembered that much. She had stuck the knife into him, deep into him. That was certain. But what had she wanted? He frowned, trying to concentrate. The bitch must have been some kind of psycho; just came at him for no reason with the knife. Suppose she got it from the kitchen. Yes, from the kitchen. Like he did once. He'd taken one of Ma's knives and used it to cut a piece of string to length. She had fallen into one of her rages when she saw him.

*Boy, you never, never, never touch those knives again, you hear me? If I see you with one I shall use it to cut a piece off you. Cut a piece of you off, I shall.*

She didn't specify, but even at six he had had some idea which particular piece she was planning to sever.

The bitch. Not Ma. Oh, no. Not Ma. *This* bitch. She tried to kill him and he didn't know why. Well, there *was* something. He had been bad and that was why, but somehow he couldn't assemble the various parts of his badness. What *was* it? Did he steal? Did he lie? Did he blaspheme? Did he kill?

*Thou shalt not kill, and as far as I'm concerned they should all be strung up.*

Ma was a convinced capital punisher, and had brought Maurice up to believe in the rope as passionately as she did.

*Yes, and when they die, they roast in Hell for all eternity. All eternity, Maurice, think of that, won't you? Because with the company you keep, that's where you're headed for.*

It was during Maurice's first bit of adult bird that they'd hanged Hanratty. It was in another prison hundreds of miles away, but at the hour of the hanging Maurice's wing had suddenly and eerily fallen silent. The hush was intensely painful, as if every prisoner in every cell there were Hanratty himself, standing on the trapdoor with the iron eye (through which the loop passed) under his ear, the bag over his head, holding his breath, waiting for the drop.

So it had been, a chill silence as they counted down the chimes of the prison clock. And exactly on the stroke of the last one there had been a single harsh yell. It echoed down from the fours, the top landing of the wing. It could be heard by every prisoner incarcerated there.

'*Swing, you bastard! Swing! You got exactly what was coming.*'

The yell was followed by a hammering of tin plates and spoons and chamber pots against walls, doors and windows, and an uproar of screams, shouts, hoots and curses was kept up for twenty minutes. He knew what it meant, they all did. 'Welcome, Hanratty,' the cacophony was saying. 'Welcome to Hell.'

If Maurice was a murderer, a multiple murderer, then he

should die too. Hanratty killed a man; Maurice had killed – what? A man, two women, yes. And *more*. He killed a – an *it*. Yes. Maurice should hang, he should hang several times over. He should dangle and roast in Hell.

Maurice had known what he was doing. There was right and there was wrong, and he was wrong. He had made a pact with himself at fifteen to that effect. Wrong was what he was, and there was nothing the Christian Brothers or the probation service or the prison padre or the shrink or Ma or any other bugger could do about it. He was just wrong. He had chosen this of his own free will.

The phone was down there, beside him on the floor. If he made a supreme effort he could pick it up and dial zero. They would get help, a hospital, clean sheets, sexy nurses. His lips twisted into a smile. He wouldn't do it, though. Snafu: the situation was normal; he was all fucked up.

His position against the wall was getting increasingly painful, his back was no longer merely throbbing but pounding, his legs were numb and now his head too felt unbearable in its weight. He knew he must rest it for his brain to go on working. He therefore edged his body sideways, using his arms to buttress his trunk and prevent a sudden lurch to the floor. Grunting with effort, trying to move away from the place where he knew the pain would suddenly scythe into him, he lowered himself. Now he was leaning entirely on his right elbow, but to get down further he would have to twist, and to do this would be unimaginable torture. He stopped like that, panting. He didn't know for how long. His brain was swelling and contracting. When, finally, he toppled off the stanchion of his arm and dropped down to an untidy, twisted-round position, his nose was first to hit the carpet, followed by his forehead, chin and mouth. He lay still, no longer capable of feeling the pain which would otherwise have blitzed nerve-ends throughout his midriff. He heard nothing. Not the beginnings of the whimper that threaded under the door from the next room, nor the shrill mouse-squeaks of the telephone on the floor beside his left ear.

At first, as the child sat up on the quilt he had been sleeping on, the hunger tickled at him pleasantly. Soon the Mama-person would come in, open the curtains, lift him from the cot, bring him food. And then the good feeling would be back inside him. After that the Mama-person would rock him against her breasts and croon into his ear, and he would inhale again the smell on her hands and face, which was a smell he enjoyed, like the smell he got from the slippery stuff she put all over him with her tickling fingers in the bath.

Yet he had a faint sense of unease. It was tucked away out of immediate reach, but it was in there, inside him, somewhere. It was because he had not seen the Mama-person for a while. OK, if he wanted her he could open his mouth and let the noise come out. That would bring her. But there was something else. He hadn't *heard* the Mama-person either. He should at least have heard her because she liked to whistle and sing a lot, and say things to him, calling out from the kitchen or from the far end of the room where she was folding clothes or standing by that high, thin table with the clothes on it in front of her. The unease began to disturb his concentration on the plastic toys she had left in the cot. Idly he used a rattle to batter the roof of a toy lorry, then stuck his fingers in the telephone dial on the rectangular box of tricks which was screwed into position halfway up the cot bars. Using the purchase of his fingers, he pulled himself up and began shaking the thing, rattling, and wrenching it until it slid down, still attached to the bars but resting now on the mattress.

He hooked his fingers over the rim of the cot, planted a foot on the plastic box and heaved himself up. He was standing now with his round stomach pressed against the rail, and both feet placed on top of the plastic box. He released a cry, a thin, reedy noise which he always used when feeling sorry for himself and in need of the Mama-person to come and pick him up. Nothing happened. He did it again, a longer, more emphatic cry, while shaking the cot rail as hard as he could.

He raised his right leg, the knee and foot going over the rim, his trunk leaning forward into empty air. He could climb out. He knew he could climb out. And if the Mama-person wouldn't come, he'd have to climb out and go and fetch her. He used his left foot like a spring, at the same time pulling at the cot rail so that he jerked upwards. Then he started tumbling over and down, and it was, suddenly, too fast. He was falling into gaping space and he couldn't control the way he was overbalancing, however much he flailed his arms. Then his back and the back of his head struck the floor with a dull thump.

He lay motionless and silent. Then his face darkened and distorted, and he let out a scream of shock and fright. It took a moment or two more for his screaming to hit maximum power. When it did, he was screaming without any inhibition, and at the same time making a grotesque face and bouncing his feet against the floor. He screamed and kicked, kicked and screamed. But still the Mama-person did not come.

As the first tide of sobs retreated, he got up. He was panicky, his empty stomach fluttered. He launched a long, elided sequence of searing vowels. He meant the Mama-person to run to him, to snatch him up and cuddle him. It must happen now, now, now.

He wandered into the small kitchen that opened into his room, but she was not there. The door of the washroom, off the little bit of passage on the other side of the kitchen, was open, but she wasn't in there either. The other two doors he ignored. They were shut. Anyway he had never been through them so they left him incurious and unmoved. He returned to the room with the playpen and cot. The other door was where Big Bad had his lair. He knew *lair* because of the book the Mama-person had read him. A lair was a dark house, and something frightening, something not to go into.

Nevertheless, he went to the door. It was the only place left. Hesitantly he put his fingers on it. There was a band of light down the left-hand rim of the door. He pushed and the door moved gently open, hinges ticking lightly as it swung. He stood blinking into the lighter room.

Big Bad was over there, and over *there* was the Mama-person. They were not moving, either of them. What was she doing?

He ran over and flopped down on top of her, forgetting his fright, laughing from relief. He had found the Mama-person and soon he would be happy.

The telephone company had come up with an answer right away, a Mr M. Fielding who had become a subscriber only last week. They provided Sim with the number – sorry, they couldn't divulge the address as that was against the regulations on confidentiality.

Sim dialled and let the phone ring for half a minute before

handing it to Madeleine. She put the receiver to her ear and then hung up.

'Try it again.'

He did, and still the phone was unanswered. He held it to his ear, that insistent falsetto squeaking, then he moved close to Madeleine and held it again to hers. He had put his body close to hers, they were side by side on Sim's bed. He put a hand on her shoulder.

The Mama-person wasn't moving. She just lay there, still, not speaking, not giving him any of the hugs and cuddles he wanted, not giving him any *food*. He called to her, in the rude, prototype language he'd developed for himself. He was trying to get her to move for him, to turn over from this stupid position she was stuck in. But the Mama-person went on being still and stuck.

He was so hungry. It was the feeling he knew best, of course, and the one he best knew how to cure. You put things in your mouth – nice-tasting things, not just any things – and you let them go down inside you.

He bit a fold of the Mama-person's blouse and sucked it into his mouth. He tried to chew it, but it tasted of nothing and he knew it wasn't dinner. He spat it out and climbed off the Mama-person. What was this? Red sweeties on the floor? Good, good. Sweets were for eating. He picked one up and popped it in his mouth. He sucked for a few moments, but there was only the slightly disappointing taste he got from his toys – the dry, mastic taste that he knew wouldn't fill up the emptiness he felt inside. Nevertheless, it was better than nothing and he went on sucking as he stood next to the Mama-person. He was looking around him.

Now there was something new, a noise. A trilling noise, and one he'd often heard before. It was from that button-thing that big people were always playing with, but would never let *him* play with. His eyes searched for it. There it was, next to Big Bad. The button-thing was making its noise next to him. He was lying still, almost on top of it, the same way as Mama-person was lying. They were playing some game, and it was a game he didn't like. That was normal. He didn't like any of the games big people played with each other, only the ones they sometimes –

and very rarely – played with him. He went over to Big Bad and stood uncertainly next to him, looking down.

Big Bad's shirt was covered in wet brown paint, all sticky and sopping. A housefly was walking over it. He heard a slight buzzing and another fly banked and dropped down to join the first. They were walking around on Big Bad's shirt. They seemed to be drinking the paint. He forgot about the button-thing for the moment and crouched down and grabbed the flies, trying to catch them. He missed. His hand went down with a smack on to the sticky, shiny brown paint on Big Bad's shirt, a loud, wet noise. He gasped and jumped up.

But Big Bad didn't move.

He looked at his hand. It was covered in paint, and he wondered if the paint was nice-tasting. He'd tasted a few different types of paint before and some of them were better than others. He spat out the red bead and started to lick his hand.

The paint tasted like no other paint he had ever licked. It tasted warm and good. It tasted like food. He licked his whole hand clean and then knelt down near Big Bad's shirt again. He must be ready to dart away if Big Bad moved.

He leaned forward and gingerly took a fold of Big Bad's sopping shirt in his teeth. Just as he'd tried earlier to suck on Mama-person's blouse he sucked on this too. He enjoyed the thick, foody taste – it wasn't exactly like, but it did resemble, dinner. He sucked contentedly for a while, then he tried another wet fold of cloth.

And now, as he was sucking, he became aware of the button-thing again. It was still chirruping. He let the twist of shirt drop from his mouth and he shuffled across to the big people's toy. He lifted the bit they always lift and said, 'Lo.'

He'd heard big people when they played with the button-thing. They always either pressed a lot of the buttons and then said 'Lo' or they waited until the button-thing chirruped and they picked it up and *then* said 'Lo.'

He said it again, and again, and then put the receiver back in its bed again.

'For Christ's sake, Sim, *stop* it. Something's happening.'

Sim removed his hand and she stood with the receiver jammed to her ear, listening intently.

'Hello?' she said. 'Hello?'

She put the phone back.

'Shit, someone answered, then hung up. What's the *matter* with you? I thought you wanted to find your Dad, stop him doing something stupid.'

'I don't care about him, I told you. Let him do anything stupid he wants. He was always a complete bastard to me.'

'Well, don't you want to get the child back, then?'

'Oh, yes, I want to do that. Take him back home.'

'So stop messing about with me and think about what's in hand.'

'It's just that I don't really believe it can work. He wouldn't be so easy to track down. In fact, I'd say he must be impossible to track down if he's trying to do a kidnap and get away with the ransom. We ought to wait for the ransom note or something. We'll never get him otherwise.'

'Don't be so sure. Listen.'

She had dialled again and now she held the phone to his ear.

He heard a cooing noise, then a string of gobbledegook ending in a hiccup or a suppressed sob. Suddenly Sim was back in the Moxon Chinese chip shop, with little Kevin down on the floor zipping and unzipping his various pockets and burbling away in his own private language. To Madeleine he breathed, 'It's the kid. It's *him*.'

'Is it? Can you really tell, Sim?'

'But it *must* be. Kevin? Is that you, Kevin?'

There were further incomprehensible sounds. They didn't even sound like English. Sim raised the pitch of his voice in excitement.

'Where are you, Kevin? It's Sim here, Sim from home in Moxon. Tell Sim where you are.'

'Look, the child's not yet two. He can't talk. He can't tell you anything.'

But now Sim was calling out in a louder voice.

'Hello! Hello! Is anyone there? Could you pick up the receiver, please? Could you talk to me please?'

There was a bump and he knew the child had dropped the receiver. He could hear some other sounds, voices. One of them came near.

'Hello! Hello! Talk to me, please. Hello!'

He heard breathing and someone calling out, not into the receiver but as it were across the room. He couldn't make out a word. Another voice answered. Then the telephone was replaced.

'Shit, Madeleine, there was someone there, in the room with him. They put the receiver back. I think they were talking Cantonese. At least, I don't think it was English. We've *got* to get this address.'

Madeleine was already dialling. There was an old police colleague who would help her.

'Don't worry,' she said. 'Police have no trouble locating an address from a phone number. They do it all the time.'

## 24

'Mr Craike? How very pleasant to have a visitor. Come right in.'

Jane Johnson's apartment in Happy Valley was on a scarp looking down at the oval racetrack. By a steep, twisting approach road Craike's taxi came to the unkempt block which, though elderly, was not as old and tottery as Mrs Johnson herself. Standing at the apartment door to greet Craike, in polo neck and loose cotton trousers, she looked skeletally, breakably thin. Her breath came and went through lungs crackling with mucus. Her cheeks were scored and leathery and the whiteness of her straight hair, straggling in wisps, was streaked with the urine-stain colouring of tobacco smoke.

'I can manage instant coffee,' she said, beginning to lead him through the hallway but suddenly stopping at a thought. Craike, following close behind, nearly collided with her.

'Or perhaps a drink?' offered Mrs Johnson.

She offered this like some outlandish hypothesis.

'Oh, no, I –'

'I think there's some Cinzano somewhere, although it *might* be a bit long in the tooth. *I* never bother with it.'

She smiled. Her teeth had gone completely to hell, ragged pegs of seasoned walnut which had spread along the gums at all the angles of Easter Island stones.

Craike repeated, 'No. No, thanks. A coffee would be fine.'

The old lady opened the door of a sitting room and ushered Craike in, then drifted off towards the kitchen, leaving her visitor to take stock. It was a book-lined room, apart from a section of wall where half a dozen four-drawer filing cabinets stood. On top of these were piles of bulging document-wallets tied up with string. A micro-computer stood on a wheeled trolley, shrouded in its plastic cover, and a desk under the window had a typewriter on it. Craike's scan through the bookcases yielded at first only names he didn't know – Odets, J. P. Bishop, Trilling, McLeish – until he came upon plenty of Hemingway and Henry Miller. There were, too, a great number of more specialized reference works: *An Index of US Army Regiments*, *A Military Who's Who*, *The Army List*, *The Official History of the Korean War*.

Mrs Johnson meandered back with a tray and two mugs. A lit cigarette hung insecurely from the side of her mouth.

'Yes, I wish I had more money for books, you know. There's so much coming out about the war even now that I can't afford to get.'

'Here, let me.'

Craike stepped forward and took the tray. He put it on a glass-topped coffee table, whose shelf, visible through the glass, was loaded with research papers and technical journals.

'I know. Books are a terrible price. How on earth do you finance all this? The campaign?'

She looked again at the filing cabinets and the computer.

'You mean the computer and stuff? It's well-wishers. You know, 8,000 prisoners of war have been lost – that's a lot of families. I've got 350 subscribers – not as many as I used to have, but that's balanced by the fact that quite a few have died and left me small quantities of money.'

'How are you getting on with the computer?'

'Oh, I bought it two years ago, but can't work the damn thing. Somehow I can't get around to learning how to operate it.'

A wheeze emerged instead of a laugh.

'Anyway I've got a part-time secretary Tuesday and Thursday mornings who does the correspondence. I *was* told the computer would replace her, and, you see, I wouldn't like to do that. So –'

She sighed, holding out Craike's mug of coffee.

'There it stands, waiting to be used. Sit down, won't you.'

Craike found a chair and sipped his coffee. It was weak and tasted of clay.

'What exactly do you do with it all, Mrs Johnson?'

'I try to get to the truth.'

'About?'

'About the war, of course. The North Koreans and the Chinese were rather unscrupulous, you know, in the way they treated the prisoners. Quite a lot were simply murdered. Others ended up being used as slave labour. Many, many were brainwashed.'

'Do you know why they didn't send them back at the end of the war?'

Jane Johnson crushed out her cigarette in a small brass bowl balanced on the armrest of her chair.

'Well, for one thing the war never really did end, not formally. Technically it's still going on. But there was a ceasefire and a demarcation line between the forces, and Eisenhower was so relieved at having got the US forces out, he kind of forgot about the lost POWs. One of them was my own son, Pete.'

She nodded at the metal cabinets. On top of one was a framed studio portrait of a young GI, grinning smugly at the camera, as if to say *Good buddy, I'm a-goin out there and waste me some gooks.* Craike had known the type only too well.

'He was reported missing all right, but they never found his body or heard anything of him again. He just vanished into thin air. Taken to prison in China, or even Russia, that's *my* guess.'

Craike raised his eyebrows, playing the rank innocent.

'Not Russia, surely? I thought –'

'No, Russia was in cahoots with the Chinese then. They supplied them with war materials and so on. And they probably agreed to take shipments of American prisoners into Siberia, to get them as far away from the war zone as possible.'

'But why would they do that?'

'I guess to use them as hostages. But the funny thing is, they never were used that way. No one's ever acknowledged that the 8,000 even existed. The CIA know. Obviously the KGB knew. *We* know, through very careful research work and piecing together the evidence. Otherwise it's a brick wall. No one wants to knock a hole in it for fear of what they'll find there. Except me, and the families, of course.'

'What sort of thing might they find there?'

The shrivelled old woman shrugged, and her scraggy shoulders lifted almost up to her earlobes.

'That some of the men may have defected voluntarily, of course. Others by extortion, to save their skins. There are quite a few known defectors like that around Beijing – I've been there and met them. But they're not really the issue, because we *know* what happened to them. It's the disappeared ones I'm concerned with. I think a lot of them must have been massacred, when it was obvious they couldn't be useful any more. Some may have been detailed to do slave labour in the good old salt mines. Coal mines, actually. There have been quite a few reports of isolated groups of Americans spotted in remote parts. God knows, my son could be there.'

'And you know the names of *all* the 8,000?'

'8,177 to be precise. Yes, I got all my boys filed in those drawers. Like I said, I was hoping to get them on the computer but, well, maybe I'll leave it for someone else to do when I'm dead.'

Craike couldn't help it. He always felt excited at the moments of breakthrough. He was very close now and the adrenalin was flowing. Just a simple question and what a coup he would have pulled off!

'I wonder if you could possibly look up a name for me in your records?'

'Certainly could. I guessed it was something like that you wanted.'

Jane Johnson carefully pushed herself up from the chair, dislodging the brass bowl with her elbow. It fell to the floor and bounced, spilling butts and ash. She stood still for a moment, holding herself bent a little forward, catching breath. Then she shuffled towards the files. Her progress was agonizingly slow as she fumbled to get a pair of spectacles to her nose.

'I am quite frequently asked to look people up, but generally by mail. It's usually relatives of the poor boys, trying to do their family trees. I'm a genealogical resource, that's what I am.'

She stiffened her back, ready to plunge in among the records.

'So, what name was it, dear?'

'Swann, James Swann, with two *n*s.'

'American, British, Canadian or Other?'

'Oh, American, I think. I mean, he could be Canadian at a pinch, but American is the most likely.'

Craike remained sitting. He didn't want the woman to spook at his over-enthusiasm. He heard a drawer being pulled open.

'Swann, Swann, Swann. Any middle name?'

'No. At least, I don't have one.'

'No matter, no matter.'

Craike could hear the dry fingers rifling through the closely packed papers.

'Smith, Smith, endless Smiths, Standing, Stanton, Stovoulos, Strasburger, Stromberg, Sullivan, Svenson – ah! Yes.'

She drew a beige folder from the drawer and opened it.

'Here we are! We do have a Swann. James Eddison Swann. Born 1931 in Chicago.'

She looked up at Craike and began to come back towards him, her step wobbly, the mottled hand shaking as it gripped the file.

'Does that sound like your feller?'

'Yes, it does. He's about the right age. Is he the only Swann?'

'Yep. The one and only.'

'What else does it say about him?'

Jane Johnson reached her chair and manoeuvred until her back was towards it before flopping down. She reopened the folder.

'Oh dear. I'm sorry to be disappointing, but I don't have much on this one. I can tell you where he was lost and that's about it.'

She sighed.

'It's the same with so many of them, so many. That's what I hate about it, the not knowing anything. If you know something, you can accept it. If you don't know, you always go on, on and on, hoping.'

She took off her spectacles and looked at Craike. The eyes suddenly had a penetration that Craike had missed before. Now he saw not a raddled old geriatric, but a fighter, a never-take-no-for-an-answer campaigner, and a shrewd intellect.

'What do you know about the war, Mr Craike?'

Craike's old regiment – before his time – had fought in Korea, so he knew a little, at least about the British effort. But he couldn't claim any specialist knowledge and he continued to let Jane Johnson think he knew even less than he did.

'Well, I don't know much. Or, to put it another way, practically nothing.'

'Well, your Private Swann, he disappeared very early in the campaign, in summer 1950, during the American retreat to Pusan. That was around Taejon, just after things started to get very fouled up indeed. The GIs were in full retreat south. It was chaos out there, so we are told. Utter confusion and chaos. But wars were ever thus. Little boys' games.'

'What do you think could have happened to Swann?'

'A few of the American prisoners in that year were shot or beaten to death by North Korean troops. He could have been one of those. If not, he would have been taken north to Pyongyang and held in some kind of primitive prison. A lot of them were requisitioned schools which quickly turned into disgusting animal pens. Then, when the American counter-attack reached that area – that was the next year – he would have been spirited away into China for safe-keeping, and thence to God alone knows where. And that's near enough all I can tell you about the fate of your James Swann, I'm afraid.'

She handed the paper across to Craike, to show just how thin the information was. There were no details beyond the name, date of birth, GI number, unit and the date and place where Swann was last seen – 18 July 1950, Taejon, South Korea. He had vanished without trace.

Jane had laboriously got back into her chair.

'Forgive me asking, but why do you want to know about this poor young man? He's not a *blood* relative, so what's your connection with young Private Swann?'

Craike had thought about what he would say in answer to this question. It would be much the easiest to claim kinship, so avoiding the need for laborious explanations. He had therefore planned to tell Jane Johnson that Swann was his uncle – his mother's younger brother. Now the lie had been pre-empted. Craike frowned and then smiled. What did it matter?

'How do you know he's not a blood relative?'

Jane Johnson opened her eyes wide, surprised by the question.

'Well, just from looking at you. I mean, you're a white boy.'

'I'm sorry, I don't –'

The old lady was delighted at wrong-footing Craike, hugging herself with pleasure at the thought of it.

'You mean you didn't know?'

'I'm sorry? Didn't know what?'

Jane Johnson had fished a squashed packet from the recesses of her chair and was fumbling for a cigarette. Her eyes were sparkling with a kind of triumph.

'See, it was like this. The US army was racially segregated until May 1951. I know that Swann couldn't be a blood relative of yours, or of mine, or of any white person, because of the *unit* he came from. It was a black unit, honey. James Swann was a *black* man.'

Sim found himself a little turned on by the flush on Madeleine's cheek. He remembered a nineteenth-century novel in which were described the symptoms of 'detective fever'. It was clearly what Madeleine had now: the hunter's hots, the inquirer's itch. It was an almost sexual excitement making her tremble and fidget and flash her eyes. Yet she forced stillness and restraint on herself.

'I've got to tell Craike. I'm sorry, Sim, I know how much you want to scoot right round there and cop the lot, but I absolutely can't keep this from my boss any longer. I've suddenly got a conscience about it. He's going to flay me alive for this as it is, except that it's such good news he might let me off with a flogging.'

'I'd like to meet this boss of yours.'

'It's time you did. Come on, we'll go to the office, and then we can get after your father. I'll say this for Ed Craike, he may be a bit thick but he's very good at the biff-biff bits.'

They found Craike at his desk. He was replete with generosity after his success with Jane Johnson, and he welcomed Madeleine like a prodigal returned.

'My dear girl, come in, come in. Who is this? Oh, Mr Fielding? Ah, well, are we not looking for you, young man, in connection with a little matter?'

'No, you're not. That's my father. I came from England to find him – to help find him, I should say.'

'And it was you who is putting up at the Mama-Bunny bar in Wanchai, I take it?'

'Yes, that's right.'

'Funny sort of address. I must say. Be that as it may –'

Madeleine butted in impatiently.

'The point is, Ed, Sim and I have found him. We not only know where he is, we know he has C. P. Cotton's supposed grandson with him.'

'Maddy.'

Craike was not fazed by Madeleine's sensational news, as he had some of his own. He lay back in the big executive chair, his only serious indulgence in this office, and put together his fingers in approved Holmesian manner. He fixed Madeleine with a stare that would have daunted Greek heroes.

'Maddy. Why didn't you tell me?'

She looked flustered by the actorish tone of the question.

'I'm sorry, Ed. What?'

'About Swann.'

Here Craike leaned forward for emphasis, tapping the tabletop with his finger. 'About the colour of his skin.'

Madeleine took a moment to digest the point being made.

'The colour of his skin? It was dirty, sallow, old. Nothing special about it.'

Craike straightened and barked, 'Swann's skin was black, Maddy. Black.'

Madeleine was flustered by her boss's grand manner. She found herself, not understanding, stammering. 'But it wasn't. I mean, I saw him. I mean, he was a white man.'

'No, Maddy. James Eddison Swann was as black as a Jesuit's hat.'

He pushed over a photocopy of the record sheet he had obtained from Jane Johnson. Madeleine picked it up and read it closely, then handed it to Sim. Craike added the necessary gloss.

'The US army in Korea was still racially segregated when Swann was captured. He was a member of a black regiment. Ergo, Swann was black.'

'I don't get it. Because quite clearly the man I saw was –'

'Not James Eddison Swann. Not Swann at all. Some other man, Maddy. A fake, an impostor, a plant.'

She faltered.

'Oh, God. You mean, we were conned?'

'I mean just that. We have been suckered, and all I want to know is, by whom and why.'

Madeleine looked at Sim.

'Well, this is Sim Fielding, Ed, and we think his father may be able to tell us. As I just told you, we actually know where Maurice Fielding is right now – at least, we are almost certain. So perhaps we should go over there. It's in Yaumatei.'

Ed addressed his next question to Sim.

'Could your father have been the fake James Swann – the one who met Madeleine?'

'Hardly. I don't think he could have acted an American, and

anyway, I'm sure he was in England committing arson, kidnap and murder at the time.'

'Your father must be a nice man, Mr Fielding. Let's get over there and meet him, shall we?'

The cab dropped them in Kowloon, on a street to the west of Nathan Road. They found the building to be a narrow, newly refurbished office of no great pretension. Outside on the doorstep, with a joss stick burning over it from the nostril of a stone lion, was a neat pyramid of oranges on a plate. Just inside they found a uniformed policeman waiting to refuse them entry.

Craike showed his identification as an inquiry agent and began to deploy all his powers of persuasion.

'Look, I'm working on a case with my colleagues which is relevant to anything that may have happened here. Now, what *has* happened here?'

'I'm very sorry, sir, I'm not empowered to inform you at the present time.'

Craike pointed to his radio.

'Look, kindly use that thing and ask upstairs whether I can come up with my assistant, Miss Madeleine Scott, and my client, Mr Sim Fielding. Say we have information which will be of material help to the police in their inquiries, OK?'

The officer walked a little way from them into the recess of the hallway to make the call. They heard the undifferentiated chatter coming back. The officer returned to them with deliberate strides.

'All right, sirs, madam. You may go up.'

They took the lift. At the top they were met by another uniformed man, who ushered them to the door of the office suite that Maurice Fielding had taken only the previous week at such a reduced rent. The man who had rented it to him was standing just inside the doorway. He was gnawing at his lower lip and looked shattered, like one who has witnessed a fatal road smash.

The place was full of police, so that you could hardly see what was what. Two shapeless mounds were covered with white sheeting and around them buzzed plain-clothes men with cameras and other equipment. Meanwhile, uniformed people stood round idly like guards. Madeleine noted a police surgeon, a dog-handler and a dog as well.

Craike said briskly, 'Who's in charge here?'

An English type in a suit came forward.

'Are you Craike? Ah, yes, they radioed up about you, didn't they? These your people? Better all come through, will you?'

He conducted them into a second room where there was a playpen, a mattress on the floor, a child's cot, an ironing-board, some suitcases. There was a tall, solid, grey-haired plain-clothes man talking to another, whom Craike was startled to recognize.

'Vanteel? Good God, what are you doing here?'

Vanteel was looking pale, his eyes starting a little out of their sockets as if he had seen sights he wouldn't care to discuss at the golf club. Seeing Ed Craike, he tut-tutted in a civil-servantly manner.

'Sad business, Craike, quite horrible. Two dead. One might more pertinently ask, what on earth brings *you* here?'

Craike ignored the question and turned to the older man. Madeleine whispered in the side of her mouth, 'Chief Super Willingdale, Ed.'

Ed smiled and held out his business card.

'Chief Superintendent, I wonder if you know my assistant, Madeleine Scott. Used to be one of yours.'

Willingdale smiled at Madeleine and jerked his head, as if even bare civility towards ex-subordinates required excruciating effort.

'And this is Mr Sim Fielding, from London, whom I think you will want to speak to about this, er, affair. Although I would be grateful to be clued up as to what the affair exactly is, and what has actually occurred.'

Willingdale still had not spoken. From the look on his face he appeared to be in the grip of some powerful nausea. His nostrils twitched and his lips worked without opening, as if sewn together. He glanced at Vanteel, and Craike noticed the London man nod his head infinitesimally. Willingdale strode to the door and plucked it open.

'You two, get in here.'

A couple of young constables trooped in from the other room. They stood awkwardly in front of their boss, looking up at his face. His height must have almost amounted to theirs' combined. Willingdale gestured curtly at Sim, Craike and Madeleine.

'I've got a job for you, boys. Will you please take these three people down to the station and park them in three separate interview rooms until I get there? Come on, now! Sharpish.'

They were not under arrest and no one mentioned coercion. And yet, before any of them had time to get out a word of protest, they were on their way.

## 25

'Well, Craike. Sticky mess you've got yourself into.'

Vanteel's complacent, well-fed face seemed lit from within with satisfaction at Ed Craike's discomfiture.

'You bastard, Vanteel. Did you work this? Well, give me some information, for Christ's sake. Where's the child? What happened at the office building? No one's told me anything.'

It was true. The police had simply asked him to explain how he came to be visiting a site where there were two dead bodies and had taken down his statement. As a result Craike was seething with thwarted energy.

Coolly, Vanteel took a seat opposite his one-time boss.

'*I* didn't work it, Ed. I have merely been liaising with the civil power which, in this particular case, is Willingdale rather than yourself. So I'm afraid all I can tell you is nothing. You'll have to put your questions to the Chief Superintendent himself.'

'Jesus, Vanteel, Willingdale is only a flunkey. Who's really running this? London?'

'Up until now, yes – in partnership with the Governor. He's really very concerned, Craike. Allegations of the sort you've been bandying about – Beijing harassing C. P. Cotton, murdering his daughter-in-law and what-not – have the potential to really annoy the Chinese, you know. And we *do* have to work with them – 1997 and all that. There's been a lot more at stake than you realized.'

'Don't tell me what I didn't realize.'

Craike was down and he knew it. He'd lost Vanteel just when he thought he'd got the prat on a plank. The failure made him savage.

'I realized a hell of a lot, starting with the fact that you are a double-eyed whore. You owed me a bit more loyalty than this, Vanteel. But you! You'll do it with anyone who'll shake a drop of scent into your hanky. And anyway, what are you handing this back to the police for? They're all bent as fish-hooks here.'

He sat at the table with a glass of water. What he wouldn't give for a stiff Glen Grant. He qualified that thought. He wouldn't give Vanteel a curl of shit, *even* for a stiff Glen Grant.

Vanteel sat down and took a dossier from his briefcase. It was an official-issue briefcase with EIIR embossed on it in gold. But then, with Vanteel, it would be.

'All that's neither here nor there, because I came down not to bury you, but to debrief you, Ed. Let's be a little more friendly, shall we?'

He smiled, utterly without warmth, and went smoothly on, as if Craike were not staring moodily at the floor.

'It's a couple of days since I received your two reports, and I've now had a chance to put them through the system. Quite honestly, I'm *rather* disappointed. They don't seem to *me* worth the money we've been paying.'

Craike looked up sardonically.

'You don't surprise me. But then, I wouldn't look to you to distinguish value from price.'

'I mean, for a start you seem to think that Cotton represents a real threat to the PRC's media stability, which in turn, so you say, by a knock-on effect, rocks Deng Xiaoping politically. But on our information, Cotton's practically on the rocks. His debts are astronomical and his plans are defunct before they've even got off the *ground*, as it were.'

Vanteel smirked, as if the joke was funny. 'In short, Cotton's headed straight for disaster.'

'A situation which you clearly enjoy.'

'Well, one doesn't like to see a *good* man go down, but of course that begs the question, doesn't it?'

'Cotton's certainly no friend of the UK. You should hear him on the subject. And that's why you should keep tabs on him, because he's dangerous – take it from me. I tell you this as a patriot rather than a colleague, Vanteel. It's free advice.'

'I think we're on top of him, actually. We can pull the plug when we like.'

Vanteel spoke idly. He was absorbed in looking through his file.

'Pull the plug? On what?'

'On his money, naturally. On his channel of credit. It's a decidedly tut-tut channel. Leaky, you could say. And tapped by a lot of individuals for their own gain, quite contrary to the rules. We can smash them when we like, and when we do, C. P. Cotton will go down the plughole with the dirty water.'

Vanteel was licking a finger fastidiously as he turned the pages.

'So much for Cotton. Turning to the second report from your, er, *assistant*, is it? Pretty girl.'

He aimed a knowing smile at Craike over the top of the papers.

'Now, let's see. James Swann, transcript of first interview with ... notes on second and ... conclusions. *Query* American GI prisoner living or held in China since the Korean War, *may* have been or become a Communist, *may* have acted for them out of conviction or otherwise under duress. *Possible* plant by PRC to destabilize. Well, it really doesn't come home with any facts, does it? *May be* this, *possible* that. It's all boffin work, Ed. Good stuff, I'm sure, but strictly for the theoretical department. What we want is nuts and bolts.'

'Is that why you had us all brought here – to award gamma-minus for course work?'

'Don't be childish, Craike, please. I came in to tell you why I don't see the need to continue the arrangement we made last week. Actually, I'm terminating it, as of now.'

'And is this decision your own or one of London's?'

'A combined effort, shall we say? We simply don't see C. P. Cotton as a threat to anyone now. I mean, when push comes to shove, he's burned out. He'll be hauled through the bankruptcy courts on three continents, that's my guess. No one could possibly have anything but a straightforward criminal motive for pressurizing him – and *that* makes this a matter for the police, not the Service. We're dropping out of the thing, which makes you, Ed, surplus to our requirements. Sorry and all that.'

Ignoring Vanteel now, shutting him out entirely, Craike closed his eyes and began to concentrate on a yogic breathing exercise. He heard Vanteel sorting his papers, packing them into his briefcase and snapping the catches. There followed the scrape of Vanteel's chair pushed back. Mentally Craike repeated Zen epigrams: 'Zero is the greatest and the least in one figure' and 'To learn defeat is to taste victory.' Vanteel's footsteps clicked across the linoleum. Craike felt a slight draught as the door opened.

That bastard had really enjoyed rubbing salt into Craike's wounds. His conclusion, though, could hardly be argued with. The more Craike's investigation had uncovered, the more the picture looked as Vanteel had described it – a criminal not a political plot. But what sort of criminal were they dealing with? What *sort* of crime?

Vanteel had made a lot out of Cotton's leaky or dodgy lines of credit. What did he mean – his bank? Craike remembered Pappingay's words about Cotton's bank: 'If anyone's looking for a BCCI Two, I'd tell them to look no further.'

What was the bank called? At first he couldn't remember. Cursing the decline in his medium-term memory, he tried to visualize the name at the top of the cheque Cotton had signed. Then he got it. Trans-Africa Finance Bank.

His eyelids snapped open as if on springs. Of *course*. It had been stuck in a corner of his mind and now it rolled into view, the connection between the two cases. *Morrison and Cotton had the same banker*. And he would bet on Pappingay being right that it was a bent bank. Craike sighed audibly with relief. He had the angle he needed to get the investigation restarted. Thank you, Vanteel, he thought. Thanks for arresting me.

He rose and walked to the door of the interview room. He pushed it open with his fingertips and walked out. He took a cab home.

Madeleine's frustration was tempered by calculation. The police had nothing to hold her on. Even if they regarded Sim as his father's accomplice, she wasn't implicated. The police knew this too, and the inspector who questioned her, a Scot named Geraldine Quinn, was inclined at first to treat the whole thing as more of a chat than an interrogation. Anyway, the two knew each other pretty well. They'd worked together for six months in the same anti-rape unit.

'You've got Sim Fielding wrong, you know. He's no more a murderer or kidnapper than you are, Geraldine.'

Geraldine, who was fat but incredibly energetic, said briskly,

'Come on, Maddy. Tell me how you got involved. There's two dead, you know, and maybe a wee child in unsavoury hands.'

Madeleine was alarmed.

'You mean you haven't *got* the child?'

'No, did you think we had?'

'Yes, I certainly did. I was speaking to him on the telephone forty minutes before the three of us arrived there. At the end of the conversation I thought I heard your people arriving. I heard adult voices.'

Geraldine looked at her notes.

'Now look, that can't have been us. We didn't get there until 1.10. Found two dead people on the floor, and a lot of articles scattered about in the next room to suggest a young child had been staying at the address. But nowhere did we in actual fact find the child, nor any trace of any other adult. Now, *you* turned up at 1.33. And you say you were speaking to the child itself at this address just forty minutes earlier?'

'Yes, about.'

'On the phone? How did you get the number?'

Madeleine told her. The telling required the full story of her two meetings with the man who called himself Swann, his death and Sim's involvement with the whole affair. At the end of the tale, Quinn gave Madeleine a cigarette and lit one for herself. She was the interrogator again now. She puffed and inhaled once, and again. Then, keeping her silence, she inhaled a third time. Madeleine nearly laughed. It was pure Hendon Police College, like a role-playing exercise. Quinn was choosing her ground and using the silence to unsettle her prisoner. Having performed the ritual, Quinn, as the jargon had it, 're-established dialogue'.

'Do you mean to tell me that this child was abducted from a Lancashire village two weeks ago and brought here? Don't make me laugh, Maddy. It's too incredible. What on earth for?'

So Madeleine led Quinn patiently back through the narrative of the supposed Swann and his particular interest in the tycoon C. P. Cotton; about the fire in the English cottage and the fate of the Cotton grandson.

'So this child could actually *be* Mr Cotton's grandson?'

Madeleine admitted the possibility, though personally she didn't believe it. Inspector Quinn, though, regarded it as information requiring executive action. She got up at once and left Madeleine alone, saying she'd be back.

Madeleine stared at the wall, requested a cup of tea, walked about half a mile in a circle around the room. An hour passed before Geraldine Quinn returned.

'Right, you can go on your way, Maddy Scott, without so much as a spot on your character. Sorry about the high drama, but you understand. Murder, and *gwailo* murder at that.'

She took Madeleine to the front desk and gave her back her effects. Madeleine was not angry about how she'd been treated. She was thinking ahead. She was thinking about the child.

'Geraldine, how did you get the tip-off to go to that address?'

Quinn shook her head.

'Sorry, Maddy, I can't tell you that. It's a police matter just now, and I'm sure we'll nab the culprits. Forget about it, will you? Same as I'm about to forget how you used an inside contact to get that address from our computer. Have a drink some time, OK?'

Of the three taken prisoner at the scene of his father's death, Sim was the one who suffered the ignominy of a police cell.

Not that he knew his father was dead. He'd seen the sheeted humps on the floor, he'd had time to note the stains of blood. OK, he supposed his father might be dead, but he *knew* nothing. And for a long time he saw no one and was told zilch. For the moment, the police were keeping him on ice.

Sim's thoughts consumed the time. First he considered his father. Sim had grown up an agnostic as far as notions of father and sonhood went. He'd never really known what it meant to be a man's son, to be one to one with your father. Even in the early days Maurice's biological status had failed to transform itself into a social role – his relation to the family was always more like an older brother or some ruinous, black-sheep uncle. He came and went as he pleased, and bothered to please no one if he didn't feel like it. Then came his parents' final split and the death of Eva, which had pulled down the curtain on the whole shabby enterprise.

Sim hadn't even thought about all this for a long time and was busy with his own life. But then, out of nowhere, the idea resurfaced. Like a drowned and gas-bloated corpse, it floated back towards him. And who was to say whether this blotchy corpse – even as decomposed as it was – could not, zombie-like, walk and talk again?

Perhaps there was no great loss. Perhaps the whole thing was a mirage anyway.

The cell was starker than most of the public urinals Sim had seen in his life. A concrete ledge to perch on, perhaps 18 inches wide. No window. Smooth, light-green walls. A floor which sloped slightly to a drain in the corner. What were they going to do – beat him up and then hose the blood away? Such things happened, he knew that much.

But he didn't know why he'd been arrested. Not exactly. Obviously they thought he was Maurice's accomplice, but he could soon convince them otherwise – or at least plant the seeds of doubt. If only they'd talk to him. Sim went to the door repeatedly and called out, hammering with his fist. Nobody came, and after six or seven attempts he gave up.

Later his thoughts had turned to the child. The police, of course, wouldn't know who he really was. Madeleine would try to tell them, but only Sim could really convince them. The kid would be back with his grandfather by now – or with the man assumed to be his grandfather. And, if Maurice's calculations had been anywhere near the mark, C. P. Cotton wouldn't know the difference. He'd be blinded by relief, he'd embrace the child as his very own. By now Kevin Ho could be embarking on a brand-new life as Joshua Cotton. So what? Sim asked himself. He was better off. You could leave well alone, Sim boy, and say nothing more on the subject.

He got up and hammered again at the cell door. They must, he supposed, come eventually. And when they did he knew the first thing to do. You ask for your telephone call. In England it was the sole thing an arrested person could count on. All else was debatable, but this was a right – to have your last contact with the world through one all-important number.

Except that he didn't *have* an all-important number. He could phone old Worsley, of course, in Moxon. He knew that one. But he'd never have the heart, even if they did allow that statutory call to be an international one half-way round the globe. Which, he thought gloomily, they wouldn't. The tight-fisted swine.

He would have to ask for a telephone book. Then he'd call Nancy Lo.

Before too long Sim came round to thinking about himself and, soon after that, to pitying himself a little. He knew he was undergoing a trial here but he lacked any way of judging his performance. If, for instance, when they came, they were to offer him a cigarette and he should refuse it, would that be a sign of resilience, heroism? All his life he had followed appetite and impulse, and there had been enough. Even giving up smoking had been something like that – he'd wanted to assert his individuality. He tried to gain applause by doing things in an unusual way. On another day, in another place, he might have sworn that he would walk on burning coals or run a marathon.

But in here there would be no applause, no interest or feedback. Or if there was, it would be calculated and so impossible to trust. And if, perhaps, he took the cigarette, he would certainly be true to himself. But would it be right?

Jesus! He was getting light-headed and his thoughts were turning silly. He rolled stiffly from the perch on which he'd been lying and decided to hammer on the door one more time. The lack of human contact was distorting his perception of what was sensible. Shit, what was the matter with him? There were people who went for months in solitary confinement. There were guys who'd spent years blindfold, chained to the walls of Lebanese basements.

He stood in position, straddling his legs fore and aft, and raised his fist to strike the door. He filled his lungs for the necessary shout, but then he froze. There was the sound of metal on metal. He did not drop his fist. He waited.

Keys on the other side jingled and scraped. A catch was pressed against its spring, releasing door from frame. It swung towards him, giving the frame up to the uniformed policeman with the bunch of keys in his hand.

The policeman saw Sim's raised fist and did not hesitate. He leapt at Sim, cannoning him back against the rear wall. Sim's body seemed to smack the concrete and then go down unstrung, winded, sobbing for breath. The copper stood above him, looking at the precise place on the wall where Sim's head would have been, had he not gone down. The policeman addressed the wall, speaking from under his shiny peaked cap with unequivocal clarity.

'Come, please. You are wanted upstairs. And don't try that again or I will bust your balls.'

They were in the place Sim dreaded. He would rather be anywhere but in here. They had led him through cold, quarry-tiled corridors, uniformed police always fore and aft of him, hurrying him along. At length they had come to a metal door and beyond that to a long, low-ceilinged room like a vault. It was like a bank's safe-deposit vault, where the boxes, built into the walls on both sides, were man-sized.

The plain-clothes policeman rapped out a number and the white-coated attendant walked them up the room. Suddenly he lunged at one of the drawers, as if meaning to catch it off its guard. He hooked both sets of fingers round the handle, put the flat of a foot on the drawer beneath and heaved. The long drawer rolled out with a sound like encroaching thunder. Inside, swathed like dust-sheeted furniture in a deserted house, was the shape of a man, his head at the near end. The hills of the nose and chin could be clearly seen under the sheet, which the attendant now untucked from beneath the head, lifting a corner up. Sim wanted to hang back, to look anywhere but there. From behind he felt himself being pushed or prodded forward by impatient, nervous hands. The policemen, like Sim, wanted to leave as quickly as was decent, and the only way to do it was to get the business over quickly. Sim understood he must perform with speed.

'Is this your father? Is this Maurice Fielding?'

Trying to control the tightening and the curling-up of his lip, Sim peered downwards. Maurice's face was mottled, grey shading into the colour of raw liver, but of course it was unmistakably his. To Sim the face had no expression he could recognize from life. Yet there *was* an expression, all the same, and Sim had seen it in an art gallery somewhere. It was the face of a St Sebastian shot with arrows, pained and yet serene, the expression of a dead saint.

'Yes,' he affirmed. 'That's him. That's Maurice Fielding. Now can we please get out of here?'

Not yet, they couldn't. The CID man mentioned a second

number and the attendant led them all off again, turning back as he went to ensure they were in tow, the way an usherette leads ticket-holders through a darkened cinema to their seats. Soon he came to the required place and pounced on the handle once again. It contained an identical shape beneath another cotton dustsheet and Sim took up his station beside it.

It was a woman, a young girl really. Her face, framed with lush black hair, was a gargoyle – the purple tongue protruding, the lips splayed, the bloodshot eyes pumped up almost to bursting. A blood vessel in her nose had burst and one of the nostrils was plugged with the black congelation. Her raised-up chin gave the neck the appearance of having been stretched, and Sim could clearly see the blue and yellow bruises, spaced in such a way as to suggest unmistakably a man's fingers on either side, and thumbs at the centre, pressed down on her windpipe. The policeman cleared his throat.

'Do you know this woman?'

Sim shook his head and turned away. He could not have felt more sickened and ashamed if he had strangled her himself.

It was Nancy Lo who stood bail and came to get him the next day. She guided him through the hall of the police station, past the desk where only three days ago he'd reported the theft of his passport, and out into Nathan Road. He walked with marked uncertainty and she needed to propel him with her hand in the small of his back.

'They have nothing to hold you on, and they know it. They couldn't answer the real question – what were you doing with Craike and Miss Scott if you are a criminal? Well, you bet they won't press any charges now. I'm sure of it actually, but even if they do, I know some pretty hot lawyers, Sim, who will get you off, no problems.'

He felt dazed. The traffic poured past on its stinking way, the people jostled and jockeyed, the money chased itself around from hand to hand. The police cell had been a sort of haven, and he hadn't realized it.

'Thanks for standing by me, Nancy. Really, thanks a lot.'

'It isn't only me who supports you, Sim. You got other friends, you know. Look.'

A small soft-top Mercedes saloon swooped up to the kerb in

front of the police station and stopped, with cars on the inner lane honking behind it. Sim bent to see who was rolling down the window. He saw first the flash of a beautiful even set of teeth, and then the rest of the beautifully even features.

'Hi, Sim,' called Madonna Lee, showing her palm and shaking it in the air. 'You didn't let those bastard policemen get you pissed off, I hope? Get in, both of you. I take you back to Wanchai.'

# 26

'Hello, Hong Kong and Shanghai Bank. How can I help you?'

'Is Caroline Jenks there, please?'

Almost instantaneously, Craike was put through to Caroline's office.

'Caro, it's Ed. You free to talk?'

'No, I've got people with me.'

'Lunch, then?'

'Today?'

She sounded doubtful, but this was no time for deference.

'Yes, today, Caro. Drop whatever Taiwanese bagman you're entertaining and meet me.'

'Life and death?'

'That's just about what it's worth, yes.'

'OK, Ed, same old place, 1.15.'

The same old place was a *dim sum* restaurant where they served particularly succulent *siu ling bau*, a steamed bun with pork, crab meat and bamboo shoots. He and Caroline had discovered this dish together a year ago and had gorged themselves shamelessly on several occasions since.

Craike arrived at 1.10 and the place looked already full. Arguing and shouting, the customers crammed together, shoulder to shoulder, their chopsticks clashing as they helped themselves to the *dim sum* baskets which littered the tables. Mealtimes were approached here with a passion which, in other cultures, is reserved for sex.

Luckily, just beside where he was hovering, a couple got up to leave. Craike commandeered the table and sat, waiting for Caro. He looked at his watch. 1.20.

At last she came, breathless.

'Sorry, Ed. I couldn't get rid of the bagman. He was Korean, not Taiwanese, by the way. Bloody mulish, too. Wouldn't give in.

He insisted I must advance him the cash he needed to export a load of surfboards to Russia. I ask you!'

They stopped a couple of waiters, chose from their trolleys and stacked the first four steaming baskets on the table between them. Caroline leaned across the squat tower of bamboo and clicked her sticks in Craike's face before helping herself to a deep-fried chicken foot.

'You want something from me, Ed. What is it? Information, education or entertainment?'

'All three, Caro. Have you got the time?'

'Sorry. I have to be on the phone to Sydney in thirty-five minutes.'

'Then I'll be brief. It's information. Trans-Africa.'

Caroline frowned.

'What?'

'The Trans-Africa Finance Bank. I want the dope.'

'What dope would that be, Ed?'

She spoke cautiously, as if wary of a trap. Craike lowered his voice to conspiracy pitch.

'I had a little whisper from someone, who may or may not have been trying to mislead me, that Trans-Africa have got an enormous mound of shit, and that a very big team of chuckers is about to go in there carrying with them a very large fan.'

She shook her head and compressed her lips.

'I'm not sure how much of this I can tell you.'

'All of it.'

She took a deep breath, shut her eyes, then opened them again.

'Promise me I'm not going to read it under your by-line in the *South China Morning Post* tomorrow morning.'

'World Chief Scout's honour. That was Baden-Powell himself – there's no more powerful oath.'

'Well, OK. It's like this. Trans-Africa almost certainly *are* deep in shit. I don't know about the chuckers, but I wouldn't be surprised if the fan's already started turning.'

'Tell me about it.'

'A bit of background first. We're talking about a Bahamas-based company which originated in Lagos. It grew fat handling American and West European cash transfers to the sub-Saharan drought regions, some of the money governmental aid, the rest from charities. They transferred to the Bahamas to cash in on off-shore investment in 1987, and opened a big branch out here in Hong Kong – what, three years ago – for no clear reason, since it's way outside their traditional patch. They claimed it was an obvious expansion move. So they went ahead, gobbled up a small local bank or two and set up shop. There's a mega-rich Nigerian oil-trader at the top of the Trans-Africa, several of his cronies, a couple of sheikhs and a few Hong Kong locals who bought in when the outfit hit town.'

'Was C. P. Cotton one of them by any chance?'

She lifted her eyebrows.

'No, not a shareholder. But he's a very big client. Is *he* your interest?'

'Were you – I mean, the HK and S – suspicious of Trans-Africa at all? When they first came out here?'

'Yes, we've always been a bit suspicious, but we've had nothing concrete to go on, or nothing until recently. Of course, a great deal of their business, perhaps the core of it, is reasonably clean. But we're now beginning to get hard indications of what we always suspected – that there's plenty of drug money and protection money being washed into those numbered accounts.'

'Triad money?'

'If you like. But gambling and guns too. All sorts of shenanigans, in fact.'

'Whose accounts? You mentioned numbered accounts.'

'Well, a lot of them are accounts belonging to the directors and their friends, you may be sure. If the clients you deal with are a little bent, you can get away with a high level of creative accountancy. The more bent they are, the more creative you can afford to get. Criminals can be incredibly trusting, you know. They find it touchingly hard to believe anyone like a bank would ever want to rip *them* off. Then, when they do tumble to what's going on, it's too late. They've got nowhere else to park their spondulicks. It's a form of blackmail. You are a bank creaming your account-holder, but he's got to put up with you because *you* know what he's done. You could turn him in.'

'So the problem was always getting the proof? Until now, that is.'

'One of the problems. Another is that financially Hong Kong is like an overloaded *dim sum* cart. See that one over there?'

She pointed a chopstick at a waiter who was trundling a cart out of the kitchen towards them. The round *dim sum* baskets, in which the food is both steamed and served, were stacked until their tops leaned at crazy angles and seemed bound to fall.

'One wheel hits a hole in the floor, the whole bloody thing could go over.'

'So if Hong Kong can't afford a banking scandal –'

'It tries its damnedest to avoid one.'

She put out her arm as the encumbered cart drew level with their table and chose another basket. She held it up for him to see.

'Mostly for you, Ed. I just wanted a taste of the *yeung chen chui*.'

She tapped the table for thanks and the waiter trundled on his way.

'But it does depend on the nature of the scandal. Rumour is amazingly potent here. A run on the banks is triggered if the HK and S chairman leaves work fifteen minutes early with his flies open.'

On extended sticks she offered one of the pork-stuffed green peppers to Craike. He took it in his mouth, laughing, and almost choked.

'Has he ever done it?'

'God, no. There'd be panic. Tellers committing suicide, computers suffering melt-down, me yelling down the phone at the head of the Bank of Australia when he's drunk on four-X in the middle of a beach barby.'

She shook her head. Craike took her hand, still laughing.

'I'd like to see it.'

'What, blood all over that lovely money? No, you wouldn't. Nasty sight.'

'So anyway, are you going to mark my card, please? The Trans-Africa Finance Bank? *Is* it about to go phut?'

'Well, I don't know what dicky-bird you've been talking to, but he was a pretty topical dicky-bird. There's been a high-level crisis meeting only this morning. It was chaired by His Excellency himself, and top of the agenda was a plan of action against certain problem banks, of which Trans-Africa is the most problematic. My guess is that we won't be holding the lid on

Trans-Africa much longer. The stink would be a hell of a lot worse if we did nothing and the thing blew of its own accord.'

Craike whistled. His hand was still lightly gripping her fingers and she shook it in warning.

'And *nobody* inside the bank must know about it. If HE is going to shut down the Trans-Africa, and I say *if*, it has to be a coup, a complete surprise. OK, Ed? A *complete* surprise.'

He smiled.

'All right, Caro. No one on the inside of the bank will know from me. May I be impaled on my scout knife and pulled through my woggle. Now, another of those delicious chicken feet, please.'

'To the *theatre*? Shit, I've just been in the cooler, Robert. I was set to serve years on a kidnapping rap. I can't go, really. Sell the tickets.'

When a successful theatrical production from London or New York hits Hong Kong, the round-eyes queue round the block. The actors may be a few fathoms down from top notch, the sets may be crumbling, the costumes crumpled and the whole thing several years after its sell-by date, but you miss the show at your peril.

*Guys and Dolls*, the revival of the revival that had been at the National in London several years before, had run into town a month before. It was due to run out some time after Christmas, by which time every English, Australian and American resident in the Territory could have been relied on to have seen it once at least. Tonight Robert had got himself and Madeleine a pair of prime tickets.

'Look, sugar plum, this is just the thing to take your mind off those nasty rozzers and their nasty questions. It's all about a girl who can't persuade her man to take his life and her devotion to him seriously, OK? Just like me, in fact.'

'God, I don't go to the theatre to be reminded of you. And what do you mean, "just like me"? Is it that *you* can't take life and devotion seriously, or that you can't get me to?'

'Both.'

'Well, you can't get me to take you seriously because it isn't serious. I've told you that hundreds of times. I'm not about to settle down with a drunken solicitor and have babies in Solihull.'

'Not Solihull. I thought we might go and have babies in Canada after '97. Or even stay here.'

'The Communists won't let you stay. You'll be expelled for being a drunken slob.'

'Fair enough. Canada, then?'

'Almost as tough. To get in you've got to be third-generation workaholic at the very least.'

'Oh, come on, baby. Just come to the play. When was the last time we had a night out?'

She sighed.

'OK, pig-head. I'll come.'

---

Sim had been sleepless at the police station all night and half the morning. Now in his room above Mama-Bunny he slept and dreamed that he had had phone sex with Madeleine Scott.

Nancy Lo woke him with brutal suddenness.

'Come on, Sim, it is evening now and you must wake up. There's something for you to see downstairs in the bar. Come first to my sitting room.'

She left him to roll out of bed painfully. He was stiff from lying on the concrete ledge. Down his back, where he'd been smashed against the cell wall by the policeman, there was the dull discomfort of bruising. His head throbbed.

In the mirror he didn't look good. There should be nothing more familiar than one's own eyes meeting themselves in the glass. But Sim's eyes were disturbing to him, like those of someone he was meeting for the first time. The stranger was, moreover, someone who had to be confronted sooner or later.

He put the discomfort to one side and splashed his stubbly face with cold water. Then he shaved and dressed and went down. Nancy Lo was waiting for him in her sitting room.

'Sim, tell me, I want to know your plans. Do you intend to stay here? Do you need money to go back to England?'

'I'm not going just yet, Nancy. I have found my father, OK, but I still have something to do here. The kid is still around. Someone's got him who shouldn't have, and I don't want to go back without him. Hasn't Madeleine Scott been in touch?'

The first thing Sim had done when he returned from the police station was try to contact Madeleine. The police had simply informed him that she had been released the previous day. So had Ed Craike. But when he phoned her flat and the office, there was no reply. 'No,' said Nancy, shaking her head sadly. 'We have not heard from that young lady. But we do have news from another place. Come on.'

She took Sim to the ground floor, not into the bar itself but along a corridor that ran behind it. It was narrow and dingy. At a point about half-way down the length of the saloon the corridor came to an end abruptly in front of an unmarked door. It led nowhere else. Nancy produced a bunch of keys and unlocked the door.

Inside was a narrow room, carpeted and quiet, with a curtain drawn across much of the wall, the wall shared with the saloon. Below the curtain was a shelf, and on this stood a line of small cassette tape units, each one numbered. Below that again was a table on which stood a small audio mixer-unit beside a loudspeaker. The mixer had sixteen channels and he saw that the tape units, too, numbered sixteen.

'I'm showing you this because I trust you and because you still need my help.'

She drew back the curtain. It ran on silent plastic runners, and concealed a long window which looked, as through smoked or slightly darkened glass, out over the bar and into the Mama-Bunny saloon. Looking past the upended spirit bottles in their brackets and the glass shelving around them, they could see the back of Jackie the barman arranging two glasses and an ice bucket on a tray. He turned around and was facing them as he bent to take a bottle of champagne from the refrigerator.

'Can't he see us?'

'He doesn't even know what is back here. For him it is only a mirror. Most of the ladies know about this equipment, since I have to trust them, but Jackie is just a boy. He's still new here.'

Sim peered at the tape-machines. Three of them were running. The mixer had an up-and-down sliding fader for each channel, and three of the faders, corresponding with the three tape-decks, were pushed up. A small green light winked over each of them.

Nancy was expressionless, competent, like a technician showing a visitor round her plant.

Sim said, 'Well, I'm gobsmacked, Nancy. This is a spyhole and a *half*. There are sixteen of your tables with microphones planted on them, am I right?'

She nodded.

'Not on them, *in* them. Embedded.'

'What's it all for? Blackmail?'

Nancy dealt with his question as once, in bed, she must have parried the sexual impertinence of the johns.

'I am not a blackmailer, OK? Just don't ask. This is part of our work here, that's all.'

'I thought you were a bar-owner, Nancy.'

'I am. There are different kinds of bars.'

'So why are you showing all this to me? Why am I being let in on the secret?'

'Because I want to help you. I still think of John Worsley and what I owe to him. I am paying him like this, because this is my risk.'

'Risk of what?'

She laughed. He hadn't heard this laugh before and there was nothing humorous about the harsh stabbing sound she made.

'It's better to ask me how I can help you, Sim. And OK, I'll show you. Listen.'

She punched a button at the base of channel three and twisted one of the mixer's knobs. A voice came up on the speaker at a very low volume. It was a man's voice. Behind him hummed the background noise – piped music, other conversations, laughter, the clink of glasses and ice. He was talking fast and urgently.

'He's Japanese?'

She nodded.

'What's he saying? Who is he?'

'The man is a little unusual among our customers. Most of them are executives. He is a servant, although he is a very well-paid one. He has been here in Hong Kong for almost a year now working for one of the many wealthy people in the Territory. We see him on his evenings of freedom. He left all his family at home in Tokyo, he has no friends here, he is not a very young man. So naturally he is lonely. He has two ways to enjoy himself – he goes to massage parlours, where they look after his body needs, and he comes here to the Mama-Bunny, where we massage the spirit. Here is such a good place to relax, like one's own living room actually. Except better because there is no sexual tension, no possibility that his virility will be challenged. He simply gets drunk and talks into a sympathetic female ear, maybe cries a little, complains a lot about his boss, his boss's family, the other servants he has to work with. At last he goes home late at night, feeling he has unloaded all his fears and frustrations, and he is ready for another week of being kicked around.'

'Fine. So what is this man to me?'

'To you he is a window on to a world very difficult to penetrate. But it is a world you *have* to penetrate if you want to complete your task.'

She touched her long, lacquered fingernail delicately on the glass and pointed through the window, to a booth on the opposite side of the room.

'There he is, see? Talking to his favourite Mama, whom we call Gloria. He is complaining, of course. He is telling her how Americans are so stupid, how they tolerate the worst excesses in their own family and lack any sense of discipline. You see, he works for an American, a very rich, very arrogant American.'

'Oh?' said Sam. 'Who's that?'

'Sim, he is the Japanese butler of Charles P. Cotton. And tonight he is very hysterical indeed.'

Bovine contentment settled over the audience as the show started. A pukka London show, set in New York. What could be more perfect?

Song, dance, jokes. The dolls clucking over the guys' gambling habits, the guys desperate to find a game, any game. You *could* see the story as an allegory, for this is exactly the relationship between the matronly Hong Kong Government and its gambling-crazy people, who can get a game only by taking the fast Jetfoil to Macao, a Las Vegas across the water founded by the far less matronly Portuguese colonists.

The plot had hardly begun to unfurl yet. They were still in the scene in which a bunch of low-life characters mooch around wondering where they can go and shoot craps. Ideas are suggested and rejected. Benny Southstreet offers a thought, and it is rejected. Nicely-Nicely Johnson counters with a second, but there's nothing doing there either. The game behind the garage has been closed down by the cops. The only other crap-game in town requires them to flash a minimum wad of $1,000, which none of the guys has even a tenth of. They all agree, it feels so unnatural. With no place to go shoot craps, they are like fish out of water. They cannot fulfil their destiny. They are even threatened by the horrors of domesticity. Deep in gloom, Harry the Horse, with his chin sunk morosely in his hand, intones from the back of the group.

'Yeah. An' don't I feel like a pig in a chicken-house, sittin' round my place so useless all day?'

Madeleine, who had been drooping in her seat, her lids beginning to close, sat up sharply. She narrowed her eyes to get Harry the Horse better in focus. He was a thin actor in late middle-age. His character wore a big-shouldered, striped suit under a large Borsalino hat. *A pig in a chicken-house* was his phrase and it was striking. Where had she heard it? She examined Harry the Horse again with minute attention. *A pig in a chicken-house.*

At the interval the bar talk was of parallels between Damon Runyon's New York and the Hong Kong of today. Robert, as usual, had set off on a different tack.

'Of course, Runyon was only half right about men and women. I mean, in his universe there's no female sexual drive, is there? Runyon's dolls only want money and marriage from the guys, while the guys only want the dolls to give them sex.'

He looked around, as if his audience might break into spontaneous applause. They didn't, so he pressed on.

'I mean, these dolls are all out to *getya*, aren't they? Getya to give up the booze, getya to give up shooting craps, getya to work and settle down. But what the hell's behind all that? What do the dolls ultimately want after the final getya? Just a great big nothing. Not *sex*, that's for sure, not in this play. And that doesn't square with my experience, actually. So I think there should be a lot more *bonking* in it.'

But Madeleine wasn't listening. She was examining the programme.

Henry Sinclair (*Harry the Horse*) has appeared in plays around the English-speaking world, as well as on television in his Australian homeland. Having trained at Brisbane's Studio Thespis, his professional debut was as Laertes to Strawson Corrigan's Hamlet at Hobart, Tasmania. Highlights of his subsequent career include the following roles: one of *The Two Gentlemen of Verona* at Weston-super-Mare; co-author and performer of *Laughter is the Best Cough Medicine* (revue) at Baltimore and subsequently on tour throughout the American Midwest; Colonel Pickering in *My Fair Lady* at the BNF Sellafield Theatre,

Cumbria; Sir Henry Baskerville in *The Hound of the Baskervilles* at the British Playhouse, Kuala Lumpur.

In the second half she waited eagerly for the appearances of Harry the Horse, but his role, already a bit-part, began to shrink further and further until finally all that issued from his lips were assorted 'Hurrahs', 'Oh yeahs?' and some indistinct grumbling in the background of Sky Masterson's great love scene. By the final curtain he had become an element of the chorus, a walk-on player whose great line about *a pig in a chicken house* had receded and probably died in everyone's memory but hers. In hers, it lived.

She stood in the foyer while the audience flowed out around her, Robert having a piss somewhere. In no time Madeleine made up her mind. She *had* to be sure.

The theatre was incorporated into the lobby of one of the Central District hotels, a spacious atrium with vertiginous sides and a shopping mall attached. Madeleine moved swiftly. She swept past du Maurier and Armani boutiques until she found a small illuminated sign reading STAGE DOOR. There were, in fact, two swing-doors made of glass. She pushed through.

'Henry Sinclair, please,' she told the old Chinese man on the desk. He rang up.

'You go up please,' she was told. 'Number chowve.'

Dressing-room twelve was the last in the corridor. She didn't knock.

There were six actors using the cramped space, hardly wider than a corridor, and for the most part they sat or stood in silence. They were all doing the same post-thespian things, scrubbing at their make-up, dragging at cigarettes, passing and swigging wine directly from the bottle. The door swung open faster than Madeleine had intended and hit the wall with a crash. The actors all looked up.

She advanced into the room. Harry the Horse was the furthest from her, standing in his off-white T-shirt by a washbasin. He had a towel draped around his neck like a boxer's second and a roll-up smouldering between his lips. He knew and didn't know Madeleine, just as she had not been absolutely sure of him until this moment. She watched recognition dawn in his eyes, followed up in fast succession by alarm and outright fear. Yet as they stared at each other, the only thing initially that moved between them was the yellow-blue smoke of his cigarette.

And then he took off. He had seemed to her paralysed and incapable of it, but he whipped the towel from his neck, lunged forward and, taking Madeleine utterly by surprise, darted between her and the greasy wall. Before she could utter a sound or do anything to stop him, he was through the dressing-room door and out.

The other actors stared, but still they remained silent. Madeleine smiled.

'Very sorry to disturb you. Loved the show.'

Then, in Harry the Horse's wake, she too was gone.

## 27

Henry Sinclair was not in the corridor. Betting against the possibility that he'd entered another dressing-room, Madeleine raced back to the theatre foyer. The audience had almost dispersed but Robert was there, standing alone and intently reading his programme. He held it close to his nose, as if it contained a hidden code he couldn't crack. She ignored him, speeding past the plate-glass doors and cut into the high marble expanse of the atrium.

The huge space was less bustling at this hour, but there were still numbers of shoppers, pedestrians, hotel guests and idlers moving through it. She spotted Henry Sinclair almost at once, an elongated figure in T-shirt and jeans, stalking with rapid, scissoring strides towards the foot of an escalator. In the next moment he was ascending, two moving stairs at a time, with the enhanced speed of a puppet swung through the air by its operator. He was being taken to a mezzanine deck, a kind of wide balcony on which stood a parade of shop units. Had he seen her? Madeleine didn't care either way; she knew only that she would have to sprint to catch him up.

She reached the foot of the moving staircase ten seconds after he had disembarked. At the top she leapt off and found herself braking like a javelin-thrower in front of the shops. These were small but snazzy, selling the kind of value-added goods you read about in credit-card magazines – vanity luggage, high-concept telephones, novelty calculators, stainless-steel toys. She looked to left and right. A woman was emerging from a picture-framers. A jeweller was hauling sailor-like on his steel-mesh shutters. An elderly couple were window-shopping. Then down to the right she saw a leg encased in blue denim as it disappeared round the corner at the end of the row of shop-fronts.

'Hey!'

She reached the corner. The man stood at a stainless-steel lift, watching the lights on the lift-door lintel as they counted down to him. He turned when Madeleine called. He was a round-eye, but twenty years younger than Sinclair, and 40 pounds heavier.

She smiled and said, 'Sorry. Thought you were someone else. You haven't seen a guy in a white T-shirt around anywhere?'

The heavy man shook his head. He leered at her.

'I wish. But won't I do, honey?'

She laughed.

'Sorry. Not tonight.'

She could go no further in this direction as the lift-bay was at the extreme end of the balcony, so Madeleine retraced her steps to the head of the escalator, scanning into each of the shops she passed. They were small boutiques, in effect little more than kiosks. None offered much space for a fugitive actor to hide in, or escape through. She glanced down the moving stairs as she arrived there but he was not on them, so she walked past, towards the other end of the mezzanine deck.

There was a row of payphones and a cardboard display stand with leaflets advocating home security. There was also a pair of double-doors leading to a stairwell.

She made towards the stairwell, then stopped, glancing at the display stand. It was a free-standing screen in box-strength card and carried an illustration, in grainy monochrome, of a stereotypical masked criminal, complete with stripped jersey and swag-bag. Superimposed on this icon were high-definition coloured images of security devices – locks, chains, bars – and a number of pockets in which were stacked publicity material for the products on offer. Madeleine looked at the criminal's face. He seemed to be shaking.

She moved towards the stand. The shaking stopped as Madeleine approached, and then, when she was not quite near enough to reach out and touch it, there was a convulsive heave. The entire stand toppled forward, dumping wads of glossy leaflets and application forms on the floor. Some fluttered up into the air on impact, others fanned out where they fell. Madeleine planted her foot on one pile and it slid forward. She lost her footing and performed a perfect banana-skin pratfall. The box-cardboard screen came down on top of her.

She was struggling free when she heard the staircase double-doors swing and bang. She got to her feet, kicking the fallen screen away, and made it to the stairwell. She could hear the feet pounding down two or three flights below and set off in pursuit.

She had descended half a dozen flights, each a 180-degree turn clockwise from the last. Somewhere below her the footsteps continued. They must be going deep into the earth by now, for they were well below the ground-level theatre. Every two flights there were yellow-painted doors with numbers on them, but her quarry left these alone until he had plunged through five levels. Then she heard the door resounding against its frame, the shock waves travelling up the stairs to meet her as she plunged downwards. When she reached the door that had made the noise, she saw that this was where the stairs ended.

It was a deep-level car-park, hardly full but with a few gleaming Mercedes and Rollses scattered throughout its grey, well-lit area. At the far end Madeleine could see an attendant's cabin, with two security guards hunched inside. They were smoking and, perhaps, playing cards. Between them and her she could not see Sinclair. She glanced the other way.

The basement ended a few yards beyond the stairwell door at an oil-stained concrete wall. Numbered bays were marked out in yellow paint on the floor, but between herself and the wall no cars were parked. She saw, too, that there was a low door let into this wall. Sinclair must have gone to ground in there, she decided. It was the only possible place.

Slowly, as quietly as she could, she moved towards it. She had chosen court shoes for her night out with Robert – he expected a show of femininity on these occasions – and in spite of her efforts, the hardened rubber of the narrow heels clipped on the concrete ground. She wished she had a torch. It would almost certainly be dark in there and, with the light behind her, he would have the advantage. Trying not to think too hard about what this might mean, she reached the door, grasped the handle and pushed.

She had been right about the darkness. When she opened the door and, in a single, practised movement, slid inside, she darted instantly to the right and knelt on one knee, keeping her back pressed against the wall. She froze, listening and trying to force her eyes to adapt quickly to the intense darkness. The air was musty and hot. Mixed into it were oily smells.

Still unable to see anything, and with her palms flat against the breezeblocks, she now began to inch sideways, noiselessly straightening herself as she went. When she had gone no more that a foot, her right hand encountered a round metal pipe fixed vertically to the wall. This had to be a duct for an electricity cable, leading either downwards to a power socket or upwards to a light switch. She patted the wall up and down, taking one more half-step as she did so. The point of her shoe met something and moved against it. There was a hollow, ringing scrape and then an echoing smash, as the bottle she had gently kicked toppled over. At the same moment she found the light-switch and pulled it down.

A series of ticks and pings was followed by flickers of blue light. As the fluorescent tubes in the ceiling worked up to ignition, fingers of illumination touched the darkness. Madeleine saw rearing black silhouettes, shapeless masses, star-like metallic glints, slabs of pale reflection. The fracture of her senses was heightened by adrenalin and for a moment her imagination kicked in. She pictured for herself a Gothic cellar or cavern of nightmares: that pale-red spot in the dark seemed to be a witch's face lit by burning brands; that gently swinging silhouette could be the shadow of a suspended corpse. Then the room was flooded with light.

Before she began to take it in, Madeleine blinked. Gradually dull normality reasserted itself. The torture chamber was a dusty storeroom, full of discarded equipment, tools and builder's parts – aluminium ducting, copper piping, stacked sheets of plasterboard. The witch's face was a red teapot standing on a plywood chest. The hanged man was a collection of rusty spades, forks and pickaxes bunched together and hung from a hook. She saw no Henry Sinclair, but plenty of places to hide him. She called out.

'Hey! What are you running from? I want a little talk, that's all. Come on, show yourself. Let's see you.'

For a moment she doubted herself. Perhaps he wasn't in here. Perhaps there was another way out. Then a shoe scraped grittily and Sinclair edged into view from behind some cardboard cartons stacked near the far end of the room. He was carrying a heavy plumber's iron ring-spanner at least a foot long, with the handle gripped in one hand and the head cradled in the palm of the other. His face was a grim mask as he walked towards her. With her back to the wall, she looked to right and left. There was no obvious escape path; she was unarmed. She could do nothing but simply wait for him.

He stopped in front of her, so near she could smell his breath. She tried not to flinch or to look at the spanner, meeting his eyes instead. They flicked searchingly about her face.

'You play a great death scene,' she said.

Then, all at once, she knew she was safe. The hardness of his expression was only a carapace and suddenly it cracked. The mouth twitched. The eyes shut, lids squeezed together, and opened again. He was no longer acting. The mask dissolved entirely, breaking down into a slop of fear and grief. His arms swung to his sides and the heavy spanner left his fingers, bouncing and ringing like a massive tuning-fork before lying dead on the floor between them.

He said, 'I wish I could – well, explain. But it's useless, isn't it?'

Madeleine adopted the brisk manner of a psychiatric nurse.

'Well, let's give it a try, shall we?'

In the apparent secrecy of the velour upholstered booth at the Mama-Bunny bar, C. P. Cotton's harassed servant poured out a litany of American dissimulation, sloppiness and hard-heartedness, while Sim had sat on in the control room with Nancy. Sim wondered what the whole thing was about. *I'm not a blackmailer* Nancy Lo had said. What, then, was she? Surely not simply a voyeur who got pleasure just from knowing the secret fears and shames of others? A man might, perhaps, fit the part. But no woman would be interested.

After a few minutes of listening to the slurred torrent of Japanese complaint – Sim could almost feel the saliva hitting him – they moved back to the sitting room.

'Gloria will come up when he has finished and left. She will brief you.'

'Why are we interested, Nancy? Is this so fascinating?' he asked.

'Oh, yes. You want to know where the boy is, don't you?'

'Hasn't Cotton got him?'

She shrugged.

'If he had, he would simply tell the world. Maybe he will. But if he *hasn't*, he'll be looking for him. And with this neurotic butler, we have our ear to the keyhole of the house. And it's a strange house, too.'

'So what do we know?'

'The boy's father is called Chuck Cotton, C. P. Cotton's son. He is really crazy, you know. He throws and smashes things. Or else he sulks for days and days. Withdrawn, crazy, withdrawn again. On top of that he's a cocaine addict, which the father encourages. In fact, the butler has to obtain the stuff for him.'

'Hey, if *that* got out! I did wonder about the father.'

Nancy said, 'He's part of the reason Elizabeth, Chuck's wife, left and went to England. C. P. wouldn't let them go as a family, he wanted to keep Chuck and young Josh with him always. But he hated Elizabeth. He doesn't like women period, but rich and intelligent ones are real poison to him. She wanted to have her own house after she got married but he said no. He kept the couple living with him. In the end she couldn't take it any more and just took off with the boy to England.'

'It sounds like C. P. Cotton had reason to kidnap the child himself,' said Sim lightly. Nancy immediately lowered her tone almost to a whisper.

'Exactly,' she hissed. 'And I think he did. Chuck could never have got custody by legal means. There would have to be social reports on the family, and that could ruin C. P. Cotton for good.'

Sim considered for a moment and shook his head.

'But this *isn't* his grandson. Wouldn't he, or Chuck, know?'

'Chuck might. C. P. – I wouldn't bet on it.'

'Well, what about this guy James Swann? Doesn't it look more like the kidnappers fell out, my father got himself killed and Swann – whoever was behind him, I mean – is holding out for the ransom?'

Nancy only smiled and said, 'Wait for Gloria, Sim. Just wait.'

'I said no at first.'

It was the best Henry Sinclair could do by way of justification. They had gone back up the stairwell in silence to the atrium. Now they were in one of the hotel bars.

'It was before the *Guys and Dolls* part came along. Like, I'd been based out here for quite a few months trying to get together a one-man show.'

He sat forward on his chair in a confidential attitude, legs splayed, forearms resting on his knees and a tumbler containing a large vodka and tonic dangling between them. He looked into the drink as he spoke, as if reading from it. In his voice the Australian was overlaid with soft, West Coast American rather than the forced New Yorkese of Harry the Horse, of the hoarse Chicago of James Swann. He looked older now than he had on stage.

'I was broke, and I was facing a dental operation. You know, root canal work. Jesus, it was gonna be so expensive, and like an actor's gotta look after his mouth, I mean *gotta*. So when they came back a second time and pressured me a bit more, I guess I said yes.'

He flashed her a dilute smile. 'You know how it is, doncha?'

But Madeleine wanted facts, not excuses.

'Who? Who came to you, who pressured you?'

'It was like this. A Chinese guy came to my apartment one morning, said he could give me a part and asked was I interested. I said yes, in principle, I was. So then he laid it on me. He described the part – an old American guy in the Far East, sick and broke, almost like a refugee. And this refugee has a secret, and he wants to pass it on to a certain person. So he fixes up a meet at a flop-house where he's staying. I'd have to ad lib, he said, there isn't a script, and I said fine, I'm comfortable with that, what theatre is it? Or was this TV or film? And then he told me. It wasn't fiction or drama at all, it was real life. He said I shouldn't ask the details, just learn what I had to say, do the meet and then report back. That was when I said no for the first time. A definite no, because obviously this wasn't kosher. Obviously this stank. But later I said yes.'

'Did the man identify himself?'

'Not at that time?'

'Was he small, slim with wire-rimmed glasses, good suit?'

'Look, I know his name. I discovered it by chance when he came back the next day and he answered his portable phone. His name is Lee Hung, and he's a big shot in the Triads.'

Madeleine fetched a deep breath. *At last!*

'Lee Hung?'

'Yes. And OK, he *is* small, sharp dresser, glasses.'

'And what about our meeting on the boat?'

Sinclair rubbed at his eye, as if trying to remove a speck of dust.

'Well, then Lee came back and said I was doing one more performance, but he stressed it would be the last. I was to tell you all that I did tell you – you know, feed you the name Fielding, ask for the money, all that shit.'

'Did he tell you to chat me up?'

'I'm sorry?'

'Did he tell you to make advances?'

'Oh, no. That was my idea. Not too serious advances, I don't think. Did I overdo it? I thought it might be in character.'

She said severely, 'Well, you frightened me.'

Sinclair mumbled something apologetic and took a gulp of his drink. Madeleine lit a cigarette, businesslike. She took her allowance, her single inhalation, then ground the thing out.

'So then someone was to burst in and pretend to shoot you, making me think you were dead.'

'Yes. I was scared you'd leave before they came in, that's why I played for time. I didn't like tricking you, Miss Scott. I've agonized over it. The number of times I've all but picked up the phone.'

'But you didn't, did you?'

'No. Then this show opened and I was sort of busy.'

'What did you think it was all about, Mr Sinclair?'

'What did *I* think? Some sort of scam, I guess. I got well paid, quite a few grand, which paid my debts. Lee liked the money, I mean the money he got from you, and some more money he was getting from – who? C. P. Cotton? But there was more to it than money. I sussed it when Lee was on the phone that time. He was talking to someone who had it *over* him. He wasn't the big boss. There was another, above him.'

'Any ideas who?'

'Nope. Do you?'

Madeleine ignored the question.

'So now I want to know where you met Lee Hung? Was it your place?'

Sinclair was getting more sure of himself as the vodka took effect. His defeated manner had been replaced by one which, though still anxious to please, was marginally more assertive.

'I could be garrotted with barbed wire and dumped in the harbour for telling you this.'

'If you don't you're going to jail. You may be an accessory to murder and kidnapping. So tell and your involvement might just get lost in the wash.'

A minute earlier Sinclair had waved his fingers at a passing white-coat and ordered more vodka. Now it arrived. He dipped his nose into the glass greedily.

'OK, got a pen? I'll write it down. It's over Kowloonside, a very crummy neighbourhood. I wouldn't go in there alone, if I was you.'

He picked up her cigarette packet and pulled out a cigarette. With the pen held lightly in his hand, he wrote quickly along the shaft. Then he handed them both back to her.

'Memorize and destroy. This is one Marlboro you'll have to smoke all the way down.'

At last Cotton's butler had lurched into the night, his equilibrium shot to hell by whisky. But now he was happy again. He had been given permission by Gloria, his chosen Mama, to potter off and find himself a special whore with firm, reassuring fingers for the massage.

Gloria was tired, every muscle, every nerve. She was too old for this. She dragged her weariness up the stairs and into Nancy Lo's sitting room. The *gwailo* who had come to stay at the house was there. She looked at Nancy questioningly and Nancy nodded.

'It's all right, Gloria. Tell us. What news from the Cotton butler tonight?'

Gloria flopped into an armchair and accepted a glass of champagne.

'The usual complaint. Too much to do, the son of C. P. Cotton's a crazy bastard, the butler has to clean up after him and on top of that buy him cocaine the whole time.'

Sim said, 'Was there any mention of the grandson, little Josh? Does Cotton have a young boy about two years old at the apartment with him?'

Gloria looked surprised.

'Well, no, the butler didn't say anything about that. It's all about Chuck Cotton, the son. He's been dragged off to a mental hospital again and the butler has to go over there and take him stuff – drugs, maybe, I don't know. Anyway, when he gets down there, some place in the New Territories it was, the son of a bitch has gone, disappeared. The hospital says he discharged himself.'

'So now Cotton's lost his son as well as his grandson,' said Sim. 'Life is not being very nice to him at the moment, is it?'

'Oh yes, and there was something else,' broke in Gloria, after another long swallow of champagne. 'Another big fuss he's making. Along with the whole of the rest of the staff, he should receive his wages on Friday. But they haven't been paid for a month, none of them. For the last few days the atmosphere has been really tense. Nobody tells him anything, which makes him always very frustrated. And *now*, Cotton phones the butler up from his office and tells him to pack a bag for him because he's going away.'

'Nothing very strange about that,' said Sim. 'Cotton does a lot of travelling.'

'Yes, but he always says when he's coming back. This time he doesn't know when he is coming back. The butler thinks he may never get paid.'

Sim whistled.

'So Cotton's going, is he? But where?'

His question was directed to the place Nancy had been sitting, but she was already standing by the phone, dialling.

## 28

Ed Craike had pondered deeply on the strategy of kendo. The good swordsman or kendo player must, as Musashi counsels, know the degree of spirit mustered against him – he must know his opponent's courage. Craike's opponents were, in fact, multiple. There was Vanteel, of course, and the anti-Craike forces crouching behind London's defensive wall of briefcases. In that battle Craike had suffered a setback, but he wasn't lost. The amount of courage in a briefcase was limited.

More immediately there was Cotton. Cotton wasn't so much an opponent as a winning-post. Craike was after Cotton's hide, like a bounty-hunter, but in doing so he had Sim Fielding to reckon with. Fielding looked a lightweight, yet he had Madeleine in his corner.

Somewhere he'd read a fragment of gnomic Japanese wisdom to the effect that 'True victory means defeating one's allies.' Had Madeleine Scott meant to do him down from the very start? Maybe not, but Craike certainly had no illusions about her now. She had dropped him into Vanteel's open hand at the Kowloon police station. She had become untrustworthy, out of control, *competition*. And the struggle was for C. P. Cotton. The one who first cut into the monster's guts and wrapped them around his neck would carry the day. But, as Craike knew perfectly well, this wasn't a winning-post that you just cantered past. You had to move up on Cotton first, tangle with him, tread him down.

And to pull this off you had to know the spirit of C. P. Cotton. Craike puzzled over it until he was forced to admit that the spirit was obscured. The true force, the nature of Cotton's resources, was hidden in shadow. So Craike must, in the words of Musashi, 'move the shade to get the insight'.

He'd left Caro Jenks feeling good. He was in the mood to put on a pair of steel-capped boots and kick the shade all the way to hell. He went to a payphone, dialled and hummed to himself as he waited. When a voice came on the line, Craike said, simply, 'Craike. By the statue of King George VI, the zoo, half an hour.'

He was there sooner, taking up position on a contoured, green-slatted bench exactly like those in St James's Park in London. Opposite him a grove of magnolia trees thrust out their blooms in various shades of violet, and to one side was an enclosure containing a captive pair of leggy, long-necked, black-and-white cranes. He watched them stalking around their cage like a brace of foppish courtiers, tilting their heads to flash the bright scarlet skull caps adorning the narrow crowns of their heads. He was so absorbed that Jonathan Pappingay was upon him before he knew it.

'What's happened, Mr Craike? Has there been any development?'

'Sit down, Pappingay.'

'Have you made the drop of Cotton's ransom money yet?'

Craike frowned. 'The what? Oh, *that* ransom money. Forget about that. I rather think I may be donating it to the Poor Evangelists' Benevolent Society, what d'you say?'

Pappingay's face became wary. Was Craike trying to get a rise out of him? He remained standing.

Craike rapped out, 'Sit *down*, boy. I've come to settle our account. It comes in the form of some news for you.'

Pappingay sat, as nearly sideways-on as he could manage, at the far end of the bench. It was the most uncomfortable posture he could have adopted on a park bench of this type, the knees pressed together and aimed towards Craike, the buttocks resting on different slats of the seat.

'What do you know about Trans-Africa Finance?'

'It's a bank we've been using, I think I told you. A Nigerian outfit but getting very big out here. Currently we keep most of our money there. Why?'

'Just that the bank is about to be given a very large official-type tranquillizer and put to sleep, by order of the Attorney-General.'

Pappingay started and the tan of his face lightened a shade.

'My God. When? Why?'

'Any day now. There's been every kind of corruption and

fraud, I imagine, going right up to the top.' He lifted his eyebrows, as if he expected more of Pappingay. 'Do you mean to say you had no inkling of this?'

One of the cranes suddenly issued a harsh, clicking cry like an old-fashioned football rattle. Craike looked past Pappingay and saw that the birds were engaged in some sort of courtship ritual. The male spread his wings and danced up and down, bowing obsequiously to the female, his beak almost stabbing the dust. She seemed disdainful. She turned and machine-gunned her suitor with her stuttering cry.

Pappingay had shifted his position, slumping back as if some stiffener had given way inside him.

'Sure, I had an inkling. Trans-Africa was obviously corrupt. But I always assumed it was that way with the connivance of the Hong Kong Government.'

'Maybe it was, but now they've decided to cease conniving. They're pulling the plug.'

There was a smile on Pappingay's lips now. He was savouring his thoughts.

'Well, this will be the end of Cotton.'

'It certainly looks that way.'

'No, I mean this could actually *kill* the old bastard. Everything he has is locked up in Trans-Africa.'

But then Pappingay's face changed, from savour to suspicion.

'So how do I know it's true? It can't be generally known or all hell would have broken out at the office by now.'

'I have a source who told me – well, told me indirectly. Chap called Plummer. Mean anything?'

Pappingay shook his head.

'Well, I can't prove there's any direct connection. There may be none. But Plummer gave me the idea.'

Pappingay was looking at Craike as if he was talking a foreign tongue.

Craike said, 'But never mind that. I've kept my side of the bargain – I warned you as requested. In return I still want two little things from you, as a sign of appreciation if you like.'

'Oh no, no, no! I gave you all I'm going to give you, Craike. We're quits now.'

Craike held up his hand.

'But I only want you to do something for me. Now come on,

Pappingay. You'll be packing your bags for home tonight, I have no doubt. It won't cost you anything to help me. On the other hand, to *refuse* might just bring about a little problem at passport control in Kai Tak.'

Pappingay sighed.

'What do you want?'

The cranes had begun an ungainly dance, prancing around the enclosure in mutual pursuit. Craike was smiling, putting Pappingay's last question on hold as he watched them. At last, as the cranes' flap subsided and they began to preen themselves, Craike got up from his seat and pulled a small notebook from his breast pocket.

'Do you set up meetings between Cotton and Lee Hung?'

'What d'you mean, set *up*?'

'You *are* Cotton's personal assistant? So is it part of your function to set up these meetings at Cotton's behest?'

'I guess I've done it a few times.'

'Well, before you scuttle off to buy your air ticket, I want you to go back to the office and set up just such a meeting, as if on Cotton's instructions.'

He unclipped a claw-pencil from the same pocket and wrote briefly on a blank page.

'Get Lee Hung to come to this place. Tell him Cotton wants to see him – tonight, at ten o'clock. Tell him it is essential he is there.'

He ripped out the page and gave it to Pappingay.

'About Cotton, there is no incipient pity for the man, I hope? In *spite* of his impending misfortune, you do still hate him?'

Jonathan Pappingay smiled bleakly.

'Does a bear shit in the woods?'

'Then fine. Don't tell him he's meeting Lee Hung. Only tell Lee.'

He had left Pappingay then, walking away past the bronze of the Queen's father in all his ceremonial robes. Poor old stammerer. He looked more than ever as if he was determined to hold his breath until someone would let him stop being king.

Craike went down to his office. Inch by inch he was pushing back the shade.

*

Craike watched the Cotton apartment block. He saw the butler leave. He saw the other servants, also, go out. He saw C. P. Cotton's helicopter land on the roof.

It took him a while to convince the man in the hall to telephone up to C. P. Cotton. The tenant of the penthouse never received visitors in his apartment, Craike was assured. There were no exceptions.

'Look. You are aware that Mr Cotton has just had a bereavement. His daughter-in-law and grandson in England? Well, I have news of them, news of a very important nature that I cannot pass on any other way. If you block me and *he* gets to hear about it, your life might as well be over.'

At last, grudgingly, the man in the hallway used the house phone and was told, also grudgingly, to frisk Craike and send him up. Ascending to Cotton's penthouse, Craike felt an extraordinary lightness, as if he had inhaled laughing-gas. He was sure of himself, with the certainty of the calligrapher, Yasaburo, in the samurai manual. It was Yasaburo who had ordered his pupils to write so boldly that you filled the paper with a single character – with so much dash that you might even destroy the paper itself.

Once, at nineteen, Craike had been in love with a woman, Anna-Francesca, twelve years older than he was. This decisiveness, the sense of being charged up with unstoppable energy, was precisely how he used to feel as the lift floated him up to her tenth-floor apartment in that Paris block. His legs had been strong, his stomach flat, his brain clearer than it might be after a toot of cocaine.

The last time he'd gone there her husband had opened the door and stood breathing heavily, unable to speak in his fury. Cocking his head, Craike had seen the repentant wife lying behind him on a sofa, weeping. So Craike hadn't waited, he hadn't negotiated. He had stepped forward immediately and fought. The fight was to a standstill. There had been blood everywhere, not an ornament or picture undamaged, not a curtain unripped. They had used knees, chins, fists and feet, they had thrown furniture and porcelain and books. The place had been wrecked, utterly trashed, until at last the husband was kneeling before him, bleeding and begging.

Craike smiled. Cotton must be fairly groggy himself by now.

He would know that Trans-Africa might go phut. The edifice of his life, so carefully created and furnished, was toppling.

Craike stood on Cotton's threshold and pounded the door. Cotton took no precautions. He opened the door wide, then turned on his heels and waddled back inside. He was wearing a shiny silk tracksuit.

Craike closed the door and followed.

The place was large and decorated throughout in spare, angular furniture. Here and there were globules of glass. On the walls post-modern works of art hung self-consciously, as if they were on loan or approval. There was nothing antique in the room. Nor was there anything personal, anything that might have been chosen for its own sake rather than for overall effect.

'You've come to return my money, I hope.'

He said it in a low voice, near to a mumble.

Craike replied brightly, 'Your money?'

'The fucking ransom money. Where is it?'

'It's safe, in my safe.'

Cotton turned and raised his voice by one notch.

'So what do you want, Craike? You fuck up my life and then you got the nerve to come here into my house. What do you want?'

'*I* fuck up *your* life? Not me, Cotton. You fucked it up all by yourself.'

Cotton stood and bared his teeth. They were unnaturally, comically white. Craike went on.

'I wanted to issue you with an invitation. To bring you down to see someone who can help us in our inquiries about your grandson.'

Cotton's face returned to its usual set, lips jutting, nostrils hitched up. He did not register interest. The question he asked was weary, a matter of routine.

'Who is this guy?'

'He's Fielding.'

Cotton snorted and ambled across to a round, glass-topped table on which stood a pitcher of water. He poured himself a glass.

'You gonna introduce me to a *stiff*, Craike? See, I know what happened to this Fielding, he's dead. We going to a seance?'

Craike felt like laughing in the man's face. Cotton's fearsome-

293

ness depended so much on context. His office, approached the way it was, surrounded by personnel and the trappings of power, gave a structure of support to his power games. But this performance, in this place, was a joke. The apartment looked like a show flat for a 1970s development in Milton Keynes. Cotton was diminished here, because for all his swagger Craike could see the poverty of the man himself.

'Why not just come along and see Fielding? You will not regret it. You ought to come.'

'I *ought*? I ought to do shit by your say-so.'

'It's in your interest.'

'Mr Craike, when that murderer and kidnapper Fielding wrote me his ransom note, I knew what my interest was. It was in seeing him roasting in hell with a pointed stake rammed up his ass. Well, now he's there. I don't need to see him.'

'But, you see, I'm talking about a different Fielding.'

Cotton's train of thought rattled to a halt.

'A different Fielding?'

'Not the Fielding being spit-roast in hell. Another Fielding, who is alive and well.'

'Which other?'

'His son.'

'His *son*? He's got a son? All of a sudden, this is a Fielding family affair?'

He passed a hand wearily over his brow.

'I don't get this. I don't need this.'

'Well, I realize you would think that. But consider, just for a moment. You may soon be broke, you may soon be banged up, you may soon be envying the beggar in the gutter. Your options are closing down rapidly, Cotton, one after another. You *do* need this.'

Cotton did not speak at first, and when he did it was carefully.

'How so? What exactly is it that you know?'

'I know about Trans-Africa Finance, I know about the secret accounts, I know about the phantom account-holders. I know the whole fraud, and I know it's about to blow, because it's not just me who knows it – the Hong Kong and Shanghai knows it, the *South China Morning Post* knows it, the Hong Kong Governor knows it. And by tomorrow, or the next day at the latest, the whole world will know it.'

Cotton shut his eyes and froze. He took a deep breath and let it out like a release of brakes. Then, slowly at first, the locomotive began to move towards Craike, his arms outstretched.

His face was pulled back in rage, a blind rage. He came with a stumbling tread and, like a bicycle that keeps upright only by its momentum, he would have fallen over had he not kept moving forward. Craike stood in Cotton's path and held out his palm to check the man.

Cotton met the buffer of Craike's hand. He looked up. His lips were flecked with yellow, frothed saliva. His eyes stared. He blinked.

He was looking down the barrel of a Smith and Wesson 61 pocket pistol.

'OK, Cotton, I've heard enough of this. Let's go. My car is outside. You won't be needing anything except your delightful self.'

# 29

The child's head contained a buzzing, like a huge trapped housefly. So much echo. Two big people craning over him. They talked to each other in whispers but spoke loudly down to him, in that sing-song which meant they wanted his attention. What they were saying he didn't know, but several times he heard the word 'mama'. He was rather distracted and listless about everything. Yet 'mama' excited him.

Physically his mama had already become a vague figure, her reality diluted by the child's watery, elusive memory. He could still get her hair, a flowing, black, silky caress which smelt ticklish when his head was hoisted up to it. The assembled image of her face had receded from him, but he could visualize some of the parts, especially her lips. He saw them red as fruit, coming down to touch him. More dimly he remembered her breasts, playthings to paddle with his hands and mash his nose against laughing; and also, in some even vaguer epoch, to flood him with that warm, sticky, sweet yoghurt whose flavour he couldn't now recall.

But he had complete recall of a *feeling* connected with mama. This inner state was quite the opposite of the dark, clogging, fluffed-up buzz that filled his skull now. It was a buoyancy. He felt able to float away from the ground, if he wanted.

He clung to the memory of this most special feeling, wishing it had not gone. There were toys which sometimes went away and would then come back again, in some unexpected place. Perhaps this would come back too. So he turned over cushions and clothes that were strewn on the floor and hammered at the piece of tin that was screwed on to the door. He longed to stumble on this feeling of mama that he had lost. It was around here somewhere, of course it was.

These big people who loomed over him, one of them was Mama-type with a small, musical voice. The other was Big Bad type with a deep voice whose breath wrinkled his nostrils. Once the child had eaten a sour nut and spat it out, and the taste this Big Bad breathed on him was nasty, like that.

The light that came through the window was dirty and cold, though he preferred it to the hot, black light that came from the bottle on the wooden box. There were no toys. He didn't mind lying on the floor because it had the cushions and all the soft clothes which he pulled from some boxes in the corner. They smelled musty and friendly. Some of them were clothes with pockets, and he found things in the pockets – little balls of silver paper, buttons, metal discs.

They kept forgetting to change him. For hours the nappies would hang between his knees, cold, stinking and sodden, before one of them would look down and do the changing. Mostly the Mama-type did this. Once the Big Bad tried, but the child had ended up screaming and almost took a chunk out of the man's sour-nut finger with his teeth.

The Mama-type was always half asleep and sad, but she was nicer than the Big Bad. She got the child a pair of wooden sticks and a metal saucepan. She put the saucepan on the floor like a drum and hit it with the sticks. The child got the idea right away. But the Big Bad came at him angrily and shouted until his ears hurt. He took away the sticks and the pan then.

The Mama-type and the Big Bad did not like each other. They screamed at each other and they fought. The Big Bad sometimes hit the Mama-type. He made her lie down and he stabbed her. She spoke very softly except when the Big Bad was stabbing her. Then she screamed and cried. She mostly lay in the room sleeping. She could sleep with her eyes open.

The child spent much of the time on his back, looking up at the ceiling. The walls had no pictures, only red stripes. But the ceiling had pictures that he could talk to. In this way he tried to drown out the buzzing fly, and the sound of the big people quarrelling. He made images of food with the cracks. There was another inner state to do with food and he hadn't felt it since the Mama-person lay down and never got up again. They did give him biscuits and pieces of bread. He had cold rice too. But he never had enough. He wanted enough, and for the bluebottle to crawl out of his head and fly away.

*

When Madeleine came home she found her answering machine had trapped an angry message from Robert.

'You cow, Madeleine. I go to the trouble to take you out and you piss off on your own, leaving me looking like a pillock. Or should I be worried? Where the fuck are you? Call me.'

Pulling the telephone plug out of the wall, she changed into jeans and sweatshirt. She made tea, sat at the kitchen table and opened up a Hong Kong police street-plan to locate the address Henry Sinclair had supplied. It was the place where he had met Lee Hung and the place, she hoped, where Lee had the child stashed away. But it wasn't just any place. It was one of the most sinister locations in Hong Kong.

She reckoned she could rough in the picture now. 'Swann' was Lee's camouflage. Behind it he'd hired Fielding to go to England, abduct the Cotton grandson and bring him back to Hong Kong. Fielding had cocked it up and accidentally killed the child. He then tried to restore the situation by finding a look-alike, but somehow the plot had misfired. Back in Hong Kong Lee Hung had disposed of him, along with a Filipino whore he had recruited to do the feeding and bum-wiping during the child's captivity.

There were plenty of loose ends. The use of a disappeared Korean POW's identity was puzzling. For whose benefit was it? Cotton's? Craike's? Fielding's? And why the elaborately staged 'murder' of Swann? As for Maurice Fielding's death, Madeleine could guess at the reasons. He must have become greedy, branched out on his own. But did Lee know that Fielding's hostage wasn't the real grandson?

One thing was sure. Lee was now sitting on the child, waiting for his street value to appreciate. And where was he keeping him? Madeleine tapped the map spread out on the table. The perfect place, the only place, the obvious place: the Walled City.

For years there had been no maps of the Walled City, no real addresses, just the system of signs and numbers used by the postmen to locate the thousands of addresses hidden within it like the cells of a termite nest. The police had created the map during the early 1980s, when they had started quietly and systematically to clean the place up. You couldn't clean it up really, of course. The Walled City was a kind of human cesspit and the only real option was the one the Government had now decided to take. After years of wrangling, the Walled City had been cleared of its inhabitants. It was a ghost city now and, in a matter of months, it was due to explode in the largest simultaneous charge of dynamite ever seen in peacetime Asia. She had to go there and see, but she could not go alone. She would need a guide, and she knew just who to ask.

The taxi journey brought her back into the alley-world of Kowloon. Three blocks from the junction of Nathan Road and Boundary Street the driver dropped her and pointed to an opening between a duck-dinner place and a small foodstore. He shook his head, muttering darkly some words she did not particularly want to catch. She stood on the kerb and looked up and down the street, which was dirty, decayed and in full use, even at half past midnight. Men and women hurried by at a clip or strolled, window-gazing. The lights of an electronic-goods shop dazzled. A street-vendor stood beside a board festooned with fake jewellery and watches, calling plaintively to each pedestrian who came within his ambit. In the restaurant's window a line of roast duck turned on a spit, their skins glistening like burgundy leather.

She crossed and plunged into the alley. Madeleine wished she hadn't come out on her own. Why the hell did she not ring Sim Fielding and get him out here with her? But he would be in bed with that girl. That girl had subdued Madeleine's interest in Sim and brought the plight of the child back to the front of her mind. What the hell was he thinking of, playing Casanova at a time like this?

Madeleine climbed to a second-floor apartment 30 yards down the alley. A woman answered her ring.

'Barbie?'

The woman seemed not to recognize the name at first. But then, when she knew her visitor, she embraced Madeleine with a broad smile.

'Ah Madeleine! Madeleine! How good to see you. Come inside, I give you tea.'

Madeleine followed the woman into the flat, which was painted white, spotlessly clean but lit only by three or four stubby wax candles and the blue light of a neon cigarette sign suspended on the wall just outside the window.

'Sorry about the lights. I got no electricity right now.'

Barbie was short and broad and rolled when she walked with

the gait of a sailor in high heels. She wore a red V-neck dress which was stretched into radial corrugations by its tightness around her plump thighs and the swell of her stomach.

Her legs were sheathed in spangled stockings and the backs of her fat, brandy-glass calves shimmered now as she strode across the room to a sideboard where lay a pack of American cigarettes. Sliding one out she lit it and swizzled round in a movement stolen years back from some Hollywood screen coquette. She leaned backwards against the black-lacquered piece of furniture and looked Madeleine up and down.

'It's been so long.'

'Yes. *Are* you still calling yourself Barbie?'

'Barbie?'

She considered the name, as if for the first time. Then she shrugged. 'Sometimes. It depends. You may, if you like.'

'Barbie, I want to go here.'

Madeleine brought out a used envelope on which she had transcribed the address and showed it to Barbie. She took it, held it up so that the light caught the writing and handed it back with another shrug. She couldn't read English. But when Madeleine read the details aloud, the reaction was instantaneous. Barbie shook her head firmly enough to rattle the gold that dangled from her earlobes.

'Oh, no! No, no! This the Wall City.'

'I know. Please, Barbie, I want you to take me in.'

'You cannot go there.'

'Oh, come on, Barbie. You owe me this. Think of all I've done for you. I found you this place, *and* I got those charges dropped when you desperately needed to stay out of jail.'

'I don't go in the Wall City now. Too dangerous.'

'Do you think it's too dangerous for a tiny child, a two-year-old child? Well, there's a child in there, and I want to go and get him out.'

'There's nothing in there. The place has been cleared. They're going to blow it up.'

'Yes, but it's still being *used*, isn't it?'

'By rats.'

'Exactly, Barbie. Rats and all their human relatives.'

Their eyes met. Barbie did not dispute the point. Madeleine went on.

'So there's a *gwailo* child, a kidnapped child in there, and I want to go in and find him. He's at this address. He must be terrified and we must help him.'

Barbie looked up at Madeleine sternly, her lips pressing together. The face was washed with the blue light, the lipstick turned black by it, the thick rope of beads gleaming like teeth from her throat.

'You don't know what goes on there, specially night-time.'

'But you do. You can take me safely. I know you, Barbie. There's nowhere you don't go.'

Madeleine touched the woman's arm.

'Please. You take me there. You show me what goes on.'

She dug her other hand into her pocket and found a banknote, $1,000.

'I have a present for you if you will come with me. This big orange.'

The woman hesitated, looked at the money. It was probably as much as she could earn in a week. It was enough to buy a new dress and a pair of shoes. She turned away from Madeleine and walked to the door. She called along the passage.

'Hey! Come in here. Look who's here.'

There was a pause of perhaps ten seconds during which neither Madeleine nor Barbie spoke. Then feet were heard, creaking the floorboards outside and a girl in pyjamas stood in the doorway. Madeleine's face took a moment to register.

'Is it Li Na? Oh, my God, how brilliant. I thought you were abroad, Li Na. When did you get back?'

She went up to the girl and kissed her. Li Na stood a little stiffly in the embrace.

Barbie said, 'My daughter's been back in Hong Kong for two weeks now. She was just visiting. It's her night off.'

As Madeleine backed away Li Na lifted her arms from her sides and let them fall back. She smiled that vague, lop-sided smile that Madeleine remembered so well from her days on the Family Crimes Squad.

'Madeleine. Good to see you.'

Barbie took a pull on her cigarette and walked across to a velour sofa.

'Why don't we all sit down?'

But Madeleine was too excited to sit.

'Li Na, you could take me down there. I came to Barbie as a last resort. She was the only one I could think of who really knows the Walled City. But now I come and find you here –'

Li Na stood unmoving, playing with the long end of the drawstring on her pyjamas. Her mother spoke rapidly to her in Cantonese and Madeleine gathered she was telling her about the kidnapping. She broke in.

'You see, I think the boy was taken from an Englishman as he lay dying. I think it was Lee Hung who took him. You know him?'

Li Na nodded.

'I was told by the actor that Lee Hung uses the Walled City sometimes, and that if he had the kid, it would be where he'd have him.'

Madeleine showed the envelope again. Li Na read it, screwing up her eyes to see in the flickering light, and handed it back.

'Li Na, do you know who we might find there?'

'Like my mama told you already, the Wall City has been cleared. But I know one bad guy who you would find at the place on that paper.'

She nodded at the envelope in Madeleine's hand.

'He is called Ho Yu Ching, but the people round about have another name for him. He is a very stupid but very dangerous bastard.'

'Then we must lose no time. Will you take me there?'

Li Na seemed to make up her mind only now. She smiled more warmly and reached out to touch Madeleine's hand.

'All right. Let me get changed. Mama will make you some tea.'

She turned in the door and then completed the rotation until she was looking at Madeleine again.

'Oh, by the way, I am not using the name Li Na at the moment. I go by another name. Did you hear?'

'No. No, I didn't. What is it?'

'I chose after the great American star – Madonna.' She laughed with enjoyment. 'I am Madonna Lee now. Do you like it?'

Sim had the feeling this was a vigil. He sat alone in the Mama-Bunny bar, drinking and trying not to think. Something was about to happen, a test was going to present itself, a question be asked.

Ever since he'd arrived in Hong Kong he had felt the current of events running against him. The business he had set himself – to find Kevin Ho and restore him to the bosom of his family – had got caught up in and swallowed into a much larger set of problems – the fate of the Cotton empire, the future of Anglo-Chinese relations.

After all, what had he really done since he got here? Fucked Madonna Lee one time. Anything else? Been robbed, imprisoned, had things done to *him*. The others were so much more effective. Madeleine – wherever she was – away like an angry hornet after hints and moving shadows. But she got results. Then there was Craike, with his hard shell of urbanity. Christ, he sometimes thought he would like to *be* Craike and have command of that supercilious smile and those pale, cold eyes.

But it was not over yet. The boy was still not free and the key fact was that nobody except Sim knew who the boy really was. Well, Madeleine did, yes. He wished in a way he hadn't told her now. He wanted his share of the test to perform. He wanted to *be there* and he knew he would have to follow Craike if he was going to be. So when Craike phoned earlier, Sim's obedience had been instinctive. The current was about to sweep him up again and drag him towards the action.

'There's someone you should meet. I'll bring him round to the bar, so don't go out.'

The bar was very quiet, unnaturally so. There was a Japanese who looked like an oriental Edward G. Robinson sitting quietly by himself on a stool. Every now and then he would sip brandy, smack his lips and smooth his silk tie as if performing some compulsive ritual. After a few minutes Nancy Lo bustled out and talked to him rapidly and softly. He left.

About 10.30 there came a new noise from the entrance hall, a growling voice. A bandy-legged man in a tracksuit was followed in by Ed Craike himself. Bandy-legs was talking seamlessly.

'I made a smart move in late '90 when I got out of BCCI, cause I figured the market for corrupt Middle Eastern banks was about to go into free-fall, so what I do? I fucking do Trans-Africa is all. I pile into Trans-Africa, so now I'm saying to myself here's an outfit that's got a great scam going for it with

Government-to-Government aid packages for the drought zone and the entire Peace Corps payroll in the region. Also the guy on the bridge was some kind of Harvard MBA financial genius. So what I'm trying to say to you, the whole shmear was looking good, really good.'

He saw Sim and stopped short. Craike took his elbow and steered him towards the bar.

'How pleasant this is,' he said brightly. 'Drink?'

'I'll take ice-water,' said Cotton. Craike ordered a malt for himself and called Sim over.

'Sim, I want you to meet Mr C. P. Cotton, God's own studio-floor manager. I brought you two nice people together because you have so much in common. Most particularly, you share an interest in a certain little child, an unfortunate who appears to have got lost in the washing. Cheers.'

Sim looked at Craike. The man sounded chipper and pleased with himself, Mr Punch with a Sandhurst accent. Cotton simply glowered at Sim. For once he seemed at a loss for words.

The pair behind the two-way mirror had nothing to say to one another, just short, transactional statements and questions.

'You sure the doorman knows his instructions?'

She gestured impatiently through the glass.

'Well, look out there. We're keeping the place dead quiet. It'll kill off my profit for the entire week, but these men won't be disturbed.'

He looked intently at the drinkers ranged around the bar.

'I wish I knew what they were saying.'

'You could ask Jackie.'

'Jackie's too young, too stupid.'

'He's listening to every word.'

'He won't remember. You should get the bar stools wired.'

'I did. The microphones kept getting squashed, then breaking. Anyway there was never anything interesting, so I had them taken out.'

'Have them put back then.'

'So what is it you want to know?'

He ignored this. He stood watching Craike, Cotton and Sim, trying to lip-read. He leaned forward.

'Perhaps I should go out there.'

Nancy Lo was not going to stop him.

'You know the way.'

The man looked at her.

'But if I did they wouldn't be talking freely, would they? Can't you get them round a table, near a mike?'

So she tried. She went out into the bar and fussed around them, suggested they take their seats in a booth. But Cotton and Craike were too edgy to sit down, while Sim, knowing about the microphones, looked at her strangely. She fetched pretzels and nuts and asked if they required female company. They said no.

She went back to the man to confess her failure.

'Well, blast it, then. I'll have to go out there. Shock tactic. It might prise something loose.'

'What *is* it you want to know?'

'I want to know who else was in on the Trans-Africa fraud. I want to know how deep Cotton was in. I want to know who in the *Government* was in on it. I want names and numbers.'

'But they're talking about the kidnapped child. They're not interested in that stupid bank.'

'Oh no? Cotton is. His life depends on it. And my guess is that Craike has picked up a hint I gave him — deliberately, of course — and tipped Cotton off. Wish me luck.'

He rose and left the narrow room. Nancy waited. From here she could not see the connecting door between the back rooms and the bar, but she knew when her companion had passed through it, because she could see the look on Craike's face. His mouth had sagged open.

What was Craike up to? Was he requiring Sim to explain that the kidnapped boy wasn't Josh Cotton? *Now?* Wouldn't it be better to get the child back first? Sim was trying to make his mind up what to do when Nancy bustled in. He could hazard a guess why she wanted them to occupy a table, since that was where the microphones were. Nancy Lo was a spy, that was obvious. Who she spied *for* was a more difficult question, but Sim didn't much care anyway.

For the next few minutes there were more comings and goings. Then Nancy Lo had just left them quietly, and Cotton was speaking.

'So this here is the son of Fielding?'

He had got no further down this line of inquiry when the backroom door swung wide again and a plump, clean-shaven beige-suited man in his thirties glided through as if on wheels. Craike, who was about to reply, never uttered the words. In astonishment his face suddenly lost muscle-tone. The others saw it and looked from the newcomer to Craike and back, waiting for elucidation.

'Jesus Christ, Van*teel*. What are you doing here?'

Vanteel gave a cold smile, like the benediction that a poker winner gives to a loser.

'Hi, Ed. Now, I *could* say the same about you.'

Craike had his hands extended a little way from his sides, and was looking with emphasis from one palm to the other.

'I don't get it. Everywhere I go, I find this man.'

'I am your genie, Ed. You rubbed the lamp and I came.'

Vanteel laughed, a very satisfied laugh. Cotton frowned, then spoke.

'Who is this guy, Craike? Another of your British spooks?'

'That's exactly right. Pathetic, isn't it? It's all the Service can recruit these days: men with second-class Polytechnic degrees.'

'Did the Army teach you snobbery, Ed?' asked Vanteel, his eyebrows arcing. 'It shows how long it's been since you saw service. I mean, the Army's so democratic these days.'

Craike stepped forward and took Vanteel by the arm. Beckoning Sim over to join them, he moved a little distance from the others.

'What exactly are you doing here?'

As Sim came close, Vanteel tapped his shirt front with forefinger and spoke to Craike.

'He'll have to sign the Official Secrets Act, you know.'

'Fuck that, Vanteel. What do you know of this place?'

'What do *you* know of it, Ed? In a manner of speaking I'm the proprietor. The ladies – well, they work for me, for us. It's so much more salubrious than running brothels. Don't you remember? We used to do that in quite a big way – pillow talk and all that. But Granny Thatcher put a stop to it, said it was degrading to the Service. This idea came up as a substitute and it worked a treat, even better than the knocking shops, you see, because the whole *idea* of this place is to blab your mouth off.'

Craike closed his eyes and swayed slightly back, bending his knees.

'Jesus. I should have known.'

'Mrs Lo has been a splendid servant of the Crown, really splendid –'

He was making like the departmental head he was, with a citation for dedicated service and unstinting loyalty for some retiring office dragon. Any second now he would produce the engraved salver.

'Keeping an eye on the expat Jap population for us, and actually making a profit into the bargain.'

Sim too had shut his eyes and, for an instant, saw in his mind Madonna Lee under him, arching her back and writhing from side to side, calling in rhythmical litany, 'Harder, Sim! Oh, break me! Fuck me, Sim! Fuck me, Sim!'

It was she who had fucked *him*, of course. He touched Craike's arm.

'Ed, there's more going on here than I knew. Where's Madeleine, Ed? Do you know if she's all right?'

At which point two polite young men in jeans and spotless polo shirts came noiselessly in. They looked like articled clerks or accountants. One wore tortoiseshell spectacles. They bowed and asked for Mr C. P. Cotton, Mr Ed and Mr Fielding. When these three spoke up the young men presented Mr Lee Hung's compliments. He was so sorry he could not come to the meeting as requested. But would the gentlemen kindly be conducted to where he is? The youths were very persuasive and everyone agreed without argument. The youths carried Uzi 9-mm sub-machine-guns.

The one in spectacles frisked each of them in turn, finding the small automatic in Craike's jacket pocket and removing it delicately, as if lifting a dead bluebottle by its wing. He then led the way to the door, leaving Vanteel behind. At the sight of the guns Vanteel had slid into a crouch and was whimpering in disbelief. Perhaps they took him for one of the Mama-Bunny's everyday clients.

After they had left, he sat still for a while, licking his lips compulsively as if the action would draw some semblance of moisture back into his tongue.

# 30

'Is it an apartment?'

Madeleine's voice came out too loud. It bounced up and down the stairwell. Madonna jammed an upright finger violently against her lips so that she appeared to kiss it. Then, in answer to the question, she shook her head.

'No. Rooms, just rooms here.'

She spoke in a spluttering hiss like a steam iron. In the thin electric torchlight Madeleine saw how she was sweating; beads of it were forming on her temples. Madeleine patted her shoulder for reassurance and they continued.

It had taken ten minutes to reach the bottom of the stairwell they now were climbing. The network of damp and malodorous alleys had been bewildering. There was little headroom because of the huge bunches of pipes and cables which were slung above the passageways. These sagged down to shoulder height in many places, forcing the women to walk stooped.

Around them was silence, and thousands upon thousands of crumbling, empty dwellings, a jam of crazy, unplanned, piled-together architecture. These conditions – silence and emptiness – are alien to any place in metropolitan Hong Kong; they were absolutely unthinkable here, or had been. It had once been the most densely populated slum in the world – $6\frac{1}{2}$ acres and 33,000 people in buildings so tightly packed that even bicycles and handcarts couldn't use the network of alleys that tried to divide and give access to the area.

The Walled City was a diplomatic blind-spot whose ownership between Britain and the PRC could never be determined. It had survived by developing a kind of practical anarchy, so that – without direction, without lawgivers, without a flag or a bunch of Founding Fathers – an order and a code of living had been created. It was highly effective, though impossible for outsiders to understand, for the Walled City had no call for officials or police. The Triads deployed their own crude enforcers, but they were superficial, not essential. The Triads needed the Walled City more than the City needed them.

There had been no *stone* barriers around it since the Japanese demolished the walls to give landfill for Kai Tak's runway during the Second World War, but the walls had lingered on as phantoms in the minds of the people. The phantom walls were still there for the Government, too, and for its servants, the Hong Kong police, who rarely went in except in force. Only now, with the whole colonial game played out for ever, had these mental ramparts melted away and had the Walled City yielded up at last its people and its secrets.

On the fourth floor of the stairwell, Madonna whispered that they had reached their goal. In Madeleine's life, how many dingy landings had she lingered on, doors hammered at, door bells fruitlessly prodded? Never grimmer, less human ones than these. The damp had stained the walls with lichen and mould, the concrete floor was pooled with rusty water and spotted with oil, the doors' paintwork was cracked and their wood was rotten. Madonna gestured at them, miming uncertainty. Behind one of those Ho Yu Ching, whom Madeleine was by now picturing as the Minotaur himself, might be holed up, but she didn't know which one. Madeleine shone her torch about her. Two of the doors had no distinguishing marks apart from their distinctive patterns of decay. The third, the right-hand one, sported a pair of flyblown rectangular cards, advertising the services and attractions of a girl called Mimi. One card was a short menu: PEEP-HOLE GAMES; HOT MASSAGE; ALSO CANING. The other boasted of SURGICALLY ENLARGED BREASTS; CORSETS WORN ON REQUEST; AIDS-TEST CERTIFICATE.

Madeleine went down on one knee and put her eye to the keyhole. Faintly, a light was visible within. She felt a tightening inside her ribcage.

'That's your soul shrinking,' an instructor in hostage-relief and siege-busting at Police College had once told her. 'You need that reflex to help you do things against the interests of your own safety.'

She tried the handle and it turned easily. Then she felt the catch give, and to her surprise the door swung suddenly open. Madeleine, whose training had also told her that at such moments hesitation could kill, simply walked in. At her back she could hear Madonna tut-tutting. It might have been for Madeleine's boldness, or for the occupant's not having locked the door.

The smoky orange light of an untrimmed oil lamp flickered with sinister effect from a tilting, upended tea-chest. It hardly illuminated what was, in Hong Kong terms, fairly spacious accommodation. Yet the air was foul, not only coarsened by oilsmoke but fetid. A bed stood in the centre, with a chaos of garments strewn thickly around it, as if someone had been sorting donations for a church jumble sale. Madeleine waded to the window and, touching the dust-caked drapes a crack apart, looked out. The view was clogged with gloom. The building opposite, just a few feet away, showed no lights, and it climbed too steeply for her to see the sky. Hak Nam. The city of darkness.

She turned and swept the whole space with her torch beam. The shaft of light jinked back and forth, always returning to the bed, the only obvious focus of attention. It took some time to make out the confusing layers of material and colour which were heaped there. Madeleine had thought at first she'd seen a raincoat which someone had discarded on the bed. Now, stumbling quickly towards it, she found it was something else.

'Madonna. Oh, Christ. Madonna, I think I've found him.'

But as soon as she approached she saw this was someone else. The lower part of the body and legs were covered by a shredded blanket. The upper part wore a ragged T-shirt. The hair was dark and close-cropped and the eyes rested open, vacantly. The head, chin pushed up at a slightly strained angle from the neck, lay in profile and seemed too large to fit the rest of the visible body.

The back was uppermost. The backbone and shoulderblades stood out in high relief from the shrunken remnants of flesh and muscle. One small hand, protruding from the blanket, was half closed as if around an imaginary treasured object.

The visible skin seemed like parchment wrapped and stretched around a disinterred skeleton. Madeleine stretched out her hand to touch it, but as soon as her fingers made contact she jerked them back, an electric shock caused by reversed expectation. She knew she would find the skin cold and dead. In fact it was warm.

'Come here, Madonna, quick. I think she's alive.'

Madeleine looked up at the door and received her second jolt. She stepped back and her fingers slackened around the torch. It dropped soundlessly into a heap of clothing.

'Oh, my God.'

The outline that, in the corner of her eye, she had taken for Madonna was not Madonna. Madonna had gone. The figure in the door stood with his feet apart, his hands open at his sides. He was very thin, dressed in a ripped T-shirt and tracksuit pants. His eyes glittered with rancid delight as they raced up and down Madeleine from her hair to her feet. She had seen the man before, of course. It was he who had passed her that message from Swann outside the Golden Fortune Boarding House.

Then he had seemed a cowed and passive, even simple-minded, member of the Hong Kong underclass. Now the intent on his face could not be mistaken. Madeleine bent and retrieved her torch. She backed away from the bed.

'Who is this? Hey, you! Who is this on the bed?'

The man smiled, his head just very slightly nodding from side to side. He had few teeth. He tapped his breast bone and said, 'Ho Yu Ching.'

She shone her torch back on the bed and repeated, 'Who is this? You know?'

At once the man walked into the room, his step springy and confident. Madeleine backed away to the window. Ho Yu Ching ripped the tattered blanket away from the figure on the bed, put his hand on the uppermost shoulder and pulled it over. It came round so that the front of the body was visible.

She was tiny; her age could be anything between twelve and thirty. She had bruises to neck and legs. There were smears of blood around her abdomen and thighs. And, as Ho moved her, something rolled out from beneath her and bounced off the bed. It was a hypodermic.

Ho said, 'Junkie.'

He began inspecting her carefully, as a poultry butcher inspects his handiwork. He prodded her stomach and then lower down, pushing his finger into her body. He withdrew and tasted the finger. He smiled and said, 'I, Ho Yu Ching, yes?'

He laughed, a high squawk. Madeleine went completely numb with horror and disgust. It was as if forethought had drained from her mind into her feet. He had *laughed* when he'd done that! She blurted out a yell. It was inarticulate and not half as terrible as she would have wished. Then she rushed him.

He was much stronger than he looked. Her first assault had him falling back over the bed, but he somersaulted and came back at her. She grappled him as he came close, fought and resisted him, tried to get her nails to his face and her feet to his balls. But slowly he brought her round, step by step like a catatonic dance, until the bed was behind her. He gripped her wrists and began to force her slowly backwards until she was bent like a bow. With one punch he could easily have smashed her down on to the mattress on top of the comatose girl, but he chose not to. He was enjoying himself too much to hurry.

In spite of the hellish light she could see his gappy smile there above her, and feel his spattering saliva on her face, as he panted with effort. Then she realized he was speaking to her.

'Fuck you now. Fuck you now good.'

He was saying it over and over and it stung her to push back against him with desperate strength, sobbing to breathe. Now her buttocks were touching the mattress and the only thing to prevent her from falling back was his grip on her wrists.

'Fuck you now. Fuck –'

'Fuck *you*!' she screamed. And then, from above him, there came a splitting sound, like a crowbar entering a packing case. Spots of moisture hit her face, warm and tacky. Ho's face crumpled, the eyeballs rolled up and then the lids dropped shut. His mouth fell from a grin to a lop-lipped drool in one instantaneous change and the neck seemed to hinge sideways like a broken twig. Then he slid from her, letting go her wrists and slumping silently to the floor.

Released by his hands, Madeleine crashed backwards on the bed, just missing the folded-up girl. Her consciousness was interrupted by phantom flashes loosed off amid plumes of black fog. With all her remaining strength, she bunched her fists and hammered the mattress, letting rip a nerve-searing five-second scream. Then she lay still.

'Hey,' said the voice. It came from somewhere among those black gauze windsocks which fluttered impenetrably above her face.

'Hey, can you hear me? Madeleine?'

One thing she could see. A piece of heavy, rusty pipe was hanging down from the voice. It swung this way and that as it spoke again.

'Where's the boy, Madeleine? Tell me, won't you? Where's Josh?'

The journey to Lee Hung had been in a stretched Mercedes, of the type with two rows of rear seats. From the front passenger seat the young man watched his three detainees, all the while fingering the barrel of his sub-machine-gun like an unconscious masturbator.

They drove through the cross-harbour tunnel and branched right past Kowloon Railway Terminus. Ten minutes later they were being herded across an area of newly laid parkland, sand-strewn and dry, its immature trees looking apologetically sparse and provisional in the moonlight. One thing was certain – they were near to Kai Tak. From the west a 747, like a gargantuan bather lowering her rump to test the water, inched down almost to the rooftops.

By the time the aircraft had dropped out of sight on to the runway, they were walking in the shadow of an urban superstructure, 100 yards of it in each direction, which stood surrounded by this new parkland. Only close up could Sim make out any detail in the walls of buildings. They had until recently been living quarters, but were now entirely unlit and seemed uninhabited. The façades were clothed in caged balconies, rusty and sagging. Some had become partly detached from their rivets and hung askew. Others still showed traces of their former use – Sim could see desiccated hanging plants, the rags of clothes pegged out to dry months or years before, the rusty, empty songbird cages lashed to the balustrading. He had no time to dwell on this. Their escorts switched on powerful flashlights and bustled them through a narrow entrance and into the abyss.

It was like walking up a concrete rat's arse – narrow, stinking and treacherous. Months of vacancy had accelerated the dilapidation to dangerous levels, so that they constantly tripped over fallen rubbish, masonry, window-fittings, the ironmongery of balconies. Passage after passage, turn after turn, the same dereliction and slippery decay. Actual rats big as rabbits slithered over their feet. Geckos 10 inches long scuttled into the cracks and ledges of the walls. Bats hung in crevices. And all the time Sim was aware of the hidden people who must be in there, in the shadows, watching them pass. Not the true inhabitants, as in the old times before this slum was condemned. Old ways could never return to this place now – it had no power, water or light. But they would be in there, nevertheless, in their hundreds perhaps – the illegals, the dispossessed, the desperate, the cave-dwellers, the catacomb people.

They moved through this dripping city of ghosts in single file and came at last to a huge door with ceremonial stone lions on guard by its post. Sim was walking second in the line, behind Ed Craike. At one turning the two had exchanged signals, just a look, a fractional nod, which said *I'm looking for the right moment too*. They passed through the door and into a small, square marble hallway. The bespectacled young man put his Uzi down and bolted the door behind them, while the other kept his weapon and torch trained on the prisoners. Prisoners? Hostages? What was their status?

From the flashes of torchlight which wheeled around the room Sim could see another closed door, which led, presumably, into the interior of this relatively imposing building. For a second the attention of the leading escort was distracted as he began to open this second door, another heavy one. To do so he had to pull it towards him, and to get maximum purchase he transferred his flashlight to the hand that held the gun, at the same time involuntarily lowering the Uzi's barrel. Craike and Sim, aware that Four-eyes had still not retrieved his own gun, saw their opportunity simultaneously.

They rushed the opening and put their shoulders to the door, which was already swinging back. They succeeded in pushing the gunman into the corner between the door and the side wall and trapping him there.

'Come on, *move*,' yelled Craike coarsely. Sim needed no further encouragement. He darted through and flung himself to one side of the opening. Cotton was slower. He seemed bewildered and demoralized, but he tripped forward and was helped through the door by Sim's fist grasping his collar and pulling him while Craike pushed from behind. Then, as the guard behind the door kicked and yelled and the other scrambled to retrieve and aim his piece, Craike and Sim pulled the door to. It crashed into the jamb just as bullets from Four-eyes's gun splattered the wood. Craike and Sim looked for bolts on the inside of the door and found them, at top and bottom. They slid them home.

It was Cotton who first turned and scanned the room. As he did so he reached out a hand and clutched Craike's arm.

'Take a look, willya?'

The room was lit by oil lamps, three of them set on an ornamental round table in the middle of the room. Slightly to one side of this, half-lit in the penumbra of light, was a carved wooden armchair. Someone was sitting in it. They could see the highly polished Italian shoes gleaming, the carefully pressed trousers from knee to ankle, the silk socks. The upper torso and face were shadowed, however.

They moved nearer. The shadow above the knees began to resolve into the appearance of a dapper, small-headed, middle-aged man. He did not move to acknowledge the presence of the three. The reflected glare from a pair of spectacles hid his eyes, and Sim thought he was dozing – the angle of the head and the way the hands dangled over the ends of the carved armrests suggested sleep.

The man was formally dressed, like a judge or senior politician, in a charcoal three-piece suit. It was the dark of the waistcoat that concealed the blood which had gushed down over the seated man's chest and stomach. A gleam at his midriff might have been mistaken in the gloom for a glinting fob-watch, but was in fact the brass pommel of a 12-inch hunting-knife. The knife had been driven right through the man's body at an upwards angle of 45 degrees from the level of the fourth button, nailing him to the back of the chair like a carcass on a gamekeeper's gibbet. This was what kept him upright.

Sim had never seen so much human blood. It was like a fall of lava from a volcano, a thick and caramelized pool dumped in his lap. In the shock he nearly laughed out loud. Cotton, standing beside him, took the experience another way. He was breathing hard after his exertions. As soon as he could spit out words he said, 'Sweet Jesus, it's Lee Hung.'

Then he turned aside, jutted his chin and threw up. The yellow arch of puke splashed down 3 feet from him.

'Jesus, Dad, give us a *break*. There's no one to clear that up round here.'

A powerful, athletic man in his thirties stepped out of the shadows. He was smiling benignly.

'Hi everybody. I'm Chuck Cotton and this disgraceful old drag-ass is my dad.'

Chuck waved one hand, palm upwards, in a gesture of inclusive welcome. In the other hand he balanced a second hunting-knife, the pair to the one that had abbreviated Lee Hung's existence.

# 31

'Chuck, son. What's going on here? What you doing outa the hospital?'

Despite having been financially shipwrecked, hijacked at gunpoint, dragged into a decayed ghost town and introduced to the butchered corpse of a business associate, C. P. Cotton momentarily became an American father again. He was all concern for an errant son bunking off school and mixing with bad company. At first Chuck seemed to play along with the role, whining his self-justifying excuses.

'Dad, I tunnelled out. Like it was doing nothing for me, OK? Those doctors and nurses spent too much time playing doctors and nurses to take care of the poor crazy bastards they got in there.'

'But that's the most expensive goddamn private facility in Hong Kong.'

'Most expensive screw-palace, Dad.'

Cotton looked around at the others, his cheeks puffing out, preparing to release a blast of righteousness. Then he remembered where he was, the Uzis, the death of Lee Hung, the ochre blot of vomit on the carpet. He plumped his face into his two palms and held it there. Chuck walked across and, releasing the bolts, pushed the doors open.

'I mean, when they weren't jumping each other, they only wanted me to talk about Liz and Josh, you know? They wanted to know all sorts of – *private* things, you know?'

He spat.

'Bletcherous creepos.'

The two gunmen had entered a little sheepishly. They shuffled sideways along the wall, cradling their Uzis. The one without glasses had a nose so reddened by its impact with the door that it seemed to glow. Chuck smiled at them indulgently.

'Meet my good buddies, Adam and Michael Lee, adopted

children of Mr Lee Hung. Welcome back, boys. You near as goddammit screwed us up, but I saved our ass. You frisked these guys?'

Michael Lee pulled Craike's small automatic from his pocket and handed it to Chuck, who pocketed the piece.

'These boys hated their pa like you wouldn't believe, so –'

He gestured at Lee's butchered remains and shrugged.

'I guess there's no feeling like when you've truly cleared the path to your inheritance.'

He turned back to C. P. Cotton.

'I found it a real drag in the hospital, Dad, having to talk. Same as I always found *you* a drag, making me talk about business and such. Liz is dead and Josh is alive, that's all I got to say on the subject, but they wouldn't believe me.'

Cotton seized on this.

'How you know Josh is alive, Chuck?'

'Why, because Lee Hung told me. Told me days ago. Came to see me in the hospital, told me *he* had my son, and would I be interested in paying? He tried to sell me my own boy. Well, look over there, Dad. Look.'

He pointed dramatically at Lee's skewered body.

'I paid him all right, in the currency he understands. Bank of Hell.'

He snickered.

'Now I got a whole lot more to say – to you guys, that is.'

'What about?' his father asked. 'You gonna tell us why you brought us here?'

'Well, I got to talk a little about murder, kidnaps, life and death. Suchlike important things.'

'Yes, but isn't the important thing the child?'

It was Sim who voiced the obvious challenge. Chuck came right up to him, nose to nose.

'Listen, you fuck. Don't try to tangle assholes with me. The main important thing is blame. Hey, who *is* this guy?'

He looked around at the others.

Michael Lee said, 'Fielding's son, from England.'

'From England, wow.'

Chuck snorted. Then he seemed to relax, smiling thinly all around, using the point of the outsize Bowie-knife to scrape the underside of a fingernail.

'So it's a family affair every which-way. I like that. What say we have us a little inquiry now? Judge Chuck Cotton presiding.'

He swivelled and walked over to where the lifeless Lee was spitted. He grasped the knife's handle with doubled fists, placed his foot on the chair's leading edge, between Lee's knees, and powerfully tugged. Out came the dagger with a dull *pock*. He took Lee by the hair and heaved him forward, using his foot to roll the body to the floor on one side of the chair. He bent and stabbed the knife into the mess of blood and fluids that pooled the seat, then he turned.

'And the object of this little trial, friends, is to determine which among you should be the next to sit in this chair.'

And once more he smiled his winsome, college-boy smile.

'I had no idea. No idea at all. God, what a squalid place.'

The man's lips were drawn back from his teeth. The sniffing-muscles above his nostrils were pulled tight. Madeleine tried to get him in focus. From where she lay, still on the bed, she could see *who* he was, but it still didn't make sense. Sim, yes, she could fancy him as a white knight, riding up in the nick of time to forestall the rape and avert the murder. Or Craike for that matter. But she didn't want to owe her life to *this* slug – not to Vanteel!

She hoisted herself up and sat on the side of the bed, trying to reconcile everything. Vanteel was a British government man. What was he doing in the Walled City at some godawful hour after midnight anyway?

'I expect you're wondering what I'm doing here?'

Vanteel sounded rueful, as if he had baffled himself with the question.

She said, 'I owe you thanks, whatever.'

Vanteel produced a squirming twist of the lips to show he acknowledged her gratitude. She looked down at Ho Yu Ching, sprawled in an ungainly attitude among the chaos of unravelled sweaters and moth-eaten blankets.

'Have you killed him?'

Vanteel hadn't considered this yet. He frowned.

'I don't know. Could I have? I just picked up this piece of pipe. I didn't know what was best to do. So I just –'

'If you have killed the swine, it'd be no less than he deserves. So. Why are you?'

'What?'

'Why are you here?'

'Madonna fetched me.'

'Madonna?'

'Yes. Before she brought you in, she phoned me. It's rather a long story, and I'm not sure there's time to tell it. She's gone to look for the child now. We ought to find him.'

He got up and began looking around the room – in the corners, under a particularly dense pile of clothes, covers and other materials.

She said, 'He's not in this room anyway. I think he *was*. This girl –'

She lifted the bundle of covers to show the emaciated nude. Vanteel returned to the bed, looked and then looked away hurriedly, as if he had seen exposed intestines. He shut his eyes and opened them again.

'Is she dead too?'

'No, unconscious. She's been shooting up. And that guy's been taking full advantage of her condition – but I guess he's been doing that for quite some time. They were the "couple" hired to be the kidnapped child's surrogates.'

'Surrogates?'

Madeleine let out a bitter laugh at the word she had chosen.

'Well, minders. They obviously minded him a treat. Anyway, the kid's not here, is he?'

'Is he dead then?'

She looked at Vanteel sharply.

'I wouldn't know. Whoever hired those two deadbeats might have him.'

'No, that's not so.'

'I'm sorry?'

Vanteel wandered over to the window and pushed his hand between the curtains, moving them aside to view the blackness outside. His voice, as he spoke, was distant and despairing, the voice of the administrator who had arranged things and seen them go wrong, a can-carrying voice.

'You see, the person who hired them is me. And I haven't got the child.'

Vanteel thrust his knuckles into his eyes and rubbed, as if vainly trying to erase the after-images of all he had seen in the room.

'I just didn't realize. God, it's far worse than I could ever have guessed. I thought it would be just a couple of days lying low where no one could find them. Then we'd produce the child on condition Cotton got out of Hong Kong and went back to the States.'

Madeleine stared at him, her face a blank. His explanation blundered on.

'We didn't want the Trans-Africa Finance scandal exposed. He would have done that. We couldn't afford to have it exposed. You do see that, don't you?'

She flopped backwards on to the mattress and closed her eyes in despair.

'Oh, no. No, no.'

Vanteel turned and lifted his arms, holding them in semaphoric appeal away from his sides.

'It was such a simple little exercise, Madeleine, in essence.'

'It was you? *You?* And I thought Lee Hung had the boy!'

'I fixed it up with Lee Hung,' said Vanteel sadly. 'Lee Hung belonged to us. We gave him a free hand, of course, he demanded no less. And he controlled this animal here – if control is the word. I never came down to check what he was doing, that was the whole of the trouble. I *trusted* people, d'you see? It's . . . well, it's bloody dishonest, what they did, isn't it?'

After a few more moments, Madeleine found she could walk. She went to the door, still open, but when she reached it something made her stop. She listened. There. There it was again, coming from the other side of the next door on the landing: the soft, thoughtful mew of a cat. Or not a cat. Something else again, more human than cat.

And then, from down below them, not far away, the rapid *thud-thud-thud* of gunfire.

# 32

Chuck Cotton, abandoning the role of prodigal son, was playing the attorney. He strode about the room, he gestured busily, he posed rhetorical questions. Chuck looked the part all right – handsome in a lantern-jawed, football-playing, comic-book way, dressed in a fashionable silk suit, Oxford shirt and light brogues.

'First,' he began, 'I'll tell you about Mr Lee Hung. See, someone hired him to hassle my family. But it was a real spaghetti-type scam. He had to make out there was some old Korean War vet who made out he got classified information about the Red Chinese to pass on. *They* were supposed to be so pissed off with Cotton Corp's satellite project, they wanted to take my father down. This brought in Mr Craike here and his organization. They were the *channel* for this communication and they were intended to get the British intelligence agencies involved –'

He nodded to Craike.

'That right? Anyways where was all that supposed to lead? We don't know. But we will, oh yes. And in the meantime Lee Hung went ahead with the next phase of the operation. He hired this deadbeat Brit called Fielding to go to England and kill my wife.'

He paused dramatically and studied the others' faces one by one.

'*Kill* my wife and kidnap my son, a defenceless child who was just learning to talk? Oh yes, he did.'

He took a tour of the room, passing behind his audience.

'So what happened next? Fielding arrived back here with Josh. Why didn't he contact Lee Hung? We don't know. But maybe out of greed he tried to lift the ransom money alone. Lee found him first, as we know, and he paid for *his* crime in the most horrible, painful and appropriate fashion.'

He had arrived back at the chair. His eyes were now gleaming with satisfaction.

'Lee's sons here have been so much help to me. Michael! Come up here.'

The bespectacled young man came forward slowly. His face showed no emotion at the proximity to Lee Hung's corpse. Chuck addressed him as if he were a witness taking the stand.

'What's your relationship to the dead man, Michael?'

'He bought my mother, me and my brother from China, PRC. He told us he married my mother, we were his sons.'

'He *bought* you or he *brought* you?'

'He bought us, he paid a lot a money. My father was just a farmer. He wouldn't let us go so Lee Hung had him killed.'

He spat briefly. The saliva landed beside Cotton's vomit. Chuck looked at it for a moment reflectively, as if metaphorically weighing the worth of an exhibit produced in court. Then he continued.

'How long have you been looking for a chance to get your revenge?'

'A long time. We are happy now.'

'Tell us about the kidnapping of Josh Cotton.'

'Lee Hung, like you said, was hired to do this.'

'Who did he work for, Michael? Do you know?'

'Different people hired him, different times. Lee Hung worked for anybody who paid good hard currency.'

'So do you know who hired him to kidnap the child in England and kill his mother?'

'Yes, I know.'

Sim could hear C. P. Cotton breathing heavily now, with a barely perceptible moan in the outbreath.

'It was him.'

Michael Lee pointed to C. P. Cotton.

'He did it.'

In the brief silence which followed, Cotton's moan developed into a choked cough, or gulp, or some other convulsion in the throat. Sim could see the sweat bubbling to the surface of his brow and temples. Then Cotton cried out, 'No, no, don't think it, Chuck. It wasn't that way, I swear it.'

'You killed my *wife*, Dad! You took away my *son*.'

'She had already left us, Chuck. She was worthless trash

anyway. I only wanted to bring the boy home to you. I knew we'd never get him back through no lousy British court of law. It was my best shot.'

'You killed Lizzie, Dad. Did you have to do that?'

'I wasn't there! I mean, was I? It wasn't any part of the fucking plan. He was supposed to knock her out before she knew what was happening and dump her some place safe in the garden. He *had* to torch the cottage so everybody'd think the child was – '

Chuck's eyes sparked. His college-kid lawyer style was rubbing thin as he spoke between tightly closed teeth.

'How could you think of my kid, your grandson, burnt? How could you *think* it? You're a fucking psycho, Dad.'

'It was a scam, son, like you just said. Then we could have him back. That's what you *wanted*, isn't it? Little Joshie back home again? I don't know what went wrong, but I didn't mean for Elizabeth to die. The goddamn bitch must've wakened up and fought him and then he killed her. Or maybe her fancy-man – '

Chuck's reaction was instantaneous. He grabbed the sub-machine-gun from Michael Lee, who was standing just beside him, and fired a burst into the ceiling. They all ducked or flinched at the overwhelming thunder of the sound. He let the echo die and took hold of his father's ear, pincering it between finger and thumb.

'Don't ever, *ever*, talk about him. Never say a fucking *word* about him in my presence.'

He spoke low, jerking his head viciously up and to the side. Then he let go of the ear and snickered again.

'But you won't have much chance to do so in the future, because you *have* no future, Dad. Just tell me one more detail. Why did you not get the child home, like you *say* you wanted?'

It seemed as if most of the fight had gone out of Cotton and that he could only shrug helplessly.

'I don't know what happened. I didn't know where he was, I swear. I *still* don't know.'

Chuck stopped in mid-walk. He hit his forehead, his jaw slack.

'You don't *know* where he is? Right now, you don't know?'

'All I know is someone screwed up – Fielding, Lee Hung, maybe this bastard Craike.'

He turned to Craike and stabbed his finger at him.

'*You* were supposed to find the child. Make it look like an ordinary investigation, make it look like the Chinese intelligence had got the kid and you got him back from them. *You* got the heroic scene to play. You didn't perform.'

Craike said drily, 'You should have shown me the script, Cotton.'

'I didn't want to do that. See, Chuck boy, you gotta believe me. I wanted the thing to look watertight. No collusion, no need to *trust* anybody.'

Cotton shook his head and worked his lips, licking and squeezing them together. Suddenly Chuck slapped the chair-back.

'OK, we've frigged around enough. Sit in the chair, Dad.'

Cotton looked at his son aghast.

'What for?'

'Just sit in the fucking *chair*, Dad. Adam!'

He beckoned and Adam Lee came forward, putting a hand under C. P. Cotton's armpit. His brother Michael passed his sub-machine-gun to Chuck Cotton and took the other. Then they lifted the old man off the ground.

He writhed, his feet bicycling, his face the colour of the sick he had deposited on the floor a few minutes earlier.

'For Christ's sake, I'm your *father*, Chuck. Don't you love me?'

'I never loved you, Dad. Now I'm going to show you how much I don't love you. Put him in the chair.'

Chuck had the Uzi trained on Sim and Craike. They could only stand and watch as Cotton was turned and hoist into the oak seat, with the great hunting-knife buried in the wood between his thighs. Chuck handed the machine-gun back to Michael Lee and plucked the knife out of the wood with vicious ease as Cotton was being cuffed in place by Adam, the arms going around behind the high chair-back. The old man's voice had gone up an octave and his pleading came out in squeals.

'You can't get away with this. How can you think –'

'Don't you know about the Walled City, Dad? It's a sanctuary, an area of liberty. Soon it will be demolished. In the meantime, what we do here is privileged. Normal rules count for diddly in here. Any or all of you guys can die and the world will be none the wiser.'

Cotton was gasping for breath now, his head back, his chin shifting from side to side as he saw his son approach with the hunting-knife, smeared with dark, tacky blood from Lee Hung's belly.

'Help me, you guys. Don't let him do this. Help me, for God's sake.'

Chuck had the point of the knife within an inch of his father's body now, just below the breastbone and midway between two shirt buttons. He circled it round, as if searching for a sweet spot at which to strike. The heaving breath of his father was coming in an undulating moan, interspersed with mucous clicks. His face was ghastly, the eyeballs churning in their sockets, the slug-like lips straining outwards as if they could in some unimaginable way ward off the blade that was about to punch him into non-existence.

People talk about windows of opportunity, but windows are for seeing through, and what Craike knew he needed was a door, or at least some opening, some breach in the concentration of the man with the machine-gun. There was no possibility that Chuck Cotton would let any of them live unless Craike could make something change. He waited. He had decided when the break would come. At the moment that C. P. Cotton died, *that* would be when he sprang.

There was, after all, dick he could do for Cotton. He was going to die, and nothing could stop it. But at least he would die in a good cause. If Craike played it right, just as Cotton's worthless life was spluttering out in a gush of blood between his shirt buttons, the rest of them would be saved.

There was a second of suspense, like the gap between lightning and the crack of thunder. Even old Cotton's tortured breathing was suspended. Chuck Cotton pulled the arm back in the attitude of a piston. Son and father looked into each other's eyes. Then, into the silence, came something unmistakable: the scream of a child.

Chuck Cotton swung around. So did the two Lee boys, Craike, Sim. Only C. P. Cotton hardy reacted. He sat there, his eyes staring straight ahead, moaning, unable to rise, unable even to see. His legs shook, his eyeballs were pumped up.

\*

Madeleine stood at the door holding a boy in a filthy red tracksuit to her breast. Behind her stood Vanteel. In the moment of pure, surprised silence they could all hear the trickle of C. P. Cotton's piss running to the floor.

Craike yelled with all the force he could muster.

'Sim! Get the other guy!'

He whip-lashed to his right and brought his forearm smashing up against the snub muzzle of Four-eyes's Uzi. The gunman lost his balance and, as he tottered backwards, his forefinger tripped a smattering of bullets across the ceiling. In one movement Craike closed him down, his kick smashing into the man's stomach and his fist on to his nose, making the glasses fly from the face. As Michael Lee actually fell, Craike took hold of the gun and wrenched it from the man's failing grip. Then Craike turned, but quick though it was, his recovery was still too slow. He took a rake of shots in his legs from across the room. The shells smashed both his shins and put him tumbling down in a roaring blaze of pain.

Sim had sprinted forward as soon as Craike shouted. He reached Chuck as he was bending to pick up Adam Lee's gun. Sim kicked out and then got behind him, tearing at his cheeks, his ears, trying to find the eyes. Then he brought his hands down with all the force he had to prevent Chuck from firing. He failed to abort the burst which stopped Craike, but he then got a hold on the gun and heaved it up, cracking it into Chuck Cotton's chin.

Chuck let go of the gun and wrenched free of Sim's grasp. Now Sim saw Adam Lee coming. He parried the first kick and jabbed at Lee's face with the protruding magazine of the gun. Adam Lee, whose physique was slight, did not last long. He was already staggering back when he slipped in the pool of urine and blood beside the death-chair in which C. P. Cotton was shackled and, striking his head on the carved wooden armrest, slumped and lay still.

Chuck had crossed the room and reached Madeleine so fast that she was completely unready. Since stepping into the room she had not had time to put together any of the messages her eyes were relaying to her brain. She took a step back and her grip on the boy loosened, so that it was as easy as if she had actually handed the child to him. Chuck took the boy, cradled him momentarily in his arms. With a look backwards, a flash of excitement, a challenge perhaps, he barged past Vanteel, who stood amazed and useless at the door. Then he was gone into the night.

Sim wasn't very far behind Chuck Cotton on the stairs. Chasing out past the stone lions, blind instinct had made him go right along the black alleyway, rather than left. When he was about 50 feet down, he stopped and listened. He could hear feet pounding wooden stairs somewhere above him, somewhere nearby.

He had one of the Lee brothers' torches in one hand, the sub-machine-gun in the other. He shone the torch in an arc, and then spotted the open door. It swung drunkenly away from its jamb a few paces ahead of him. In a couple of strides he was through and sprinting up to the first floor, where he stopped and listened again. Muffled thuds four, five floors above him and a metal door crashing into its frame. Silence. Sim took a step towards the next flight.

His foot hooked a cat. With a yowl the creature slid away from him. In or beyond the walls he could hear smaller presences also – scuttling rodents, urban squirrels, toads, the scrape of pigeons' claws. He started to sprint upwards once more, two steps with each stride, until he reached the top.

The metal door that faced him had a fire-escape release bar, a strange control device in a place where fire regulations had been scoffed at for generations. He settled the wooden stock of the small gun into his armpit and closed his fingers round the magazine-cum-handgrip. Running the torchlight down the gun, he found the safety catch in the grip itself. He moved it into the firing position and felt ready. He hit the bar and walked out on to the rooftop.

The distant grumble of an aircraft could be heard approaching from the south. The roof was like a plantation of blasted trees imagined by a bric-à-brac sculptor. Lashed to every conceivable protuberance, stapled to every vertical plane, were television aerials, their guy-wires creating a treacherous criss-cross undergrowth for the unwary. He began to pick his way towards a loose mound of discarded objects piled up in the centre of the asphalt-covered roof – rusted refrigerators, disembowelled computers and TV sets, rolls of linoleum, cruddy mattresses, fractured deckchair-frames, bottles, cycles, over-flowing bin-bags.

Sim had reached the foot of the mound and was edging round it when he spotted Chuck Cotton. He was silhouetted against the sheen which glistened in a wide band between the roof's parapet and the sky – the lights of harbourside high-risers and their shimmering reflection in the harbour waters. Chuck was visibly poised on the very edge of the roof.

'Hey, Chuck. Just put him down and move away from him, why don't you?'

Chuck's elbow bent as his hand came up his side. Sim could see he was groping inside his jacket pocket. Then the hand came out, the arm came up and a series of sharp cracks split the air. Sim saw small flickers at the end of Chuck's arm, like flint-sparks from a spent butane lighter.

There was nothing spent about the bullets. They smacked and stung the heap of junk some way to the left of Sim's head and he dropped to one knee. With the dark mass behind him Chuck couldn't be sure where Sim was, but there was no point in inviting a random hit.

'Come on, Chuck, let the boy go. He's not who you think he is.'

What was Chuck doing? He had clearly been hoping to cross from rooftop to rooftop, before plunging back down into the stinking network of passages, landing in an alley far from the one he had left, clear and free and away, safely possessed of the child he thought was his son.

But it wasn't as simple as that. He had chosen a rooftop and a direction at random and had been checked at an uncrossable chasm 10 feet wide between buildings. Unlike most gaps separating the closely packed blocks in the Walled City, here there was no span of plank or walkway to escape by.

'What you doing, Fielding? What's *your* percentage?'

Chuck's voice was coarse with strain. Sim tried to sound relaxed, to communicate control.

'I came for the child. He's not a percentage, Chuck, he's flesh and blood. And you've got to let him go.'

'Crap, he's my son. I gotta right.'

The boy was whimpering very slightly in Chuck's grip. Chuck, like Sim, went into a crouch, his back to the chasm. The boy was held by one restraining arm in front of him.

'No, Chuck. You got it wrong. He's not your son. Take a look at him. He's been switched, Chuck. Take a look.'

Sim held his torch at arm's length to his right, so as not to give away his exact position. Then he switched it on. Its beam fell on Chuck and the tiny, red-suited figure, who looked by now like a much-mauled rag-stuffed doll bent sideways in Chuck's grip.

But Chuck was not looking into the child's face. He was staring into the beam of light, trying to see what it concealed. He let go another volley of inaccurate fire and Sim switched the torch off, looking for a place where he could put it down. He found a rusty cooker, the oven door ripped away. It was possible to stabilize the torch on the bars of the oven-rack in such a way that it would point directly at Chuck and the boy.

'Chuck, don't look at me. Look at the boy. You know your own boy, Chuck. This isn't Josh. It's another kid. Look at him in the torchlight.'

Sim switched the torch on and moved instantly crabwise away from it, carefully slithering towards Chuck's left under cover of the torch's glare. Chuck fired again and again at the source of the light, his slugs twanging like snapped guitar strings.

The sky's rumble was increasing now as the aircraft lined up for the landing run. In gradual increments the volume was stepping up as Sim came near the roof's edge some 20 yards from Chuck, his movements covered by the airliner's noise and the glare of the still-undislodged torchlight.

He stopped moving. He was unsure what to do next. There were half a dozen taut guy-wires grounding at all angles between himself and his prey, giving him no chance of making a clean rush. How accurate was the Uzi? Could he put a bullet into Chuck's head and be sure of missing the boy?

He got rid of the thought as soon as he had it. Even if Chuck Cotton was killed, he would quite likely fall backwards from the roof still holding the child.

The roar of four huge Pratt and Whitney power units had reached a crescendo, a terrifying, all-encompassing descent of thunder. Sim saw, suddenly, the child begin to squirm. He slid downwards, as all small children know how to do, writhing out of Chuck's arm. Then he flopped forward on to all fours. Sim raised the Uzi, lined up the sights at Chuck's head. He was prepared to fire, and to kill if he could. All he had to do was choose his moment and squeeze the trigger.

Chuck spoiled the chance. He half stood up, groping to retrieve what he had lost. His sight was still dazzled by the powerful torchbeam. Sim could see that the boy had crawled a small distance along the parapet, in the other direction from Sim. Then he stood up, wobbled, turned. He was giving Chuck, for the first time, sight of his face. Sim, stationed behind and to the right of Chuck, tried to imagine the effect this would have, the failure of recognition, the bewilderment, the crashing of Chuck's hopes. Sim could at any event clearly see Chuck's head shaking from side to side in disbelief. He heard him speak.

'C'mon, Joshie. Come here to your daddy.'

The aircraft had gone from overheard now, and in the relief of its passing Sim heard the child's voice, too.

'No. Don't *want* to.'

It was spoken like a battlecry. The boy charged forward and, with both hands up in front of him, he collided with Chuck, ramming him as hard as he could in the chest. Chuck, who had frozen in the crouch position, was jolted on to his heels, and from there, in perfect slow motion, he toppled over. In normal circumstances he would have crashed on to the asphalt under his rump and then rolled on to his back, his feet coming up in the air. But there *was* no asphalt under his rump, there was only 140 feet of air, and Chuck – overbalancing helplessly backwards – sat in it. He went down, all the way down, a look of terminal astonishment lighting his handsome features. Then he was swallowed by the darkness of the hole he'd fallen into. Sim heard a wet crump as he hit the ground.

The boy had braked cleverly after impact. He now stood and watched Chuck's fall with interest, but without emotion. Then he saw Sim rearing up, stepping over the criss-cross obstacle-course of wire rigging which divided the space between them.

The boy whimpered. His lips quivered. He started to cry.

# 33

The Mama-Bunny was almost silent. There was just the chink of glasses as Jackie, behind the bar, carried out some last-minute polishing before the place opened for business.

Nancy sat with Madonna in one of the booths, drinking champagne. Not the rubbish they served up to their customers, but vintage Pol Roger. A suitcase stood packed beside the table.

'Well, here's to you,' said Nancy. 'I shall miss you, Madonna.'

'Me too, Nancy. I know I wasn't around too long, but I liked it here with you. You've got a neat operation.'

Nancy sighed and drank. The bubbles effervesced in her mouth, like the illusion of youth.

'I don't think I can keep it going much longer. I'm getting old. Why don't you come back and manage the place, Madonna?'

'Why not?' said Madonna. She raised her glass again. 'You keep it warm for me, just a year or two.'

'That how long they say they want you in San Francisco?'

'Yes, there's a politician I've got to get to know. Ah well, it doesn't sound too bad. Yankee politicians are always loaded, at least. Here's to California, Nancy.'

Nancy glumly filled her glass and raised it again.

'OK, sweetheart. Here's to California.'

She tipped the entire contents of the glass down her throat and called out.

'Hey! Jackie, time we opened up for business. Switch on the muzak, will you?'

They got up and walked to the door. Jackie was ahead of them with Madonna's case, loading it into the back of the waiting taxi. Madonna Lee and Nancy Lo kissed and Nancy watched the car go bumping gently down the narrow alley, until it disappeared around the corner. Then she turned and walked back into her bar. The familiar, silky strings were oozing into the opening bars of 'Moon River'.

Tommy Plummer hated Yanks, which is what made it so inevitable that he should wind up spending most of his exercise time with C. P. Cotton. Although they hadn't previously met, both were on charges connected with the collapse of the Trans-Africa Finance Bank.

The remand prisoners were unlocked at 10.00 and went to the exercise yard, where they spent the next two hours. There was a games hut too, although in wet weather, when it was useful but crowded, the carbon dioxide level of its atmosphere was apt to climb. Cotton complained of shortness of breath.

So it was invariably in the open air that Plummer and Cotton used to play draughts – or checkers, as Cotton called it. On fine days they sat out in the shade of the compound's only tree, a sad-looking evergreen much kicked and abused by frustrated inmates. On wet days they would huddle under the overhanging eaves of the hut. But always, while they played, they engaged in noisy and passionate transatlantic disputes, audible from one end of the compound to the other.

'Whenever I'm with Brits, Plummer, I hear them crowing about their system. Health? Best in the fucking world. Banking, Law? Likewise. Democracy? Also. Corruption? What *are* you talking about?'

He spat in the dirt.

'You kidding yourselves? The rest of the goddamn world knows Great Britain's been a loused-up shit-heap for years.'

'We criticize ourselves, Cotton. We don't like to hear it from foreigners. Your move.'

'Yeah, but you don't know your own country, you don't know what goes on. This bank that we both got mixed up in. That's a symptom of the corruption of an entire nation –'

'It's not a British bank. It's Nigerian, by way of the Bahamas.'

'That's the same lousy, stinking *thing*. Ex-fucking-colonial, circles of interest. You bastards have poisoned half the world. You're a cancer. Israel is yours. So are all the offshore sneak-holes, Bahamas, Barbados. You're clever, I'll give you that. Your Zionism is maybe the cleverest idea of the twentieth century, even Hitler couldn't beat it. Your atheism is disguised as this

Episcopalianism crap. I seen your Bishop of Durham. We had him on one of my TV stations. I fired the station manager's ass next day.'

Cotton leaned across the draughts-board and began to count on his spread fingers.

'That so-called bishop makes out *one*, there was no Garden of Eden; *two*, there was no Noah's Ark; *three*, there was no parting of the Red Sea. He says, *four*, there was no healing of the sick by Jesus, no making the lame walk and the blind see. And finally, *finally*, there was no Res-urr-ection. That ain't no Christian thinking, Plummer. There's atheist degeneracy.'

'Isn't it freedom of speech? That is big in the States, so we are led to believe.'

'Don't get fancy with me, Plummer. I know what I know. The one country you Brits've been longing to get your wrecking paws on is the US of A. So cocaine comes creeping through *your* West Indies. Dope is pipelined straight out of *your* Hong Kong. Why d'you think I came here in the first place? I wanted to crack that bastard drugs pipeline open and lay it waste. Zionists, bootleggers, drug-pushers, industrial takeover artists, assassins.'

'Assassins? Sometimes I don't know what you're on about, Cotton, I really don't.'

'I'll tell you straight, then, Plummer. You sons of bitches killed John F. Kennedy, that's God's truth. He finally stopped taking the orders of that murdering deviant Macmillan, so you took out a contract.'

'*We* did that?' asked Plummer drily. 'Well, stone me.'

And he jumped three of Cotton's pieces.

'Think that's my game, old man. Another?'

Roller blinds of yellow-ochre gave the room a warm glow. Craike thought of it as a healing light.

He was left alone much of the day, simply left to heal, his legs encased in plaster. They had begun to rebuild both his legs below the knee, which would take several operations. He was told the series of reconstructions might take weeks but after that he would walk again.

He kept finding his eyes drawn to a picture on the wall, a nineteenth-century engraving of Whitehall. It showed a view down Northumberland Avenue from Trafalgar Square, a very uninteresting view to most people – to almost any conceivable patient at this hospital, except himself. But it was in Northumberland Avenue, in an office whose windows he thought he could just make out, half-way up the steeply pitched roof of one of the grey Victorian edifices, that he had been given his marching orders out of the Civil Service. His departure from London had been a matter of days later. What crassness. Allowing those computer-jockeys, those political fuss-pots, those jobsworths and time-servers, to run him out of town.

So he lay there and plotted. He would walk again. And when he did, he would not be farting around here any more.

# 34

'Here it is, Madeleine, the hub of northern civilization.'

The taxi dropped them at the bridge-head beside Moxon Field. Sim hadn't telephoned in advance. He'd not been in touch with the village at all since leaving it. He hadn't wanted them to know where he was. He just wanted to return in triumph and show them what he'd got for them.

He felt a little high, disorientated, detached after the long flight. Was it only ten days ago he'd left? Ten weeks, ten *months* seemed more likely. New lives had metaphorically started, old lives had actually ended. Moxon seemed exactly the same, but Sim would never be.

Madeleine held the child sitting in the crook of her arm. She stroked the hair out of his eyes and he looked at her, then at Sim, then at the village green. He looked warily, without response or apparent recognition.

'Come on, my lad,' she said. 'You're going home.'

He buried his face in her shoulder. He had developed a huge, irrational trust for Mag-Lay, a bond greater than he'd had with anyone since the Mama-person – even more than the Mama-person. After he'd lost the Mama-person, and after he'd been a long time in that sad room, the one with the bed and all the clothes and blankets on the floor, he was put in the room next to it, a bare, bad room. The Big Bad had eaten a lot of white sticks in there. The parts he couldn't eat, the brown bits, he spat out; they were all over the floor. It was just as dark as the other room, but there were only hard surfaces and edges here. He hadn't liked it. When he was left alone there he started to cry. And Mag-Lay had rescued him and taken him away from the bad room.

Things kept changing fast then. Another Big-Bad had tried to run away with him, but he'd pushed the Big Bad down a hole and then he'd got Mag-Lay back and he'd clung to her and come with her. It was satisfactory.

Sim pointed to the fish and chip shop and they started to walk diagonally across the Field towards it. Already, from a distance, they could see it was open. Now, as they came close, they smelt the hot oil and heard the sizzle of deep-frying.

'We'll have cod and chips to celebrate, shall we?' said Sim.

'Mmm, yes. I'd like that. It's been a long time since I had the indigenous product.'

The plate-glass door was wedged open. Behind the food warm-cabinet and the great, ornate, old-fashioned till was Jackie Ho, riddling a heap of cooked chips in the warming-drawer to keep them from going soggy. As they entered, Jimmy lumbered through the bead curtain from the back-store, humping a large polythene sack of cold-stored chips. The Hos looked up. Their recognition of Sim was a little slow in dawning.

'Hi, Jackie, hi, Jimmy. I've just come from Hong Kong. And look who I've brought back.'

He hadn't prepared this at all. He hadn't thought about the best way to tell people you're giving them back their only child, who they thought was dead. So the words were just blurted out, they spoke themselves. They seemed farcically inadequate, but what words *would* have been right?

What didn't seem right, what didn't seem to match the occasion at all, were the reactions of the two Hos. Jackie froze. Her face was a mask of horrified suspicion. Her husband dropped the sack of chips and took a step forward. He stared frankly, uncomprehendingly, for four or five seconds. He put a hand to his hair.

'Jesus *Christ*, for a moment I thought it was –'

His face clouded and his teeth clenched. He swung round and waved angrily at his wife, a wide, desperate gesture of abandonment.

'Worra you trying to do? Worra you fucking trying to *do*? Because I've got a very, very sick feeling in my stomach.'

Jackie turned to her husband slowly, shaking her head. Tears filmed the surface of her eyes.

'I don't – I mean, it's nothing to do with me, Jimmy. For a second I thought the same as you. I don't know what this is about, honest I don't. Some idea of Sim's.'

Jimmy swung around again. He swayed and swung his body this way and that like a bewildered bull. Then he trained his fierce gaze on Jackie again, leaning towards her, his fisted hands propped against his sides.

'Look, Jackie, he's *gone*, remember? G-O-N-E!'

He lashed his head downwards with each letter as he spelt the word out.

'Nothing can replace him. This boat-people idea of yours is shit. *Shit!* And I want nothing to do with adoption.'

He gestured towards Sim, Madeleine and the child, standing in the door. He spoke directly to Sim, his face already crumpling with pain. At first he seemed not to know what to say to them.

'This is cruel, pal. Cruel. This makes me vomit.'

He turned and strode into the back-room. The beads rattled behind him.

Jackie turned back to Sim and Madeleine. Her voice was robotic, almost like an airport announcement.

'If you have brought this child with the idea of us doing an adoption, then I'm afraid you've made a mistake. My husband and I have so recently lost our little boy that we cannot think of such a step at the moment. I'm sorry.'

Sim stepped forward. His triumph had all evaporated now, his thoughts had become scattered and chaotic.

'But, Jackie, look. Look who we've brought. We've brought you Kevin. He's back. He's here. He was taken to Hong Kong and now he's back with you. Look!'

Jackie did not reply immediately. She whisked a glance over the child, flicked another at Madeleine and rested her flat gaze again on Sim.

'I don't get you. I don't know this child. Whoever he is, wherever he comes from, will you take him out of here? Please?'

'But Jackie, this is Kevin. Don't you recognize him?'

Jackie's mouth hardened. Her eyes narrowed to discourage her tears.

'If *this* is my son, Sim Fielding, they fished a little kid out of the river, 8 miles down. Who was that? Just tell me, because I'd be glad to know who we buried in the churchyard over there last Wednesday morning. I really would.'

On the wall behind her was a framed colour photograph of Kevin. It was the same snapshot – a recent one – that the police had had blown up and circulated during the search for the child. It was only three days since Sergeant Caldwell had brought it round to the shop, having purchased out of his own pocket the gilt, ornamental frame at the Clitheroe Woolworths. The Hos had cried over it together and then Jimmy had put it up on a stretch of blank wall above the shelf of sauces.

Sim looked at the photograph now, then he turned sideways and looked at the child Madeleine was holding. He saw that Madeleine was making the same comparison. She twitched her head at the photograph and mouthed the name at him.

'Kevin?'

He nodded. Then he shook his head. He could see it now, what he should have seen at first. He had been so *sure* that Kevin Ho was the child abducted by Maurice Fielding that he hadn't been able to see the truth. He'd seen Kevin so many times. He'd carried him in his arms, let him play with the zip-pockets on his leathers, tried to teach him words. He *knew* Kevin Ho.

And now he knew this wasn't Kevin Ho. He was like him – same size, same kind of hair, similar-shaped head. But it wasn't him, that's all.

He took Madeleine outside. They walked to the Field and crossed it, until they were standing beside the water.

'They must have found the dead child just after I left here. There was a hell of a flood, worst we've seen here for generations. He fell in and was carried downstream. We all searched for days but nothing was found.'

Madeleine bounced the boy in her arms. She tried to sound cheerful.

'Well, the question now is, who's *this* and what are we going to do with him? Eh, my lad?'

She tried to put him down but he didn't want to be released. He clung and clung.

Sim couldn't bear the thought of using his house, so they borrowed old Worsley's van and went to Preston. The hotel was a modern link in a chain, a featureless place of the no-surprises school, every room identical. They booked just the one double room, with a truckle bed for the kid. It was cheaper.

The boy had slipped down beneath the covers so that only his straight, busby-black hair could be seen. He was asleep. Sim and Madeleine were sitting opposite each other, one on each bed.

They were searching one another's faces. Suddenly Sim stretched out his hand. He touched her face. He stroked the side of it from temple to chin, and let his thumb trail her eyebrow, and the ridge of her nose. Madeleine raised her hand to his face too, momentarily. Then she twisted her hand and found his thumb with her lips, kissing it lightly. She rose and went into the bathroom.

He did not move. He let his hand fall to his knee and sat still, listening to the boy's even, snuffling breaths. Developing a cold. Apart from that, the kid was suffering no physical effects, though the ones in his mind would be hard to calculate, of course.

Who was he? Would they ever know? Would *he* ever know? Tomorrow they would have to go to the police, who would search their computers for missing children. And even if they couldn't find out who he was, they wouldn't let Sim or Madeleine keep him. They would take him into the care of the local authority. Sim sighed. After tomorrow he wouldn't see the child again. But who *was* he?

The bathroom door opened. Madeleine was dressed in a silk dressing-gown. She held her arms out from her sides very slightly.

'Shall we push the beds together? What do you want to do?'

Sim sat and stared. Madeleine was beautiful, sexy. He'd already decided he wanted to make love with her. Yet now he didn't see her. She might have been transparent.

*What do you want to do?*

Who had stood in a doorway and asked him the same question? Then suddenly the scene was there in front of him, the room, the other room, the things in the other room: scrambled bedding, empty bottles, a hair-drier, a plastic potty.

A plastic *potty*.

And when he'd left, what had she said?

*Bring him back. Oh please. Bring him back!*

'Good God!'

Sim leapt to his feet and dug in his pockets for the van's ignition key.

'Sorry, Madeleine. You've got to get dressed again. Get the kid up. We're going to take this boy home.'

Nothing had changed. The tower block was dripping with

internal condensation. Oil spills, broken glass, sweet papers and condom packaging littered the floors. In the hallway Sim kicked a plastic hypodermic. Still no lifts.

'Sim, this place is awful!'

They were trudging up the stairs, Sim with the boy asleep on his shoulder, his weight soft and warm.

'You must have seen worse in Hong Kong.'

'Yes, in the Walled City! Sim, what's his mother *like*?'

'She's a whore. A local Chinese. Very pathetic and young.'

Madeleine stopped Sim impulsively, putting her hand on his sleeve.

'What are we doing? He can't have much of a life here. Why don't we try to keep him? We could try to adopt him? Or if you won't, I'll do it.'

'No, Madeleine, it's not –'

'Why not? If, as you say, she *sold* the child to Maurice Fielding –'

'That's only a guess. I don't *know*.'

'But if she did, she won't have reported it to the police. There was no hue and cry, was there? We could take him to the authorities and, if there was no trace of any missing boy with this description, I would say I was interested in adopting him.'

'They'd never let you. Come on.'

He started to climb again. He wished there was some way, but there was no way.

At the sixteenth landing he could see a band of thin light under Treeze's door. He walked firmly across to it. Madeleine came up and stood beside him. They could smell the spicy cannabis smoke drifting under the door.

'Maddy, she begged me to bring him back. I didn't realize what she was saying at the time. But she begged me.'

Sim put his hand into hers and tightened before letting go. Then he knocked firmly on the door.

# READ MORE IN PENGUIN

In every corner of the world, on every subject under the sun, Penguin represents quality and variety – the very best in publishing today.

For complete information about books available from Penguin – including Puffins, Penguin Classics and Arkana – and how to order them, write to us at the appropriate address below. Please note that for copyright reasons the selection of books varies from country to country.

**In the United Kingdom**: Please write to *Dept. JC, Penguin Books Ltd, FREEPOST, West Drayton, Middlesex UB7 OBR*

If you have any difficulty in obtaining a title, please send your order with the correct money, plus ten per cent for postage and packaging, to *PO Box No. 11, West Drayton, Middlesex UB7 OBR*

**In the United States**: Please write to *Penguin USA Inc., 375 Hudson Street, New York, NY 10014*

**In Canada**: Please write to *Penguin Books Canada Ltd, 10 Alcorn Avenue, Suite 300, Toronto, Ontario M4V 3B2*

**In Australia**: Please write to *Penguin Books Australia Ltd, 487 Maroondah Highway, Ringwood, Victoria 3134*

**In New Zealand**: Please write to *Penguin Books (NZ) Ltd, 182–190 Wairau Road, Private Bag, Takapuna, Auckland 9*

**In India**: Please write to *Penguin Books India Pvt Ltd, 706 Eros Apartments, 56 Nehru Place, New Delhi 110 019*

**In the Netherlands**: Please write to *Penguin Books Netherlands B.V., Keizersgracht 231 NL–1016 DV Amsterdam*

**In Germany**: Please write to *Penguin Books Deutschland GmbH, Friedrichstrasse 10–12, W–6000 Frankfurt/Main 1*

**In Spain**: Please write to *Penguin Books S. A., C. San Bernardo 117–6° E–28015 Madrid*

**In Italy**: Please write to *Penguin Italia s.r.l., Via Felice Casati 20, I–20124 Milano*

**In France**: Please write to *Penguin France S. A., 17 rue Lejeune, F–31000 Toulouse*

**In Japan**: Please write to *Penguin Books Japan, Ishikiribashi Building, 2–5–4, Suido, Tokyo 112*

**In Greece**: Please write to *Penguin Hellas Ltd, Dimocritou 3, GR–106 71 Athens*

**In South Africa**: Please write to *Longman Penguin Southern Africa (Pty) Ltd, Private Bag X08, Bertsham 2013*